# FIGHTING SLAVE OF GOR

Again Krondar charged, as though maddened, but now I knew he understood how dangerous I could be. This time I stood to the right, and as he thrust forth his hands to seize me I struck upwards with my left fist. I struck crosswise with my right, and then again with my left to the gut. This brought his head into position for the upward stroke of my right fist again. The combination was swift. The crowd was screaming. Krondar struck against the palings and twisted away. He suddenly lunged towards me and we grappled. He grunted, savagely trying to hurl me off balance into the palings. We stood locked together, swaying, breathing heavily, on the sand.

Other titles in the
CHRONICLES OF COUNTER-EARTH
by John Norman

# FIGHTING SLAVE OF GOR

John Norman

**A STAR BOOK**

*published by*
the Paperback Division of
W. H. ALLEN & Co. Ltd

A Star Book
Published in 1981
by the Paperback Division of
W. H. Allen & Co. Ltd
A Howard and Wyndham Company
44 Hill Street, London W1X 8LB

Reprinted 1984

First published in America by
Daw Books, 1980

Copyright © 1980 by John Norman

Printed in Great Britain by
Hunt Barnard Printing Ltd, Aylesbury, Bucks

ISBN 0 352 30838 9

# CONTENTS

# 1 THE RESTAURANT; The Cab

"May I speak to you intimately, Jason?" she asked.

"Of course, Beverly," I said.

We sat at a small table, in a corner booth. The small restaurant is located on 128th Street. A candle burned on the table, set in a small container. The linen was white, the silver soft and lustrous in the candlelight.

She seemed distracted.

I had never seen her like this. Normally she was intellectual, prim, collected and cool.

She looked at me.

We were not really close friends. We were more in the nature of acquaintances. I did not understand why she had asked me to meet her at the restaurant.

"It was kind of you to come," she said.

"I was pleased to do so," I said.

Beverly Henderson was twenty-two years old and a graduate student in English literature at one of the major universities in the New York City area. I, too, was a student at the same university, though pursuing doctoral studies in classics, my specialty being Greek historians. Beverly was a small, exquisitely breasted, lovely ankled, sweetly hipped young woman. She did not fit in well with the large, straight-hipped females who figured prominently in her department. She did her best, however, to conform to the standards in deportment, dress and assertiveness expected of her. She had adopted the clichés and severe mien expected of her by her peers, but I do not think they ever truly accepted her. She was not, really, of their kind. They could tell this. I looked at Beverly. She had extremely dark hair, almost black. It was drawn back severely on her head, and fastened in a bun. She was lightly complexioned, and had dark brown eyes. She was something in the neighborhood of five feet in height and weighed in the neighborhood of ninety-five pounds. My name is Jason Marshall. I have brown hair and brown eyes, am fairly complex-ioned, am six feet one inch in height, and weigh, I conjecture, about one hundred and ninety pounds. At the time of our meeting I was twenty-five years old.

I reached out to touch her hand.

She had asked if she might speak to me intimately. Though I appeared calm, my heart was beating rapidly. Could she have detected the feelings I had felt towards her in these past months since I had come to learn of her existence? I found her one of the most exciting women I had ever seen. It is dif-ficult to explain these things. It is not, however, that she was merely extremely attractive. It had rather to do, I think, with some latency of hers that I could not fully understand. Many were the times when I had dreamt of her naked in my arms, sometimes, oddly enough, in a steel collar. I forced such thoughts from my mind. I had, of course, many times asked her to accompany me to plays, or lectures or concerts, or to have dinner with me, but she had always refused. It did not seem, however, that I was unique in collecting this disappoint-ing parcel of rejections. Many men, it seemed, had had as little luck as I with the young, lovely Miss Henderson. As far as I could tell she seldom dated. I had seen her once or twice about the campus, however, with what I supposed might be male friends. They seemed inoffensive and harmless enough. Their opinions, I suppose, conformed to the correct views. She would have little to fear from them, save perhaps bore-dom. Then, this evening, she had called me on the telephone, asking me to meet her at this restaurant. She had not ex-plained. She had said only that she had wanted to talk with me. Puzzled, I had taken a subway to the restaurant. I would take her home, of course, in a cab.

She had asked if she might speak to me intimately. I touched her hand.

She drew her hand back. "Do not do that," she said.

"I'm sorry," I said.

"I don't like that sort of thing," she said.

"I'm sorry," I said.

I was irritated. But I was now more puzzled than ever.

"Do not try to be masculine with me," she said. "I am a woman."

"Did that come out right?" I asked, smiling.

"I mean 'I am a person'," she said. "I have a mind. I am not a sex object, not a thing, a toy, a bauble."

"I'm sure you have a mind," I said. "If you didn't, you would be in a very serious condition."

"Men do not value women except for their bodies."

"I did not know that," I said. "That sounds like something that would be said only by a woman whom it would be very difficult to value for her body."

"I do not like men," she said. "And I do not even like myself."

"I do not understand the purport of this conversation," I said.

In so brief a compass it seemed to me that she had touched on two of the major ambiguities afflicting the politics she espoused. First there was the insistence on womanhood coupled simultaneously with the suppression of womanhood, exalting the neuteristic, sexless ideal of the person. One must be insistent on being a woman, rhetorically, and yet the last thing one must be is honest to one's womanhood. The ideal of the person was the antithesis to honest sexuality, a device to inhibit and reduce, if not destroy, it. It was, of course, a useful instrumentality to certain types of women in the pursuit of their political ambitions. In a sense I thought this wise on their part. They had the good sense to recognize that the sexuality of human beings, and love, was the major obstacle to the success of their programs. The desire of women to find love might yet prove fatal to their designs. The second major ambiguity in the politics involved was the paradoxical combination of hostility toward men coupled with envy of men. Most briefly put, on the level of primitive simplicity, such women hated men and yet wished to be men. They hated men because they were not men. A natural consequence of this, of course, was that they, unhappy with themselves, felt hostility toward themselves as well. The answer to this latter difficulty might be a simple one, namely to accept what one is, in its fullness and depth, for the man to accept manhood, and the woman womanhood, whatever it might involve.

"The sexes are identical," she said.

"I did not know that," I said.

"I am just the same as you," she said.

"I see no point in entering into an argument on this issue," I said. "What would you accept as counterevidence?"

"Some unimportant, minor differences in anatomical details are all that divide us," she said.

"What of ten thousand generations of animal ancestry and

evolution, of the genetic dispositions in billions of cells, not one of which is the same in your body as in mine?"

"Are you a sexist?" she asked.

"Perhaps," I said. "I do not know. What is a sexist?"

"A sexist is a sexist," she said.

"That is a logical truth," I said. "An apple is an apple. The argument is not much advanced."

"The concept is vague," she said.

"There is little if any concept involved," I said. "The expression is a 'signal word,' a word selected for its emotive connotation, not its cognitive meaning. It is to be used as a slander tool to discourage questioning and enforce verbal agreement. Similar expressions, once meaningful, now largely of value as rhetorical devices are 'chauvinist', 'sex object', 'person', 'conservative' and 'liberal'. One of the great utilities of these words, long since evacuated of most of their cognitive content, is that they make thought unnecessary. It is little wonder men value them so highly."

"I do not believe you," she said. "You may not share my values."

"Does that disturb you?" I asked.

"No," she said, quickly, "of course not!"

I was growing angry. I slipped from the booth.

"No," she said, "please do not go!" She reached forth and took my hand. Then, swiftly, she released it. "Forgive me," she said, "I did not mean to be feminine."

"Very well," I said, irritably.

"Please, don't leave," she said. "I do wish, desperately, to talk to you, Jason."

I sat down. We scarcely knew one another, and yet she had used my first name. I suppose I was weak. I felt mollified. Too, I was curious. Too, she was beautiful.

"Thank you, Jason," she said.

I was startled. She had thanked me. I had not expected that. I felt then that perhaps, truly, she did wish to speak with me, though for what reason I could not conjecture. Surely our politics were insufficiently congruent, as she must now understand, to motivate any expectation on her part that I would supply much positive reinforcement for her own views.

"Why do you wish to speak to me?" I asked. "Before you scarcely passed the time of day with me."

"There are reasons," she said.

"Before you would not speak with me," I said.

"You frightened me, Jason," she said.

"How?" I said.

"There was something about you," she said. "I do not know really what it was. There is a kind of power or masculinity about you." She looked up, quickly. "I find it offensive, you understand."

"All right," I said.

"But it made me feel feminine, weak. I do not wish to be feminine. I do not wish to be weak."

"I'm sorry if I said or did anything to alarm you," I said.

"It was nothing you said or did," she said. "It was rather something which I sensed you were."

"What?" I asked.

"Different from the others," she said.

"What?" I asked.

"A man," she said.

"That is silly," I said. "You must know hundreds of men."

"Not like you," she said.

"What were you afraid of," I asked, "that I would tell you to go into the kitchen and cook?"

"No," she smiled.

"That I would tell you to go into the bedroom and strip?" I asked.

"Please, Jason," she said, putting her head down, reddening.

"I'm sorry," I said. Inwardly, however, I smiled. I thought it might be quite pleasant to direct the lovely Miss Henderson to enter the bedroom of my small student's apartment and remove her clothing.

"There are various reasons I wanted to speak to you," she said.

"I'm listening," I told her.

"I don't like you, you understand," she said.

"All right," I said.

"And we women aren't afraid of men like you any more," she said.

"All right," I said.

She didn't speak, though. She put her head down.

This evening she was dressed as I had never seen her before. Normally she wore garb of the sort tacitly prescribed for her in her intellectual environs, slacks and pants of various sorts, and shirts and jackets, sometimes with ties. Imitation-male clothing, interestingly enough, is often adopted by individuals who are the most vehement in their claims to be women. It is possible, of course, that those who make the most noise about being women are the least feminine of all. But such matters are perhaps best left to psychologists.

"You look very lovely tonight," I said.

She looked up at me. She wore an off-the-shoulder, svelte, white, satin-sheath gown. She had a small, silver-beaded purse. Her wrists and neck were bare. She had lovely, rounded forearms, and small wrists and hands. Her fingers were small, but lovely and delicate. She did not wear nail polish. On her feet were golden pumps, with a wisp of golden straps.

"Thank you," she said.

I regarded her. She had lovely, exciting shoulders. I saw that her breasts would be very white. Her bosom, small, but sweetly swelling, concealed, strained against the tight satin sheath. I felt I would like to tear the garment from her and throw her on her back, naked and helpless, on the table. When she was crying to be used, I could throw her to the floor, there to make her mine. I thrust such thoughts from my mind.

"But that is surely not the standard uniform in your department," I said.

"I do not know what is going on with me," she said, miserably. She shook her head. "I had to talk to someone."

"Why me?" I asked.

"There are reasons," she said. "Among them is the fact that you are different from the others. I know what the others will say and think. I want someone who thinks for himself, who can be objective. In our short conversations it became clear to me that you are one who thinks not in terms of words but in terms of things and realities. Your thinking is less analogous to the playing of tapes than it is to the photography of facts."

"Many thousands of individuals think in terms of the world, its nature and promise," I said, "not in terms of slogans and verbal formulas. Indeed, those who control the world cannot afford not to. They may use verbal formulas to manipulate the masses, but, in their own thinking, they cannot be limited in this fashion or they would not have come to their positions of power."

"I am accustomed," she said, "to those who think only verbally."

"The academic world, too often," I said, "is a refuge and haven for those who cannot manage more. Academic thinking does not have the same sanctions of success and failure as practical thought. The aeronautical engineer makes a mistake and a plane crashes. A historian writes a stupid book and is promoted."

She looked down. "Let us order," she said.

"I thought you wanted to talk," I said.

"Let us order now," she said.

"All right," I said. "Would you like a drink?"

"Yes," she said.

We ordered drinks, and later, dinner. The waiter was attentive, but not obtrusive. We drank and ate in silence. After dessert, we sipped coffee.

"Jason," she said, breaking the silence, "I told you before that I didn't understand what was going on with me. I don't."

"You wished to talk to someone," I said.

"Yes," she said.

"Proceed," I said.

"Don't tell me what to do," she said. "Don't tell me what to do!"

"Very well," I said. "Shall I call for the check?"

"Not yet," she said. "Please, wait. I—I do not know where to begin."

I sipped the coffee. I saw no point in hurrying her. I was curious.

"You will think that I'm mad," she said.

"If you will forgive the observation," I said, "you seem to me, rather, to be frightened."

She looked at me, suddenly. "A few months ago," she said, "I began to have unusual feelings, and urges."

"What sorts of feelings and urges?" I asked.

"They are the sort of thing which people used to think of as feminine," she said, "when people still believed in femininity."

"Most people still believe in that sort of thing," I said. "Your official position, whatever its political values, is a perversion not only of truth but of biology."

"Do you think so?" she asked.

"Clearly," I said. "But I would be less worried, if I were you, about what people believed to be true than about what was true. If you have deeply feminine urges you have them. It is that simple. Let people who have never truly experienced femininity argue about whether it exists or not. Let those who know it exists, because they have experienced it, set themselves to different problems."

"But I am fearful of the nature of my femininity," she said. "I have had frightening dreams."

"What sort of dreams?" I asked.

"I hardly dare speak of them to a man," she said, "they are so horrifying."

I said nothing. I did not wish to put her under any undue stress.

"I have often dreamed," she said, "that I was a female slave, that I was kept in rags or naked, that a steel collar was put on my neck, that I was branded, that I was subject to discipline, that I must serve a man."

"I see," I said. My hands gripped the table. My vision, for a moment, swam. I looked at the small beauty. I had not known I could feel such sudden lust, such startling, astonishing, maddening desire for a woman. I dared not move in the slightest.

"I went to a psychiatrist," she said. "But he was a man. He told me such thoughts were perfectly normal and natural."

"I see," I said.

"So I went to a female psychologist," she said.

"What happened?" I asked.

"It was strange," she said. "When I spoke to the psychologist about this she became quite angry. She called me a lewd and salacious little bitch."

"That was scarcely professional of her," I smiled.

"In a moment," said the girl, "she apologized, and was again herself."

"Did you continue to see her?" I asked.

"A few times," said the girl, "but it was never really the same after that. Eventually I stopped."

"You apparently touched a raw nerve in her," I said. "Or perhaps what you said threatened her in some way, perhaps as not being obviously compatible with some theoretical position." I looked at her. "There are many other psychiatrists and psychologists," I said, "both male and female."

The girl nodded.

"There is a variety of positions in those fields, in particular in psychology," I said. "If you shop around you will doubtless find someone who will tell you what you wish to hear, whatever it is."

"It is the truth I wish to hear," she said, "whatever it is."

"Perhaps," I said, "the truth is the last thing you wish to hear."

"Oh?" she asked.

"Yes," I said. "Suppose that the truth were that you were, in your heart, a female slave."

"No!" she said. Then she lowered her voice, embarrassed. "No," she said. Then she said, "You are hateful, simply hateful!"

"That you might be in your heart a female slave is not even a possibility that you can admit," I said.

"Of course not," she said.

"It is politically inadmissible," I said.

"Yes," she said, "but beyond that it cannot be true. It must not be true! I cannot even dare to think that it might be true!"

"But you are very beautiful, and very feminine," I said.

"I do not even believe in femininity," she said.

"Have you told it to your hormones," I asked, "so abundant and luxuriously rich in your beautiful little body."

"I know I'm feminine," she said, suddenly. "I cannot help myself. I simply cannot help it. You must believe that. I know it is wrong and despicable, but I cannot help it. I am so ashamed. I want to be a true woman, but I am too weak, too feminine."

"It is not wrong to be yourself," I said.

"Too," she said, "I'm frightened. Last summer I did not even take a pleasure cruise in the Carribean."

"You feared the famed Bermuda Triangle?" I asked.

"Yes," she said. "I did not want to disappear. I did not want to be taken away, to be made a slave girl on another planet."

"Thousands of planes and ships, year in and year out, safely traverse the Bermuda Triangle," I said.

"I know," she said.

"You see, you are being silly," I said.

"Yes," she said. Then she asked me, "Have you ever heard of the planet Gor?"

"Certainly," I said, "it is a reasonably well-known fictional world." I laughed, suddenly. "The Bermuda Triangle and Gor," I said, "have, as far as I know, absolutely nothing to do with one another." I smiled at her. "If the slavers of Gor have decided to take you, my dear," I said, "they certainly will not sit about waiting for you to take a trip to the Carribean." I looked at her carefully. She was beautiful. I wondered, if there were Gorean slavers, if she might indeed not be the sort of woman they regard as suitable for their chains. Then again I tensed myself, scarcely daring to move. The thought of the lovely Miss Henderson as a helpless Gorean slave girl, at the mercy of a man, so aroused my passion that I could scarcely dare to breathe. I held myself perfectly still.

"You are right," she said. "Gor and the Bermuda Triangle have presumably nothing to do with one another."

"I think not," I said.

"You are comforting, Jason," she said, gratefully.

"Besides," I smiled, "if the slavers swoop down and carry you off, perhaps you will eventually, sometime, find a master who will be kind to you."

"Gorean men," she said, shuddering, "are strict with their slaves."

"So I have heard," I said.

"I am afraid," she said.

"It is silly," I said. "Do not be afraid."

"Do you believe Gor exists?" she asked.

"Of course not," I said. "It is an interesting fictional creation. No one believes it truly exists."

"I have done some research," she said. "There are too many things, too much that is unexplained. I think a pattern is forming. Could it not be that the Gorean books are, in effect, a way of preparing the Earth and its peoples for the revelation of the true existence of a Counter-Earth, should it sometime be expedient to make its presence known?"

"Of course not," I said. "Do not be absurd."

"There are too many details, too," she said, "small things that would not occur to a fictional writer to include, pointless things like the construction of a saddle and the method of minting coins. They are not things one would include who was concerned to construct spare, well-made pieces of fiction."

"They are more like the little things that might occur to one, not a writer, who had found them of interest, and wished to mention them."

"Yes," she said.

"Put it from your mind," I said. "Gor is fictional."

"I do not believe John Norman is the author of the Gor books," she said.

"Why not?" I asked.

"I have been frightened about this sort of thing," she said. "I have met him, and talked with him. It seems his way of speaking, and his prose style, may not be that of the books."

"He has never claimed," I said, "to be more than the editor of the books. They purport, as I understand it, to be generally the work of others, usually of an individual called Tarl Cabot."

"There was a Cabot," she said, "who disappeared."

"Norman receives the manuscripts, does he not, from someone called Harrison Smith. He is probably the true author."

"Harrison Smith is not his true name," she said. "It was changed by Norman to protect his friend. But I have spoken with this 'Harrison Smith.' He receives the manuscripts, but he apparently knows as little as anyone else about their origin."

"I think you are taking this sort of thing too seriously," I said. "Surely Norman himself believes the manuscripts to be fiction."

"Yes," she said. "I am convinced of that."

"If he, who is their author or editor, believes them to be fiction, you should feel perfectly free, it seems to me, to do likewise."

"May I tell you something which happened to me, Jason?" she asked.

Suddenly I felt uneasy. "Surely," I said. I smiled. "Did you see a Gorean slaver?" I asked.

"Perhaps," she said.

I looked at her.

"I knew you would think me mad," she said.

"Go ahead," I said.

"Perhaps foolishly," she said, "I made no secret of my inquiry into these matters. Dozens of people, in one way or another, must have learned of my interest."

"Go on," I said.

"That explains, accordingly, the phone call I received," she said. "It was a man's voice. He told me to visit a certain address if I were interested in Gorean matters. I have the address here." She opened her purse and showed me an address. It was on 55th Street, on the East Side.

"Did you go to the address?" I asked.

"Yes," she said.

"That was foolish," I said. "What happened?"

"I knocked on the apartment door," she said.

"It was on the fifth floor," I said, noting the apartment number.

"Yes," she said. "I was told to enter. The apartment was well furnished. In it there was a large man, seated on a sofa, behind a coffee table. He was heavy, large handed, balding, virile. 'Come in,' he said. 'Do not be afraid.' He smiled at me. 'You are in absolutely no danger at the present moment, my dear,' he said."

" 'At the present moment'?" I asked.

"Those were his words."

"Weren't you frightened?" I asked.

"Yes," she said.

"Then what happened?" I asked.

"He said to me, 'Come closer. Stand before the coffee table.' I did that. 'You are a pretty one,' he said. 'Perhaps you have possibilities.' "

"What did he mean by that?" I asked.

"I don't know," she said. "I started to tell him my name, but he lifted his hand, and told me that he knew my name. I looked at him, frightened. On the coffee table, before him, there was a decanter of wine and a heavy, ornate metal goblet. I had never seen a goblet of that sort. It was so primitive and barbaric. 'I understand,' I said to him, 'that you may know something of Gor.' 'Kneel down before the coffee table, my dear,' he said."

"What did you do then?" I asked.

"I knelt down," she said, blushing. Suddenly I envied, hotly, the power of that man over the beautiful Miss Henderson.

"He then said to me," she said, " 'Pour wine into the goblet. Fill it precisely to the second ring.' There were five rings on the outside of the goblet. I poured the wine, as he had asked, and then placed the goblet on the coffee table. 'Now unbutton your blouse,' he said, 'completely.' "

"You then cried out with fury and fled from the apartment?" I asked.

"I unbuttoned my blouse," she said, "completely. 'Now open your slacks,' he said."

"Did you do this?" I asked.

"Yes," she said. " 'Now remove your blouse, and thrust your slacks down about your calves,' he said."

"Did you do this?" I asked.

"Yes," she said. " 'Now thrust your panties down about your hips,' he said, 'until your navel is revealed.' I did this, too. I then knelt there before him in my panties, thrust down upon my hips, that my navel be revealed, my slacks down about my legs, and in my brassiere, my blouse discarded, placed on the rug beside me."

I could scarcely believe what I was hearing.

"Do you understand the significance of the revealing of the navel?" she asked me.

"I believe on Gor," I said, "it is called 'the slave belly'."

"It is," she said. "But Gor, of course, does not exist."

"Of course not," I said.

" 'Now take the goblet,' he said, 'and hold the metal against your body, pushing inward.' I took the goblet and held it, tightly, to my body. I held the round, heavy metal against me, below my brassiere. 'Lower,' he said, 'against your belly.' I then held the goblet lower. 'Press it more inward,' he said. I did so. I can still feel the cold metal against me, firmly, partly against the silk of my undergarment, partly against my belly. 'Now,' said he, 'lift the goblet to your lips and kiss it lingeringly, then proffer it to me, arms extended, head down.' "

"Did you do that?" I asked.

"Yes," she said.

"Why?" I asked.

"I do not know," she said, angrily. "I had never met a man like him. There seemed some kind of strength about him, such as I had never met in another man. It is hard to explain. But I felt that I must obey him, and perfectly, that there were no two ways about it."

"Interesting," I said.

"When he had finished the wine," she said, "he replaced the goblet on the table. He then said, 'You are clumsy and untrained, but you are pretty and perhaps you could be taught. You may stand now, and dress. You may then leave.' "

"What did you do then?" I asked.

"I stood up, and dressed," she said. "Then I said to him, 'I am Beverly Henderson.' I felt, I suppose, I wished to assert my identity. 'Your name is known to me,' he said. 'Are you fond of your name?' he asked. 'Yes,' I said to him. 'Relish it while you can,' he said. 'You may not have it long.' "

"What did he mean by that?" I asked.

"I do not know," she said. "I demanded, too, to know. But he said to me merely that I might then leave. I was then angry. 'What have you to tell me of Gor?' I asked. 'Surely you have learned something of Gor this afternoon,' he said. 'I do not understand,' I said. 'It is a pity that you are so stupid,' he said, 'else you might bring a higher price.' 'Price!' I cried. 'Yes, price,' he said, smiling. 'Surely you know that there are men who will pay for your beauty.' "

"Go on," I said.

"I was terribly angry," she said. " 'Never have I been so insulted!' I said to him. 'I hate you!' I cried. He smiled at me. 'Being troublesome and displeasing is acceptable in a free woman,' he said. 'Be troublesome and displeasing while you may. It will not be permitted to you later.' I turned then and went to the door. At the door I turned. 'Have no fear, Miss Henderson,' he said, 'we always save one or two capsules, aside from those allotted to our regular requisitions, in case something worthwhile shows up.' He then grinned at me. 'And you, I think,' he said, 'with the proper training, exercise and diet, will prove quite worthwhile. You may go now.' I then wept and ran out the door."

"When did this happen?" I asked.

"Two days ago," she said. "What do you think it means?"

"I think, obviously," I said, "it is a cruel joke, and it could have been a dangerous joke. I would advise you never to enter into such a rendezvous again."

"I have no intention of doing so," she said, shuddering.

"It is over now, and there is nothing to worry about," I said.

"Thank you, Jason," she said.

"Did you inform the police?" I asked.

"I did," she said, "but not until the next day. No crime, of course, had been committed. There was nothing I could prove. Still it seemed to warrant an investigation."

"I agree completely," I said.

"Two officers and I went to the same address," she said.

"What occurred in the confrontation?" I asked.

"There was no confrontation," she said. "The apartment was empty. It was not even furnished. There were no drapes, nothing. The superintendent claimed it had been empty for a week. There was no reason for the officers to disbelieve him. Perhaps he was paid off. Perhaps he was in league with the heavy man. I do not know. The officers, angry, gave me a stern warning about such pranks and let me go. The entire matter has been a pain and an embarrassment to me."

"It certainly seems an elaborate hoax," I said.

"Why would anyone go to such trouble?" she asked.

"I do not know," I said.

"Do you think I have anything to fear?" she asked.

"No," I said, "certainly not." Then I lifted my hand, to call the waiter.

"I must pay half the check and leave half the tip," she said.

"I'll take care of it," I said.

"No," she said, suddenly, irritably. "I will be dependent on a man for nothing."

"Very well," I said. I saw that Miss Henderson had a sharp edge to her. I supposed that a Gorean slave whip, if there were a Gor, would quickly take that out of her.

We then, at the hat-check counter, secured our wraps. The girl behind the counter was blond. She wore a white blouse and a brief, black skirt; her legs, well revealed, were clad in clinging black netting. Miss Henderson received her light cape. She placed a quarter in the small wooden bowl on the counter. I received my coat. I gave the girl a dollar. She had lovely legs. She had a pretty smile. She pleased me. "Thank you, Sir," she said. "You're welcome," I said.

"Scandalous how some women exploit their bodies," said Beverly, when we had stepped away from the counter.

"She was very pretty," I said.

"I suppose you would not mind owning her," said Beverly.

"No," I said, "I wouldn't mind owning her at all. She might be very pleasant to own."

"All men are monsters," said Beverly.

I donned my coat. She held her wrap.

"Why are you dressed as you are tonight?" I asked. "Are you not frightened that some of your "sisters" in your department will see you? Can you afford the risk?"

She seemed momentarily apprehensive. I had been joking. Then I saw that it was not truly a joke. One student can, subtly, belittle and undermine another student in the eyes of her peers and in the eyes of the faculty. It can be done with apparent innocence in the dialogue in a seminar, by an apparently chance remark at a coffee or tea, even by an expression or a movement of the body in a classroom or a hall. The rules for conformance and the sanctions against difference are seldom explicit; indeed, it is commonly denied that there are such rules and sanctions. They are reasonably obvious, however, to those familiar with the psychology of groups. Such things, unfortunately, can ruin graduate careers. Most obviously they can be reflected in the evaluations of the student's work and in his letters of recommendation, particularly those written by strict professors of the correct political persuasions, whatever they happen to be at the particular institution in question.

"Surely it is all right," she said, "for a woman, sometimes, to be a little feminine."

"Perhaps," I said. "The question is indeed a thorny one."

"I have heard it debated," she said.

"Are you joking?" I asked. I had thought I had been joking.

"No," she said.

"I see," I said.

"In my view," she said, "it is all right for a woman, once in a while, to be feminine, if just a little bit."

"I see," I said. I wondered if there were a world anywhere where women, or at least a certain sort of woman, would have no choice but to be totally feminine, and all the time. I smiled to myself. I thought of the fictional world of Gor, which obviously did not exist. Gorean men, as I understood it, did not accept pseudomasculinity in their female slaves; this, then, left the female slaves no alternative but to be true women.

"But you are not just a little feminine tonight," I said. "You are deliciously feminine."

"Do not speak to me in that fashion," she said.

"Even if it is true?" I asked.

"Particularly if it is true," she said.

"Why?" I asked.

"Because I am a person," she said.

"Would you settle for a 'deliciously feminine person'?" I inquired.

"Do not demean my personhood," she said.

"What about 'deliciously feminine little female animal'?" I asked.

"What a beast you are," she said. "It sounds like you want to put a collar on me and lead me away to your bed."

"That would be pleasant," I said.

"You think I'm sexually attractive, don't you?" she asked.

"Yes," I said. "Does that disturb you?"

"No," she said, "not really. I am aware that some men have found me sexually attractive. Some have even tried to take me in their arms and kiss me."

"Horrifying," I said.

"I did not permit them to be successful," she said.

"Good for you," I said.

"I insist on being totally respected," she said.

"Have you ever considered," I asked, "that your desire to be respected may interfere with the development of your sexuality?"

"Sex," she said, "is only a tiny and unimportant part of life. It must be seen in its proper perspective."

"Sexuality," I said, "is radically central to the human phenomenon."

"No, no," she said. "Sex is unimportant, irrelevant and immaterial. Better put, it must be placed in its proper perspective. This is something which is understood by all politically enlightened persons, both men and women. Indeed, sexuality is a threat and a handicap to the achievement of a true civilization. It must be ruthlessly curbed and controlled."

"Nonsense," I said.

"Nonsense?" she asked.

"Yes, nonsense," I said. "Sex may be a handicap to the achievement of a certain sort of civilization," I admitted, "but I do not think I would relish that sort of civilization in which it would be a handicap. Surely it is possible to at least consider a civilization which would not be inimical to the nature of human beings but compatible with their desires and needs. Perhaps in such a society sexuality would not need to be suppressed but might be permitted to flower."

"It is impossible to talk with you," she said. "You are too unenlightened."

"Perhaps," I said. "But one thing, amidst all these complexities, stands out clearly."

"What is that?" she asked.

"That you," I said, "undeniably and nonrepudiably, are an extremely lovely and exciting young woman."

"You are terrible," she said, head down, smiling.

"It is easy to see why the slavers of Gor would be interested in you," I said.

"What a beast you are," she laughed.

I was pleased to see that I had relieved her mind on this issue.

"And your outfit tonight," I said, "like yourself, whether you like it or not, is deliciously feminine."

She looked down at herself. She, without really thinking, smoothed the sheath on her hips. It was a very natural gesture. I supposed slaves might be taught such a gesture. But with Miss Henderson it was totally natural. I found her very exciting. I wondered if there were such things as natural slaves. If there were, I was confident the lovely Miss Henderson would qualify.

"What a hateful and unteachable brute you are," she smiled.

"I have never seen you wear anything really feminine before," I said. "What brought about this sudden change of heart, that perhaps it might be all right for a woman to be just a little bit feminine?"

She put down her head.

"Surely this represents a change," I said.

"Yes, perhaps," she said. "I do not know."

"You bought this outfit recently, didn't you?" I asked.

"Yes," she said.

"When?" I asked.

"This morning," she said. She looked up, angrily, defensively. "I thought it wouldn't hurt to have something that was just a little bit pretty."

"You are more than just a little bit pretty," I told her.

"Thank you," she said.

"And you are wearing a bit of make-up and eye shadow," I said.

"Yes," she said.

"And perfume," I said.

"Yes," she said. "I truly hope," she said, "that none of those in my department see me as I am now."

"They would deride your attractiveness," I said, "and attempt, in envy, to avenge themselves on you in the department?"

"Yes," she said. "I think so."

"This change in you is sudden," I said. "It has to do with your experiences with the heavy man, who, so to speak, interviewed you, doesn't it, he whom you saw in the apartment?"

She nodded. "Yes," she said. "It is strange. I never felt so feminine as when he ordered me, so complacently, to kneel and serve him."

"It released your femininity?" I asked.

"Yes," she said. "It is so strange. I cannot explain it."

"You had been put under male domination," I said. "For the first time in your life you probably found yourself in a fully natural biological relationship."

"I repudiate your analysis," she said.

"Too, you were sexually aroused," I said.

"How could you know that?" she asked. "I said nothing of that."

"You did not have to," I said. "It was evident in your expressions, your tone of voice, the way you recounted the experience."

"You are hateful," she said, irritably.

"May I help you with your cape?" I asked.

"I can manage it myself," she said.

"Doubtless," I said.

She glanced back at the girl at the hat-check counter. The girl then looked away.

"Yes," she said, clearly, a little more loudly than was necessary, "you may help me with my wrap."

She then stood there quietly, and I, standing behind her, lifted the cape about her shoulders. For an instant, the barest instant, after the cape had settled about her, I rested my hands on her upper arms. In that brief second she knew herself held. Then I had released her. Her body was tense, rigid, defensive. "Do not think to put me in your power," she whispered, angrily. "I will never be in the power of any man." Then she said, clearly, pleasantly, a bit loudly, for the benefit of the girl at the counter, "Thank you."

Then, suddenly, she half moaned. Then she said, delightedly, "Hello, how are you! How nice to see you here!" Introductions were exchanged. I looked at the two horselike women, in one another's company, a large one and a small one, who had entered. They regarded me, angrily. They beamed on Beverly. "How pretty you are tonight, Beverly," said the larger woman. "It is all right to wear a dress sometimes," said Beverly. "It is a freedom." "Of course it is," said the larger woman, "don't you worry about it. You look lovely, just lovely." The smaller of the two women said almost nothing. Then they had entered the main dining room, and were being greeted by the head waiter.

"I should never have come here," said Beverly.

"You know them from school?" I asked.

"Yes," said Beverly, "they are in two of my seminars."

"You look ill, miserable," I said. "Do you care, truly, what they think?"

"They are politically powerful in my department," she said, "especially the big one. Even some of my male professors are afraid of them."

"So much for them," I said.

"Many without tenure fear their student evaluations," she said, "and, more importantly, their influence on the evaluations of others. Most of our young male teachers, and female teachers, too, do what is expected of them, and try to please them. They do not wish to lose their positions."

"I'm familiar with that sort of thing," I said. "It is called academic freedom."

She tied the strings of her cape. We then left the restaurant.

"I will hail a taxi," I said.

"I am not really a true woman," she said, outside the restaurant, miserably. "I am too feminine." She looked up at me. "I have tried to fight my femininity," she said. "I have tried to overcome it."

"You could redouble your efforts," I said. "You could try harder."

"I am finished in my department," she said. "They will undermine and destroy me."

"You could transfer to another school," I said, "and start over."

"Perhaps," she said, "but I fear that it is hopeless. It might just begin again. Or the word might be conveyed to the new department that I was not, truly, of the right kind."

"Of the right kind?" I asked.

"Of their kind," she said.

"That of the two women you met in the restaurant?" I asked.

"Yes," she said. "They are so strong and manlike, like men used to be, before."

"Femininity is wrong in a woman, and masculinity in a man?" I asked.

"Of course," she said, "it interferes with personhood."

"But it is all right for women to be masculine and men to be feminine?"

"Yes," she said, "that is all right. Indeed, men must be taught to be gentle, tender and feminine."

"Can you not see," I asked, "that women who wish that of a man are not truly interested in what men happen to be, but want, perhaps, actually not a man but a woman of an unusual sort?"

She looked at me, with horror.

"The thought has an alarming plausibility, doesn't it?" I asked.

"I have never known anyone like you," she said. "You confuse me."

"Frankly," I said, "you are not of their kind, that of the two women in the restaurant you met. You are extremely different. Indeed, most women are extremely different from them. They are not even, truly, women. They are something else, not really women or men. It is little wonder they are so hostile, so filled with hatred, so vicious and bellicose. After centuries of disparagement why should they not now, with a vengeance, set themselves up as models for their sex? Why should they not now, so long denied the world, attempt now through rhetoric and politics to bend it to their designs? Can you blame them? Can you not understand their hatred for women such as you, who seem a veritable biological insult and reproach to their pretensions and projects? You are their enemy, with your beauty and needs, far more than the men they attempt through political power to intimidate and manipulate." I looked at her, angrily. "Your desirability and beauty," I said, "is a greater threat to them than you can even begin to understand. Their success demands the castigation and suppression of your sort of woman."

"I must not listen to you," she said. "I must be a true woman!"

"I have little doubt that you are more intelligent, and have a greater grasp of reality, than they," I said, "but you will not, in all likelihood, compete successfully with them. You lack their aggressiveness and belligerence, which are probably indexed to an unusual amount, for a woman, of male hormones in their bodies. They will, through their cruelty and assertiveness, crush you in discussion, and, when it is to their purpose, demean and humiliate you."

"I do not even enter into discussion with them," she said. "I am afraid."

"You do not wish to be verbally whipped," I said.

"I do not know what to think," she said.

"Try to understand and interpret your feelings," I said. "Consider the possibility of being true to yourself."

"Perhaps they are really women, only latently so," said the girl.

"Perhaps," I said. I shrugged.

"What is a woman, truly?" she asked, angrily. "A slave?"

I was startled that she had asked this. I looked down at her. She was emotionally overwrought. There were tears in her eyes. I knew that I was supposed to reassure her and deny vehemently what had been suggested in her fantastic question. But I did not reassure her nor deny, as I was expected to, what she had suggested. Indeed, it suddenly struck me as not only strange that she had addressed this question, presumably a rhetorical question to me, but, too, that this was precisely the sort of thing which, for no reason I clearly understood, women of her political persuasion spent a great deal of time, excessively in my mind, denying. I wondered why they should be so concerned, so frequently and intensely, in denying that they were slaves. Why should they feel it necessary to deny this apparently fantastic allegation so often and so desperately?

"Do you think we are slaves?" she demanded.

I looked down at her. She was small and exquisitely beautiful. She wore a bit of lipstick and eye shadow. I could smell her perfume. The whiteness of her breasts, as I could see them, and of her throat, was striking. How marvelously the white sheath concealed and yet suggested her beauty. I wanted to tear it from her.

"Well?" she demanded.

"Perhaps," I said.

She spun away from me, in fury and rage.

I did not speak to her then, but watched her, as she stood, angrily, outside the restaurant.

I considered her. Thoughts slipped through my mind. I wondered what she might look like, her clothing removed, standing on the tiles of a palace.

How strange it then seemed to me that society should ever have developed in such a way that such delicious and desirable creatures should have ever been permitted their freedom. Surely they belonged in steel collars at a man's feet.

She was aware of my eyes on her, but she did not look at me directly. She tossed her head. It was a lovely gesture I thought, of a girl who knew herself inspected, a slave's gesture.

"Are you going to apologize?" she asked.

"For what?" I asked.

"For saying that I might be a slave," she said.

"Oh," I said. "No," I said.

"I hate you," she said.

"All right," I said. I continued to regard her, her clothing removed in my mind. I tried, in my mind, various sorts of collars and chains on her.

"You are a rude and hateful person," she said.

"I'm sorry," I said. I then considered how she might look in a market.

At last she turned to face me, angrily. "What are you thinking about?" she asked.

"I was considering how you might look on a slave block," I said, "being exhibited by an auctioneer who knew his business."

"How dare you say such a thing!" she cried.

"You asked me what I was thinking," I said.

"You needn't have told me," she said.

"You would prefer dishonesty?" I asked.

"You are the most hateful person I have ever met," she said.

"I'm sorry," I said.

She walked angrily to confront me, but then she looked away.

"I do not see any cabs," she said.

"No," I said.

She turned to face me.

"Was I pretty?" she asked.

"When?" I asked.

"In your imagination," she said, archly.

"Sensational," I said.

She smiled. "How was I dressed?" she asked.

"You were exhibited naked," I told her, "as women are sold."

"Oh," she said.

"If it is any comfort," I said, "your wrists were joined by a long length of chain. The auctioneer showed you off with a whip."

"With a whip?" she asked, shuddering.

"Yes," I said.

"Then I would have had to obey him, wouldn't I?" she asked.

"You did obey him," I said.

"Perfectly?" she asked.

"Perfectly," I said.

"If I had not, he would have used the whip, wouldn't he?"

"Of course," I said.

"Then it was wise of me to obey."

"I would suppose so," I said.

"I was pretty?" she asked.

"Marvelously exciting and beautiful," I said.

She blushed, and smiled. How feminine she was.

"Jason," she said.

"Yes," I said.

"Would you have bought me?"

"What else was for sale?" I asked, smiling.

She struck me with sudden fury and my face stung. "Hateful monster!" she said.

She turned angrily away from me.

"I am not a slave!" she said. "I am not a slave!"

At this point I noticed that a car's headlights went on. It had been parked down the street about a block away. It had been there for some time.

"Hey!" I called, raising my arm, suddenly seeing that, as it approached, it was a cab.

The cab pulled to the curb.

"I will take you home," I said.

"It is not necessary," she said. She was angry, distressed, upset.

The driver came about and opened the back door on the right.

"I have been very rude," I said. "I'm really sorry. I did not mean to upset you."

She did not even look at the driver. "I'm not one of those females you have to patronize," she said. "I am a true woman."

She climbed angrily, distressed, into the cab. The glimpse of her ankle was exciting. I forced from my mind the thought that its lovely slimness would look well inclosed in a loop and ring.

"Please give me an opportunity to apologize," I begged. I was, myself, suddenly upset. I realzed that she might be angry, and might not see me again. I could not bear the thought

of losing her in this fashion. I had admired and desired her
from afar for months. Then tonight we had met, and talked.
I found her irresistibly attractive. "Please let me apologize," I
begged. "I was thoughtless and rude."

"Don't bother," she said.

"Please, please," I said.

"It is not necessary," she said, icily.

I was miserable. She was an intelligent woman. How offended she must have been by my foolish audacity. How scandalized she must have been by the pretensions of my boorish
and foolish masculinity. Did I not care for her feelings? Did I
not respect her mind? How tiresome and obnoxious she must
have found my inopportune and unorthodox views. Surely
there was still time to change them, to please her. I hoped
that I had not ruined everything that might have been between us. Was I not strong enough to be solicitous, sweet,
gentle, tender and feminine? I hoped she would still like me,
that she could still permit me a chance to try to please her. I
realized then, with a force I had not felt before, probably because I had not found a woman so exciting as she before,
that, in this society, men must strive to please women, that
they must, if they wish to relate to them, be and do exactly
what the women wish and require, else the women will simply remain aloof. The women, now, were of a whole new
breed, somehow magically different from all women of the
past, free and independent. It was they who would set their
terms, and it was the men who would, if they wished to know
them, comply with their wishes. But was this not all right?
Surely women have a right to demand that men comply precisely with their wishes. If the men do not do so, the women
simply need have nothing to do with them. In my society it
was women who called the tune, and the men who would
have to dance. If the women, for some reason, wished us to
be just like women then we would have to do our best to be
just like women. They could decide matters, by the device of
granting or withholding their favors.

"Please," I begged.

"You are despicable," she said.

"Please forgive me," I begged.

The driver went to close the door. "Wait," I said to him. I
held the door open. For some reason, it seemed, he wished
for me to remain outside the cab. He did not ask me if I
were getting in, or accompanying the lady. It seemed he

wished to be on his way, leaving me behind. I did not understand this, but I did not stop to consider it.

"Please, Miss Henderson," I said. "I know I must have truly offended you. For this I am extremely sorry." I was thinking quickly. "But it is late now, and it may be hard to find another cab. If you will not let me take you home, let me, at least, share the cab, so I can get back to my apartment without a great deal of inconvenience."

The driver reacted irritably. I did not understand this. It seemed to me in his best interest to have an extra fare.

"All right," she said, looking straight ahead, "get in."

I entered the cab. The driver shut the door, it seemed to me a bit angrily.

Miss Henderson and I sat side by side in the cab, not speaking.

The driver went around the cab. In a moment he had slipped behind the wheel.

We then gave him the addresses. Miss Henderson lived closer to the restaurant than I. Although the driver was not facing us I could tell that he reacted angrily when I gave him my address, which was farther from the restaurant. His irritation made no sense to me. What difference could it make which fare was let off first? He seemed a surly fellow. Too, he was a large man.

"I am sorry, Miss Henderson," I said.

"That's all right," she said, not looking at me.

In the top of the seat in front of us, that against which the driver's back rested, there was a long, lateral slot. In the top of the cab, interestingly, there was a similar slot. The slot was about an inch in width.

The cab pulled away from the curb and entered the traffic on 128th Street.

"I am a woman," said Miss Henderson, speaking very precisely and very quietly. "I am free. I am independent."

"Of course," I said, hastily.

"In the restaurant you held me for an instant, when you were helping me with my cape. I did not like that."

"I'm sorry," I said.

"You tried to put me in your power," she said. "I will never be in a man's power."

I was silent, miserable.

"Too, you insulted me, when you wished to pay for the meal and leave the tip."

"I'm sorry, Miss Henderson," I said.

"I will never be dependent on a man for anything," she said.

"Of course not," I said.

"I am free and independent, and a person, and a true woman," she said.

"Yes, Miss Henderson," I said.

She looked at me. "Do you think I am a slave?" she asked.

"Of course not!" I said. "Of course not!"

"Do not forget it," she said.

"No, Miss Henderson," I said.

We drove on in silence.

"Do you think I might see you again, sometime?" I asked.

"No," she said. Then she looked at me, in fury. "I find you utterly contemptible," she said.

I put down my head. I was miserable. My behavior, so boorish and gross, and my foolish attitudes and opinions, so crudely expressed, so unenlightened, had ruined our possibilities for a meaningful relationship. I was miserable. I was not pleasing to her.

"I am free and independent, and a true person, and a true woman," she said.

"Yes, Miss Henderson," I said.

"And I will never be dependent on a man for anything," she said, "nor will I ever be in a man's power."

"Yes, Miss Henderson," I said, my head down.

"Driver," she said, suddenly, "you have taken a wrong turn."

"Sorry," he said.

He reached under the dashboard and pulled two levers. I heard a movement of metal in the door beside me. An instant later, as he had pulled the second lever, I heard a movement of metal within the door on Miss Henderson's side.

He continued to drive in the same direction, not circling about.

"Driver," said Miss Henderson, "you're going in the wrong direction!"

He continued to drive.

"Driver," she said, irritably, her small voice imperious and cold, "you are going in the wrong direction!"

He did not respond to her.

"Turn back here," she said, as we neared a corner. But he continued to drive straight ahead.

"Can you hear me?" she asked, leaning forward.

"Be silent, Slave Girl," he said.

"Slave Girl!" she cried.

I was startled. Almost instantly, as he threw a lever which must have been beside him, a heavy glass screen or shield sprang up, from the top of the seat in front of us, against which his back rested. It locked in the lateral slot in the top of the cab. At the same time I heard two sudden hisses, coming from the back of the seat in front of us, one on each side. I started to cough. A colorless gas, under great pressure, was being forced into the rear of the cab.

"Stop the cab!" I demanded, coughing, pounding on the glass shield with the flat of my hand. It rang softly. It was thick. I do not even think the driver could hear me, or well hear me, through its weight.

"What is going on?" cried the girl.

The cab had now begun to accelerate. I suddenly discovered that there were no handles by means of which the windows might be rolled down!

"Stop the cab!" I cried, choking.

"I can't breathe," cried the girl. "I can't breathe!"

I struck down at the door handle on my side. It would not move. I tried not to breathe. My eyes smarted. I lunged to the other side of the cab, leaning across the girl. I tried to force down the handle on her side, but it, like that on my side, did not move. I then understood the meaning of the two metallic sounds I had heard earlier, one within each door. Two bolts, one on each side, had been thrust home, securing the doors.

I lunged back to my side of the cab, where I might exert more leverage on the handle of the door on my side.

The girl wept and coughed.

I am strong, but I could not begin to move the steel.

I then, again, this time with the side of my fist, began to strike at the heavy glass. It did not yield.

"Please, stop, driver!" cried the girl.

My lungs felt as though they must burst. I tore off my coat, and my jacket, to thrust it against one of the circular apertures, some four inches in diameter, set flush with the back of the seat, now a barrier, in front of us. It was through these apertures that the gas entered our portion of the cab. Each aperture was protected by narrowly placed steel slats. Because of the slats I could not thrust the jacket into the opening. Gas continued to flow in, permeating the cloth, and seeping about and through it. Gas, too, hissing, continued to flow unremittingly into our portion of the cab through the other aperture.

"Please, stop, driver!" wept the girl, choking. "I will pay you!"

I tried to tear loose then the steel slats from the aperture, to wad the jacket inside. I could not get my fingers behind them.

The girl crouched forward, pressing her hands and face against the heavy glass separating us from the driver. "Please, please," she wept, "please, stop, driver! I will pay you!" She scratched at the window. "I'm pretty!" she said. "I will even let you kiss me, if you want. Let me go! Let me go!"

I began to pound at the glass on my side. It, too, as I instantly realized, with a sickening feeling, was unusually thick. It was not a standard safety glass. The door, though it had appeared a normal door, had been especially constructed to receive it.

Suddenly, spasmodically, miserably, my lungs bursting, I expelled air. Then, as new air rushed into my lungs, I felt sick and half strangled. Whatever the molecules of the gas might be I knew they would be soon, and in volume, within my blood stream. I shook my head. My eyes watered.

The girl shrank back, coughing. She drew her legs up on the seat. She looked at me, miserably. "What do they want of me, Jason?" she asked. "What are they going to do to me?"

"I don't know," I said. "I have no idea." The only thing that occurred to me was so horrifying and fantastic that I could not even bring myself to consider it as a possibility, let alone mention it to the terrified girl. It was simply too horrifying even to think about. I looked at her, she so frightened, in the cape and sheath dress, her feet drawn up beneath her on the leather of the seat of the cab. She was a lusciously beautiful young woman, of the sort that might drive men mad for her. I drove the thought from my mind. No, it could not be! They could not want her for that! But what man would not? No, I told myself, no! It could not be! I dismissed it from my mind. The possibility was too horrifying to even consider as a reality.

"Jason," she said. "Help me!"

I turned from her and, with my fingers, tried to find some crack or crevice between glass and steel, to the side and in front of me, anything that I might be able to exploit. I could find nothing.

I turned back to look at her.

"Jason," she said. "Help me."

"I can't," I said.

She knelt now on the leather of the seat, facing to the side, toward the opposite window. She turned her upper body to face the driver's back. "Please let me go," she cried out, miserably. "I will let you make love to me," she said to the driver, "if you will let me go."

I do not know why I then said to her what I did. For some reason I was furious.

"Shut up," I said to her, "you stupid little slave!"

She looked at me with horror.

"Do you, who are owned," I asked, "think to bargain with masters?"

Did she not know that she, if her captors wished, was theirs in her entirety?

Why had I been so angry with her? Why had such terrible words sprung up so wildly and spontaneously from hitherto unfathomed depths within me?

I looked at her beauty. I saw it then, suddenly, and deliciously and marvelously, as a slave's beauty. In every woman there is a slave, in every man a slaver.

She put down her head, not daring to meet my eyes in that moment.

Why was I so angry with her? Was it because it was others, and not I, who owned her?

She knelt, head down, on the leather of the seat. Gone then was the pretense of her politics. Gone then was the illusion of her freedom and independence, and her arrogance and pride. She was then only a frightened girl and perhaps, I feared, a captured slave.

Then, suddenly, I was again the male of Earth, apologetic, miserable, self-castigating, overcome with anguish. How cruel I had been to her! How grievously I had demeaned her! Did I not know she was a person?

"Forgive me, Miss Henderson," I wept. "I did not know what I was saying."

She sank down on the seat. I was kneeling then on the floor of the cab.

"I'm sorry," I said. "I'm sorry." Indeed, I was truly sorry. I had no idea why I had said what I had. In the stress of our strait circumstances it had just welled up from within me, cruelly, insuppressibly, explosively.

Of course she was not a slave! Yet, as I looked upon her, now slumped down, unconscious, on the leather, naught but a pathetic captive, I could not help but remark how maddeningly luscious were her small curves. I could not help but wonder what they would look like, owned, in silk and steel. I could not help but wonder if girls such as Miss Henderson, so fantastically beautiful and feminine, might not, in actuality, be slave girls. If so, why, then, should they not be enslaved? Then I put such thoughts from my mind. The cab, moving swiftly, continued on its way. I could see why men might want Miss Henderson. She would be a prize for the collar. They would not, of course, presumably, want me. I realized now, from the driver's behavior earlier, that he had not counted on my being in the cab. The quarry had not been me, but the beautiful Miss Henderson. It had been an accident that I had been captured as well. Things began to go black. I fought to retain consciousness. I recall looking again at Miss Henderson. I recall, as things began to become dim, the last thing in my field of vision, her lovely ankle. It would look well, I thought, in a loop and ring. I wondered what would be done with me. Then I lost consciousness.

# 2    SYRINGES

I felt a bit of cold air, as the door of the cab was opened. Slowly, painfully, I began to come back to consciousness.

I was aware of Miss Henderson being lifted from the cab.

Then I, too, was removed from the cab, two men dragging me by the arms. We were inside a garagelike structure. The floor was cement. Miss Henderson was laid on her stomach on the cement. The light in the building was furnished by four bulbs overhead. They hung on cords from the ceiling. They had dark metal shades with white-enameled interiors, and were protected by wire frames.

I, too, was placed on my stomach on the cement. I felt my hands being drawn behind my back. They were then, to my consternation, locked in handcuffs.

I saw, from my position on the floor, five men. There was the driver of our cab, three burly fellows, two in jackets and one in a sweater, and one other man, dressed in a rumpled suit, his necktie loose about his throat. He was a large man, and heavy. He had, too, large, heavy hands. He seemed very strong. He was balding, virile.

"Awaken the slave," he said.

One of the men then, from behind, put his hands in Miss Henderson's hair and, rudely, with two hands, pulled her up backwards, she crying out suddenly with pain, awakening, finding herself kneeling, held by the hair, before the heavy man.

"It is you!" she said. "The man from the apartment!"

"You have not been given permission to speak," he said to her.

"I do not need permission to speak," she cried. "I am a free woman! I am not a slave!"

"Oh!" she cried, in pain, as the man's hands, he who held her, tightened in her hair, pulling her head back.

Her small hands, clutching at him, were helpless on his thick wrists.

"You had best form the habit early, of addressing free men as 'Master,' Slave Girl," said the heavy man.

"I am not a slave girl," she cried. Then she cried out in pain, as her hair was twisted. Then she added, "—Master."

The heavy man gestured to the man who held the girl. He released the tension in the girl's hair, but he did not take his hands from it. She gasped. She looked up at the heavy man.

"That is better," he said.

"Yes," she said, "—Master."

"To be sure," he said, "the point is moot, and interesting. There is a sense in which you are a slave, and a sense in which you are not a slave. The sense in which you are a slave is the sense in which I am justified in addressing you as a slave, and referring to you as a slave. That is the sense of the natural slave. Do not react so, my dear. It is true. You are a natural slave. This is fully clear to anyone who is familiar with such matters. Any slaver, any master, anyone who knows women, even another woman, but one knowledgeable in such matters, could tell it at a glance. Do not fret. It is simply true. And, indeed, if you derive any reassurance from this remark, you are one of the most obvious natural slaves I have ever seen. Your slavery, already, lies almost at the surface."

"No," she said, "no!"

"Your culture has provided little scope for the satisfaction and fulfillment of your slave needs," he said. "Other cultures, you will discover, are more tolerant and generous in this respect."

"No!" she cried.

"The sense in which you are not a slave, of course," he said, "is a trivial one. You have not yet been placed within the actual institution of slavery. You are not yet a legal slave, a slave under law. You have not yet, for example, been branded, nor have you been put in a collar, nor have you performed a gesture of submission."

She looked at him with horror.

"But do not fear," he said, "you will eventually find yourself in full compliance with any necessary legal pedantries. You will eventually find that you are, fully and legally, under law, a slave, totally a slave, and only a slave." He smiled at her. "You may now say, 'Yes, Master,' " he said.

"Yes, Master," she whispered.

"Put the slave on her stomach," he said.

The man who held her hair threw the girl forward. She broke her fall with her hands. He then, with his foot, pressed her down to her stomach. I could see the mark of his boot on the back of her white dress.

"Put your hands at the sides of your head, palms down on the cement," said the heavy man.

"Yes," she said.

"Yes, what?" he asked.

"Yes, Master," she said. Then she cried out, "You can't enslave me!"

"Slavery is neither a new nor unusual phenomenon for women," he said. "In the course of human history many millions of lovely women have been enslaved. They have found themselves at the feet of masters. You are not special. Your fate is in no way historically unique."

He then removed a leather case from a white-enameled cabinet to one side. He placed the contents of the case on a steel table against one wall, on which there were certain tools. It contained two vials, cotton and a set of disposable syringes.

"I can't be a slave," she said. "I'm Beverly Henderson!"

"Enjoy your name while you still have it," he said. "Later you will be called only by those names by which masters please." I then understood, as I had not before, the remark of the heavy man in the apartment, which had been reported to me by the girl, that she might not have her name long. A slave, of course, would have no name in her own right. She must wear, docilely, any name her master might see fit to put upon her.

The girl moaned.

The heavy man then poured some fluid from one of the vials onto a piece of cotton.

"But, perhaps," he said, "your master will choose to call you Beverly. That, it seems to me, is a lovely name for a slave."

He nodded to the fellow who had held the girl's hair. That fellow, as she whimpered, tore open her dress at the waist on the left side. He then jerked back the sides of the dress, exposing a portion of flesh.

"The name then, of course, would be only a slave name," he said, "affixed on you by the will of the master." He smiled down at her. "Say, 'Yes, Master,'" he said.

"Yes, Master," she said.

He crouched down beside her and, with the cotton onto which he had poured some fluid from one of the vials, swabbed a portion of her exposed flesh.

She shuddered.

"It's cold, isn't it?" he asked. "It's alcohol."

"Yes, Master," she whispered. He left the cotton on her body and went back to the leather case on the steel table. With another piece of cotton and some additional alcohol he sterilized the rubber diaphragm sealing the second vial. He then broke off the sanitary seal on one of the disposable syringes and, holding the second vial, now sterilized, upside down, inserted the long needle through the rubber diaphragm. He drew a greenish fluid into the needle.

"What are you doing?" begged the girl.

He replaced the second vial on the steel table and approached her. He crouched down beside her.

"I am preparing you for shipment," he said.

"Shipment!" she cried.

"Of course," he said. He lifted away the cotton he had left on her body.

"Where?" she asked.

"Can you not guess, you little fool?" he asked.

"No," she whispered.

"What a delicious, but stupid little slave you are," he said.

"Where, Master?" she asked. "Oh!" she cried, as the needle was entered into her body, in her back, just behind and above the left hip.

I tried to struggle to my feet. But a booted foot, that of one of the men behind me, pressed me down.

The girl began to sob. The heavy man, after a few moments, drew the needle from her flesh. The syringe was then empty. He again swabbed the area into which the needle had penetrated.

"Where, Master?" begged the girl, shuddering from the coolness of the alcohol. "Where?"

"Why, to the planet Gor," he said.

"Gor does not exist!" she cried.

"Let us not enter into fruitless controversy," he said.

"It does not exist!" she cried.

"You will better be able to adjudge the truth of that matter later," he said, "when you awaken chained in a Gorean dungeon."

He rose to his feet. He handed the cotton and the used disposable syringe to one of the men, who discarded them.

"I can't be a slave. I can't be a slave!" she wept.

"You are a slave," he said, looking down on her.

"No!" she said.

"Indeed," he said, "you are one of the most luscious and exquisite natural slaves I have ever seen."

"No," she said. "No!"

"Do not rise from your stomach," he cautioned her.

"Yes, Master," she wept. She trembled, and moaned. "You have drugged me," she said.

"It is kindness that we have done so," he said. "The trip, otherwise, would be very difficult for you."

She began to sob, uncontrollably.

"Relax, relax, little slave," he said to her, soothingly.

"Yes, Master," she said. Then she was unconscious.

I watched in horror as Miss Henderson's clothing was cut from her, completely. A crate was then brought forward. It opened from the side. Inside it were various straps. One of the men busied himself with gagging the girl. The gag was of leather, black, and effective. It buckled behind her neck with two buckles. I gathered they were taking no chances on the possibility of the effects of the drug prematurely wearing off. The heavy man then brought forth a long, narrow, rectangular leather case. In it, aligned, each held in its place by the construction of the interior of the case, each in its cushioned slot, was the remainder, some six or so, of what must once have been a series of something like twenty steel anklets.

Miss Henderson, now gagged, lay unconscious on her back on the cement.

The heavy man put the case down on the steel table, made a note of something in a small notebook, and then threw one of the steel devices to the fellow who stood by Miss Henderson, he who had gagged her unconscious body.

I saw then that the device was indeed a steel anklet. The man snapped it snugly about Miss Henderson's ankle, her left ankle. The snap was heavy, sharp, businesslike. Her ankle was then locked in the device. To my horror I realized she could not remove it. She would have to wear it until men chose to take it from her.

"H-4642?" asked the heavy man.

The other man lifted Miss Henderson's ankle, inspecting the steel locked there. "Yes," he said.

The heavy man closed his notebook.

He nodded to the man at the side of Miss Henderson, and to another man, as well.

Not speaking these two men then, as I watched, from my helpless, prone position, placed Miss Henderson in the crate. They placed her sitting in the crate, its open side to her left. Her head was first drawn back and fixed in place. There was a ring on the back of the gag straps and a ring within the crate. These two rings snapped together, holding her head back. A heavy black belt then, attached in the container, was looped about her waist. She was thrust back in the container further. Then the belt was tightened about her and buckled shut. Each of her wrists was then strapped back, her left wrist on her left side, her right wrist on her right side, the back of each wrist against the side of the container against which her back rested. Because of the smallness of the container her knees must be thrust up. Both ankles, then, one on the left, one on the right, were strapped in place.

The heavy man looked at the girl.

The heavy belt, buckled tightly about her belly, held her body back against one wall of the container. Her head, too, by the two rings, was held in place. Her wrists were strapped back, her ankles were strapped down. She was gagged.

The heavy man smiled. There was little doubt but what the fair prize was well secured.

I suppose I should not have looked upon her, but I could not help myself. Clothed, she had been beautiful; naked, she was fantastic. I could scarcely imagine the joy and power a man would feel, having such a woman at his feet.

"Close the crate," said the heavy man.

I saw the hinged side of the crate swung shut, inclosing Miss Henderson within it, a steel anklet, numbered, apparently an identificatory device, locked on her left ankle.

When the side of the crate had swung shut, it had snapped shut. Two fastenings had been engaged. Two men, now, twisted some ten screw bolts shut. There would be no way the container could be opened from the inside. There were two small, round holes, each about a half of an inch in width, in the upper half of the side of the crate which had served as its door. It was through these that the girl would breathe.

I looked at the crate. It occurred to me that its contents, Miss Henderson, if she were truly a slave, would one day, doubtless, be put up for sale. The thought of Miss Henderson on a slave block, actually, not just in my imagination, was almost overwhelming.

"Put the crate in the van," said the heavy man.

Two men picked up the crate and carried it from the room. Another man preceded them, presumably to facilitate their passage and, perhaps, open the van.

I felt, along the floor, a flood of fresh air. Somewhere a door had been opened. I tensed. I felt, then, a boot in the small of my back, pressing me down. "Don't try anything," said a voice, that of he who had been the driver of the cab. The fresh-air draft then ceased. I heard a door shut in another room.

The heavy man then turned and looked at me.

"You treated her like merchandise," I said, angrily, to the heavy man.

"She is merchandise, a slave," he said.

"What are you going to do with her?" I asked.

"She is to be shipped to another world, one called Gor," he said, "where she will be branded as what she is, a slave, and then sold on the open market for whatever she will bring."

"How can you do this?" I demanded.

"It is my business," he said. "I am a slaver."

"But have you no pity for your pathetic captures?" I asked.

"They deserve no pity," he said. "They are only slaves."

"But what of their happiness?" I asked.

"It is unimportant," he said. "But, if it is of interest to you, no woman is truly happy until she is owned and mastered."

I was silent.

"Free a woman," he said, "and she will try to destroy you. Enslave her, and she will crawl to you on her belly, and beg to lick your sandals."

"Madness!" I cried. "False! False!"

The heavy man smiled at the man behind me. "He seems a typical man of Earth, does he not?" he asked.

"He does, indeed," said the man behind me. I then felt again the draft of fresh air, which then, in a moment, ceased. The other three men then re-entered the room. "The crate is in the van, with the others," said one of them.

I was startled. There must, then, be other girls, too, who were to share the sordid, horrifying fate of Miss Henderson.

I then found myself the center of the attention of the five men. I became suddenly very frightened. I began to sweat. I realized that neither Miss Henderson nor myself had been blindfolded. The men, thus, had not apparently been concerned that we would, at a future time, be able to identify either themselves or the interior of the large structure in which we had found ourselves.

"What—what are you going to do with me?" I asked.

He who had been the driver of the cab now walked about me, until he stood some eight or ten feet in front of me. I saw, then, that he carried a revolver. From his jacket pocket he took a hollow, cylindrical object. He spunt it onto the barrel of the revolver. It was a silencer, which would muffle the report of a pistol.

"What are you going to do with me?" I demanded.

"You have seen too much, and you are of no use to us," said the heavy man.

I tried to struggle to my feet, but two men held me down on the cement.

Out of the corner of my eye I saw the revolver, with its silencer. Then I felt the blunt end of the silencer pressing against my left temple.

"Don't shoot me," I begged. "Please!"

"He is not worth a bullet," said the heavy man. "Put him on his knees. Use a wire garrote."

The man who had driven the cab removed the silencer from his revolver. He dropped it back in his pocket and put the revolver in his belt. I was thrown to my knees, two men holding my arms, my hands helpless behind my back in the confining steel cuffs.

The fifth man, the one who had opened the door for the others with the crate, was then behind me. I felt a thin wire suddenly looped about my throat.

"I have another pickup to make tonight," said the fellow who had driven the cab.

"We will meet you on the highway," said the heavy man. "You know where."

He who had driven the cab nodded.

"We are to be at the new point of embarkation at four A.M.," said the heavy man.

"She gets off work at two," said he who had driven the cab. "I will be waiting for her."

"It will be close," said the heavy man, "but proceed. We can strip and inject her, and crate her, in the van."

I felt the wire loop tighten about my throat.

"Please, no, please, don't!" I cried.

"It will be swift," said the heavy man.

"Please, don't kill me!" I begged.

"Do you plead for your life?" asked the heavy man.

"Yes," I said, "yes, yes!"

"But what are we to do with you?" asked the heavy man.

"Don't kill me, please don't kill me," I begged. I squirmed on my knees, the wire on my throat.

The heavy man looked down at me, on my knees, helpless, before him.

"Please," I said. "Please!"

"Behold the typical man of Earth," said the heavy man.

"We are not all such weaklings and cowards," said one of the men.

"That is true," admitted the heavy man. Then he looked down at me. "Is there any hope," he asked, "for males, not men, such as you?"

"I do not understand," I stammered.

"How I despise your sort," he said, "fools, cowards and weaklings, guilt-ridden, confused, smug, meaningless, pretentious, soft, males who have permitted themselves to be tricked out of the prerogatives of their sex, robbed of the birthright of their own manhood, who dare not be true to the needs of their own blood, males too weak, too frightened and ashamed, to be men."

It startled me that he had said these things, for I had thought myself unusual among the men of Earth in my manhood. Indeed, I had often been castigated and belittled for having been too masculine. Now he spoke of me as though I had not even, as yet, begun to glimpse the meaning of true manhood. I was shaken. I began to tremble. What then could be biological manhood, in the fullness of its rationality and strength? I had, already, begun to suspect that manhood was not a mere pretention, as I had been taught, but soomething selected for, as seems reasonable, like the nature of the eagle and the lion, in the long, harsh realities of a brutal evolution, but now, for the first time, I had begun to suspect that my conception of manhood, so advanced I had thought, did little more than begin to hint at the possible glories of a suppressed, thwarted, tortured reality, a reality genetically dispositional in every cell in a man's body, a reality feared and castigated by a counterbiological culture. I came from a world in which eagles cannot fly. I put down my head. Lions do not well thrive in a country of poisons.

"Look up at me," said the heavy man.

I lifted my head.

"I find you guilty of treason," he said.

"I have committed no treason," I said.

"You are guilty of the most heinous of treasons," said the heavy man. "You have betrayed yourself, your sex, your manhood. You are a despicable traitor, not only to yourself but to true men, everywhere. You are an insult not only to your own manhood but to that of others. You are a sniveling coward and a weakling, worthy to be held only in the most profound of contempts."

"A man must be strong enough to be weak," I said. "He must be brave enough to be sweet. True men must be gentle and tender, and considerate, and solicitous, and do what women wish. That is how they prove they are true men."

"True men give orders to women, and women obey," said the heavy man.

"It is not what I have been taught," I said.

"You have been taught lies," said the heavy man. "Surely your own misery and unhappiness should tell you that."

"He has been found guilty of treason," said one of the men holding my arms. "What is the sentence?"

The heavy man looked at the others. I felt the wire on my throat. "What should the sentence be?" he asked.

"The termination of his miserable existence," said one of the men, "death."

The heavy man looked down at me. "I wonder," said he, "if there is any hope for such as you."

"Let the sentence be death," said another one of the men.

"Or something else," said the heavy man.

"I do not understand," said the fellow who had first suggested that I be slain.

"Look at him," said the heavy man. "Does he not seem a typical male of Earth?"

"Yes," said one of the men. "Yes," said another.

"Yet, beyond that," said the heavy man, "his features appear symmetrical and his body, though soft and weak, is large."

"Yes?" said one of the men.

"Do you think a woman might find him pleasing?" asked the heavy man.

"Perhaps," smiled one of the men.

"Throw him on his belly and tie his legs," said the heavy

man. I felt the wire whipped from my throat. I was thrown forward on the cement. My belt was loosened and torn from its loops. My ankles were crossed and, with the belt, lashed together, tightly. In a few seconds I felt my shirt being jerked away from my left side, and felt the cold swab of the cotton and alcohol and, a moment later, the entrance of the needle, deeply, into my flesh.

"What are you going to do with me?" I asked, terrified.

"Do not talk now," he said.

I felt the fluid entering my body. It was apparently considerably more than he had injected into Miss Henderson. It was painful. Then he withdrew the needle from my back and swabbed the area again with alcohol and cotton.

"What are you going to do with me?" I whispered.

"You are going to be taken to the planet Gor," he said. "I think I know a little market where you might be of interest."

"Gor does not exist," I said.

He rose to his feet and discarded the cotton and the second syringe.

"Gor does not exist!" I said.

"Put him in the van," he said to the men.

"You are mad, all of you!" I cried. I was lifted by two men. "Gor does not exist!" I cried. I was being carried toward the door. "Gor does not exist!" I cried. "Gor does not exist!"

Then I lost consciousness.

# 3 THE LADY GINA

I screamed with pain, awakening suddenly. I tried to get to my feet. I could not do so. My wrists and ankles seemed confined. There was something heavy on my neck. I got to my hands and knees. I could not believe my senses. I was collared, and naked and shackled. Then the lash fell again, and I cried out with misery, slipping to my stomach. I lay on a flooring of large blocks of fitted stone. My wrists were chained to one iron ring, my ankles to another. I felt wet straw beneath my body. The stones were damp. There were no windows in the room. The light was dim, being furnished by a tiny lamp in a small niche. The place was dank, and smelled of wastes. I thought it might be far below the ground. I was intensely conscious of the heavy metal collar I wore. There was, attached to it, as I conjectured, hearing the tiny sound of its movement and its clink on the stone beneath my body, a smaller piece of metal, perhaps a ring of some sort.

Then the lash, as I wept from the pain, struck me again and again.

"Please, stop!" I begged. "Please, stop!"

Then I no longer felt the disciplinary tearing of the leather at my flesh.

The gravity of this world was different from that of my own, being slightly less. I knew then I was no longer on Earth.

I turned, frightened, in the chains, to see who had struck me.

A strong woman stood there, perhaps some five feet ten inches in height and one hundred and forty pounds in weight. She was breathing heavily and, in two hands, held the whip tightly gripped. She was dark-haired and dark-eyed. She was muscular and strong, but her figure was striking. She wore a leather halter and tights of black leather. Her midriff was strikingly white, and her arms and legs. There was a golden armlet on her left arm. Her hair was held back by a leather band. She wore a heavy, studded belt, tightly buckled, and heavy sandals, almost like boots, with thongs. From her belt there hung a ring of keys and a coiled chain, with a snap. On her belt, toward the back, on her right side, in a snap strap, hung a pair of steel manacles.

I tried to turn away from her, for I was naked, but she drew back the whip and, suddenly, again struck me.

"You are a woman," I said, half turned from her, stung by the fierce stroke of her whip. There were tears in my eyes.

"Do not insult me," she said.

She then struck me again with the whip. I cried out with misery.

She then changed her position, walking about me, until she stood a few feet ahead of the forward ring, that to which my hands were chained. Again I tried to turn to the side, that I might not be so shamefully exposed to her.

"Kneel facing me," she said. "Spread your legs."

I did so, miserable with embarrassment.

"Free persons may look upon you as they please," she said.

"You speak English," I said.

"A little," she said, "not much. Some four years ago my superiors thought that it might be useful for me to learn the language. A female captive, a graduate student in linguistics, kept under close discipline, was acquired to teach me. When I had learned a sufficient amount she was disposed of."

"Slain?" I asked.

"No," she smiled. "She was intelligent and attractive. Thus we made her a slave and sold her. She was purchased by a strong master. She will serve him well."

"But you do not much use your English?" I asked.

"No longer," she said. "For a time we used it in the training of Earth wenches, slave girls. But now, from this facility, as from others, they are simply scattered, after two or three days' training, to various markets, sold, for most practical purposes, ignorant and raw. They are then forced to learn the language of their masters directly, as a child learns, not through the medium of their old tongue. The method is efficient. The girls become quickly acclimated to their chains and collars in a unilingual environment, that of their masters."

"Are you holding, here," I asked, "an Earth girl named Beverly Henderson?"

"Slaves have no names," she said, "unless it pleases the masters to name them."

"She is dark-haired and dark-eyed," I said, "very pretty, about five feet in height and ninety-five pounds in weight."

"Oh, the exquisite little beauty," she said.

"Yes," I said.

"I wish that I had been able to get my hands on her," she said.

"Where is she?" I asked.

"I do not know," she said. "She and the others, hooded and chained, have already been separated and sent to various markets, to be sold. They will quickly learn to be superb slaves."

I looked at her.

"It was a lovely shipment," she said. "Masters will be pleased to own them."

I moaned. What a miserable fate awaited the lovely Miss Henderson and, of course, her fellow captives, or slaves.

"You know nothing of where they were sent?" I asked.

"No," she said. "I am not privy to that information."

I shook my head in misery. Miss Henderson, the helpless little beauty, now totally in the power of men, could be anywhere on this world.

I lifted my chained wrists. "Why am I chained?" I asked.

"What a stupid fool you are," she said. Then she walked about me, whip in hand. "Yet you are a pretty one," she said. "To a woman you might not be unattractive."

Then she stood again before me.

I shrank back in the chains. I was acutely conscious of the clasp of the steel on my wrists and ankles.

She approached me and, with the coils of the whip, tapped the metal on my neck. "This is a collar," she said. Then, with her left hand, she jerked at the metal piece attached to the collar. From the way it felt I gathered that it was, as I had suspected, a ring. Then it fell back against the collar and against my collarbone. She then stepped back, and regarded me. Never had I been looked upon so objectively by a woman. "I think you will do very nicely," she said.

"Release me, please," I said.

She then struck me twice, viciously, with the whip.

I fell to my stomach on the stone and straw. I tried to cover my head with my chained hands. Five times more the whip fell, mercilessly.

"On your back," she said.

I rolled on my back, and lay, miserably, at her feet. She caressed the side of my body with the coils of the whip. "Yes," she said, "I think you will do very nicely. Now, again on your knees, legs spread, before me!"

Then again I knelt before her, precisely as she had commanded, obeying her. Frightened, I lifted my eyes to those of my sturdy jailer. Her eyes frightened me. They were cruelly hard, uncompromising, dominating. Never in my life had I seen such inflexible will manifested in the eyes of a woman. I put down my head. I realized that her will was stronger than mine. I feared she would be strict with me. I trembled. I was afraid of her.

I felt the whip under my chin, lifting my head. Again I looked at her. "Do not be afraid," she said, soothingly, "Slave."

"I am not a slave," I said.

She stepped back, and laughed. She went to my left. The wall there had the shape of a large, conical arch. The area which would have been open, however, was closed by heavy bars, reinforced every six inches or so by sturdy, lateral crosspieces. In this wall of bars, itself also formed of bars and crosspieces, was a heavy gate. Beyond the bars and crosspieces I could see a corridor, some eight feet wide. On the other side of the corridor I could see another cell. As nearly as I could tell, it was empty. My jailer stood very straight and proudly, whip in hand, by the heavy gate. Her flesh seemed very white. I saw the keys and the coiled chain which hung at her belt and, toward the back, on the right side, in their snap strap, the steel manacles she carried.

"Prodicus," she called. "Gron!"

In a moment two extremely large and powerful men had responded to her call. They were dressed not unlike her, save for the halter and the leather band which bound back her hair. Their chests, bare, were large and broad. The chest of one was hairy; that of the other was smooth. Their arms and thighs were like iron. They carried no whips. One seemed Caucasian and the other Oriental. The Caucasian had shaggy, brown hair and the Oriental had had his head shaved, except for a topknot of black, shiny hair. They pushed into the cell, for she had apparently left the gate unlocked following her entrance. Or, perhaps, it had not been locked, considering the confinement of my chains. She spoke to them rapidly in a language I did not understand. I heard her use the expression 'sleen'.

"What are you going to do?" I asked, frightened. The men approached me and I tried to pull back in my chains. I heard the clink of the metal piece, presumably a ring, on my collar. The men handled me like I was a child. I had never encountered such strength. I was thrown on my stomach. The chain and manacles fastening me to the forward ring were then removed and my hands were jerked behind my back. My hands were then locked anew in manacles, taken from the belt of one of the men. Then my ankles were freed of their impediments, and I was jerked to my feet, my arms held by the two men, one on each side of me.

"What are you going to do?" I asked the woman.

She did not respond, but turned and led the way from the cell. The two men holding my arms, I was forced, stumbling, rapidly, to follow her.

"No!" I screamed. "No!" I lay on my side. My ankles were crossed and tied. I saw a large side of meat being hoisted by me, hung on a dangling hook. I had looked into the pit. I heard the raging of the animals. "No," I begged. A rope was tied, tightly, about my waist, and then tied about the linkage between the manacles confining my hands behind my back. My hands, then, must be held close to the small of my back. "Please, no, please, no!" I begged. Two men took another side of meat, large and heavy, and thrust it on a new hook. Then it was lifted up and swung, on a set of ropes, over the edge of the barrier and toward the center of the circular, sunken enclosure, whence it was lowered. I heard the snarling, the squealing, the frenzied feeding. "Please, no!" I begged. Never had I seen such beasts. They were darkly colored, usually brown, and some were black. They were, some of them, as much as twenty feet in length. Several must have weighed between twelve and fourteen hundred pounds. They were six legged, clawed, and doubly fanged. Their heads were wide and triangular, like those of vipers, but their bodies, long and sinuous, were thickly furred. They twisted and squirmed about one another. I had been held by the two men at the edge of the barrier, to see the attack on the first piece of lowered meat. The animals leaped for it, some of them thirty or more feet into the air. Some even caught and clung to it as it was being lowered, tearing at it and cutting at it with their hind pairs of feet. There was a stink in the place of the animals, and the noise of their snarling, their hissing, their squealing and challenge screams was ear-piercing and horrifying.

"No!" I screamed. One of the two men slipped a hook under the ropes that bound my ankles. In a moment it began to ascend and I was lifted, feet upward, above the walkway encircling the sunken enclosure. I hung, helpless, head downward.

"Please, no!" I wept.

The woman in the black leather, she whom I had taken as my jailer, gave a signal.

"No, please!" I cried.

Helpless I felt myself lifted higher and, on the system of ropes, carried out over the sunken enclosure, the floor of which was some seventy-five feet below me.

I could sense the animals below me, their large size, the fetid smell, almost overwhelming, swirling upward, their energetic stirring, their twisting in and about one another. I put my head back and could glimpse several of the furred bodies below. I saw their heads raised, their eyes blazing, their long, dark tongues, triangular, their distended jaws, the two rows of fangs. Then I felt the rope give a hitch and I was lowered a foot toward them.

The first of the beasts leaped upward toward me, falling short by several feet, falling back, scrambling, among the others.

I was then lowered some five to seven feet again. I wept with misery. I could feel the heavy collar now against the bottom of my chin, as it had slipped down. The metal attachment, which I took to be a ring, lay against my chin.

I was then lowered some ten more feet, then another ten feet.

The animals were now much more frenzied, save for some, here and there in the enclosure, in small groups, snarling and scratching, tearing apart meat already lowered into the pit.

The rope then again slipped, being lowered again.

"Please, stop!" I begged. I could see the woman with such white skin, she in the black leather, with the whip, at the height of the barrier. Behind her were the two brutes who had taken me from my cell. I had never seen such strength as theirs. I had been helpless in their hands. They had controlled me with utter ease.

I was now, squirming and crying, some forty feet above the floor of the pit below.

The rope lowered again.

I screamed with misery.

The animals, then, began to leap upward. I heard jaws snap not more than a yard or so below my head. I saw the raking of broad claws, exposed, curved and white, pass sweeping below me. I was certain they could, with a single, wicked blow, half tear my head from my body.

My screams mingled with the raging snarls and piercing hunger screams of the beasts.

The rope gave another hitch, and I was lowered another foot.

Then I was lowered another foot.

I cried out with misery.

Then I felt my body, suddenly, swung to the side and drawn upward. I was hoisted up, on the system of ropes, then, to the barrier, and over it. The two brutes who had taken me from my cell removed me from the hook. They then unbound my ankles. They then removed the rope from my belly, which had held the manacles close to the small of my back. Two men placed a large piece of meat on the hook from which I had been removed and, in a moment, on the system of ropes, had hoisted it over the barrier, out over the enclosure, and down to the animals. I heard them fighting, tearing at it. The large Oriental fellow pulled my hands, manacled behind my back, toward him. He then, with a key, removed them from me and replaced them in the snap strap at his belt. They had been his.

"Kneel," said the fair-skinned, leather-clad woman, my jailer.

I knelt, terrified. I could hear the animals tearing apart the meat below.

"Legs spread," she said.

I complied, shuddering.

"Do you know now you are a slave?" she asked.

"Yes," I said, "yes!"

"Yes, what?" she asked.

"I don't know," I said. "I don't know!"

" 'Yes, Mistress,' " she said.

"Yes, Mistress," I said.

"Say now," she said, " 'I am a slave, Mistress.' "

"I am a slave, Mistress," I said.

"Say now," she said, " 'I am your slave, Mistress.' "

"I am your slave Mistress," I said.

"You may now put your head down and kiss my feet," she said.

I did so. I was terrified of her.

"Do you know on what world you now find yourself?" she asked.

I dared not answer her.

"It is called 'Gor'," she said.

"Yes, Mistress," I said. I trembled. I almost fainted. There was truly a Gor.

"Look up, Slave," she said.

I looked up.

"And on Gor," she said, "you are a slave."

"Yes, Mistress," I said.

"On Gor," she said, "we do not accept disobedience in slaves, not the least disobedience, is that clearly understoood?"

"Yes, Mistress," I said.

"Beyond that," she said, "a slave is expected to be fully pleasing, fully. Is that understood, perfectly?"

"Yes, Mistress," I said.

"The animals you have seen are called sleen," she said. "They are used for many purposes on Gor. One purpose they are commonly used for is to hunt down and destroy slaves. That is the purpose, incidentally, for which the animals you have just seen have been trained."

"Yes, Mistress," I said.

"It is common also on Gor to take troublesome or disobedient slaves, or recalcitrant slaves, or slaves who have not been fully pleasing, perhaps even in a quite minor way, either male or female salves, and feed them to sleen. Indeed, sometimes slaves are fed to sleen simply for the amusement of the masters."

"Yes, Mistress," I said.

"Do you understand now, just a little, what it might be to be a slave on Gor?" she asked.

"Yes, Mistress," I said.

"Get on your hands and knees," she said.

I did so.

One of the men, the strong fellow with brown, shaggy hair,

said something to her. She laughed, and shook her head. They exchanged a remark or two, and then the two men, the fellow with brown, shaggy hair and the other man, the large Oriental fellow, turned about and left.

"He was asking," she said, "if I wished him to accompany me back to the cell." She hung the whip on her belt, folding back its blades. There was a small ring on the butt end of the whip which fitted over a hook on the belt. The blades of the whip fitted under a clip, also on the belt. She turned the collar on my throat, so that the metal attachment, or ring, was at the back. "I told him it would not be necessary," she said. She unslung the metal chain from her belt. "I told him you were tame," she said. She then snapped the chain on the collar. She jerked it. I was on my hands and knees, leashed. "You are tamed, aren't you?" she asked.

"Yes, Mistress," I said.

"Come along now," she said. "We are returning to the cell."

"Yes, Mistress," I said.

"Kneel here," she said.

I knelt where she indicated. She took the shackles from the rear ring and snapped them on my ankles.

She came around in front of me, and crouched down. "Put your wrists here," she said.

I put my wrists where she had indicated and she snapped them into the waiting manacles, those attached to the forward ring. She had already removed the chain leash from my collar and, coiling it, slung it on her belt.

I then knelt chained before her. I was again in my cell. Again my ankles were shackled to a ring. Again my wrists were manacled to the forward ring. Things were much as they had been before, before she had called the men to fetch me forth from the cell. There was, however, one important difference. Before there had knelt on that spot a free man in chains. There knelt there now only a chained slave.

She stood up and backed away a bit, and stood there, regarding me.

"You will commonly," she said, not unkindly, "when kneeling before a free woman, keep your knees spread, unless your lady wishes otherwise."

"Yes, Mistress," I said.

"That is right," she said. "I find that good. But remember, the whim of the Mistress is everything."

"Yes, Mistress," I said.

"You are, as far as I know," she said, "the first male of Earth brought to Gor as a slave."

"It is an accident that I am here," I said. "I fell across the path of slavers. Please send me back to Earth."

"Be silent, Slave," she said.

"Yes, Mistress," I said.

She walked around behind me, where I could not see her.

"I was once, for a time, on your planet," she said.

"Oh?" I said.

I heard a very tiny sound, almost inaudible, metallic.

"Did you hear that sound?" she asked.

"Yes," I said.

"It is the sound of the whip being removed from my belt," she said.

I said nothing.

"You will learn to know it well," she said. "Yes," she said, "a year and a half ago, in the service of my superiors, I spent several months on your world. Are you afraid you are going to be lashed?"

"Yes, Mistress," I said.

"It was there," she said, "that I learned the nature of the males of Earth, and to despise them."

"Yes, Mistress," I said.

I heard a tiny sound again, very similar to the first.

"I have replaced the whip on my belt," she said. Then she came again in front of me, where she might look down on me. The whip hung again at her belt.

"I'm not going to whip you now," she said.

"Thank you, Mistress," I said.

"What is your name?" she asked.

"Jason," I said. "Jason Marshall."

"You have no name," she said.

"Yes, Mistress," I said.

"But 'Jason' will do," she said. "You are Jason."

"Yes, Mistress," I said.

"The name is now a slave name," she said, "put on you because it pleases me."

"Yes, Mistress," I said. I was now a named slave.

She went to the side of the cell. There, on a shelf, were two shallow pans. They had been there before. She carried one of them over to me. It contained, as I now saw, pieces of meat. She held the pan in her left hand and, with her right hand, picked out a piece of meat.

She looked down at me.

"The transition to slavery will be easier for you than for a true man," she said, "but it will still, doubtless, not be easy for you."

I looked up at her, miserably.

"Feed, Jason," she said, putting the piece of meat in my mouth.

"I have been to Earth," she said. "I have seen the males there. There are so few men among them. Is it so hard, I wonder, to be a man. Why is it that so many of the males of Earth have given up their manhood, and pretend to rejoice in their mutilation. Doubtless there are complex historical causes. It is interesting, the grotesque shapes into which culture can shape a tortured biology."

As she spoke, she continued to feed me.

"But I feel no pity for you sorry males of Earth," she said, "for you have permitted this to be done to you. What despicable weaklings and cowards you are. You have little left to you but the vestiges of your manhood, and you let even those, bit by bit, be taken from you."

She thrust another piece of meat in my mouth.

"Poor, pretty Jason," she said. "He does not know what to think." She smiled at me. "I will tell you a secret, Jason," she said, "you were a slave before, but did not know it. You were the slave of a culture, of values, of propaganda and women. Your chains were invisible, so you pretended they did not exist. But did you not, nonetheless, feel their weight? Are things so different here than there for you? There is, surely, little true difference. The whips here, of course, are of real leather, and the chains of honest iron. When you feel them you need not pretend they are something other than what they are." She stopped feeding me. "They are precisely what they seem," she said, "true leather and iron. And you are precisely what you seem to be, a slave."

"Yes, Mistress," I said, miserably.

She then put the pan of meat down on the stones, where I might reach it. She then went back to the shelf and brought the other pan to where I knelt. She placed it within my reach, on the stones. It contained water.

"Put your head down and drink," she said. "Do not use your hands."

I put my head down and drank.

"Stop," she said.

I stopped.

She then, with her foot, white in that high, bootlike, thonged sandal, slid both the pan of meat and the pan of water out of my reach.

"The slave is completely dependent on the master or mistress," she said, "even for food and drink."

"Yes, Mistress," I said.

She then, again, with her foot, slid the pan of meat and the pan of water to where I might reach them.

"Say 'Thank you, Mistress,'" she said.

"Thank you, Mistress," I said.

"Put your head down again, and drink," she said.

Again I put my head down and, frightened, drank.

"Oh," she said, "how I despise you, and how I shall enjoy working with you."

I trembled.

"Look up, Jason," she said.

I looked up.

"Look into my eyes," she said.

I did so. It was difficult to meet her gaze.

"Who is stronger?" she asked.

"You, Mistress," I said. I had never encountered such inflexible resolve in a human being. I knew I could not begin to match the power and strength of her will, her stern character. I could only bend helplessly before it. She was totally superior to me. She was mistress; I was slave.

"Do I frighten you, Jason?" she asked.

"Yes, Mistress," I said.

"You need only try to be totally pleasing," she said. "You will then, to some extent, improve your chances for life."

"Yes, Mistress," I said.

"The matter rests with me," she said, "with whether I am pleased or not."

"I will try to please you, Mistress," I said.

"I'm sure you will, pretty Jason," she said. She then stepped back from me. "I am not so terrible," she said. "I can be kind."

I looked at her, startled.

"Oh," she laughed, slapping the whip roughly at her side,

"do not think I will not be strict with you. I am strict with all my charges. All, like yourself, must obey perfectly. All must be fully pleasing."

"Yes, Mistress," I said.

"But, too," she said, "I can be kind. There are worse mistresses on Gor than I."

"Yes, Mistress," I said.

"On this world, as on yours," she said, "there can be rewards for pleasing slaves. For example, perhaps in the future, you need not be chained like a raw slave, naked, in a stinking cell. There are better accomodations in the pens."

I put down my head. How conscious I was of the chains I wore.

She went to the heavy door of the cell, which she had left open. There she stopped, and turned to face me. I turned to my left, to see her.

"Rewards, like punishments," she said, "lie within the prerogatives of the mistress, to distribute, both with respect to type and abundance, as she pleases."

"I understand, Mistress," I said.

"You understand, too, do you not," she asked, "that you are in my total power?"

"Yes, Mistress," I said.

"Whether you live or die is up to my whim," she said.

"Yes, Mistress," I said, miserably.

"You are a slave," she said, "fully. Do you understand?"

"Yes, Mistress," I said.

"But I am not cruel," she said. "If you please me, totally, I may even be kind to you."

"I will try to please you, Mistress," I said.

"It is in my power to make your life more pleasant, if I choose," she said. "Rewards can be many and varied, different sorts of chains and cells, clothing, and of various sorts, a lighter collar, different sorts of food. I can even have a woman thrown to you." She smiled. "Or would you, a male of Earth, know what to do with one?"

She turned about then and went through the heavy door of the cell, that door formed, like that wall of the cell itself, of bars and heavy, lateral crosspieces, set some six inches apart. She swung shut the door and it closed, with a heavy metallic ring that reverberated in the cells and corridor. She stood behind it, looking at me.

"Yes," she said, "you are pretty, Jason. I think you will do very nicely."

"Who are you?" I cried.

She looked at me from the other side of the bars. She was a large woman, tall and strong. She stood very straight. Her figure was striking. Her skin was very white. It contrasted vividly with the brief, confining black leather she wore. She wore, too, a headband of leather. At her waist was the heavy belt, from which hung a coiled chain, a ring of keys, a pair of manacles and a whip. "I am the Lady Gina," she said, "your trainer."

"Trainer?" I cried.

"Yes," she said.

"I do not understand," I said. "What is your work?"

"Have you not guessed?" she asked. "I train men to give pleasure to women."

I looked at her with horror.

She then took the ring of keys from her belt and thrust a key into the lock on the cell door, and turned it, locking the heavy door.

"Sleep well, pretty Jason," she said. "Your lessons begin in the morning."

She then replaced the keys on her belt, and left.

# 4    LOLA AND TELA

"Put your wrists behind you," she said.

I stood in my cell. I had been freed of my chains. I put my wrists behind me, obeying the Lady Gina. She took the manacles from her belt and expertly, almost casually, in one motion, threw them on me, snapping them shut. I gathered she had manacled many men.

She tied a belt of soft, rolled cloth about my waist. She then took a long strip of cloth, some five feet long and eight inches wide, thrust it over the cloth belt in front, took it under and between my legs, passed it under and over the cloth belt in back, and, adjusting it, drew it snugly tight.

"This is not for your modesty, Jason," she said. "It is because your lessons in Gorean will largely be conducted by slave girls."

"Slave girls, Mistress?" I asked.

"Yes," she said. "They are stinking, meaningless, lascivious little sluts who have been as slaves in the arms of Gorean men. It has spoiled them for freedom. They are worthless, sensuous little beasts whose passions Gorean men have seen fit, as cruel masters, to ignite. Their sexuality, their shamelessness, their needs, their helplessness, makes them an insult to free women. I do not want them falling to their knees by you, to seize you, to fawn upon you, to hold you, to lick and kiss you."

"No, Mistress," I said.

She then removed the chain from her belt and snapped it on the metal ring attached to my collar. I had, this morning, when my chains had been removed, felt the attachment. It was as I had conjectured, a ring. It was about a quarter of an inch thick. It was sturdy. It was of iron.

"Come along, Jason," she said. She then led me, manacled and leashed, from the cell.

"This is Lola. This is Tela," said the Lady Gina, pointing, respectively, to the two girls.

I was startled. Never would I, of Earth, have believed such women could exist. I could scarcely breathe. I was stunned. I beheld, for the first time in my life, Gorean slave girls.

I met their eyes. They beheld me with a sullen interest. Both girls were incredibly beautiful, and almost naked, but that tells little about them. I suppose, if you have never looked upon a slave girl, it will be impossible for me to convey to you more than an inkling of what it is to see one, particularly for the first time. Imagine, if you will, the most exciting and desirable woman you have ever seen; then imagine her standing stripped before you in a steel collar, and that the collar is yours, and that you own her, and that she must obey. That will convey to you something of what it is to see a slave girl. I looked on the girls. Surely their bodies were graceful, curvacious and vital; surely they were both unusually, even incredibly, beautiful; surely, too, both had been limited in their raiment to the rags of half-naked slaves; yet it was not these things, strange as it may seem, which so set them apart from other women; it was not these things which made them so different. What set them so apart from other women, what made them so different, what made their beauty ten thousand times more devastating and exciting than that of other women was that they, in full actuality, in full reality, were owned slaves.

Both girls knelt before the Lady Gina. She spoke to them in Gorean. I heard the word 'Kajirus', which I would later learn was an expression for a male slave, and I heard the expression 'Jason', which was the name I had been given. How I envied the Lady Gina, having two such beauties kneeling before her.

The two slaves looked up at her, deferentially, attending to her every word.

I could not take my eyes from the two slave girls. They were the first slave girls I had ever seen.

The Lady Gina spoke to them rapidly, and in detail.

Slave girls are unlike and beyond all other women. Earth, with its frigid, competitive, frustrated females, trying to be men, has not even prepared one for the understanding that such fantastic, owned beauties could exist. What wonders

does the collar work upon a woman! How it transforms her!
The Goreans say that no woman is a true woman until she
has submitted as a slave, and that no man has experienced his
full sexuality until he has thrown her to the foot of his couch.
Looking upon the girls I wondered if it were not a madness
that any woman is let out of the collar. Are they not all,
truly, the property of men? Should they not all, truly, be
owned by men?

One of the girls, Lola, asked a question of the Lady Gina,
to which she promptly replied. She continued then with her
instructions, whatever they might be.

I clenched my fists in the manacles that confined my hands
behind my back. I wanted to scream with pleasure that I had
been brought to a world on which such women could exist.
They were deeply sensuous, profoundly feminine, excruciat-
ingly luscious, and slaves.

The Lady Gina turned her right hand, back down, to the
floor, and lifted it slightly. Both girls, obedient to the gesture,
rose together to their feet.

They turned to regard me. Both girls were dark-haired and
dark-eyed. Lola's hair was darker than that of Tela. Goreans,
male and female, like most of those of Earth stock, from
which they are doubtless derived, or derived for the most
part, are brunet types. Statistical deviations in large numbers
from this type occur only in Torvaldsland and in certain
other areas in the northern latitudes. Lola, I conjecture, was
in the neighborhood of five feet four inches tall and would
have weighed about one hundred and twenty pounds; Tela,
who was a bit smaller, I would conjecture would have been
about five feet three inches tall and would have weighed a
pound or two less, perhaps about one hundred and eighteen
pounds.

"Do you like the girls, Jason?" asked the Lady Gina.

I looked upon the two girls. They were sweetly slung, with
truly feminine bodies, luscious and curvacious. Their breasts
were bared. Each, about her hips, wore a gray rag, knotted
high on the left hip, to expose the left hip and thigh. Each,
on her throat, wore a light, locked steel collar. The collars
had writing on them, incised in the steel, which I could not
read. The rag at their hips and the steel on their neck were
all they wore. Both were barefoot.

"Yes, Mistress," I said.

"They will be your principal tutors in Gorean," she said.

"Yes, Mistress," I said. "Thank you, Mistress."

"Beware of them," she said.

"Mistress?" I asked.

I saw quirts thrust in their hands.

"Kneel, Jason," said the Lady Gina.

In consternation I knelt.

The quirts were thrust to my face.

"Kiss the quirts," she said.

I did so, commanded by the woman whom I feared, who was my mistress.

"In the time of your lessons," she said, "they will be to you as I, your mistresses. You will obey them, perfectly. You will learn swiftly and well."

"Yes, Mistress," I said.

"Look upon these slave girls," said the Lady Gina.

I looked upon them. What fantastically attractive women they were, their lovely faces framed in cascades of dark hair, their throats, closely encircled by steel collars, their shoulders, their breasts, bared, their narrow waists and sweetly flared hips, the bit of rag they wore, their thighs, calves, ankles and small, high-arched feet.

"Do you find them beautiful?" asked the Lady Gina.

"Yes, Mistress," I said.

"Do you desire them?" she asked.

"Yes, Mistress," I said.

The Lady Gina nodded to the two girls and they, suddenly, viciously, began to lash at me with the leather quirts.

I put my head down, miserably. I was startled. When I looked up, confused, frightened, my body stung in a dozen places.

The Lady Gina spoke to the slave, Lola. Immediately the girl placed her hands behind her head and threw her head back, arching her back and body, legs flexed, before me. I supposed that it was sometimes in such a fashion that slave girls were ordered to display themselves for the pleasure or inspection of masters. I almost sobbed with the pleasure of seeing her.

"Your hands are manacled, Jason," said the Lady Gina. "Too bad. You would like to touch her, wouldn't you?"

"Yes, Mistress," I said, miserably.

The Lady Gina nodded to the girl Tela who then, crying out angrily, struck me twice with her quirt. Lola meanwhile broke her pose and looked at me, impassively.

I looked up at the Lady Gina. There were tears in my eyes, from the stinging of the blows of the quirt.

"Poor Jason," she said, soothingly. Then, again, she spoke to Lola. Lola, the beautiful slave girl, then tore away the rag from her hips and lowered herself to the tiles. She lay then on her back before me. She threw her ankles apart and put her wrists to her sides, their backs to the tiles. It seemed she struggled, as though she might be chained in place, and then resigned herself to her helplessness, and turned her face to me. I looked down at her. It was as though she lay chained before me. Again, suddenly, it seemed she tried to free herself, but could not do so. Then her struggles, it seemed, grew weaker, and she lay before me, as though awaiting whatever fate a master might choose to bestow upon her. Suddenly tears sprang to her eyes. She tried to hold herself still. She bit her lip, to control herself. She, a slave girl, lay before a man.

The Lady Gina, suddenly, viciously, kicked her, and spoke sharply to her. The girl closed her eyes and lay perfectly still. Again the Lady Gina spoke to her. She opened her eyes and looked up at me. She lifted her body to me. Then she lay back on the tiles, watching me, her sweet breasts rising and falling with her breathing.

I could scarcely believe how beautiful, how desirable, was the female slave lying before me. I, a man of Earth, wanted to cry out with wonder that a woman could be so beautiful. I, a man of Earth, wanted to scream with joy that a woman could even begin to be so desirable. And what I did not understand at the time was that the girls, Lola and Tela, though surely astoundingly lovely, were only a little above the average for Gorean slave girls.

"Would you like to take her in your arms?" asked the Lady Gina.

I began to squirm. "Please, don't hit me," I begged.

"Speak, Slave!" commanded the Lady Gina.

"No, Mistress. No, Mistress," I said. "I would not want to take her in my arms."

She suddenly cuffed me, angrily, and kicked me. "You can be slain for a lie, Slave," she said.

"Forgive me, Mistress," I begged.

"Did you lie?" she asked.

"Yes, Mistress," I said. "I lied! I lied! Forgive me, Mistress. Please, forgive me!"

"You would, then," she asked, "like to take her in your arms?"

I looked at the supine girl before me, holding her body as though chained. What a desirable female she was, exciting far beyond anything I could have believed existed.

"Yes, Mistress," I said.

The Lady Gina then spoke to the two girls. Lola rose to her feet. She tied the brief rag again about her hips. Both took their quirts well in hand. They were long quirts, some two feet in length. They held them now, each of them, with two hands.

"You will now be beaten twice," said the Lady Gina, "once for having, as a frightened, ignorant slave, dared to lie to your mistress, and once for having desired to take a beautiful girl in your arms."

I was then twice beaten, each time with twenty strokes. The Lady Gina, then, placed the chain leash which was snapped on my collar in the hand of Lola. As I lifted my head, miserable, cringing, my back and legs lacerated and bloody, I saw, truly noticing it for the first time, a deep mark, a lovely mark, about an inch and a half high and a half of an inch wide, incised in Lola's left thigh. I was startled. It was a brand. Lola had been branded. The mark was exquisite in her flesh. The design was rather floral. It consisted of what seemed to be a straight line, rather severe, with what appeared to be, adjacent to it, to its right, two fronds, curled and graceful. I would later learn that this was, in cursive script, the initial letter of the Gorean expression 'Kajira', which is the most common Gorean expression for a female slave. The design also, according to some, is supposed to have symbolic significance. The straight line is supposed to represent the staff of discipline and the two fronds the beauty of a woman. The significance of the whole, then, would be beauty subject to the staff of discipline. Interestingly, the design also bears a remote resemblance, if one thinks about it, to the English letter 'K'. Since the first sound in the expression 'Kajira' would be represented in English by the letter 'K' it is quite possible that this resemblance is more than a coincidence. Certain letters of the Gorean alphabet, not all of them, bear a very clear resemblance to certain letters in certain of the alphabets of Earth. This, I suppose, was to have been expected, given the doubtless Earth origin of all, or

most, of the human Goreans. The Gorean name for the letter
in question, if it is of interest, is 'Kef'.

I was gasping from the beating. My body stung. But I
could not, for the moment, take my eyes from the exquisite
mark, the brand, in the girl's thigh. It was clear upon her,
and beautiful. She wore it in her very flesh. Lola was clearly,
decisively and beautifully marked. Anyone who looked upon
that mark would know what she was, a female slave. I looked
to the thigh of Tela. That same mark, lovely and identical,
was burned into her thigh. She, too, was well marked as a female slave.

Suddenly Lola struck me in the belly with her quirt, a
vicious, lashing blow. Tela, too, then, hit me with her quirt,
though on the left shoulder. I cried out with misery. I looked
up, puzzled, at my mistress.

"You looked upon their brands," said the Lady Gina to
me. "Do not forget you are only a slave, Jason."

Lola jerked on the chain leash and thrust her quirt under
my chin, pressing upwards. I stood. She tapped me on the
belly and at the small of the back. I stood straight, frightened.

"Look upon the slaves," commanded the Lady Gina. "See
their ankles, their legs, the sweetness of their bellies, the loveliness of their breasts, the beauty of their shoulders, their
throats and faces, their hair."

"Yes, Mistress," I said. The hair of slave girls is commonly
worn long and loose, unbound. The hair of both Lola and
Tela was long, falling well to the small of their backs.

"They are desirable, aren't they?" asked the Lady Gina.

"Yes, Mistress," I said, tensing myself.

"You would like to own them, wouldn't you?" asked the
Lady Gina.

"Yes, Mistress," I said, clenching my body against the blow
or blows to come.

Then Lola, at a sign from the Lady Gina, struck me with
the quirt.

"I am confused, Mistress," I cried. "I do not know what to
do! Why are you doing this to me?"

"It is not different from what is done on Earth," she said.
"Only there, except for children who can be, and often are,
physically abused, the whips are social and verbal."

I looked at her with horror.

"It is the type of conditioning to which a male of Earth is
almost certain to have been exposed," she said. "Would you

like me now to remove your manacles and give you one of the girls for an hour or so, for your pleasure?" she asked.

"No," I said, honestly, shrinking back.

"Lola?" she asked. "Or Tela?"

"No," I said. "No, Mistress!"

"Suppose that I ordered you to perform with one of them, for my interest?" she asked.

I looked at her, terrified. "I could not do so, Mistress," I said.

"A few minutes ago," she said, "you could have used them well."

"Yes, Mistress," I said.

"And now?" she asked.

"Not now," I said. "Not now."

"I am teaching you, as men of Earth are taught," she said, "to fear and suppress your sexuality. The process is simple. Tantalize and punish. Tantalize and punish. Soon, by natural psychological linkages, an association will be formed between sexuality and punishment. You will come to fear your sexual feelings, as being precursors to pain, physical or mental. This will induce anxiety in sexual situations and impair sexual effectiveness. In children, of course, the punishments are commonly forgotten, at least on conscious levels. Inexplicable anxieties, however, often remain. These anxieties, and the rules that seem associated with them, pertaining to the suppression and inhibition of sexuality, must, of course, by thinking organisms, be rationalized. An entire structure of myths is then raised to protect the individual from the insight that he was, long ago, when defenseless, mutilated and crippled. You are familiar with the nature of such myths, such superstructures and defense mechanisms. They are many and varied. These range from the praising of an idiotic celibacy in the interests of a presumably nonexistent spirit to the genres of dirty jokes and stories, in which a vengeance is taken on the thwarted sexuality by trying to make it appear small and dirty. Between these two madnesses is a variety of more dangerous antisexisms, more pernicious because subtler, recrudescent Puritanisms masking themselves under the garbage of trigger rhetorics, the usage of such expressions as 'persons' and such, designed to suppress thought and enforce social conformity."

"But what would be the point of all this madness and cruelty?" I asked.

"Why do the ugly disparage beauty?" she asked. "Why do the weak belittle strength?"

"I do not understand," I said.

"Masculinity in the male," she said, "is closely allied with sexuality. Masculinity may be best attacked by an attack on male sexuality, and the more pervasive and pernicious it is the better. Men are the natural masters. This is obvious in the study of primate biology. Thus the male must be hobbled, broken and crippled. He must be, as a male, destroyed. Women can then assume their place as his equal, or superior."

"Why do you hate men so?" I asked.

"I am not one of them," she said.

"Why do you not carry your cause outside the pens?" I asked.

She laughed. "I am not a fool," she said. "Do you think I want to be branded with a hot iron? Do you think I want to be put in a steel collar and thrown naked to the feet of men beneath their whips? No, my dear Jason, I do not wish that. Those are not men of Earth up there, who will consider the arguments for their own castration with reflective care. Those are Gorean men up there."

"You are afraid of them," I said.

"Yes," she said. "I am afraid of them."

I wished that I was such a man.

"You are then," I said, "trying to make me fear my sexual feelings that I will suppress them, and with them my manhood."

"It is the best way we know," she said, "to reduce a male's effectiveness in all socially competitive situations. He is then crippled, of course, not only sexually, but, often, in many other ways, too. When his sexuality does not give him spine he becomes timid and manipulable. He is then useful to ambitious women who, at another time, might scarcely have dared to speak to him."

"What is the true point of depriving men of their sexuality?" I asked.

"Is it not obvious?" she asked. "It is to make them slaves."

"Can biology be so perfectly eradicated?" I asked.

"Not with mere conditioning techniques," she said. "There is more to be hoped for, eventually, on your world, with punishing implants, chemical alterations, the castration of unsuitable male infants, hormone injections, sex control, genetic engineering, and such. It should not be difficult, with power in the hands of women, presumably an inevitable eventuality in your type of democracy, to bring about the success of these programs."

"Why, then," I asked, "do you not wish to go to Earth and take up your abode there?"

"I am not insane," she said.

"Do you not, truly, wish for the success of such hideous programs?" I asked.

"No," she said, "for, for all practical purposes, it would be the end of the human race."

"You look then," I asked, "beyond your own selfish interests?"

"I cannot help myself," she said. "There is in me left a little bit of the human being."

"I do not think Earth will succumb to such a nightmare as you have outlined," I said.

"It is already on its way to doing so," she said. "Can you not see the signs?"

"Men, and women, will prevent it," I said.

"Earthlings," she said, "are manipulated organisms, helpless in the flow of social forces, slobbering to slogans and rhetoric. They will be the first to celebrate their own downfall. They will not discover what has been done to them until it is too late."

"I hope that you are wrong," I said.

She shrugged. "Perhaps I am wrong," she said. "Let us hope so."

"More likely than your scenario for the future," I said, "would be times of great conflict and tumult, the precipitation of horrifying and vast wars."

"Perhaps," she said. "I suppose there will always be recalcitrant brutes who will not willingly surrender their manhood."

"Does the future not portend barbarism?" I inquired.

"Barbarism or the lawn party," she smiled. "You may have your choice."

"Any rational person must surely choose the lawn party," I said.

"Is that true?" she asked.

"I do not know," I said.

"I would choose barbarism," she said. "Lawn parties are boring."

"Your sex," I said, "might not fare well under barbarism."

"We might fare better than you think," she said.

"But you might then be little better than slaves," I said, "if you were not fully slaves."

"That might suit us quite well," she said.

I was silent.

Then she looked at me, angrily. "How foolishly I have spoken to you," she said, "a mere slave!"

She then turned to the two girls. They had understood nothing of what we had been saying, of course, for they did not speak English.

"Why, Mistress," I asked, "have you spoken to me as you have? Surely your techniques would be more effective if I were imperfectly aware of them? It is as though you were warning me of your intentions."

She did not look at me, but she spoke to me. "On Gor," she said, "we would not even break our male slaves as the men of Earth are broken."

She then spoke to the two girls and they conducted me swiftly from the presence of the mistress, Lola pulling me, stumbling on the chain, and Tela, behind, prodding me with her quirt.

My lessons in Gorean were soon to begin.

I tried not to look at the beauty of the girl who led me. I knew that if I looked upon either of them as a man I would be punished. I must not permit myself to have sexual feelings. I must control myself ruthlessly. I must keep fully in mind that I was a slave.

Then it occurred to me that it would not be right for me to look upon their beauty. They could not help that they were slaves, no more than I could help it. They were, despite their beauty and rags, the brand and steel collar, true persons, like myself. I must respect them. I must not look upon them as beautiful women are biologically looked upon by strong, aggressive males. I must look upon them as persons. This was not, then, weakness on my part, but evidence of my respect for them, my nobility, my understanding, my sweetness and tenderness. That I suppressed my feelings toward them, thus, was not now evidence of my cowardice but rather of my strength and courage. I was now strong enough and courageous enough to control and conquer myself. How wonderful I was, really. I was not to be despised. No, rather I was to be congratulated and commended. Perhaps Goreans might not understand the sacrifice I had made, and how noble I was, but I was certain these things, my sacrifice, and my nobility, would have been well understood, and appreciated, by a woman of my own world.

Content then I went with the two women who were to me now, in the time of my lessons, as mistresses.

Never must I permit Goreans to rob me of my true self. I knew what was my true self, for I had been taught what it was on Earth. Years of careful conditioning and training, and a pervasive social and cultural milieu, had taught me what my true self was.

I did not think it would interfere with my slavery.

# 5   I AM TAUGHT TO POUR WINE;
# I AM PUNISHED;
# I HEAR OF THE MARKET OF TIMA

"Pour, Jason," said the Lady Gina.

"Yes, Mistress," I said. I left the line of kneeling male slaves and approached the table, carrying the vessel of wine Tela had given me. Behind the table, kneeling with her knees together, as a free woman, was Lola. She had a bit of white rep-cloth thrown about her shoulders, serving to represent the robes and veil of a free woman. Near the table, in her leather, with her whip, was the Lady Gina.

I approached the table deferentially. I knelt before Lola.

"Wine, Mistress?" I asked.

"Yes, Slave," she said.

"You look nice this evening, Jason," said the Lady Gina.

"Thank you, Mistress," I said.

I now wore a short, silk tunic, white, trimmed with red. My hair, longer now, though I had worn it long before, was combed back and tied behind my head with a white ribbon. I had been in the pens, I estimated, some five or six weeks. The heavy iron collar I had worn was now replaced with a lighter collar, enameled white. It had writing on it, in yellow, but incised, too, into the steel. I could not read the writing, for I was illiterate. I had been told the writing read 'Return me for punishment to the House of Andronicus'. I did not think I would care to be caught wearing it outside the pens. I did not know the location of the House of Andronicus. I had once been beaten for asking. I had been told that curiosity was not becoming in a slave. This collar, too, though much lighter

75

than the former collar, had, too, a ring upon it, for the snap of a leash.

Lola regarded me with contempt.

I heard a stirring behind me, of the other male slaves, in their silks and ribbons. They had not been pleased that the mistress had commended such things. They were jealous of such things, and of their handsomeness.

"Again, Jason," said the Lady Gina, "more softly, more deferentially."

"Wine, Mistress?" I again asked.

"Yes, Slave," said Lola.

"Good," said the Lady Gina. "Now, pour."

Carefully I poured the wine into the cup before Lola.

"You are pouring it too swiftly, Slave," said Lola.

I looked to the Lady Gina. Surely I was not pouring it too swiftly.

"The whim of the Mistress is everything," said the Lady Gina.

"Forgive me, Mistress," I said to Lola. Lola looked at me, smugly. "Slip your tunic down to the waist," she said.

I did so.

"A blow for the clumsy slave," Lola called to Tela. Tela took a slave whip from its ring on the wall and, coming up behind me, struck me across the back. The tunic had been slipped down to the waist that it not be bloodied.

"Forgive me, Mistress," I said.

I looked at Lola. How imperious she seemed, pretending to be a free woman. She knelt there behind the table, almost naked save for the rag at her hips, the bit of cloth about her shoulders and, locked on her lovely neck, a steel collar. Her breasts were very exciting. What a slut she had been to me. How vicious she had been in my training, far beyond anything required of her. My nights had often been filled with pain from the blows of her quirt. In comparison Tela had been very businesslike and efficient with me, treating me with no more than the same severity and contempt than would have been accorded to any other miserable slave who might have been in her power. I did not know why Lola so hated me. She seemed to hold me in an incredible contempt. She lost no opportunity to belittle or strike me. I had tried not to look upon her. I had tried, constantly, to respect her, and I had reminded myself, a thousand times a day, that she was, as I, a person. Yet, to be honest, I was not the only slave to whom she was petty and vicious. She was not popular in the pens, either with the slaves or keepers. I knew she was a person. Yet it was hard not to see her as a girl, and a slave. At times I suspected even the Lady Gina might be growing impatient with her.

"He looked at me!" cried Lola, triumphantly, pointing to me, turning to Lady Gina.

That was true. I had looked at her. Interestingly, given the weeks in the pen, the simple food, the constant training and exercising, perhaps the Gorean milieu, I was beginning to feel a return of my sexuality. I had fought this, of course. But, sometimes, it seemed to me that perhaps it was pointless to keep fighting and torturing myself. What, truly, was the point of it? What was so wrong, really, with being a man?

"Twenty strokes!" cried Lola to Tela.

Tela looked at the Lady Gina.

"One will do," said the Lady Gina.

Lola suddenly turned white.

"Do not forget, Lola," said the Lady Gina, "that you are not really free. Do not grow pretentious."

"Yes, Mistress," said Lola, frightened. It pleased me to see the fear in the female slave.

"You may now administer the disciplinary blow," said the Lady Gina to Tela.

The blow was delivered. I winced. Tela, being a woman, could not strike me overly hard with the whip. She had only a woman's strength. A woman cannot punish a man too efficiently with a whip. A man, on the other hand, with his strength, may punish a woman terribly with it, should he choose to do so. No true man I knew, of course, would choose to do so.

"Pour the wine back into the vessel," said the Lady Gina, "and pour it forth again."

"Yes, Mistress," I said.

Then, a moment later, again, I poured wine into the cup before Lola.

"You are pouring it too slowly, Slave," said Lola.

"Forgive me, Mistress," I said. But she did not call for Tela to strike me again.

As I drew back Lola reached forth and, with her hand, knocked the cup over on the small table. "Clumsy slave!" she cried, aghast.

I was startled.

Lola looked to the Lady Gina. "See what he has done!" she cried.

I looked at Lola with a sudden fury.

"Are you not a slave, Jason?" inquired the Lady Gina.

"Forgive me, Mistress," I said, hastily, to Lola. "I will clean this up immediately."

"Hurry, Slave," said Lola, triumphantly. "And, meanwhile, I shall consider what your punishment shall be."

In fury I went to the side of the room and put down the vessel of wine. There, at the side of the room, I fetched cloths and water and returned, quickly, to clean the table and floor, where Lola had struck over the cup. "Clumsy slave," whispered one of my fellow male slaves, kneeling at the line, to me. When I had cleaned the table and floor and replaced the water and cloths I again knelt before Lola.

"Head down," she said.

I put my head down.

"What punishment shall I mete out to you?" she mused. "I have it! Return to your cell and remove your clothing. There, have yourself placed in close chains. There will be no food or blanket for you tonight. Too, tell the guard you are to receive twenty strokes." She paused. "Of the snake," she added, thoughtfully.

I looked up at her, in disbelief. Men could die under the blows of the snake. She was smiling at me, contemptuously.

"Five will do," said the Lady Gina.

"Very well, five!" said Lola.

"Thank your mistress, and obey," said the Lady Gina.

"Thank you, Mistress," I said to Lola.

"Run," said Lola. "Run, Jason, Slave!"

I rose to my feet and, angrily, ran from the room.

"Tandruk," I heard, from the Lady Gina, behind me, "you are next. Pour the wine, Tandruk."

I lay on the stones of the cell, naked, in blood, my wrists and ankles chained. I could scarcely move my body. I had received five strokes of the snake, wielded by a man.

"Jason," I heard.

I struggled to my knees and looked to my left. There, on the other side of the bars, was the Lady Gina.

"Why did you not point out that Lola had spilled the wine?" she asked.

"You know that she did it?" I asked.

"Of course," she said. "Her small hand, though quick, was not so quick as my eye. Too, your hands, as they were placed on the vessel of wine, could not have struck the cup."

"I did not want you to punish her," I said.

"Good!" she said. "I see you are learning. You wished to reserve her for yourself, that you yourself might later, if the opportunity presented itself, mete out her punishment. Good! You are learning something of being a man."

"I would not have punished her," I said. "I am a man of Earth. A woman is not to be punished no matter what she does."

"How then do you control your women?" she asked.

I shrugged. "We don't," I said.

"You men of Earth well deserve the lives you lead," she laughed.

"Mistress," I said.

"Yes," she said.

"Why does Lola so hate me?" I asked.

"You are different from the other men she has known," said the Lady Gina. "She finds you despicable. You do not master the slave in her."

"She is a person," I said. "She has feelings."

"Of course she has feelings," said the Lady Gina. "She has the deep, exciting, profound feelings of a woman who knows herself a slave. Have you answered those feelings in her?"

"No, of course not," I said.

"You are a male of Earth," she smiled.

"Yes!" I said. "She is not supposed to have those feelings!" I said. "She is supposed to be a person!"

"Women are slaves," said the Lady Gina. "They long for their masters. That is far deeper than your myths and political inventions, regardless of their expediency in your form of society."

"How can you speak in such a fashion?" I demanded. "You yourself are a woman!"

"Look upon me, Jason," she said. "See my size and strength, my severity. I am not as other women. I am for all practical purposes a man, but one trapped by some cruel trick of nature in a woman's body. It is painful, Jason. That is perhaps why I hate both men and women so."

"I do not think, Mistress," I said, "that you truly hate either."

She looked at me, puzzled. Then she said, "Beware how you speak, lest you be lashed and burned with irons."

"Yes, Mistress," I said. "Yet I think you are, strangely, a woman of both vision and kindness."

"Beware, Slave," she warned me.

"Forgive me, Mistress," I said.

"Keep clearly in mind, Jason," she said, "that women are slaves, longing for their masters."

"They are persons!" I insisted.

"You insist on seeing women through sexless and demeaning categories," she said. "By doing so, you will prevent yourself from knowing them and understanding them. You will, by using such categories, miss their richness, their depth, their latency, their womanhood, and you will be forever unable to satisfy them in the fullness of their biological needs, which include the need to submit themselves as a slave to a strong male."

"False! False!" I cried. "False! False! False!"

"I am sorry if I have caused you distress, Jason," she said. "That was not my intention. You have had a difficult and cruel day. Doubtless I should not speak to you as I sometimes do. Sometimes, for some reason, I seem to forget that you are only a male of Earth, and a slave."

I did not speak.

"You are large and strong to be a slave, Jason," she said. "Perhaps that is why I sometimes forget that, as a male of Earth, you are small and weak inside."

"It requires courage and strength to be small and weak," I said, angrily.

"Perhaps," she said. "I would not know. I am neither small nor weak."

I put my head down, angrily.

"It is an interesting way to view matters," she said. "Perhaps the fool has the strength to be a fool. Perhaps the coward has the courage to be cowardly."

I looked at her.

"It is sad enough to be a fool and a coward," she said, "without making virtues of these sorry flaws. Can you not see that you have been conditioned into a morality of weakness, an invention of the weak to undermine and inhibit the strong? Is not the social utility of such a device, so congenial to the fears of the small and weak, obvious? Can you not see that a morality designed to cripple and thwart the strong, to turn them against themselves, is an ideal instrument to advance the ambitions of the small and weak? While the strong lacerate themselves and tear themselves apart with misery and guilt the small and weak, swarming unabated over the world, proceed unimpeded with their small projects and gnawings."

"No, no," I said.

"Rest now, Jason," she said. "Tomorrow you are to be appraised by woman slavers from the market of Tima."

"What is the market of Tima?" I asked.

"You will discover, soon enough," she said. Then she said, "Lie down, Jason."

"Yes, Mistress," I said. I lay down.

She stood there for a moment, looking at me. "Lola should not have attempted to embroil you in difficulties with me," she said. "The slave oversteps herself. I am growing rather dissatisfied with her performances. She is treading a thin line. I think she is growing too bold, too pretentious. The next time she displeases us in the pens, even in the least way, I think that I will have her disciplined."

I looked at her.

"We are not of Earth here, Jason," she said. "We punish slaves when they are not pleasing. Indeed, sometimes we punish them even if they are pleasing."

"But why, Mistress?" I asked.

"Because they are slaves," she said.

"Yes, Mistress," I said.

"Rest now," she said.

"Yes, Mistress," I said.

"Incidentally, Jason," she said, "I commend you on your progress in Gorean. You have a skill with languages."

"Thank you, Mistress," I said.

"And your body, too," she said, "with the exercises and the diet, is shaping up nicely. You have gained weight but look more trim, for the weight now is more that of muscle and less that of fat."

"Thank you, Mistress," I said. Muscular tissue, to be sure, was both heavier and more compact than fatty tissue. This accounted for the paradox of increased bodily weight coupled with a thinner appearance.

"You are as large as many Gorean men, Jason," she said. "Indeed, you are even larger than many of them. It is too bad you are fit to be only a slave."

"Yes, Mistress," I said.

"Go to sleep now, Jason," she said.

"Yes, Mistress," I said.

# 6    THE LADY TIMA

"Interesting," said the woman. "Promising."

I trembled, involuntarily, as the coolness of the leather of the woman's whip, its blades folded back against its handle, moved upward against my right side.

"We call him 'Jason'," said the Lady Gina, standing in the background.

My hands were manacled over my head to a ring in the low-ceilinged, torchlit room. My ankles, too, were manacled. They were fastened closely to a ring on the floor, near my feet. I was stripped naked.

"A nice name," said the woman, "but we can call the tarsk anything."

"Of course," said the Lady Gina.

Extending in a line to my left, the same line in which I formed the initial point, stripped, secured as I was, were twenty more male slaves. We were being examined by five women, veiled and robed, woman slavers.

"Open your mouth," said one of the women to me.

I opened my mouth.

She pushed up, under my upper teeth, with her thumb. The robes and veils the women wore were graceful and of silken sheens. They were predominantly blue and yellow in their colors, which are the colors of the slavers. As the lovely sleeve of her robe dropped back I saw, on her left wrist, a heavy, metal-studded wristlet of black leather. Her eyes were dark and shrewd, fierce, objective, appraising, merciless. I had little doubt but what, in her own pens, she would be as formidable, if not more formidable, than the Lady Gina. I did not meet her eyes. She, like the Lady Gina, when she chose to be severe, frightened me. Such women, I knew, would treat me with great strictness. They would not be easy with men so miserable as to fall into their power as slaves. Her hands were then at my mouth, pulling it more widely open, moving my head about that she might more easily conduct her examination. Then, her thumb and first finger at my chin, she turned my head from side to side. "Not bad," she said. She stepped back. "Hold your head up," she said. "Yes, Mistress," I said. I lifted my head. We were being examined by these women as what we were, animals and slaves.

"This one has good thighs," said a woman down the line.

"Good," said another.

"Keeper," said the woman who had been examining me.

"I am here," said the Lady Gina.

"In this one," said the woman, indicating me, "there is a mark on the upper left arm, and in one of the teeth on the left and in the back, a bit of metal. I have seen such things before almost only in Kajirae from the slave world."

"This is a male from the slave world," said the Lady Gina.

"I wondered if it might not be," said the woman. "But we will not pay the more for him, if we are interested in him, because of that."

"Such matters are between you and my superiors," said the Lady Gina.

"Your superiors are men," said the woman, mockingly.

"Yes," said the Lady Gina.

"I could use a woman like you," said the woman.

"I have my work here," said the Lady Gina.

"As you wish," she said. "Are they vital?" she asked.

"I think so," said the Lady Gina, "though we have, of course, kept them suppressed in the pens, the better to control them as slaves."

"It is a delicate matter," admitted the woman who had examined me. "Yet I think an intelligent mistress will usually manage to her own satisfaction."

"This one is alive," said one of the women down the line, laughing. She drew back her hand from the slave's body.

"Let us amuse ourselves," said the woman who had examined me. "Send for a Kajira."

The Lady Gina went to the door of the long, low-ceilinged room. "Prodicus," she said. "Send Lola to us."

In a few moments Lola entered the room. I had never seen her appearing so demure. Her hair was combed back and tied with a white ribbon. She had been washed. She was dressed in a brief, sleeveless, white tunic. She was barefoot. She still had on her throat, of course, the same steel collar. Lola fled to the Lady Gina and knelt before her, putting her head to the floor. Lola, I saw, was terrified to be in the presence of the free women. I realized then, as I had not before, something of the loathing and hatred with which the enslaved female is regarded by her free sisters.

"A pretty little slave," said one of the women.

I then realized that Lola's garb, so demure and modest for a female slave, so unlike the usual bit of rag knotted at her left hip, must be because of the presence of the woman slavers in the pens. The House of Andronicus, in which I was slave, presumably did not wish to offend the female visitors. Lola, too, I imagine, was only too happy to deemphasize her sexuality before her free sisters. She did not, after all, wish to writhe beneath their whips, the lashed object of the fury and contempt of free women, jealous perhaps of the helplessness of the slave girl before men, her beauty and her collar.

When Lola looked up, the Lady Gina directed her to the woman who had examined me. Lola swiftly went and knelt before her.

"What are you called?" asked the woman.

"Lola," said the girl, looking up, fearfully.

"Stand up, Lola," said the woman, "and take off your clothes."

"Yes, Mistress," said Lola. She stood up and slipped from the tunic, which she dropped to the tiles behind her.

"You are a very pretty slave, Lola," said the woman.

"Thank you, Mistress," said Lola.

"Let her begin," said the woman to the Lady Gina.

"Lola," said the Lady Gina, "begin at the far end of the line of male slaves. Tell each that you are his slave. Kiss them. Tell them that you love them. Address them as Master. Then, kiss them again."

"Yes, Mistress," said Lola, miserably. She ran lightly to the end of the line.

The Lady Gina followed her to the end of the line. She removed the whip from its hook on her belt. This action did not pass unnoticed by Lola.

"Be sensuous, Lola," said the Lady Gina. "I think you can manage that," she added, acidly.

"Yes, Mistress," said Lola, casting a frightened glance at the Lady Gina, and, too, at the female slavers.

Lola then took the first male slave in her arms. She looked up at him. "I am your slave, Master," she said. She then kissed him. "I love you, Master," she said. Then she kissed him again.

"Excellent, Lola," said the Lady Gina. Two of the woman slavers laughed. One of them, with a marking stick, made a notation on a paper she carried. It was clipped on a board.

"Proceed to the next," said the Lady Gina.

Lola, obedient, frightened, proceeded to the next slave. It was a great shame, I knew, for a female slave to even have to touch a male slave, let alone to perform such an act as to address him as master. Female slaves despise male slaves. They regard themselves, and correctly, I suppose, as the rightful property only of free men and women, masters and mistresses.

At last Lola stood before me. Her eyes were filled with tears. She almost choked. "Not him, please, Mistress!" she begged.

"You have hesitated in the performance of your duties, Lola," said the Lady Gina.

Swiftly Lola put her arms about me. Then, suddenly, for an instant, she held me tightly. I had then felt her body, for the instant, spasmodically move against mine. Her cheek was against my chest. "Interesting," said one of the woman slavers. "I think the little slut should be whipped," said another. "Have no fear," said the Lady Gina. "She will be punished." Lola drew back a little. She trembled. I could still feel her body, sweet in its trembling, against mine. She looked up at me. There were tears in her eyes.

"Proceed, Lola," said the Lady Gina.

"With so despicable a slave, Mistress?" asked Lola.

"Proceed, Lola," said the Lady Gina.

"Yes, Mistress," said the girl. She then, again, held me more closely. Again she lifted her eyes to mine. "Look at the little slut," said one of the women. "She is excited." "Filthy little slave slut," said another. Lola was stark naked, save for her collar. She was barefoot on the tiles. "I am your slave, Master," she whispered to me. I felt her belly against me, and her breasts. She was the sort of woman a man of Earth would scarcely have dared to let enter his dreams. I recalled that she had once been forced to lie naked before me as a slave girl. I must resist her! Then the hot, sensual, naked, collared she of her pressed to me. I felt her lips on mine, and she kissed me, with the liquid, melting, indescribable kiss of the slave girl, the owned woman. "I love you, Master," she whispered. "Aiii!" cried one of the women. I cried out with misery. The women laughed. "That one is alive!" laughed one of them. "Are you sure he is from Earth, the slave world?" asked another. "It will be a lucky mistress who gets him," said another. I looked at the women, wretchedly, shamed. I looked at the woman with the marking stick and the paper, clipped to its board. She looked at me and laughed. I saw the marking stick move, as she made a notation on her record.

"Do not put your clothing on, Lola," said the Lady Gina. "Go directly to your kennel. You will hear from me later."

"Yes, Mistress," said Lola. Then she looked at me. "I hate you, Slave!" she cried. "Slave!"

"Run, Lola," said the Lady Gina.

"Yes, Mistress," said Lola, and fled from the room.

"What a slut she is," said one of them, "to be excited by a mere male slave."

"Yes," said another.

"Let us retire to a more comfortable room," said the Lady Gina, "and discuss the slaves."

The Lady Gina then left the room, followed by most of the women slavers. One of them remained for a moment, looking at me. It was she who had most closely examined me, she who had worn, beneath her silken sleeve, the metal-studded, black-leather wristlet.

"Are you coming, Lady Tima?" asked one of the women, pausing at the door.

"Yes," said the woman regarding me. Then she turned and, with the other woman, who waited for her, left the room.

# 7  I AM THROWN A WOMAN

I sat alone in my cell. I now sat on a heavy bench, some five feet in length, before a stout, rectangular table. These things had been put in the cell for me. I wore a light, rep-cloth slave tunic. On the floor, on straw, was a blanket which I had been given. Though the cell door was locked, I was not chained. On the table was a bowl of cheap wine, some wedges of yellow bread and a wooden bowl containing vegetables and chunks of meat.

Today I had been appraised.

I was still furious with the shame of it. I was not a woman! Then I smiled to myself. The thought had been almost Gorean. I reminded myself I was a man of Earth. How shameful, too, must be such an ordeal for a woman. How piteous it was that such fair beauties should be enslaved for the pleasures of masters.

I wished I owned one. Then, of course, I thrust the thought from my mind.

I chewed on a piece of meat and drank from the shallow, chipped bowl of clay which contained the wine.

My thoughts were mixed and troubled. Today I had been appraised. I was confident, now, that I would not be kept much longer in the pens. But I did not even know the location of the pens. I did not even know the city in which I was kept. Curiosity, I had been told, was not becoming in a slave. I smiled to myself. How faraway seemed Earth now with its pettiness and vanity. I was not even, for some reason, miserable that I had been brought to Gor. I did not understand, clearly, why this should be. Surely my condition was shameful, and I had much to fear. Surely, in many ways, it was a horrifying world to which I had been brought. I remembered the sleen. I had felt the whip. Yet I was not, truly, unhappy. Earth had been a country of pollutions and poisons. The very air men breathed there, the very food they ate, contained recognized, but, incredibly, not removed, toxic elements. It was impossible, really, to do anything about such things, I had gathered. What an incredible world Earth was. Could it not understand that the environmental criminal was far more dangerous than the lonely madman or assassin, that his crime affected not isolated, tragic victims but communities, a planet, unborn generations. Was his profit so sacred, truly? Was it truly more precious than lives, and the future? The men of Earth congratulated themselves smugly on the power of their democracies, in which the people, purportedly, ruled. But if the people, truly, ruled, why and how could their planet's processes proceed in such obvious ways inimical to their welfare? How could their world be so miserable for the people if they were truly kings within it? But perhaps they were not kings within it. Perhaps they have only been told they are kings, and that satisfies them. Who, I wondered, were the true kings? Or, perhaps there were no kings, truly, only the madness of the untended machine.

I rose from the bench and walked about the cell. I felt one of the damp walls. I was grateful for the blanket I now had. I went and felt the heavy bars, with the lateral crosspieces, which formed one side of the cell. I gripped them. I was well confined within. I went back to the table. I was a prisoner and a slave. I even wore a steel collar. Yet I was not overly discontent. I was eager to see this world to which I, a man of Earth, had been brought as a mere slave. It was my hope that if I obeyed my masters or mistresses, and well pleased them, I might be permitted to live.

Why was I not more miserable than I was that I had been brought to Gor? I pondered this. Because of the diet and exercise, enforced on me in the pens, I was now healthier and stronger than I had ever been. Perhaps this had something to do with my feelings. Such homely simplicities as diet, rest and exercise can often work wonders for one's outlook. Too, I was looking forward to the adventures of a new world, even though it might be one in which I was only a slave. I laughed. Perhaps the matter was so simple as even the water and air of Gor, so fresh and pure, so stimulating, compared to that of Earth, even in the depths of the pens.

I rose from the bench again and gripped one of its legs in my fist. I lifted it from the floor by one of the legs, lifting it slowly, directly upward, until I held it at an arm's length. I could never have done this on Earth. This was not merely a

function of the reduced gravity of the planet but of newly acquired strength. "A Mistress may wish to know that she is in
your arms," the Lady Gina had told me. I laughed, and lowered the bench slowly to the stones.

I sat down again on the bench and fed myself another
piece of meat.

I looked about the cell. The greatest reason I was not more
discontent than I was, I think, was simply that I had come to
a world such as Gor. I remembered Earth, with its pettiness,
its greed and vanity, its smugness, its pretensions, its pollutions and poisons, its teeming, crowded, miserable populations, and its endemic fears, fears such as that of not having
enough energy to spin the wheels of an exorbitant and largely
unnecessary technology, and the fear, fully warranted, of the
falling of the sword of a nuclear Damocles. Earth seemed a
world of sicknesses and traps, a world which seemed con-
trived as an offense against nature, a world in which the very
air itself, by the works of men, was laden with deleterious
gases. How little surprising, then, that I should not have
found myself overly discontent with the felicitous discovery
that I had now been introduced into a quite different milieu.
I sensed that in Gor there was a youth and an openness
which had long been missing from my old world. In Gor I
sensed an ambition, a freshness and hope, a sparkle, that had
perhaps not been felt on Earth since the Parthenon was new.
Doubtless there is much on Gor to be deplored, but I cannot
bring myself to deplore it. Doubtless Gor is impatient, cruel
and heartless, but yet, I think, too, it is innocent. It is like the
lion, impatient, cruel, heartless, and innocent. It is its nature.
Gor was a strong-thewed world, a new world, a world in
which men might again lift their heads to the sun and laugh, a
world in which they might again, sensibly, begin long jour-
neys. It was a world of which Homer might have sung, singing
of the clashing of the metals of men and the sweetness of the
wine-dark sea.

I thought of the gray, blackened landscapes of Earth. How
sad it is when a world grows old, resigned and vile.

Doubtless there is much on Gor to be deplored, but I cannot bring myself to deplore it. I cannot bring myself, truly, to
deplore the exuberance, the joy, the vigor and freedom that is
Gor. Others may do that, if they wish. I cannot do so. I have
been there.

Let men again put their hands to the oars; let the low, swift ships be launched once more.

I took another piece of meat from the wooden bowl. I looked down at the straw, and my blanket, heavy and dark, upon it. I did not really wish to retire so soon.

I then heard her weeping, being dragged down the corridor. I sprang up. I then saw the guard, Prodicus, on the other side of the bars. He was a huge man. I had already had experience of his strength when he, with his fellow guard, Gron, the Oriental, had handled me with such ease. I knew he could break my arms and legs with ease, if he chose. "Stand back in the cell, Slave," he said. I stood back. At his left hip, cruelly bent over, his hand knotted tightly in her hair, he held a girl. She was naked and crying. Her small hands were fastened behind her back with slave bracelets. A key on a wire dangled downward from her collar. It was the key, I supposed, to the bracelets she wore. Also, tied about her neck, fastened there by its blades, dangling downwards, was a slave whip. Prodicus, with a jangle of keys on his ring, thrust a key into the lock on my cell door and freed the bolt. He then returned the key, on its ring, to the hook on his belt. He swung open the cell door. He entered the cell, dragging the girl. He threw her cruelly to her knees before me. "She is yours for the night," he said. "Do not kill her. Do not break her bones."

"I understand," I said.

He then, not turning his back on me, left the cell. In a moment he had locked it and, replacing the ring of keys on his belt, had disappeared down the corridor.

Lola, the slave whip tied about her neck, terrified, looked up at me.

"Please do not hurt me, Master," she said.

It startled me that she had called me 'Master,' but then I recalled that she had been given to me for the night. For the night I owned her.

"Get up, Lola," I said.

She struggled to her feet, frightened. Half crouching over she backed away from me, until she was stopped by the bars, which confined her with me in the cell, one of many such cells deep beneath the House of Andronicus.

I approached her.

She stood straight then, her back against the bars, her head turned to the side. I realized, suddenly, that she feared to look me in the face.

"I am sorry that I did you such injuries, Master," she said. I recalled her many cruelties to me in my training, the many lashings of the quirt, the blows of the slave whip she had arranged for me, the blows of her small hands and fists, her kicks, her belittlings of me. I recalled, most of all, how she had spilled the wine in the training session, had accused me of it, and had prescribed twenty blows of the snake. The Lady Gina had reduced the penalty to only five. Twenty blows of the snake, I had little doubt, might cost some men their lives.

It irritated me that she was not looking directly at me. Angrily, before I had truly thought, I took the sides of her mouth between my thumb and fingers and pressing tightly inwards, which draws the inside of the cheeks painfully between the teeth, turned her head to face me. I had seen a guard do this once to Tela, when she had not seemed to be paying him attention. This is not an action a woman fights. She complies instantly. I looked at Lola, so held, facing me. She was frightened. But suddenly I saw, too, in her eyes, that she wanted to be had as a slave. It was the first moment in which I had ever dominated a woman as a male brute, her master. I have never forgotten it.

Then, of course, I released her.

"Why did you spill the wine and accuse me of it?" I asked.

"It was a joke," she whispered.

"Do not lie to me," I said.

"I hated you," she said.

"Do you hate me now?" I asked.

"Oh, no, Master," she said, hastily. "I love you now. I want to please you. Please be kind to me."

I smiled. I did not think that Lola, in her cruelties, or when she had played the cruel trick with the wine, and had prescribed the twenty blows of the snake, had anticipated that she would, one day, be braceleted in my cell, at my mercy as a naked slave girl.

"Why twenty blows of the snake?" I asked. "Did you wish to kill me?"

"You are strong," she said, her head inclined a bit downward, but looking up at me. "Twenty blows would not kill you. It would only have punished you, terribly."

"You would have had this done," I asked, "because you hated me?"

"Yes, Master," she said. Then she added, hastily, "But I do not hate you now. I love you now. Please be kind to me, Master."

"Let me relieve you of the weight of this slave whip," I said, reaching up to untie it from her neck.

She lifted up her head, her head pressed back against the bars. Her body, her back, too, her lovely shoulder blades, was pressed against them. "Are you going to use it on me?" she asked.

"I did not hear you say 'Master,'" I said.

"Master," she said, quickly.

I untied the whip from her neck and, taking it, walked back to the table and bench. I put it on the bench. I sat down on the bench. I looked at the girl, standing with her back to the bars.

"Approach and kneel, Slave Girl," I said.

Quickly she came to the side of the table and knelt down before me.

"Am I to be whipped, Master?" she asked.

"Be silent," I said.

"Yes, Master," she said.

I looked at the girl. I felt conflicting emotions. Lola was one of the most beautiful women I had ever seen. She was now kneeling before me, frightened and obedient, naked and braceleted, mine to do with as I pleased. Yes, she had caused me much pain, and had much abused me. Yet, interestingly, the miseries and humiliations which she had inflicted upon me were not uppermost in my mind. It was not that I was unaware that I now had an opportunity to work out a well-deserved revenge upon her beautiful slave hide; it is rather that that thought did not particularly occupy me. It was not, surely, what seemed to me of overwhelming interest and importance in the situation in which I found myself.

I looked at the beautiful, kneeling, braceleted woman. What seemed to me of overwhelming significance was simply this, that such a woman, one who must obey, and who was in my power, knelt at my feet.

"Master," said Lola.

"Yes," I said.

"I have not fed since this morning," she said. "May I feed?"

I took a piece of meat from the bowl on the table. I held it out to her. "Thank you, Master," she said. Then, turning her head delicately, she took it between her teeth. I then, for a time, fed Lola. She depended upon me, in the hours of my ownership of her, for her very food and drink. I could scarcely comprehend the feelings I had, feeding the beauty by hand. I had not realized such feelings could exist in a man. Then I placed the bowl on the floor and she, putting her head down, her hands braceleted behind her, biting and licking, addressed herself to its contents. I looked down at the kneeling, feeding slave. She was in my power. In these hours she was mine. I fought against the incredible surge of power and pleasure I felt, against the power and pleasure of blood and manhood. I fought against might and passion, and glory and joy, for I was a man of Earth. But in those moments, for a brief instant, before I could deplore and castigate my feelings, before I could muster misery and guilt, I had felt what it was to stand, if only briefly, in man's place in the order of nature. I had, for a brief instant, tasted dominance. But then I recalled that I was a man of Earth, and that the world of nature, and what I was and women were, must be rejected and repudiated. Thirsting, I must not drink. Starving, I must not feed. Never should one be true to oneself. Always should one be true to the images and lies of others, fearful ones, weaklings unable to be strong themselves, whose safety lay in the bleeding and tricking of more dangerous beasts. Is it not in the interest of slaves to prohibit kings from claiming their thrones?

Then I was overcome with misery and guilt that I had even dared to think such thoughts!

How wrong nature was! How wrong to be true to the deep themes of the animal kingdom! Did I truly need to be what I was? Why should I fulfill my needs? How wrong it was to have needs! And how far more wrong it would be to dare to fulfill them! Men, I knew, must be as flowers, not as lions, not as men.

But who will tell the lion to be a flower? Surely, only the flowers. And who will tell a man not to be a man? Surely, too, the flowers, who might otherwise fear the tread of the heavy paw, the passing of the foot of the striding warrior.

Then I laughed, for it suddenly seemed to me absurd that such incredible conflicts should rage within me. Surely I, a man of Earth, knew well how to live. I had been taught how to live, and if, in abiding by the denials and negativities of my world, I was made unhappy and miserable, what did that matter, truly, in the larger scheme of things? Who did I think I was? Did I think that I was important? Is a lion, or a man, truly, more important than an insect or a flower? If there were more flowers than lions, or men, must not it be right to be a flower, and not a lion or a man? It may not be easy for lions or men to pretend to be flowers, but let them do their best. Above all do not let the flowers know that there may be a man or a lion among them. They would then be disturbed. They would flutter their petals fiercely.

Again I forced Gorean thoughts from my mind.

When I had laughed the girl, feeding, had stopped, and trembled. Then, after a time, she continued to feed.

"Here," I said. I crumbled the rest of the bread, which I had not eaten, which had been on the table, into her bowl, mixing it with the vegetables and meat which still remained there. "Thank you, Master," she said. She put down her head again, feeding. I smiled. The braceleted, beautiful slave was ravenous.

I had laughed for it had suddenly seemed to me absurd that I should even, for a moment, have allowed myself to think disapproved thoughts. Was I not of Earth? Was I not a true man, capable of conquering myself? Why, I wondered, should I conquer myself? Why should I not allow myself to be victorious? Then, again, chagrined, embarrassed, I thrust such thoughts from my mind.

But who is stronger, truly, I asked myself, he who continues to wound and bleed himself to please others, or he who refuses any longer to do so?

I shook my head, to force such a thought out of my mind.

The girl lifted her head. The bowl was clean. I picked up the bowl and carried it to the side, where I placed it on a small shelf.

"Thank you for feeding me, Master," she said.

I took a bit of her hair and, gently, wiped her mouth. To my surprise she put her teeth gently on my hand, and then licked and kissed at my hand. She then drew her head back. "You are not going to beat me, are you, Master?" she asked.

"Be silent," I said.

"Yes, Master," she said.

I looked at Lola. I forced myself to remember that she, in spite of her beauty and her collar, was a person. I looked at the small key, on its wire, dangling from her collar, between

her breasts. It was, doubtless, the key to her confining
bracelets. I must free her. Yet, as I looked down at her, I
must admit that I enjoyed having her at my mercy. I knew,
of course, despite the fact that she was a woman and I was a
man, and that she was then to me as my own slave and I to
her as her true master, that I must not permit myself this
pleasure. It hinted too clearly at my dominance over her by
nature, a dominance which I knew I must not permit myself
to exercise, indeed, a dominance which I, of Earth, was not
even supposed to permit myself to recognize. It was not congenial to the contemporary political myths of my planet.
Men, not so long ago, I recalled, had not even been permitted
to recognize that they were animals. Now, it seemed, although they might be granted a token permission to recognize
their animality, they were refused permission to recognize the
sort of animals they were. I wondered if there could be a politics which did not betray truth. Perhaps such a politics,
something beyond theater and myths, might someday emerge
upon the forge of history.

"There is a bucket of water at the side of the cell," I said.
"Go there and drink. Then return and be again before me, as
you are now."

"Yes, Master," she said. She went to the side of the room
and knelt down. There was a wooden bucket there, with
slatted sides, hooped with iron. It was full. She put her head
down and drank. Meanwhile I put the wine, that in the shallow, chipped clay bowl, on the shelf to one side. The girl did
not pay me the least attention in this. She did not expect to
receive any of the wine. She was a slave. It was more than
sufficient that she should kneel at the bucket and, braceleted,
drink from it. Indeed, I had not forced her to crawl on her
belly to a shallow pan. I wanted the table free.

I returned to the bench and sat down. In a moment the
girl, again, was kneeling before me.

"Thank you, Master," she said. She had been fed and
watered.

I rose to my feet and walked about her. I suppose I should
not have done so, but she was so incredibly beautiful. It was
a pleasure to see her displayed, fully, in her beauty and steel.
She knelt very straight before me, a bit tensely, back on her
heels, her knees wide. How marvelous it must be to own such
a slave, I thought. Then I reminded myself that she was a
person. There was something about her, subtle, in her breath-

ing and body tone, which I could not place at the time. Too, there was an exciting odor emanating from her, easily detectable in the Gorean air, even in the pens. A man of Earth I did not even fully register or comprehend these signs. I had never seen them manifested in an Earth woman, at least in such degree. As I now understand she was attempting to hold herself still and control herself, but her body was betraying her. The evidence was manifest, exposed before my senses, but I, as a naive fool of Earth, did not even fully understand what was presented before me. I had at my feet an aroused slave girl.

I put my hands on her upper arms, good-naturedly, not understanding her shuddering, and lifted her to her feet. "Master," she begged. I knew I must free her. She had caused me a great deal of bother. I then lifted her from her feet, by one arm and an ankle. I was startled. I had not realized I could handle her so easily, nor, I think, had she realized it. "Master," she begged, "please." I then, less gently than I should have, perhaps, threw her on her belly on the table. She tensed, and lay very still. I threw her hair forward. I twisted her collar about until I had the wire and the key attached to it. I unwound the wire and placed it, with its key, at the side of the girl's head. I readjusted the collar on her neck, so that the small, heavy lock was again at the back of her neck. I observed the small hairs on the back of her neck, her hair thrown forward, and the steel, with its lock, on her neck, snug. I thrust the tiny key into the locks on the slave bracelets and, with two small, heavy clicks, and an opening of metal, removed them from her. I put the key, with the wire, and the bracelets, on the bench.

"My hands are now free, that I may please you more," she whispered. She lay before me, on her stomach, her hair thrown forward. Her hands were beside her, their backs to the table. This exposed their palms to me. The palms of a girl's hands are extremely sensitive and erotic. I resisted the impulse to trace lightly in the palm of her left hand a small cursive "Kef," the staff and fronds, that letter used commonly in the branding of female slaves.

The girl lay still. She did not move. This irritated me. Had I not freed her of the bracelets? I realize now that she was waiting to be commanded to my pleasure.

She moaned.

I looked at her. She was very beautiful, and it was extremely difficult to remind myself that I must not treat her as the marvelous and exciting woman she was but rather as a person, a thing to which its maleness or femaleness was incidental and unimportant.

"Master?" she asked.

Then, suddenly, for an instant, I saw her as Lola, a stripped and collared slave, who had caused me much misery, and who now lay before me, mine to do with as I wished. She suddenly tensed, sensing the difference in my attitude. My hands, angrily, gripped the edge of the table.

"Do not whip me, Master," she begged. "Let me try to please you. If I do not please you, then whip me."

"Do you bargain?" I asked.

"No, Master," she cried. "No, Master! Forgive me, Master! Please forgive me, Master!"

"Be silent," I told her.

"Yes, Master," she said.

I enjoyed having Lola at my mercy. Then I reminded myself that she was not to be treated according to the harsh modalities of nature, those of dominance and submission, and the enforcement of order. She was, of course, a person.

Did she truly think that I, a man of Earth, would treat her as a slave?

Surely she must know that she had nothing to fear from one such as I who would treat her with dignity and respect.

Then, suddenly, looking at her, I felt a flood of anger. It was she who had wished for me to receive twenty blows of the snake.

I flung the table up and to one side, throwing her to the floor. The table was half way across the cell.

Then she was at my feet, on the stones, kneeling in the straw, her head down, her hair before her face. I felt her lips, through her hair, kissing at my feet. Never had I dreamed that I would even meet so beautiful a woman, let alone have her in my power, attempting to placate me.

I looked down at the woman, her head down. "Lola begs to please Master," she wept. I felt, looking down at her, throughout my entire body, an incredible surge of force and power, of exhilaration. I threw back my head and laughed. She kept her head down. She trembled. Lola, I think, had heard such a laugh before. The feelings which swept me were almost incomprehensible and inutterably magnificent. I looked down at her. She was at my feet. I knew then, with a clarity and force far beyond those of argument and theory, that I stood in the order of nature. Laughing I crouched down, over her. I put my hands in her hair. I pulled her head up. Her eyes were closed. Her face, to my amazement, was rapturous. "Yes, Master," she said, "yes!" I prepared to hurl her to her back on the straw and stones, and treat her as what she was, a woman, and a slave. And then I remembered that I was a man of Earth. I released her hair. I seized her by the arms and threw her back from me. I clenched my fists. I cried out with frustration and misery. She was then on her hands and knees, on the stones. She looked at me, frightened. Then, again, quickly, she knelt. "Master?" she asked.

She was so beautiful!

I dug my fingernails into the palms of my hands. I gritted my teeth.

She crawled, unbidden, to me. She knelt then, close to me. She put out her hand to touch me. "Master," she said.

"Do not touch me," I said, suddenly.

She drew back her hand, quickly. "Yes, Master," she said.

I turned away from her.

"How have I failed to please you?" she begged.

"Be silent," I snapped.

"Yes, Master," she whispered.

I strode to the wall of the cell, away from the girl. I extended my arms and, head down, leaned against the wall. I fought myself, and my desires, and my needs.

"Master?" she asked.

"Be silent!" I cried.

"Yes, Master," she whispered.

I struck the heavy stone then with my fists, moaning. I must conquer myself. I must defeat myself. I must deny, thwart and suppress my impulses, my blood and manhood. I must be my own enemy. I must make myself my own victim.

"May I serve you wine, Master?" she asked.

I turned from the wall. I then had myself under control. I breathed deeply, almost gasping.

Unbidden, she went to the shelf where I had placed the shallow, chipped clay bowl of cheap, dark wine, fit for slaves. She then, holding the bowl, knelt again, gracefully, before me. Looking at me, she tossed her head, throwing her dark hair behind her. The slender steel collar was beautiful on her throat. She, holding the bowl with two hands, pressed it back against her belly, low, below the navel. I looked at the edge of the bowl, containing the wine, pressed back, into her flesh. Then she lifted the bowl before her and, gently, turning her head, placing her lips softly upon it, kissed it. She then, with two hands, head down, proffered to me the chipped, shallow bowl.

"Wine, Master?" she asked.

I took the bowl of wine from her. She trembled. She looked up at me.

I drank then, holding the shallow bowl with two hands. Then, after a bit, I lowered the bowl from my lips and looked down at the beautiful slave. I had not finished the wine.

"The wine, and Lola, are yours, Master," she said. I knew that she spoke the truth.

I lifted the wine again to my lips and again drank. Then I placed the bowl, containing its residue of wine, behind me on the table.

I had drunk as a master before the girl, the kneeling slave.

"You have tasted the wine of the House of Andronicus," she said. "Taste now the wine of Lola."

I then realized, clearly, suddenly, for the first time, that the slave before me was sexually aroused, and helpless. Hitherto I had been impervious to the obvious, manifested to displays of her need. Signs of which I had hitherto neglected to take active account now seemed clear to me, even the odor of her begging slave body. I realized now I had registered many of her piteous signals, but, somehow, had forced them away from explicit, conscious recognition. I had been, I suppose, stupid and insensitive. It is one thing to understand clearly what is the case with one's slave and then, as one pleases, to satisfy or not satisfy the girl, using her needs to bring her more deeply and powerfully under your control as an abject slave, and quite another not even to know what is going on in her pretty head and lovely body. My ignorance in these matters was, I think, a function of complex factors. First, I was a man of Earth. Thus I was not accustomed to truly looking upon women, truly seeing them and trying to understand them. Most men of Earth do not, truly, unfortunately, pay much attention to women. Men often do not even, truly, know their mates. If they did, it seems that misunderstandings, divorces, and such, would be less frequent. An interesting contrast here is the Gorean master/slave relationship. Men tend to be extremely interested in things they own, and tend, usually, to be quite fond of them. Owned women do not form an exception to this general rule. The slave girl is commonly desired and prized by her master; she is one of his treasures. The Gorean master, interested in her and attentive to her, wants to know everything about her, in its complexity and intimacy. He wants to know her thoughts, her emotions and feelings, in their feminine, lyrical detail. Conversing with a lovely slave is one of the many pleasures of owning her. It is almost impossible for a girl to keep her thoughts or feelings from her master. He knows her too well. Most girls are extremely responsive to their masters, and love them deeply, with that incredible love which can be known only by an enslaved woman, that love which a woman can accord only to a man who is her total master. Yet I would be remiss did I not mention that even the most vital, animate slave, delightedly conversing with her master, knows that at a mere snap of his fingers she may have to tear aside her garments and serve him as a chain slut. She is owned. Too, many slave girls are kept by men who are harsh and cold to them, and who despise them as mere slaves. These girls, too, of course, must obey. They, too, of course, must perform perfectly for their masters.

"I am yours, Master," said Lola.

I looked down upon her. No, I had not, hitherto, realized the extend of her needs. I had looked at her, but I had not truly seen her. I had looked at her as might have a man of Earth, seeing her in terms of classifications and categories, and my conditioned expectations, discounting what did not seem congenial to these categories and expectations, refusing to see, or, at least, to understand, what was clearly, objectively, presented before my senses. I now saw her, however, not in terms of generalities and conditioned expectations but as what she was, startling though it might be to my Earth-trained mind, an incredibly aroused female at my feet.

I clenched my fists.

"Master," said Lola.

I had not even understood that a woman could have such feelings, in such depth and desperation. My education on Earth had not familiarized me with the complex and deep needs of women. That, I think, is the second reason I had not been hitherto alert to Lola's needs. I simply did not register what I saw. I did not know that that sort of thing, in such degree and intensity, could exist. I was furious. My education had apparently been kept deliberately incomplete in this re-spect. I had little doubt but what many specialists on Earth were familiar with such facts, facts they found it politically pertinent to suppress, or, should one say, politically pertinent to avoid bringing forward for general attention. There is much to investigate in science. Surely not all areas need be explored equally, especially if unguarded researches might, if published, bring ruin upon one's career. How much easier it is to be objective about the constituents of the atom than about ourselves.

I looked down upon the girl.

I had, of course, never seen such need manifested in a girl of Earth. But then, of course, I had never seen a girl of Earth, naked, in a steel collar, thrown to my feet in the straw of a Gorean dungeon either. I wondered if the girls of Gor were truly incredibly different from the girls of Earth. They seemed so sexually alive, so feminine and vital, whereas the girls of Earth, many of them, seemed so inhibited, so timid, so restricted, so tight, so embarrassed, so ashamed and frightened of their sex. It was as though they feared to let themselves go; as though it was terribly important for them to hold themselves in. Indeed, what was the pseudomasculini-zation of many of the women of Earth, in clothing and men-tal garb, but a hysterical attempt to deny their sexuality? What did the women of Earth fear? That a true ac-knowledgement of their deepest sexual needs would lead them to kneel at the feet of a master?

Lola looked up at me, tears in her eyes. Slavery, I suddenly suspected, releases femaleness in the woman. I did not sup-pose that Gorean free women could have brought themselves to this pitch of exposure, vulnerability and excitement, which was perhaps not unusual for a slave girl. The major differ-ence then, I suspected, lay not so much between the Gorean woman and the Earth woman, but between the free woman and the slave. I recalled that Gorean slavers brought Earth women to Gor as slaves. Surely they would not have done so if such girls did not sell well, and, of course, they would not sell well unless they proved, on the whole, to be pleasing slaves, and fully. Many an Earth girl, I suspected, who might have thought herself frigid or sexually inert on her own world discovered to her horror that, collared, stripped, she was hot, helpless, exquisite meat in her master's furs. The girl of Earth would discover her sexuality on the planet Gor, or her master's whip would know the reason why.

"Did Master enjoy his wine?" asked Lola.

"I have not yet finished it," I said. The bowl was behind me, on the table.

"Yes, Master," she said.

I had drunk from the bowl which she had proffered to me. I had been standing. She, a naked slave, had been kneeling before me. I had drunk with her at my feet, as a master. Power had been in my body when I had drunk the wine. I recalled that I should have castigated myself for the feelings of strength which had been in me at that time, but I had failed to do so. I had felt powerful and magnificent. I realized now, of course, I should have been ashamed. I wondered if it were so wrong to feel magnificent and powerful. Was it truly unworthy of a man to feel magnificent and powerful? Why, I wondered. Why is it wrong for a man to feel like a man? Perhaps, I pondered, it is not wrong for a man to feel like a man. Perhaps it is not even wrong for a man to be a man. Who could think such, save perhaps some who were not themselves men?

"Would you like me to again serve you wine, Master," asked Lola.

"No," I said.

"Yes, Master," she said. She put her head down, deferentially. I realized then she was waiting for me to take her by the arms and throw her on her back on the straw, claiming her, subjecting her to the ruthless domination, sometimes tender, sometime harsh, always uncompromising, accorded by a master to one who is only a miserable slave.

Tears came to my eyes. I wanted her. Yet I knew I must not touch her. I was a man of Earth. I must remember that. And she was a helpless girl, a person.

She looked up. "Taste me," she said.

I then realized, to my chagrin, that another reason I might not have been alert to her needs was because of my fear. He who does not recognize a woman's needs certainly does not have to consider whether or not he should satisfy them. When a girl exposes herself as a slave it would seem there is then extended to the male an invitation to her mastery. She was at my feet, a slave. Did this not, then, challenge me, in effect, to put my collar on her. He who fears he cannot satisfy a woman, or fears he will be unable to do so, often pretends he does not understand her need. If necessary he may chide her, gently, or belittle or ridicule her, attempting to make her ashamed of her need, that it will therefore be overlooked that he has not satisfied it. If the female can be tricked, thusly, into the verbal repudiation of her needs, the male, in his weakness, relieved, need not consider fulfilling them. These deceptions, of course, are seldom successful; unhappiness, conflict and frustration, accordingly, for both males and females, for the needs cannot be physiologically repudiated, become endemic. One who fears to be a master, who doubts his capacity, his power, his strength, his will, his resoluteness, will be expected to turn a deaf ear to the pleas of even the most piteous of beautiful slaves. How can he be expected to fulfill another who fears, first, to fulfill himself? No man can be truly happy who does not own a slave. No woman can be truly happy who does not belong to a master. But if, in an unguarded moment, I had suddenly glimpsed my terror at the prospect of fulfilling myself, of accepting the responsibility, the joy and incredible power, energizing and exalting, of the mastership, of answering the obvious depth needs of the lovely, surrendered female before me, I swiftly thrust such a frightening comprehension out of my thoughts. I feared to look deeply into myself, and into women. Was I strong enough to accept honestly what I might find there? Is it not safer to cower in the caves of lies than stand upon the cliffs of truth, surveying the world? Yet when one stands in the sunlight, and feels the winds of reality, how dank and shameful seem the dark shelters of falsehood, and how foolish it seems then to have once feared daylight and fresh air. But swiftly I, a man of Earth, well tutored in my myths, scoffed that I might have feared to assume my manhood. I was well aware of the definitions of my manhood, and how well I must fulfill them, that I must be gentle, solicitous, feminine and sweet, and obedient to the whims of females, lest I be a brute. But into those definitions did not enter, as I now recognize, hints of a nature formed by a harsh evolution, remarks pertaining to genetic dispositions selected for in times when the meadows were bestrode by the prowling tread of the saber-toothed tiger and the hills rang with the trumpeting of mastodons; those definitions did not tell of the dark songs and cries of hunters; they did not speak of campfires or knives of blue flint; they did not speak of warriors, or of meat turned on green spits by captured, neck-thonged women; one reality seemed to have eluded the verbal formulas I had been taught; one item had been left out of the definitions; it is called man.

"I kneel before my master," said Lola. "I await my rape."

I cried out with misery and frustration. Lola looked at me, startled, unable to comprehend the conflict which raged within me. I wanted to seize her and throw her to her back, and vent my wrath and joy upon her, uncompromisingly exercising the nocturnal rights which had been assigned to me over her, taking her hot slave flesh in my arms, making it writhe to my least touch, making her scream her submission to me as her master, but I knew that I was a man of Earth, and that she was a person.

Suddenly, angrily, stupidly, foolishly, I lashed out at her, cuffing her back with the back of my left hand. She fell backward. I was startled that I had struck her. Yet it had happened so swiftly I had hardly realized what I was doing. I had been furious not really with her, but with myself. Lola was innocent. She was only a naked, aroused, beautiful, collared slave at my feet. It was not her fault that she had been thrown to me nor was it her fault that her needs were those of what she was, a slave girl. Yet she was the obvious precipitant of my dilemma, my misery. It was thus that I had suddenly, irrationally, struck her. It was foolish, and meaningless, that I had done so. She was flung back in the straw, blood at her beautiful mouth. I expected her to look at me with horror and reproach. Instead, she put down her head and crawled swiftly to my feet. She then lay on her stomach in the straw before me, her upper body lifted on her elbows, her head down, over my feet. I felt her lips, sweet and full, kissing at my feet. There was a kind of wonder and pleasure in her voice. "Yes, Master," she said. "Thank you, Master. I am sorry if I was not pleasing to you." I then understood that she had taken the blow as a token of my mastery over her, an explicit expression of my sovereignty over her. I felt her lips kissing at my feet, happily, gratefully.

"It is enough," I said.

"Yes, Master," she said. She continued to lie at my feet, her head turned to the side, her right cheek on my feet. I felt her hair, too, on my feet.

A slave girl is subject to discipline. She may be struck with or without reason. Usually, of course, the master would have a reason, however trivial it might be. Sometimes, of course, he may strike her with no obvious reason whatsoever, even one which is trivial. This serves to remind her that she is a slave and that no reason is needed to strike her.

I looked down at Lola.

She looked up at me, and then, turning her head and lifting herself on her elbows, she again kissed my feet. She then rolled from my feet a yard or so away in the straw. She lay on her back and regarded me, happily. "It will not be necessary to strike me again, Master," she said. "I will be docile, and obedient and loving." She looked up at me, smiling, her left knee raised, her hands beside her, palms up, in the straw. "Have me, Master," she said. "Subject me, uncompromisingly, to your pleasure."

"Do you beg it?" I asked. I did not know why I asked the question.

"Yes, Master," she said, smiling, "I beg it."

"Why were you put in with me tonight?" I asked.

"To be punished," she said. She smiled. "I await my punishment, Master," she said.

Then suddenly I was afraid, and guilty, and confused. I was weak, and I reddened, and stammered. I had struck the poor thing. And surely she did not expect me to be strong, and to take her in hand, as would have a Gorean master. I was of Earth. And did she not know she was a person?

"I am sorry I struck you," I stammered. "It was a stupid and cruel thing to do. I was really angry not so much at you, as at myself. I behaved as a brute. I am very sorry."

She looked at me, frightened. She did not understand me, or the forces which moved within me. How could she have understood me, she a Gorean girl, collared, whom strong men had long ago taught her womanhood? Did she not know that I, because of my fears, was trying to make her like a man? Could she not, like many of the women of Earth, because of her own fears, try, too, to be like a man? Each sex could then, because of its fears, try to protect itself from the other, denying the obvious complementarities of nature, the fitting together of diverse dispositions and modalities. The wholeness is not achieved, the puzzle is not solved, by trying to put together pieces of the same configuration.

I looked at her. Quickly, trembling, confused, she knelt, making herself small. She put her head down to the straw.

"Do not be cruel to me," she begged. "If I have displeased you, simply whip me. I do not understand you, or what you

are doing. I am only a poor female slave. Please do not torture me in this insidious fashion. If I have so grievously displeased you, I beg to be simply put under the honesty of a
leather discipline."

"I do not understand," I said.

She moaned. "Please do not subject me to these tortures,
Master," she begged. "Lola is only a poor slave. Just tie her
and whip her. Perhaps then she will learn to please you better."

"I am not trying to be cruel to you," I said. "I am trying
to be kind to you."

She moaned.

"Look up," I said.

"Yes, Master," she said. She looked up, frightened.

"I'm sorry I struck you," I said. "I am very sorry."

"But Lola is only a slave," she said. "Slaves are meant to
be struck and abused."

"I am sorry," I said.

"Sorry?" she said.

"Yes," I said. "I am truly sorry."

She shuddered. "Tie me and whip me," she begged.

"Here," I said, hurrying to the wine, which I had left on
the table behind me. I took the wine and, as the girl
trembled, crouched near her, holding the wine to her lips.
Shuddering, she drank. "You see," I said, "you served me
wine, now I serve you wine." "Yes, Master," she said, trembling. I understand now her trepidation better than I did at
the time. My emotional conflicts and frustrations, my warring
motivations, expressing themselves in inconsistencies in
speech and behavior, had terrified her. She was a Gorean girl,
and her experiences on Gor had not prepared her to understand a male who had been taught to suspect his own nature,
and to torture and lacerate himself for impulses, desires and
feelings as natural as the circulation of the blood and the
movement of molecules through the membranes of cells.
Shame she could understand, such things as the chagrin of a
man who has failed in honor, but pathologically conditioned
guilts, instilled neurotic anxieties, used as control devices to
perpetuate sickened societies, were unfamiliar to her. I think,
now, she may have feared that she was in the presence of a
madman, one to whom her beauty, her vulnerability and
helplessness seemed meaningless, one who seemed not to understand that she was a woman and a slave, one who seemed

ignorant of her desires, impervious to her needs, one who did not seem to know what to do with her or how to handle her, one who, though ostensibly sane, and possibly dangerously strong, yet behaved unpredictably and irrationally, one who, though ostensibly a male, behaved in no fashion remotely resembling that of a man. It is little wonder she was frightened. Surely, she must have surmised, if I were not mad, I was at least a fool. Who but a fool would not drink when he was thirsty, or eat when he was hungry? But I was not a madman or a fool. I was neither, or perhaps both. I was a man of Earth.

"Forgive me," I begged the girl.

She shuddered, spilling a bit of wine. She looked at me with terror. I did not strike her.

"Are you finished?" I asked.

She nodded her head, frightened.

"There is some left," I said. "Finish it."

I held the chipped bowl, and the girl, frightened, finished the wine. I put the shallow, chipped bowl on the table.

I returned to the girl, and crouched down beside her. She feared to meet my eyes.

"Please forgive me," I begged.

She shuddered.

"Forgive me," I said, irritably.

"I forgive you, Master," she said, quickly.

"I did not mean, truly, to order you to forgive me," I said. "I would appreciate it if you, of your own free will, would voluntarily forgive me."

"Yes, Master," she whispered. "I forgive you, of my own free will, voluntarily."

"Thank you," I said.

"Don't hurt me, please, Master," she begged. She refused to meet my eyes.

"Look at me," I said.

"Please do not torture me, Master," she said.

"Look at me," I said.

"Yes, Master," she said.

She lifted her head and looked into my eyes. I was startled. The girl was genuinely frightened.

I saw the slender steel collar on her neck. My eyes must have momentarily hardened, or glinted. She shuddered. Then I again controlled myself. "You need not call me 'Master'," I said, kindly.

"Yes, Master," she said.

"Do not call me 'Master'," I said.

"I am a slave, Master," she wept. Disrespect in a slave can be punishable by death.

"Do not call me 'Master'," I said.

"Yes, Master," she said. "I mean 'Yes,'" she wept.

"Call me 'Jason'," I said.

She looked away from me, down, trembling, terrified. "'Jason'," she whispered. "Please do not kill me, Master."

"I do not understand," I said.

"You have scorned my beauty," she wept. "You refused to rape me. You have forced me to show you disrespect. Now will you not, cruelly, punish me for being insufficiently beautiful, for not having yielded in your arms as an abject slave, and for having shown you disrespect? Will you not now throw me to your feet and kick and beat me mercilessly, venting your displeasure upon me?"

"Of course not," I said.

She shrank back. "The House of Andronicus would not like it if you killed me," she said. "I am their property."

"I have no intention of killing you," I said.

She shook with relief. Then she looked at me. "I am here," she said. "What are you going to do with me?"

"Nothing," I said.

"I find that hard to believe, Master," she said.

I shrugged.

"What game are you playing with me?" she said. "For what cruel treatment and punishment are you preparing me?"

"None," I said.

She shuddered. "I know you are not of Gor," she said. "Are all men of your world like you?" she asked.

"Most, I suppose," I said.

"How their slaves must live in terror of them," she said.

"Most men of my world do not have slaves," I said. "Our women, almost uniformly, are kept free."

"Whether they wish it or not?" she asked.

"Of course," I said, "in such a matter their wishes are unimportant."

"That is called freedom?" she asked.

"Yes," I said. "I suppose so."

"But some men, strong men," she said, "must enslave their women."

I nodded. I had known of such cases. Such men, I supposed, made their own laws.

"But most men of your world," she said, "do not have slaves."

"Of course not," I said.

"Did you have slaves?" she asked.

"No," I said.

"Not even one slave?" she asked.

"No," I said.

"Are you typical of those of your world?" she asked.

"I think so," I said.

"If that is true," she said, regarding me narrowly, "how is that you know so well how to plunge a woman into terror?"

"If I have inadvertently frightened you," I said, "I am truly sorry. Such was not my intention."

"I am naked and collared, and at your mercy," she said. "Do you truly expect me to believe that you have nothing in store for me?"

"I will not abuse you," I said. "You are safe with me. Have no fear."

"You torture me so," she cried. "Why do you not just do what you are going to do and have done with it? Was I truly so cruel to you that you have seen fit to subject me to these agonies?"

I did not know how to reassure her.

"Is there some cruel caprice you intend to practice upon me," she asked, "some humiliating and degrading performance you will exact from me for your pleasure?"

"Do not be afraid," I said.

"Torturer," she wept. "Torturer!"

"Do not be afraid," I said.

She put her head in her hands, weeping. "How cruel and insidious are the men of your world," she wept. "How simple and bluff are the exactions of the men of Gor in comparison. Why could you not, simply, have made me serve you, and then raped and beaten me if you wished?"

"I have no intention of doing you harm," I said.

She, sobbing, crawled to the bench where I had left the whip. She took it from the bench in her teeth and, carrying it in her teeth, crawled to me. She lifted the whip in her teeth to me. I took it from between her small white teeth. "Whip me," she begged.

I threw the whip aside. "No," I said.

She, shuddering, lay at my feet. She did not know what would be done with her.

I did not speak to her but went to the dark blanket which lay to one side on the straw. I spread the blanket, which was heavy, and fashioned from the wool of the bounding hart, on the straw. I gestured to the blanket. "Lie on the blanket," I told her, kindly.

She crept to the blanket and lay upon it, on her back. Her body was very beautiful on the dark blanket. She touched her collar, lightly, with her finger tips. She was a slave. She looked at me. "Does it begin now?" she asked.

I stood over her, and looked down at her small, trembling body, open to whatever I might choose to inflict upon it.

I crouched beside her, and her eyes, terrified, met mine. "Please be kind to Lola, Master," she whispered. "She is only your poor slave."

Gently I took the half of the blanket on which she was not lying and drew it over her, covering her. "It is late now," I said. "You must be tired. Go to sleep."

She looked at me, frightened, disbelievingly. "Are you not going to own me?" she asked.

"Of course not," I said. "Rest now, pretty Lola." Then I realized that I, a man of Earth, should not have called her 'pretty Lola'. That she was pretty, decidedly so, and helplessly a slave, must be ignored; such things must not be recognized. They might interfere with the artificial constructions of neuteristic personhood, constructions in terms of which my conditioning required me to view her. How foolish it now seems to me that I then refused to see a beauty as a beauty, and a slave as a slave.

"Are you not going to share the blanket?" she asked.

"No," I said.

"But I am branded, and wear a collar," she said.

"Rest," I said. "Go to sleep, Lola."

I went to the far wall of the cell, that opposite the bars. I sat back against the wall.

"Go to sleep," I said to the girl, gently.

She looked at me, the blanket pulled about her neck. "Am I not to be tied, or chained?" she asked.

"No," I said.

She lay there, quietly.

"You are safe," I told her. "Go to sleep."

"Yes, Master," she said. "Master," she said.

"Yes," I said.

"I am a slave," she said.

"Yes," I said.

"Are you not going to treat me as a slave?" she asked.

"Of course not," I said. "I am a man of Earth."

Did she truly think that I, a man of Earth, would treat her as a slave, merely because she was a slave?

She was silent.

"Go to sleep," I told her.

"Yes, Master," she said.

I leaned back against the wall, sitting in the straw. The girl lay very quietly. We did not speak for a long time. Then, after perhaps an Ahn, I heard her moan, and saw her twist under the blanket.

"Master," I heard her beg. "Master."

I went to her side.

In the half light, she thrust the dark blanket down about her thighs. She half sat, half lay, on the lower portion of the blanket. She looked at me. She tried to put her small hands out, to clasp me piteously behind the neck. But I caught her wrists, and held her hands from me. "Master," she begged. "Please, Master." Her body, small and curved, was beautiful in the half light. Her breasts were marvelous. I noted the sweet turn of her body where the curve of her belly yielded to the flare of her hips.

"What is wrong with you?" I asked. Her small strength was no match for mine.

"Please have me, Master," she begged. "Please take me, and as a slave!"

I looked at her small body, and at the collar of steel on her throat.

"No," I said.

She stopped struggling, and I released her wrists. I rose to my feet and stood regarding her. She knelt now, trembling, on the blanket.

"I am a man of Earth," I told her.

"Yes, Master," she said, her head down.

I was angry, and frightened. My heart was pounding.

"You have nothing to fear from me," I said.

"Yes, Master," she said.

Surely she must know that she had nothing to fear from one such as I who would treat her with dignity and respect.

Why, then, was I terrified of her, she only a slave? I think it was because I feared she might release in me things which I feared to understand, because I feared she might release in me something proud and savage, something which would be a stranger to apologies and pretenses, something long-forgotten and mighty, something which had been bred in caves and the hunt, something which might be called a man.

I looked upon the girl, the kneeling slave. For an instant I felt a surgency of power.

Then I recalled that I must not be a man, for manhood was prohibited and forbidden; it was something to be belittled and ridiculed. One must not be a man. One must rather be a person. Lions must be snared, and castrated and bled. There is no place for them among the flowers. Let lions be taught it is their function to draw the carts of sheep. Let them then be rewarded with bleats of approval.

But, for an instant, looking upon the girl, I had felt stirring within me something dark and mighty, uncompromising and powerful, something which told me that such beauties as now knelt before me were the full and rightful properties of men.

Then I thrust such thoughts from my mind.

"I do not understand you," I said, angrily.

She kept her head down.

"I have treated you with kindness and courtesy," I said. "Yet you persist in behaving like a slave."

"I am a slave, Master," she said.

"I do not know what you want," I said. "Should I tie you to the bars, that the urts may feed upon you?"

"Please do not do that, Master," she said.

"That is a joke," I said, horrified that she might have taken me seriously.

"I thought it might be," she said, softly.

"Speaking of jokes," I said, "what a splendid jest have we two tonight played upon our jailers."

"Master?" she asked.

"They put you in with me that I might punish you, and yet I have not done so. I have treated you with gentleness and courtesy, with kindness and respect."

"Yes, Master," she said, "it is a splendid joke."

"Apparently you are having difficulty sleeping," I said. "I, too, am restless. If you like, we may have a conversation."

She put her head down, silent.

"Would you like me to tell you of the women on my world," I asked, "who are fine and free?"

"Are they happy?" she asked.

"No," I said. "But neither are the men," I added hastily.

"Surely some men and women on your world must be happy," she said.

"Some, I suppose," I said. "I shall hope so." There did not seem much point to me to tell her in detail of the broadcast misery on my world, its pettiness and frustration. If one judges a civilization by the joy and satisfaction of its populations the major civilizations of Earth were surely failures. It is interesting to note the high regard in which certain civilizations are held which, from the human point of view, from the point of view of human happiness, would appear to be obvious catastrophes.

"You are safe with me," I told her. "I shall not demean you by treating you like a woman."

"Why is it demeaning to be treated as a woman?" she asked.

"I do not know," I said. "But it is supposed to be demeaning to treat women like women."

"Oh," she said.

"They are to be treated like men, the same," I said. "It is insulting not to treat them like men."

"Who has told you this?" she asked.

"Men," I said, "some men, and women who are much like men."

"I see," she said.

"Thus it must be true," I said.

"I see," she said.

"Yes," I said.

"I am a woman," she said.

"What you want does not matter," I told her.

"I see," she said.

I was silent.

"It would seem to me very insulting to treat a woman as though she were a man," she said.

"No," I said.

"Oh," she said. She looked at me. "But are not men and women obviously different?" she asked.

"Statistically, of course," I said, "there are vast and obvious differences between them, both psychological and physical, but some men can be found who are very feminine and some women can be found who are extremely masculine. Thus, the existence of such feminine men and such masculine women proves that men and women are really the same."

"I do not understand," she said.

"I do not really understand either," I admitted.

"If a man can be found who is like a woman and a woman can be found who is like a man does this not suggest, rather, that men and women are really different?"

I was silent.

"If an urt could be found which was like a sleen," she said, "and a sleen could be found which was like an urt, would this show that urts and sleen were the same?"

"Of course not," I said. "That would be preposterous."

"What is the difference?" she asked.

"I do not know," I said. "There must be one."

"Oh," she said. "And," she said, "would not the feminine man and the masculine woman, by their comparative rarity, tend not to cancel out the obvious differences between men and women but rather, in their relative uniqueness, tend to point up the contrasts and differences even more vividly?"

I began to grow irritated. "The contrasts, over time," I said, "will grow less. Education now, on my world, is oriented toward the masculinization of women and the feminization of men. Women must become men and men must try to be like women. That is the key to happiness."

"But men and women are different," she said. She looked sick.

"They must behave as if they were the same," I said.

"But what of their true natures?" she asked.

I shrugged. "Their true natures are unimportant," I said. "Let the heads be shaped by boards. Let the feet be bound with tight cloths."

"But will there not come a time of screaming," she asked, "a time of rage, of lifting of the knife?"

I shrugged. "I do not know," I said. "Let us hope not." I did know that frustration tended to produce aggression and destructiveness. It did not seem unlikely that the frustrations of my world, particularly those of men, might precipitate the madness and irrationality of thermonuclear war. Aggression, displaced, would presumably be ventilated against an external enemy. But the trigger would have been pulled. It would be unfortunate if the last recourse left to men to prove to themselves that they were men was the carnage of contemporary, technological conflict. Yet I knew men who hungered for this madness, that the walls of their prisons might be destroyed, even though they themselves might die screaming in the flames.

But perhaps they might reclaim their surrendered manhood before they themselves, and their world, became the helpless victims of its thwarted furies.

Manhood cannot be forever denied. The beast will walk at our side, or it will destroy us.

"Am I to understand," she asked, "that the men of your world do not take their women in hand, and throw them to their feet?"

"Of course not!" I said. "Our women are treated with total honor, and dignity and respect," I said. "They are treated as our equals."

"Poor men, poor women," she said.

"I do not understand," I said.

"You would make a love slave your equal?" she asked.

"Of course," I said.

"You cheat her then of her opportunity to be over-whelmed, and to be forced to serve and love. You preclude her then from the fulfillment of her deepest nature."

I said nothing.

"If you will not be a man," she asked, "how can she be a woman?"

"Do you think that a woman is a slave?" I asked, scornfully.

"I have been in the arms of strong men," she said. "Yes."

I was stunned.

"You are wrong!" I cried. "You are wrong!" I was afraid, terribly, then, for if what she said was true then there might be within me a master. But if a woman should kneel before me and beg a collar would I not be terrified to enclose her lovely neck in its inflexible grasp? Would I not be afraid to own her, to assume the mighty responsibility of the mastery? Did I have the power, the strength, the courage, to be a master? Did I fear I would be unable to control and tame, and make mine, such a sinuous, beautiful animal? No, I surely would have, reddening and frightened, hurried her to her feet, trying to embarrass and shame her for having displayed her needs. I would have to encourage her to be a man. If she, too, were a man, then I could, with a clear conscience, leave the woman in her unsatisfied.

"And you are a fool," she said.

It irritated me that she had called me this, but I reminded myself that I was a man of Earth, and women might annoy or insult me as they pleased, with complete impunity. If they were not permitted to do this, how could they respect us?

"I am not surprised," she said, "that women are the equals of such men as you. It seems to me, Jason, that you are quite possibly the equal of a woman."

"I did not speak.

"You are despicable," she said.

"It should please you," I said, "if you are the equals of men."

"Women dream not of equals," she said, "but of masters."

I sat back against the wall, angrily.

"It is degrading to wear a collar in this cell," she said. Then she lay down on the blanket, bitterly, and turned her back to me.

She did not bother covering her lovely body. Each insolent, luscious curve of her collared slave body was displayed to me, contemptuously, taunting me. It was the insult of a slave girl to an ineffectual slave she did not fear. My fists clenched. A wave of anger swept me. I considered leaping to her, hurling her upon her back, whipping her face back and forth with the palm and then back of my hand, and then, mercilessly, raping her, reminding her that she was only a slave, and a wench that had been given to me for the night. But I did not do this. I controlled myself.

I sat back against the wall, angry. I had tried to relate to her. I looked to the bench, where lay the slave whip. I considered putting it to her beauty, until she begged to serve. Lola would understand the kicks of my feet, the blows of the whip. Those are arguments which any woman can follow. Then I forced such thoughts from my mind. I had failed to relate well to her, in spite of being solicitous and charming, courteous and attentive, in spite of treating her with honor, and with dignity and respect. I treated her as my equal and I was, in return, subjected to ill treatment and scorn. I understood almost nothing of what had occurred. I had joked with her; I had treated her with homely comraderie; I had, almost invariably, treated her as a person.

"Are you going to whip me?" she asked.

"I certainly am not," I said.

"I did not think so," she said. Then, with a twist of her body, she rolled onto her back, and stared up at the ceiling. I saw the collar on her throat.

I sat against the wall, and troubled, thought.

Lola did not understand a gentleman, I decided. She was accustomed only to the brutes of Gor. I was too good for her.

"You do not seem grateful to me," I said, angrily.

"Why should I be grateful to you?" she asked.

"You were put in with me to be punished," I said. "I did not punish you."

"How clever were the masters," she said, bitterly. "I must have displeased them grievously."

"I do not understand," I said.

"I have been most cruelly punished," she said.

"I do not understand," I said. "I have not punished you."

Suddenly, surprising me, she rolled onto her stomach and, with her small fists, struck down at the blanket spread over the straw. She began to sob, hysterically. I could not understand her.

"What is wrong?" I asked her.

She leaped from the blanket and, piteously, choking and sobbing, fled to the bars. She pressed her lovely body against them and extended her arms and hands between them, to the silent, empty corridor. "Masters!" she cried. "Masters! Let me out! Let me out! Please let me out!" Then she shook the heavy bars with her tiny, lovely hands. "Let me out!" she begged. "Please let me out, Masters!" Then, subsiding, sobbing, she slipped to her knees at the bars, holding them with her small hands. "Let me out, Masters!" she wept. "Please, my Masters, let me out!" But no one answered her cries. She knelt at the bars, her head down, sobbing. "Let me out," she whispered. "Please let me out, Masters."

"I do not understand you," I said.

She sobbed, at the bars.

"I do not understand," I said. "I have not punished you."

"Do you not know what my punishment was?" she sobbed.

"No," I said.

"It was to have been put in with you," she said. She put down her head, sobbing.

Angrily I went back to where I had sat against the wall. Again I sat down, in the straw.

She remained at the bars, sobbing. Then, later, near them, she fell asleep.

I leaned against the wall, angry. I did not sleep.

# 8  I AM SHAMED;
# I WILL LEAVE THE HOUSE
# OF ANDRONICUS

"Get in," said Prodicus.

Gron, bare chested, stood beside him, resting the point of a great, long, curved sword on the tiles at his feet.

"Wait," said the Lady Gina.

I knelt, head down, before the square iron box, the exterior of which was enameled white, one side of which, its door, on hinges, lay opened on the tiles. I tensed. On two sides of the box, in red paint, was a Kef, in block printing. Kef, of course, is the initial letter not only of the Gorean expression 'Kajira', the most common Gorean expression for a female slave, but also 'Kajirus', the most common Gorean expression for a male slave. The block printing indicated that the box was suitable for a male slave. This could also, of course, have been determined from its size which, though small, was larger than would have been that in which women would be placed. Such boxes, for women, were marked also with red on white, but the letter, of course, would be the cursive Kef, which is also used as a common slave brand for imbonded females.

"Last night, Jason," said the Lady Gina, "we threw you a slave girl." She shook loose the blades of her slave whip. I kept my head down. "I was curious to see what you would do with her. I had wondered about you. I had thought there might be a bit of manhood in you." She suddenly lashed downward with the whip and I winced. "I see there was not," she said. She struck me again. The blades, in their stroke, burned cruelly on my back. I could not help tears forming in my eyes. Yet I think the tears were from frustration and misery, and from my shame, that I knew, in my heart, that I well deserved my beating, rather than from the mere pain of the harsh strokes.

118

"May I speak, my Mistress?" I begged.

"Yes," she said.

"I am a man of Earth," I said. "We prove our manhood by denying it. He who behaves least like a man shows himself thus to be most a man."

"Do you believe that?" asked the Lady Gina.

"No, Mistress," I said, miserably. I did not really believe it. I had only been taught to say it.

"Perhaps," she said, "those who pride themselves on the denial of their manhood deceive themselves. Perhaps it is thus they protect themselves from understanding that they have, in effect, no manhood to deny."

I kept my head down. I knew that males differed much, one from the other. Some were perhaps, for most practical purposes, without manhood. It would surely be easiest for them to pretend to expertise in its denial. Some males, I supposed, incredibly enough, did not feel strong urges and powerful appetites. There was nothing in their own experience, perhaps, which prepared them to understand drives, and desires and rages which might terrify them. There was simply nothing in their own experience, perhaps, thus, which prepared them to understand the desires and rages of natures deeper and mightier than theirs. These things would be to them simply colors they could not see, sounds they could not hear, worlds which must remain to them forever beyond their ken. But perhaps I am wrong. Perhaps there lies somewhere in all men a trace of the rover and hunter; perhaps no man is so weak or lost as to have forgotten completely the feel of the grasped, bloody bone in his paw, or what it was on a windy night to throw back his head and howl at a moon.

"How can one know," asked the Lady Gina, "if one has a manhood to deny, if one has never expressed it?"

"I do not know, Mistress," I said.

"Let those who have expressed their manhood," she said, "decide then whether or not they will ever again choose to deny it."

I did not speak.

I did not know what it would be, truly, to be a man. I feared manhood. Suppose that I became a man. How then, once having dared to taste meat and blood, and victory, could I again surrender so preciously recollected a birthright? I knew that men must not be men. I kept my head down.

"Slave," sneered the Lady Gina.

I knelt naked, the steel collar of the house of Andronicus on my neck, before the small, opened slave box. On its top it had two sets of rings, each set placed along an edge of the top, through which long carrying poles might be thrust. To one side, behind Gron, and to the back, stood four carrying slaves, large, brawny, collared men, two of whom held the poles, like spears, butt down, on the tiles.

"Look up, Jason, Slave," said the Lady Gina. "Look about you."

I looked up, and at the Lady Gina, and the men in the room.

"How are you regarded, Handsome Slave?" asked the Lady Gina.

"With contempt, Mistress," I said.

"Yes," she said.

It was true. All in the room looked upon me with contempt, even the slaves, I, a kneeling man of Earth.

"Put down your head, Slave," she said.

"Yes, Mistress," I said. I lowered my head.

"How fit you are to be a slave," she said, scornfully.

"Yes, Mistress," I said. I did not know why she should be so angry with me. Somehow she seemed to feel that I had disappointed her.

What did she want of one who was only a slave?

Suddenly, crying out with rage, she began to strike at me with the whip. I knelt, naked, miserable, under the blows.

She struck me, again and again.

Then, after a time, she wearied. She hooked the whip again on her belt. She pulled up my head by the hair.

"Is there a man in you, Jason?" she asked.

I did not speak.

She smiled.

"Get into the slave box," she said.

I hesitated.

"Do you obey?" she asked.

"Yes, Mistress," I said.

"Then obey," she said.

"Yes, Mistress," I said.

I crawled into the tiny box, on my knees. It was barely large enough to contain me. The metal door, behind me, was lifted and flung shut. I heard bolts thrust in place. I pressed against the sides of the iron container. On both the right and left, about level with my eyes, the sides of the container were perforated with fifteen small holes, arranged in three horizontal rows of five openings apiece. Each opening was about a half of an inch in diameter. I heard the two long poles being thrust through the sets of rings on the roof of the box.

"Deliver him to the market of Tima," I heard the Lady Gina say.

"It will be done, Lady Gina," said Prodicus.

I felt the box being lifted into the air, suspended by the rings and poles.

I put my head down, and wept. I was a man of Earth. I was a slave.

# 9 I AM GOODS BOUND FOR THE MARKET OF TIMA

"Smell a slave girl, Master!" taunted the slave. The slave box in which I was being transported to the market of Tima had been placed on the stones near a trough at which the carrying slaves, now chained, were being watered. We were at the edge of what appeared to be a square in a city. I drew back from the perforations in the iron wall of my container as the brown rep-cloth, a thin, single layer of cloth, covering the sweetly rounded, lower belly of a female slave, thrust suddenly against the perforations. She rubbed herself insolently, closely, across the perforations. I could smell her indeed, dirt and sweat, and the hot, moist female of her.

"Smell me, too, Master," said another slave. She, too, in brown rep-cloth, rubbed against the perforations.

"Get your filthy, stinking little bodies away from there!" called Prodicus.

The two girls laughed and, turning about, ran swiftly, lightly, away.

Both were exciting, briefly tunicked, collared. One's tunic had been torn to the waist on her left side.

They did not stay to feel the whip of Prodicus.

"Slave! Slave!" called a small child, beating on the metal of the slave box. "Slave! Slave!" called his companion. They struck repeatedly on the box. Inside the noise was painful. Then they ran to play elsewhere.

"Master!" I called to a man who was passing by. I pressed my face against the perforations. "Please, Master," I called, "in what city am I?"

He spit against the perforations. I swiftly drew back my face. I wiped my cheek.

He was kind, I now realize, not to have had me beaten.

How insolent I had been, to have dared to speak to him. Some slaves have been slain for such acts.

"Are you a pretty one?" I heard. A woman's voice had spoken. I looked up, through the perforations.

"I can see very little of him," said another voice, also that of a woman. Two free women, veiled and in robes, stood near the slave box. They had market baskets on their arms.

"Are you pretty?" I heard.

"I do not know, Mistress," I said.

She laughed.

"For what market are you bound?" asked the other woman.

"The market of Tima," I said.

They looked at one another and laughed. "I'll bet you are a pretty one!" said one of the women.

"My companion would not even let me have a pet like you," said the other.

"Are you quite tame?" asked the first woman.

"Yes, Mistress," I said.

"He probably is," said the second woman. "The market of Tima is famous for her tamed slaves."

I did not tell them that I came from a world in which almost all the males were perfectly tamed, indeed, a world in which males were supposed to pride themselves on their inoffensiveness and agreeability.

"I do not trust Kajiri," said the first woman. "They can revert. Can you imagine how fearful that might be, if one turned on you?"

The second one shuddered, but I thought with pleasure. "Yes," she said.

"Consider your danger, and what they might make you do," said the first.

"Yes," said the second.

"They might treat you as though you were little better than a slave."

"Or perhaps as only a slave," said the second.

"How horrifying that would be," said the first.

"Yes," said the second, but it seemed to me that she, beneath her robes and veil, shuddered again with pleasure.

"But if the Mistress is strong," said the first, "what has she to fear?"

"One who is stronger than she," said the second.

"I am stronger than any man," said the first.

"But what if you should meet your Master?" asked the second.

The first one was silent then for a moment. Then she spoke. "I would love him and serve him, helplessly," she said.

"Beautiful Mistresses," I said, "can you tell me in what city I am?"

"Be silent, Slave," said the first woman.

"Yes, Mistress," I said.

"Curiosity is not becoming in a Kajirus," said the second.

"Yes, Mistress," I said. "Forgive me, Mistresses."

They turned away, their market baskets on their arms. The butt of the whip of Prodicus suddenly struck twice at the side of the box, sharply. I jerked away from the sound, crying out, startled, frightened. "Be silent in there, Slave," he said, "or you will be well beaten."

"Yes, Master," I said. "Forgive me, Master."

I then felt the slave box, on the rings and poles, again being lifted. I pressed my face again to the perforations. I saw the brightly colored robes and tunics of the people. The square was crowded. I saw market stalls and heard the cries of vendors hawking their goods. I smelled fresh vegetables and roasting meat. The day was bright. The air was clear. On a cement dais, at one side of the square, I saw a man selling naked, chained slave girls. They were very beautiful, and piteous, in their collars and chains. I thought of Miss Beverly Henderson. How lovely she had been. I scarcely dared to conjecture what tragic fate might have befallen her on this rude world.

"Make way," called Prodicus. "Make way for goods bound for the market of Tima!"

# 10 I FIND MYSELF SLAVE IN THE HOUSE OF THE LADY TIMA;
# I AM RECREATION FOR THE LADY TIMA, AFTER SHE HAS FINISHED HER WORK

The door of the slave box, behind me, was opened, and swung down. At the same time I was thrust forward in the box and my ankles were seized. I was dragged backwards out of the box on my belly. Four men held me. Prodicus jammed the key into the lock on the back of my collar and, in an instant, had opened the collar, which he jerked from my throat. Almost at the same time another man closed another collar about my throat and snapped it shut. I then wore the collar of the House of Tima. I saw a woman, stern and cruel, in black leather, with leather wristlets, sign a paper. Prodicus placed the paper in his tunic. Two men lifted me and flung me to my knees on the cement flooring of the large room. The door, or gate, to the slave box was swung up and shut, the bolts thrown in place. Prodicus gestured to the carrying slaves and they set their poles again through the rings and, in moments, they, carrying the box, preceded by Prodicus, had exited through an iron door.

I felt the woman's whip under my chin. It pushed my head up.

"Greetings, Pretty Slave," she said.

"Greetings, Mistress," I said.

"I am Tima," she said. "I am Mistress here."

"Yes, Mistress," I said.

Then she turned to the men about her, strong fellows, fit for keeping order in slave pens.

"Whip him," she said. "Then clean and groom him. Then send him to my chamber."

"Yes, Lady Tima," said one of them.

I was lifted to my feet and, two men holding my arms, was dragged stumbling from her presence.

"Kneel here," said the man, indicating a position before the heavy door, of iron, in the dark corridor. "When we have left," he said, "make your presence known."

"Yes, Master," I said, miserably. I had not been in the House of Tima more than a few Ehn before I had been bound at a whipping ring, suspended over my head, and, dangling, feet tethered to a second ring, well lashed. I had then been conducted to a small, low-ceilinged cell in which I was locked. I lay there, alone, miserable, I conjecture, for some Ahn. Then a man brought a pan of water and a bowl of moistened slave gruel. I was not hungry but I was ordered to eat and, kneeling, observed, did so. When I had fed to his satisfaction he made me precede him to a warm, humid chamber. In that place there were sunken baths, cisterns of water, and vessels of heating water. Too, there were strigils, towels and oils. He removed my collar and ordered me into the bath. It was uncomfortably hot but I dared not object. Gorean masters tend not to be tolerant of the feelings of slaves. An enslaved male of Earth, fool that I was, I did not even know how to take a bath. Laughing, he explained to me the use of the strigils, the rinsings and oils. Frightened though I was, I was pleased, in the lengthy process of the bath, which tends for Goreans to be a pleasant experience, and is often a social one, at the public baths, to rid myself of the stink of the pens. I had then been scented, with the colognes and perfumes thought suitable for certain types of male slaves. I was then given a white, silken tunic. "Kneel," he then said. I knelt, and again he fastened me in my collar. We left the chamber. I was then made to lead the way through the halls of the House of Tima, until we arrived at the entrance to a long, dark corridor. This entrance was protected by two guardsmen, armed with spears and swords. "Continue forward, Slave," said the man. "Yes, Master," I said. I continued to walk forward and the two guards, not speaking, fell into step behind us. The corridor was long, and branching. We walked for some Ehn. I could feel the carpeting beneath my bare feet. "Turn left," said the man. We continued to walk. I was aware of the steel locked on my neck, the silk on my body. "Turn right," he said. We continued on for another Ehn. "Stop here," he said. We stood before a heavy, iron door.

"Shall we wait?" asked one of the guards.

"It will not be necessary," said the man. "This is a man from the planet Earth."

The guards nodded, understanding.

"Kneel here," said the man, indicating a position before the heavy door, of iron, in the dark corridor. "When we have left," he said, "make your presence known."

"Yes, Master," I said, miserably.

He then turned and left, followed by the two guards. They did not look back.

I knelt by the door, miserably. I lifted my hand to knock at the door, but then my hand fell. I feared to knock. I put down my head, miserable. After I had been locked in the cell, only one man, for all practical purposes, had controlled me. He had fed me, and commanded me, and had overseen my bath, my preparation for whatever was to ensue. He had taken my collar off and then, later, had made me kneel, fastening it again on me. I knew he had not been armed, but, still, I had feared and obeyed him. Free men were to me as master, as free women were to me as mistress. I was angered, now that I thought of it, that they had seen fit to send only one man to handle me. In the beginning four or five men had, rudely and cruelly, controlled me. But then I had been whipped. They had seen me under the whip, crying out, begging for mercy. They had known then, I suppose, as slavers can know such things, that no more than one man would be necessary to see to my governance. I was only a man of Earth.

Then I was frightened, for I had not yet knocked at the iron door.

I knocked lightly, frightened, at the door. I had knocked timidly. I had scarcely heard the knock myself. I put my head down, trembling.

I looked down the corridor. The man who had conducted me to this place had now disappeared, together with the guards.

He had doubtless gone about his duties, whatever they might be, and the guards had returned to their post. I could see far down the corridor.

They did not fear to leave me at the door, alone. One man had, in effect, conducted me to this place. He, and the guards, had now left. I might as well have been a woman. They showed me no more respect than they might have accorded to a helpless, vulnerable slave girl. How shamed I was. Yet were they not right? I was a man of Earth. Are we not all well tamed?

The door had not yet been opened. I was afraid. I had been told to make my presence known.

I then, frightened, breathing heavily, my heart pounding in fear, again knocked at the heavy door. I hoped that no one would be within.

"Who is it?" called a woman's voice, distracted.

"A—a slave," I stammered.

She opened the door, and looked down at me. She held some papers, long and yellow, in one hand.

"It is Jason, is it not?" she asked.

"If Mistress pleases," I said.

"It will do," she said. She regarded me. She did not even seem to notice that I was alone in the hall. In this she apparently saw nothing out of the ordinary. "I had forgotten," she said. "You were to be sent to my chamber this evening, were you not?" she asked.

"Yes, Mistress," I said.

"Come in," she said. "Remove your tunic and kneel by the couch. Close the door behind you."

"Yes, Mistress," I said. She was wearing golden sandals and a long, scarlet robe, with a high, ornate collar, fastened by a silver clasp.

I entered the room and shut the door behind me. I removed the silken tunic I had been given and folded it, placing it on the floor. I then knelt, naked and collared, near it, in the vicinity of the couch.

She knelt before a low desk, her back to me, and gave her attention to the papers which she had now placed upon it. She held a marking stick in her right hand.

"I am attending to the details of tomorrow evening's sale," she said.

"Yes, Mistress," I said.

She worked quietly, thoughtfully. Sometimes she would remove one paper from the group, and add another. Occasionally she would make a notation on one of the papers with her marking stick. Several Ehn went by. I did not disturb her. I knew she was working. She was a businesswoman, with demanding and intricate responsibilities. I wondered if any of those papers were pertinent to me. I did not dare ask, of course. I had learned that curiosity was not becoming in a Kajirus. If I were to be sold tomorrow I would find out when masters or mistresses were pleased to let me know, perhaps as late as the moment when a sales disk might be wired to my collar.

"Serve me wine, Jason," she said, distractedly. "As a slave girl," she added.

"Yes, Mistress," I said, bitterly.

"Do I detect bitterness?" she asked, not turning about.

"No, Mistress," I said.

"Good," she said. "You are a true man of Earth, fit to be the slave of a woman."

"Yes, Mistress," I said. I found some wine, and poured a bit for her. Then, as I had seen Lola do for me, I pressed the goblet into my lower abdomen and then lifted it to my lips, where, turning my head, I kissed it. Then, head down, kneeling back on my heels, arms extended, I proffered it to the Mistress.

"Excellent, Jason," she said.

"Thank you, Mistress," I said.

She sipped the wine, and regarded me contemptuously. Then she said. "Go back to your place."

"Yes, Mistress," I said.

I went back, beside the couch, and again knelt. She turned about and placed the cup of wine on the low desk and. in a moment, was again deeply engaged in her work. I think she forgot that I was in the room. I knelt silently in the background. Occasionally, however, as the Ehn passed, she drank from the cup.

I was ignored and neglected. I would be summoned, if needed.

I glanced at the large, fur-strewn couch. I saw that there were chains, on rings, attached to it.

She at last, wearily, thrust back the papers and put down the marking pencil. She rose to her feet and stretched, and turned to look at me.

"Get on the couch," she said, "on your back."

"Yes, Mistress," I said.

She went to the right side of the couch and, in a routine and unconcerned fashion, lifted a shackle, on a chain, which she snapped shut on my right ankle. She then walked about the couch and, on the left, similarly secured my left ankle, She then, as I felt the movement through the left shackle, my leg pulled slightly to the left, adjusted that chain at the ring. She then walked about the bottom of the couch and, taking my right wrist, locked it on a manacle, at my right side. She then went about the head of the couch and, taking my left wrist, enclosed it, too, in a manacle, at my left side, which she then snapped shut. My left wrist was pulled further then to the left, as she adjusted the chain on the left manacle, fixing the length of its play by a snap ring thrust through a link and about the couch ring. My feet, then, had been well chained, and my hands, too, had been well chained, and a few inches from my sides. She had done these things with the same habitual routine, the same lack of attention and concern, with which she might have hung up a piece of wearing apparel or replaced a comb and brush on a vanity.

"Do you remember me, Jason?" she asked.

"I think so, Mistress," I said. "You were the slaver, were you not, who subjected me to such thorough assessment in the House of Andronicus?"

"You have a good eye for women, Jason," she said. "I was veiled."

"Thank you, Mistress," I said. "Yes, Mistress," I said.

"Did I frighten you, Jason?" she asked.

"Yes, Mistress," I said.

"How I despise weakness in men," she said.

I did not speak.

"You are of Earth, are you not?" she asked.

"Yes, Mistress," I said.

"The Lady Gina told me this," she said, "in the House of Andronicus. Too, it is on your papers."

"Yes, Mistress," I said.

She looked down at me, I a man of Earth, chained helplessly before her on her couch.

"Do the women of your world not despise weakness in men?" she asked.

"No, Mistress," I said. "They desire it."

"How do you know that?" she asked.

"It is what we have been taught," I said.

"Interesting," she said. "Are they, then, so different from all other women?"

"Perhaps, Mistress," I said. "I do not know."

"I wonder, then," she said, "if that is true, why the females brought here from Earth become such dreams of pleasure and submission for Gorean males."

"I do not know," I said.

"Surely you know that they, stripped and collared, thrown to the feet of strong men, make fantastic, yielding slave sluts?"

"I did not know, Mistress," I said. I knew nothing of Earth-girl slaves. I had heard, however, to be honest, that they were prized in certain markets, and often brought good prices. I supposed there must be some explanation for their economic value. I thought of poor Beverly Henderson. I hoped, somehow, she had managed to escape the cruel fate of female slavery. How piteous it would be if her beauty, so lovely and delicate, were simply to be rudely auctioned to the highest bidder. What an affront to her intelligence and personhood! Too, I thrust from my mind, frightened, the thought of what a joy it would be to own her.

"I find you interesting, Jason," said the Lady Tima. She went to a cabinet, and opened it, removing from it a slave whip.

I tensed.

"When I first saw you," she said, "I felt, for a moment, looking into your eyes, that they might be the eyes of a man. I thought this even though I had been informed you were of the planet Earth."

I did not speak.

"I thought, for a moment," she said, "looking into your eyes that they were the sort of eyes before which a woman fears that the lineaments of her features, even though veiled, may be clear to him under whose observation she finds herself. Indeed, she fears, as his eyes imperiously, casually, rove over her, that her beauty and needs, in spite of the intervening robes, the intervening layers of cloth, may be exposed as helplessly to him as those of a slave girl."

I did not speak. She moved the whip and its coils gently upon my body, half caressing it, half instructing it in its bondage.

"Please do not whip me," I said.

"But then," she said, "I discovered that you were not a man, but only a slave, and one who was despicably weak."

"Please, Mistress," I begged, "do not whip me."

She put the whip aside, on the couch beside me. "Do not fear, Jason," she said. She looked down at me. "You are not worth whipping," she said.

She put her hands to the high, ornate collar of her robes, undoing the silver clasp. She slipped the robe from her shoulders, letting it fall to the floor. She was strikingly beautiful.

"I will not play long with you, Jason," she said. "I will soon send you back to your chains."

"What are you going to do with me?" I asked.

She laughed. She went then to the wine and poured the goblet half full. Then she came and sat near me, at the top of the couch. I struggled to my elbows, as I could. I put my head back. She supported my head, and put the goblet to my lips. "Drink, pretty Jason," she said. "It will make you less tense." She then tilted the goblet and poured the wine, bit by bit, into my mouth. I drank, frightened. Then she left the couch and returned the goblet to a small table. In a moment she had returned to the side of the couch, where she stood, looking down at me.

I could already begin to feel the wine. I was still half on my elbows. "What are you going to do to me?" I asked.

"Treat you as what you are," she said, "a man of Earth, a weakling, at the mercy of a Gorean free woman."

I regarded her, frightened.

"Lie back, pretty Jason," she said. I lay back. The furs were deep about me. I felt the inflexible clasp of the steel on my ankles and wrists.

Then suddenly, lightly, like a cat, she slipped onto the couch beside me.

"I do not understand," I said. "What are you going to do with me?"

"Own you," she whispered. "Use you for my pleasure."

I looked at her with horror.

She smiled and then thrust the whip, crosswise, in my mouth, between my teeth.

She then aroused, and raped me.

# 11 THE ROOM OF PREPARATION

"Poor slave," said the girl. "How the Mistress has abused you."

I lifted my head, slightly, from the flat stones. I lay on my side. The room was quite dark. My feet and ankles were chained together, the chain joining them apparently run through a ring in the stone. I was naked. I wore my collar.

"Lie quietly," said the girl.

"Yes, Mistress," I said.

I felt a cool rag, moistened with water, bathe my forehead.

"I am not a Mistress," she laughed. "I, too, am only a poor slave."

"What has happened?" I asked. "What time is it? Where am I?"

"Last night," she said, "you were sent to the chamber of the Mistress."

I was silent.

"I wager she well taught you that you were a slave," she said.

"Yes," I said. "I was well taught that I was a slave."

The girl continued to bathe my forehead. "What time is it?" I asked.

"It is early evening of the day following that in which you were sent to the Mistress' chamber," she said.

"How can that be?" I asked.

"When the Mistress was finished with you," asked the girl, "did she not remove your chains and place a bowl of meal for you at the foot of her couch?"

"Yes," I said. I had been made to eat from it on my hands and knees, head down, not permitted to use my hands.

"Did she not then thrust your tunic under your collar and tell you to find the guards, that they would know what was to

133

be done with you? And did she not then send you from her presence?"

"Yes," I said. "But I do not recall finding the guards."

"The meal was drugged," she said.

"Where am I?" I asked.

"In one of the rooms of slave preparation," she said. "It is in such rooms as these that slaves are often readied for their sale."

"Am I to be soon sold?" I asked.

"I fear so," she said, "since you have been placed here."

I sat up, bitterly.

"I am so sorry for you," she said. "It is such a horrifying and degrading experience to be sold, almost incomprehensible."

"Have you ever been sold?" I asked.

"Yes," she said, "many times."

"I am sorry," I said.

"It does not matter," she said, softly. "I am only a slave." I sensed that she leaned back. "Do you wish me to bathe your forehead more?" she asked.

"No," I said. "But you have been very kind." I heard her wring out a rag, hearing the water drip into a pan of water. Then she got up, apparently taking the rag and water to the side of the room. In a moment or two she had returned.

"Are you thirsty?" she asked.

"Yes," I said.

She held a flask of water to my lips from which, gratefully, I drank.

"How cruelly they have chained you," she said. As I had sat up, my wrists, chained closely together, were near my ankles, similarly closely chained. A length of chain, joining my wrists and ankles, running through a heavy ring, secured me in place.

"Are you hungry?" she asked.

"Yes," I said.

From a loaf of dried bread, breaking pieces from it, she fed me.

"Would you like again to drink?" she asked.

"Yes," I said. She again held the flask of water to my lips.

"I stole some meat for you," she whispered. She then, piece by piece, fed me small pieces of boiled meat.

"You should not have taken such a risk," I said.

"Eat," she said. "It will give you strength."

"What would they do to you, if they found out that you had stolen the meat?" I asked.

"I do not know," she said. "I suppose they would only whip me. Perhaps they would cut off my hands."

"Why would you take such a risk, only for me?" I asked.

"Are you not of Earth, Jason?" she asked.

"Yes," I said. "I am of Earth. How did you know my name?"

"I have heard you called that," she said. "Is it not the name you have been given?"

"Yes," I said. "It is the name I have been given." I wore the name 'Jason' now only as a slave name. Slaves have no names in their own right. They are only animals. They are called whatever their masters wish.

"Do you know of Earth?" I asked.

"Yes," She said, ruefully, "I know of it."

"What is your name?" I asked.

She was silent.

"What is your name?" I asked.

"It is a shameful name," she said. "Please do not make me say it."

"Please," I said.

"Darlene," she said.

"That is an Earth-girl name," I said, excitedly. I trembled in the chains.

"Yes," she said.

"It is a beautiful name," I said.

"It seems to well arouse the lust of Gorean masters," she said.

"Why would they put such a name upon you?" I asked.

"To make it clear to all that I am no more than a slut and a slave," she said.

I had heard that Earth-girl names were often used as slave names on Gor, often being given to the lowest, and the most exciting and sensuous of slaves.

"How cruel Goreans are," I said. Then I said, "I am sorry. Forgive me."

"Why?" She asked.

"I did not mean to insult you." I said.

"I do not understand," she said.

"You are Gorean, are you not?" I asked.

"No," she said.

"Then what are you?" I asked.

"Only a poor Earth-girl slave," she said.

I was stunned. "Your Gorean," I said, "is flawless, superb."

"The whip has taught me much," she said.

I was silent, overcome with pity for her. How tragic, I thought, to be a girl of my own world, and be brought cruelly and helplessly to the world of Gor, to be made a slave.

"On Earth," she said, "my name was Darlene. It was then, of course, my own name, and not a mere slave name, put upon me by the whim of Masters."

"I must see you," I said. I pulled at the chains.

"Eat, Jason," she said. "There is a little meat left."

I finished the meat, her small fingers delicately placing it in my mouth.

"You have risked much, bringing me this meat," I said, "for one who is only a slave."

"It is nothing," she said. "You are a man of my world."

"You are a fine and brave girl," I said.

"I am only a miserable slave," she said.

"I must see you," I said. "Is there no way some light can be brought into this place?"

"There is a small lamp," she said. "But I would fear to light it."

"Why?" I asked.

"You are a man of Earth," she said. "I would be so ashamed to have you see me, a girl of Earth, as I am now."

"Why?" I asked.

"I am clad only in the rag and collar of a slave," she said.

"Light the lamp," I said, kindly. "Please, Darlene."

"If I do so," she said, "please try to look upon me with the gentility of a man of Earth."

"Of course," I said. "Please, Darlene."

"I will light the lamp," she said. She rose to her feet and went to the side of the room.

I heard the striking together of stones, probably iron pyrites, and saw sparks. Inwardly I gasped as I, in a flash of sparks, followed by darkness, caught a brief glimpse of the luscious, kneeling girl at the side of the room. She wore the scandalously brief shreds of a tattered slave rag, sewn of brown rep-cloth, torn open at her thighs, I assume deliberately, held but by a single, narrow strap over her left shoulder. Her breasts hung lovely, sweet and full, scarcely concealed, within the thin brown cloth. In the spark of light I had seen the glint of the collar, of close-fitting steel, about her throat. She was barefoot.

The stones struck together again, and again I saw her, kneeling over a bit of moss, tinder, which she was intent upon igniting. She had dark hair, short but full, which fell about her face. Again I glimpsed the lusciousness of her curves, her collar, her bare feet. Had I been a slaver I thought surely I would have marked her down for inclusion on a cargo manifest.

Then she had the bit of moss lit and, into it, she placed a straw. This straw, burning then at one end, served to light the wick of a small, clay oil lamp. She then shook the straw, extinguishing it and, with her fingers, moved the bit of moss about, spreading it, and the tiny flame there dissipated into scattered glowing points which then, rapidly, disappeared. She took the lamp then in her hands and approached me, then crouched down and set it to one side, then knelt back, on her heels. I looked at her then in the tiny light of the lamp, kneeling back on her heels, small, luscious, her beauty so full and sweetly curved, so poorly concealed in the tattered rag, the knees of her bared legs placed closely together.

She looked at me, in piteous protest.

How could any male, any with even a single drop of blood in his veins, any who still drew breath, look upon such a woman with gentility?

She shook her head. "Please." she said.

I wanted to thrust apart her knees and, taking her by the hair and an ankle, throw her to her back, on the stones. I wanted to have her, ruthlessly, with cries of joy. I clenched my fists. I was chained. How I envied then the rude beasts of Gor, who have such women for their pleasure.

"Forgive me," I begged her.

"You looked upon me," she said, shrinking back, shuddering, "as might have a man of Gor, one whom a woman knows is her master, one whom she knows she must obey."

"No, no," I protested. "That is not true. No."

"It is perhaps fortunate for me," she smiled, relaxing, "that you are closely chained."

"Perhaps," I smiled.

She laughed. She looked at me. She touched the rag she wore. "I suppose it is difficult." she said, "to respect a girl who wears the slave rag, the Ta-Teera."

"No," I said. "Of course not."

"Even one," she smiled, indicating her collar, "who wears the collar of a slave?"

"Of course not," I said.

To be sure, it was not easy to respect a woman who wore only the scandalous and sensuous Ta-Teera, and whose throat was locked in the lovely, exciting collar of a slave. How could one see such a woman, truly, except as a slave? And how could one treat such a woman, truly, except as a slave? And the slaves of Goreans were true slaves. How natural then that they should treat them as what they were, their owned slaves.

"Of course not," I said. "I respect you deeply and fully."

To be sure, the sight of such a woman, so clad and collared, tended to provoke not emotions of respect but deeper and more primitive emotions, emotions such as love, desire and lust, and dominance and uncompromising ownership. Such a woman was, under the enhancements of a civilization, the primitive woman, who must hope to please the brute who owns her.

"I accord you full and total respect," I said.

"A moment ago," she chided me, smiling, "you looked upon me as though I might have been a slave girl."

"Forgive me," I smiled.

"You do respect me, don't you, Jason?" she asked.

"I do," I said, "totally."

"Then I forgive you," she smiled.

"Thank you," I said. I was grateful and relieved that she had forgiven me for my lapse, for my having looked upon her, for an instant, as a man upon a woman. I had looked upon her for that shameful instant not as a person, but as a luscious, desirable female, one fitted by nature to kneel at the feet of a strong man.

She smiled at me. "I care deeply for you, Jason," she said. "You are the first man I have met, in years, who has been kind to me, who has regarded me with gentleness and respect."

I smiled, and shrugged.

"Too," she said, "you are the first man of my world I have seen in years. What lovely memories of their sweetness, their pleasantries and courtesies, you recall in me."

"Your life as a slave must have been hard," I said.

She smiled. "We serve, and obey," she said.

"Doubtless some of your masters must have been harsh," I said.

"Please do not ask a girl to speak of her bondage," she said. She put her head down.

"I'm sorry," I said, softly.

"You cannot even begin to suspect," she said, "what it is to be a slave girl on a world with such men as those of Gor."

"I'm sorry," I said.

"They are overwhelming," she said. "On occasion I have even been forced to yield to them."

I looked at her.

"As a slave," she said, bitterly.

"I'm very sorry," I said. I almost wanted to scream with pleasure at the thought of the lovely Darlene being forced to yield as a slave. How I envied the brute who would have held her in his arms!

"Jason," she said, softly.

"Yes," I said.

"No," she said. "It is nothing."

"What is wrong?" I asked. "You seem troubled, fearful."

"You know what room this is, do you not?" she asked.

"It is a room of slave preparation, you have told me," I said.

"Yes," she said. "Do you know what your presence in this room indicates?"

"That I am to be soon sold," I said, bitterly.

"I fear so," she said.

"How soon am I to be sold?" I asked.

"I do not know," she said. "I am not privy to the secrets of masters."

"But doubtless it will be soon," I said.

"I fear so," she said.

She was silent.

"Jason," she said.

"Yes," I said.

"Do you wish to be sold?" she asked.

"No," I said. "Of course not."

"I can help you to escape," she whispered.

I shook in the chains. "How?" I said. "No," I said, "It is too dangerous."

"I have stolen the key to your chains," she said, "and to your collar. I have stolen clothing for you. I can show you a secret exit from this place."

"It is madness," I said. "What escape can there be. for a slave on Gor?"

"Do you wish to try, Jason?" she asked.

Suddenly we were silent and regarded one another, alarmed. We heard two men talking, approaching.

Then two guards, gigantic fellows, brawny, stripped to the waist, their heads shaven save for a knot of hair behind the crown, stood behind the barred gate to the cell. The gate was ajar, doubtless that the girl could come and go, attending me.

The girl faced them, making herself small, kneeling, the palms of her hands on the floor, her head down to the stones. It excited me to see her in such a posture. She was a slave girl in the presence of masters.

"Have you fed the slave, Darlene?" asked one of the men, the larger of the two.

"Yes, Masters," she said, not raising her head.

"Then leave him, Darlene, Slave Girl," he said.

"Yes, Masters," she said, not raising her head.

Then the two men turned away and went down the hall.

Quickly the girl raised her head and, turning about, re-garded me. Her eyes were wide. Her lip trembled. "I fear there is little time," she whispered.

I nodded.

"Do you wish to try, Jason?" she asked.

"Surely there would be incredible danger in this for you," I said.

She shrugged. "No one knows that I have the keys," she said. "They will not believe that I could free you."

"But what if you were caught?" I asked.

"I am a slave girl," she said. "Doubtless I would be fed to sleen."

"I cannot permit you to take such a risk," I said.

"They will not know it was I," she said. "They will not be-lieve it could be I."

"Do you think you are safe?" I asked.

"Yes," she said. "I will be safe. The danger will be yours."

"Free me," I said.

She rose to her feet and ran to the side of the room, where there was a small store of moss, tinder for lighting the lamp. She snatched two keys from the moss.

I clenched my fists in the manacles.

She fled back to me, wildly, and thrust one of the keys into the shackle on my right ankle. She opened it. She then, with the same key, opened the shackle on my left ankle and the manacles on my wrists.

We listened. We heard nothing in the corridor. I rubbed my wrists.

I felt her jam another key into the lock on the back of my collar. She twisted the key, freeing the single-action double bolt.

"You would not get far in a collar," she said, whispering, smiling.

"No, I would not," I said, smiling.

I jerked the collar from my throat.

She took the collar and, carefully, noiselessly, put it to the side, where it might not be seen from the threshold. I looked at the collar, lying on the stones. It was of sturdy steel. I would not have been able to remove it. It had well marked me as a slave.

"I am naked," I said. "Where is the clothing?"

She went to the side of the room and picked up a bag, fastened with a drawstring, the knot on the string sealed with a wax plate, the plate bearing the imprint of a stamp. "The guards said," she said, "that this is clothing. They did not know I overheard them. Doubtless it is true."

I looked at her.

"I did not dare to break the seal," she said. "I did not know until moments ago whether you would be willing to attempt escape or not."

"What is this seal?" I asked, indicating the wax plate with its stamp.

"That is the seal of the House of Andronicus," she said.

"When did this come to this house?" I asked, frightened.

"The day before you arrived," she said. "Do you think perhaps it is not clothing?"

I broke the seal, breaking it away from the knot. I undid the knot. I tore open the bag, thrusting back the loop of the drawstring.

My heart sank.

"Is it not clothing?" she asked, her voice trembling.

"It is clothing," I said.

"What is wrong?" she asked. "Even if they are slave garments they might serve to get you into the streets."

"Look," I said.

"Oh," she wept, miserably. "I had no way of knowing."

I lifted clothing from the bag, dismally. This was, of all

things, my old clothing, the clothing I had worn on Earth the night on which Miss Beverly Henderson, a lovely quarry of Gorean slavers, had been abducted and I, unwittingly, had become implicated in her fate.

I held my old jacket clutched in my hand, angrily. I had not known what had happened to my clothing. I had awakened naked, chained, in a dungeon cell in the House of Andronicus. My clothing, unknown to me, even my jacket, and, as I saw, my coat, too, had apparently been transmitted to Gor with me, though for what purpose I could not imagine.

"How cruel they are," she said.

"I do not understand," I said.

"This was sent here, doubtless," she said, "that it might, for the instruction and amusement of buyers, be used in your sale."

"That is doubtless it," I said. I looked at her, miserably.

"The seal is broken on the bag," she said. "What can we do now?"

"We have no choice but to continue," I said.

"It is too dangerous," she said.

"We have no choice," I said. "Before, when I awakened, when I asked you what time it was, you told me that it was early in the evening."

"Yes," she said.

"That was some time ago," I said. "Do you think that it might be dark by now?"

"Yes," she said, trembling.

"Perhaps, in the darkness," I said, "I might be briefly unnoticed, at least long enough to obtain more suitable, less conspicuous garments."

"It is all my fault," she said, miserably.

"Do not be afraid," I said to her, reassuring her. I took her by the shoulders and looked down into her uplifted eyes.

"I shall try to be brave, Jason," she said.

I lowered my head, gently, to kiss her, but she turned her head away, looking down. "Please, don't, Jason," she said. "Though I wear a collar do not forget that I am a woman of Earth."

"I'm sorry," I said. "Do not fear. I will not take advantage of you." I chastised myself. How forward I had been. I scarcely knew her. Too, I was naked, and she wore only the scandalous Ta-Teera, and her collar.

"Thank you, Jason," she whispered.

"Men have been cruel to you, haven't they?" I asked, gently.

"I am a slave girl," she shrugged.

I could well imagine the torments and ecstasies with which the Earth beauty would have been afflicted by the brutes of Gor.

"It was my intention," I said, "to kiss you only with the gentleness, and tenderness, of a man of Earth." It had not been my intention to subject her mouth, her throat and breasts, her belly, the interior of her thighs, to the cruel, commanding, raping kisses of the Gorean master.

"How wonderful you are, Jason," she said. "If only the men of Gor were more like you."

"Please let me kiss you," I said. She was so lovely.

She turned her head away. "No," she said. "I wear a collar."

"I do not understand," I said.

"I am a woman of Earth," she said. "I would be ashamed to be kissed while my throat is locked in the collar of bondage."

"Of course," I said. "I am sorry."

"Dress now, Jason," she said. "There is little time."

"I do not understand," I said.

"The guards may make their rounds soon," she said.

"I see," I said. I removed my clothing from the bag. I began to draw on my undergarments.

"There is another reason, too, why I did not let you kiss me," she said.

"What is that?" I asked.

"I scarcely dare to speak of it," she said.

"Tell me," I said.

"You do not know what a collar does to a woman," she said. "When a woman wears a collar she does not dare to let a man kiss her."

"Why?" I asked.

"She fears she might turn into a slave girl in his arms," she said, softly.

"I see," I said.

"I want you to respect me," she said.

I nodded. One might exult in a spasmodic slave, subjecting her to the conquest of the helpless bond girl, but, it was true, how could one, in such a situation, respect her? One would surely be enjoying her too much to respect her.

"Where are you from?" I asked.

"I do not understand," she said.

"You are from Earth," I said. "I would be curious to know from what land." There is no Gorean expression for 'country' in the precise sense of a nation. Men of Earth think of cities as being within countries. Men of Gor tend to think of cities and the lands controlled by them. The crucial political entity for Goreans tends to be the city or village, the place where people and power are. There can be, of course, leagues among cities and tangential territories. Men of Earth tend to think of territory in a manner that might be considered circumferential, whereas Goreans tend to think of it as a more radial sort of thing. Consider a circle with a point at its center. The man of Earth might conceive of the territory as bounded by the circumference; the man of Gor would be more likely to think of the territory as a function of the sweep of the radius which emanates from the central point. Geometrically, of course, these two conceptions are equivalent. Psychologically, however, they are not. The man of Earth looks to the periphery; the man of Gor looks to the center. The man of Earth thinks of territory as static, regardless of the waxing and wanings of the power that maintains it; the Gorean tends to think of territory as more dynamic, a realistic consequence of the geopolitical realities of power centers. Perhaps it would be better to say that the Gorean tends to think more in terms of sphere of influence than he does in terms of imaginary lines on maps which may not reflect current historical realities. Certain consequences of these attitudes may be beneficial. For example, the average Goran is not likely to feel that his honor, which he values highly, is somehow necessarily connected with the integrity of a specific, exactly drawn border. Such borders generally do not exist on Gor, though, to be sure, certain things are commonly understood, for example, that the influence of, say, the city of Ar, has not traditionally extended north of the Vosk River. Another consequence of the Gorean's tendency to think of territory in terms more analogous to an area warmed or an area illuminated than an area laid out by surveyors once and for all time is that his territoriality tends to increase with nearness to his city or village. One result of this attitude is that most wars, most armed altercations, tend to be very local. They tend to involve, usually, only a few cities and their associated villages and territories, rather than gigantic political entities such as nations. One result of this is that the number of people affected by warfare on Gor usually tends, statistically, to be quite limited. Also, it might be noted that most Gorean warfare is carried out largely by relatively small groups of professional soldiers, seldom more than a few thousand in the field at a given time, trained men, who have their own caste. Total warfare, with its arming of millions of men, and its broadcast slaughter of hundreds of populations, is Gorean neither in concept nor in practice. Goreans, often castigated for their cruelty, would find such monstrosities unthinkable. Cruelty on Gor, though it exists, is usually purposeful, as in attempting to bring, through discipline and privation, a young man to manhood, or in teaching a female that she is a slave. I think the explanation for the Gorean political arrangements and attitudes in the institution of the Home Stone. It is the Home Stone which, for the Gorean, marks the center. I think it is because of their Home Stones that the Gorean tends to think of territory as something from the inside out, so to speak, rather than from the outside in. Consider again the analogy of the circle. For the Gorean the Home Stone would mark the point of the circle's center. It is the Home Stone which, so to speak, determines the circle. There can be a point without a circle; but there can be no circle without its central point. But let me not try to speak of Home Stones. If you have a Home Stone, I need not speak. If you do not have a Home Stone, how could you understand what I might say?

"I am from a place called England," said the girl.

I was startled that she had said 'I am from a place called England' rather than something like 'I am from England'. Her construction was Gorean in nature. Yet, of course, she did speak in Gorean.

I had now drawn on my trousers and shirt. I buckled my belt.

"I speak English," I said, in English. "I am from America. I can speak with you in English. Marvelous!"

She looked down. "I am only a slave," she said, in Gorean. "Let us speak in Gorean. I fear to speak but in the language of the masters."

I went to her and lightly touched her face.

"Do not be afraid," I said. "There is no one here but me. Speak English to me." I had spoken in English.

She looked up, shyly. "It is a very long time since I have spoken in that tongue," she said. She had spoken in English.

"I believe you," I laughed. "I would have thought you would have said something like 'It's been a long time since I have spoken English.' "

She smiled. "You see how long it has been?" she asked.

I smiled. "Your Gorean is flawless," I said.

"Is my English really so poor, Jason?" she asked.

"No," I said. "It is quite good. It is precise. But I cannot place the accent."

"There are many accents in England," she said.

"True," I smiled, "but the accent does not even sound like an English one."

"Alas," she smiled. "I fear I have been too long on Gor."

I sat down and began to draw on my shoes and stockings. "That is it," I said. "There is a Gorean flavor to the accent."

She put down her head. "I have not been permitted for years to speak my native language," she said. "We girls," she said, her voice soft, the fingers of her right hand touching the narrow, close-fitting metal loop at her throat, "must learn the language of our masters."

"Of course," I said. I stood up. "I am ready," I said. "Show me the exit."

"Please," she said. "Will you not put on this garment?" She held up the necktie which I had left on the floor.

"I scarcely think I need a necktie," I smiled.

"It has been so long since I have seen a man of Earth in such a garment," she said, "please."

"Very well," I said.

She came close to me and lifted the tie.

I looked down into her eyes. I lifted up the collar of my shirt. "Would you like to tie it?" I asked. I did not think I would mind having her arms intimately about my neck, even if but briefly, or having her so close to me, performing this simple, homely task.

"I do not know how to tie it, Jason," she said.

"Very well," I said. I took the tie, and, in a moment, had tied it. I then turned down and smoothed the collar of my shirt. I adjusted the tie as well as I could, not having a mirror.

"How handsome you look," she said.

This pleased me.

"Your thigh," I said, suddenly. "It is not marked." Her left thigh did not bear the brand. I must have noticed this before but, somehow, it had not registered with me. The Ta-Toora, as it had been torn, did not conceal the branding area on her leg.

"No," she said. "No," she then said, angrily, "I am not branded on the right thigh either." I had, almost without thinking, moved in such a way as to ascertain this. Most girls wear their brands on the left thigh, where they may be conveniently caressed by a right-handed master. Some girls, on the other hand, are right-thigh branded. Some, too, though very few, are branded on the lower left abdomen.

"Are you disappointed?" she asked.

"No," I said. "No!"

"Do you want Darlene branded?" she asked.

"No," I said, "of course not!" I was surprised that she had spoken of herself as she did, using her name. This is not uncommon, of course, among Gorean female slaves. I reminded myself that she was a female slave, and had doubtless been long on Gor, doubtless well accomodating herself to the harsh realities of her collar. How marvelous, I thought, that some beautiful women are slaves. How I then, for an instant, envied the brutes of Gor, who could own such a woman as stood before me.

"Would you prefer to have me branded, Jason?" she asked, angrily.

"No," I cried. "Of course not!" But what man would not prefer to have a beautiful woman branded? I realized she had not referred to herself, this time, by her own name. It was almost as if she had caught herself.

She looked at me, angrily.

"I was only surprised," I said, chagrined, embarrassed, "that you were not branded. The female slaves I have seen hitherto on Gor have been branded."

"Well, I am not," she said.

"I can see that," I said.

"Do you speak to me as a Gorean brute?" she asked. She, with her small hands, tried to pull together the rent fabric at her thighs.

"No," I said, quickly. "I did not mean to hurt your feelings. I am very sorry."

"Perhaps I am marked on the lower left abdomen," she said. "That is sometimes done. Would you care to look?"

"No," I said. "Of course not!"

Angrily she tore open the Ta-Teera at her lower left abdomen. She held the cloth apart. "Is there a mark there?" she asked.

"No," I said. "No!"

I wanted to take her by the arm and thrust my right hand through that rent in the garment, and, half lifting her, forcing her back to the wall, holding her against it, make her cry out piteously to be had, after which to put her to its foot and rape her as a slave.

"Please forgive me," I said. "I am very sorry!"

She looked at me.

"Please forgive me," I said. "I am very, very sorry."

"I forgive you," she said. "I should not have become angry." She looked up at me. "Can you forgive me, Jason?"

"There is nothing to forgive," I said.

"It is only that I am so sensitive," she said, "that my beauty, if I am beautiful, is so blatently exposed to the vision of masters."

"I understand," I said. "And you are, indeed, beautiful."

"Thank you, Jason," she said. "You are very kind."

"You are beautiful," I said, " quite beautiful."

"I suppose that it is not hard to tell that, if it is true," she said, "when one is clad as a Gorean slave girl."

"No," I smiled. "It is not."

"What brutes they are, to clothe us for their pleasure," she said.

"At least," I pointed out, "you have been permitted clothing."

"Yes," she smiled. It was true that often, in slave pens, and in the houses of slavers, women were kept nude, save for their collars. This effects a saving in the laundering of slave tunics. Too, it is sometimes thought to have a useful disciplinary effect on the girls. They learn that even a rag is not something they can take for granted, but must, so to speak, be earned. Too, it might be mentioned, some masters commonly keep their girls nude in their own compartments. Most, however, permit the girl some garment, usually a brief, sleeveless, one-piece slave tunic. This helps the master to control himself; should he wish to do so. Too, it is enjoyable, at a snap of his fingers, to have the girl remove it, or, indeed, if he wishes, to tear it from her at his whim.

"In the Ta-Teera though," she said, bitterly, "it is sometimes like being more naked than naked."

"I understand," I said, softly. It presented her as a displayed slave.

She was silent.

"Yet doubtless," I said, "it affords your modesty more comfort than might a mere collar."

"Yes," she smiled, "a bit more than might a collar alone."

How I then again envied the Gorean brutes who might order such a woman, at so little as a snap of their fingers, to strip to her collar.

"I was not branded," she said, "because the masters thought a brand would mar my beauty."

"I understand," I said. Actually, however, though I was not prepared to argue, I found this quite surprising. From what I had seen a brand made a woman at least a hundred times more beautiful and exciting. The brand's marvelousness, of course, is not simply a function of its aesthetic enhancement of the woman's beauty, adding beauty to her beauty, raising her almost geometrically to a new dimension of loveliness, but was doubtless as much or more a function of its meaning; it marked the loveliness into which it was burned as that of the most desirable of women, a female slave.

"I do not need the jacket," I said.

"Please, for me, Jason," she wheedled.

She was so pretty!

"Very well," I said. I drew on the jacket.

"Now, the coat," she said.

"I certainly do not need the coat," I said.

"Oh, please, please, Jason," she wheedled.

"Very well," I said. I drew on the coat.

"How marvelous you look," she said. "How long it has been since I looked upon a handsome man of my world, so smartly attired."

"I feel like a fool," I said. "These garments are so incongruous on this world. Too, they seem clumsy and out of place, almost rude and barbaric, compared to the lines and simplicity of Gorean garments."

"No, no," she said. "They are perfect!"

"If you say so," I smiled.

"You have been very kind to me," she said, "to let me see you dressed in this fashion, as a man of my old and dear world. You have pleased me very much. What lovely memories do you recall for me!"

"It is nothing," I said. Indeed, it was such a little thing to do for the girl, and she seemed so appreciative. I gathered it meant much for her. "Perhaps now," I said, "you should show me the secret exit, that I may attempt to escape from this place."

"Hurry," she said, slipping in front of me and out the barred gate, which was ajar.

"Slowly," I said. "There may be guards in the hall."

"No," she said. "It is not yet time for their rounds but it will be quite soon. We must make haste."

I followed the girl, swiftly, from the cell. Behind me I left the collar, opened, on the floor, and the chains, open and discarded, strewn about the ring.

I was well pleased to leave the room of slave preparation. I quickly followed the girl, heart pounding, through the dimly lit corridors. I thought it fortunate we encountered no guards. She knew the way well. Once we heard, in the distance, the striking of a gong. "What is that?" I asked. "It is a signal," she said, "that it is time for the guards to begin their rounds."

"Hurry," I said. She moved quickly before me.

How brave she was. She risked much, doubtless, for one who was only a man of her world.

What a fine and noble girl.

Suddenly she stopped before a large, heavy door. She turned, breathless, to face me.

"Is this the door?" I asked.

"Yes," she said.

I took her in my arms. "You must come with me," I said. "I cannot leave you here."

She shook her head. "I cannot go," she said. "Leave me! Escape!"

"You must come with me," I told her.

"I am only a half-naked slave," she said, "in a Ta-Teera and collar. I would be picked up in a moment. Go."

"Please," I said. "Come with me."

"Do you know the penalties for an escaped slave girl?" she asked.

"No," I said, frightened.

"I tried to escape once," she said. "This time my feet could be cut off."

I shuddered.

"Please, hurry," she said. "Every moment that you delay prolongs our danger."

"You are the finest and bravest girl I have ever known," I said.

"Hurry," she whispered.

I lowered my head to her, to kiss her, but, again, she twisted her head away.

"Do not forget that I am a woman of Earth," she said.

I continued to hold her. She was sensitive to the pressure of my hands upon her arms.

She looked up at me.

"Our relationship has been so beautiful, Jason," she said, "please do not spoil it."

"I'm sorry," I said. I released her.

She opened the door and peered through. It was dark on the other side of the door.

She turned about and faced me. She smiled. "I wish you well, Jason," she said.

"I, too, wish you well," I said.

"Hurry," she said.

"I will never forget you," I said. Then I slipped through the door

My arms were instantly pinioned to my sides. I heard a woman's laugh behind me.

"Light the torches." said another woman's voice. I recognized it as that of my Mistress, the Lady Tima.

Torches were lit. I found myself on a semicircular stage, in a sort of an amphitheater. My arms were held at my sides by the two gigantic brutes, guards, whom I had seen earlier. There was much laughter, that of women, which rang about me, which showered down upon me. To my left and right torches were ignited. I was well illuminated. I could not see too well into the tiers but I could see, dimly, that they were filled with robed, veiled women. I struggled, futilely. There was much laughter.

I saw the girl whom I had thought was named Darlene removing the collar from her throat with a key. She handed the collar and key to an attendant, a husky brute with a knife thrust in his belt, who handed her a loose, white gown which she, fastening a clasp at her throat, donned. Too, she was handed a whip. She shook out its blades, and snapped them once. The sound was fearful.

I looked up into the tiers.

I recalled the words of the heavy man on Earth. "I think I

know a little market where you might be of interest," he had said.

I moaned.

I felt the whip of the Lady Tima pushing up my chin. She was dressed in brief black leather. She wore leather wristlets, studded. There were keys, and a knife, at her belt.

"Welcome to the market of Tima," she said.

I looked at her with misery.

She gave a sign and an attendant, at one side, struck a gong with a hammer. It was the same sound I had heard earlier, in the corridors. I now realized its significance.

"Let the sale begin," said the Lady Tima.

The girl whom I had known as 'Darlene' strode forward. She indicated me with the whip. "This is a man of Earth," she said. "I will now take the first bid on him."

"Four copper tarsks!" I heard a woman call.

I was to be sold.

# 12 THE MARKET OF TIMA

"I have a bid of four tarsks!" called the girl in the white gown, it concealing the shameful Ta-Teera she had worn while pretending to be an Earth-girl slave.

"Five!" I heard.

"Five!" said the girl.

"Let us see him!" called a woman, shrilly.

"He stands before you clad in the barbarous garments of his own world," called the Lady Tima, stepping forward with her whip, indicating me. "Note them!"

I struggled, but futilely. I was well held by the two brutes who pinioned my arms.

"See how ugly are such garments," said the Lady Tima, "how constricting!"

There was laughter. Indeed, among most Gorean garments, with their simplicity, their flowing lines, the freedom allowed for movement, my own garments seemed rigid, confining, frightened, unimaginative and boorish. Were those of Earth really so ashamed and fearful of their bodies as such garments suggested, I wondered.

"Are they not offensive to your eyes?" inquired the Lady Tima.

"Remove them!" cried more than one lady, laughing, from the tiers.

"Some of the women of Earth even aspire to wear such garments!" laughed the Lady Tima. "It is their way of trying to be men, according to the quaint modalities of his strange world."

"Our men teach them that they are women," laughed a woman.

"It is true, and the little sluts learn swiftly," laughed the Lady Tima.

There was much laughter...

I struggled, but could not free myself. How cruel was their

153

joke, to present me clad before buyers in garb which, though appropriate perhaps to my world, could appear only homely and foolish in comparison to the garments of Gor. I was chagrined to be presented before Gorean women in what now seemed to me to be gross and stupid garments. How little charm or grace, or liberty, there seemed to me then in such cloths. That certain women, too, would hasten to don them seemed to me then a pitiful irony bespeaking the confusions of my native world. The question was less as to why women would wish to wear them than as to why anyone would wish to wear them. I wondered if the aesthetic judgment of the women who hastened to don such garments was as stereotyped and thoughtless as that of the men who wore them as a matter of course. I hoped not. But perhaps women who were determined to be male impersonators had really little choice in the matter. Did they not imitate men in their eccentricities and stupidities as well as in other features their portrayal or characterization would surely seem the less convincing and plausible. Such garments, I suspected, were a softened heritage, rather than a break from such a heritage, from the repressions of an earlier era in Earth history, repressions now denied but repressions undeniably lingering. How scandalized and shamed would be an Earthling to adopt convenient and handsome raiment. How ridiculed would such a fellow be. How little we have learned from the informal garb of Greeks and Romans. Is it truly easier, I wonder, to adopt columns and arches, philosophy and poetry, mathematics and medicine, and law, than a rational mode of dress. But the Greeks and Romans were proud peoples, so untutored as to be unapologetic concerning their humanity. It is little wonder they are so alien to the men of Earth. It is a long time since I have thrown salt into the wind; it is a long time since I have poured wine into the sea; it is a long time since I have gone to Delphi.

"A silver tarsk!" cried a woman. "Let us see him!"

"A silver tarsk!" called the girl in the white gown, who had pretended to be an Earth-girl slave. She was quite pleased. She thrust my chin up with her whip. "An excellent bid for one of the opening bids!" she congratulated the woman who had called out.

"But a moment!" laughed the Lady Tima. She signaled to an attendant, a burly fellow, who brought forth and set at one side of the platform a large, shallow bronze dish, containing cubes of wood. He set a torch into this wood, which had apparently been soaked with oil. The wooden cubes sprang immediately, briefly raging, into flame. I did not understand the meaning of the dish, or its flaming contents.

"We are ready now, are we not," asked the Lady Tima, "to remove his clothing?"

There were affirmative shouts from the tiers.

The Lady Tima nodded to the two men who held me. They shifted their grip to my wrists.

The Lady Tima then signaled again to the burly fellow who, with a knife, from the back, cutting at the back of the coat, and at the sleeves, cut and tore away the coat. He threw it into the dish of burning, oil-soaked wood. He then removed, similarly, my jacket, which, too, he threw into the dish of burning wood. I looked at the coat and jacket, burning. They had been things I had had from Earth. The men who held me returned their grip to my arms.

"More! Let us see more of him!" cried a woman.

"But first," called the Lady Tima, "permit me to congratulate you, my lovely, and generous and noble clients, for cooperating so splendidly in the joke we played upon this poor slave. You were silent. He thought himself attempting to escape to freedom, abetted by a woman of his own world, which role was played by the lovely Lady Tendite." She indicated the girl in the white gown, who had pretended to be an Earth-girl slave. She whom I had thought bore the exciting slave name of Darlene, whom I now understood to be Tendite, a lady of Gor, nodded and smiled, lifting her whip to the crowd. Many in the tiers struck their left shoulders with the palms of their right hand, in Gorean applause. "Instead," she laughed, "he finds himself only a slave being marketed." There was much laughter. "You were superb," she told them. "The House of Tima is grateful," she said. Several of the women continued to applaud her. She was clever. The crowd, enlisted in the sale, was in a splendid mood.

Suddenly I was furious.

I began to struggle wildly. To my astonishment, in spite of the two men who held me, and their large size, I almost freed myself. I think the men, too, who held me, were astonished. They were almost thrown from my body. Then, again, they held me firmly fixed between them. I looked out with rage at the crowd. I was confident that had there been only one man he could not have, in spite of his size, held me. I had not realized I was so strong.

I think the women in the tiers, and the Ladies Tima and Tendite, too, had not realized this.

They exchanged glances.

"Is he tame?" asked one of the women in the second tier.

I could see, to my surprise, that several of the women were alarmed. In the back of the tiers I saw two guards, with spears, go to the top of one of the aisles, whence they might descend quickly into the tiers if it should be necessary.

I was pleased though, breathing heavily, I gave no sign of this. I had become, in my time on Gor, given the exercise and diet, more formidable than I could have dreamed, from my sedentary, refined existence on my native world.

"Many of you own tharlarion," said the Lady Tendite, calling merrily to the crowd. "They are much stronger than he," she laughed. "And perhaps they are more clever!" she added.

There was some uneasy laughter.

"Who wants a stupid slave?" called a woman.

"The Lady Tendite jests," said the Lady Tima, quickly. "The slave is highly intelligent. The House of Tima vouches for this."

"Yes!" said the Lady Tendite. "I but jested. The slave is quite intelligent."

"Perhaps he is too intelligent," said one of the women.

"Look at his eyes," called another. "He does not look like a slave."

"Perhaps he is a master," said another woman, her voice trembling.

"Would you sell us a master for our boudoir?" inquired another. I heard several women gasp, taken aback at the boldness of the question. I was startled. There had been something unmistakable in their response, an expression of excitement, of thrilled, scandalized pleasure. Was that what they desired, I wondered, a master in their boudoir? But if that were true surely they knew that then they, in their own boudoir, would be only slaves.

I knew I must be mistaken.

"No, no, no, no," laughed the Lady Tima. "No!" She seemed amused, but I could tell she was not pleased at the sudden turn the sale had taken. No more bids, I noted, had been forthcoming. "His intelligence, which is quite high," she said, "is that of a man of Earth. He is trained to use his intelligence to anticipate the desires of women, and to obey and serve them. The intelligence of the men of Earth is at the disposal of women. They do what women tell them."

"Are there no masters among them?" asked a woman. "Are they all silk slaves?"

"That is my understanding," said the Lady Tima. "They are all the silk slaves of women."

Surely that is false, I thought. I had known large and strong men on Earth. Yet it was true that many such men, of masculine configuration and size, hastened to obey women. They had been taught that they would not be true men unless they did what women wished. On Gor, of course, it is the women who obey, if they have been made slaves.

"The men of Earth are only silk slaves," said Lady Tima.

I was certain that she was wrong. Somewhere on Earth, here and there, I was certain, there were honestly strong men, in the historical and biological sense, men before women knelt as smaller and weaker creatures, and objects of intense desire. I had thought that I had been such a man. Then I had found myself a slave on Gor. I wondered if more than a handful of men on Earth would ever recollect their manhood. I thought not. It is easier to fear and castigate manhood, than to assume it. The first is well within the reach of the weak; the second is only within the grasp of the strong.

"Only silk slaves!" said the Lady Tima.

"No," I cried, in agony. "No! There must be true men on Earth!"

The whip of the Lady Tendite, suddenly, its blades folded back against its staff, struck me on the side of the face.

"Oh, Jason," said the Lady Tima, pityingly, "did you speak without permission?"

Again I struggled, fiercely, to throw off the men who held me. Then again, helplessly, was I held.

"That is no silk slave," I heard.

"Send him to the quarries!" cried a woman.

"Chain him at a rowing bench," called another. "Let him draw an oar!"

"Bring forth the next slave for sale!" called yet another.

"Begin the next sale!" called yet another.

"Wait! Wait!" called the Lady Tima.

The crowd subsided.

"Have we truly fooled you, Ladies?" she laughed.

The crowd was silent.

She turned to me. "You did well, Jason," she said. "You played your role well, pretending to be imperfectly tamed." I looked at her, my arms held.

She turned again to the crowd. "Forgive me, Ladies," she laughed. "It seems my jest was but a poor one. I had thought all knew that the men of Earth were mere slaves. Thus, when you saw the slave struggle, obedient to my signal, I thought the farcicality of his activity would be evident. But I see that you are not truly familiar with the males of Earth, fearing that some of them might be men. Is he not a fine actor?" She faced me and struck her left shoulder, as though applauding my performance. Some of the women, too, uncertainly, in the tiers, struck their left shoulders.

"Is he tame?" asked a woman in the fourth tier.

"He is perfectly tame," said the Lady Tima. "I have used him even on my own couch."

I put down my head. I well remembered my humiliation on the couch of my mistress, the Lady Tima.

"Do you guarantee his tameness?" asked one of the women.

"We do," said the Lady Tima. "The House of Tima guarantees his tameness, fully."

"Prove to us that he is tame!" called a woman.

"We shall do so," smiled the Lady Tima. She turned to me. She smiled. She spoke softly. None but those on the platform might hear. "You have had your moment of sport, Jason," she said, "pretending, as is occasionally the wont of the males of Earth, to be a man, but it is now time to remember what you truly are, only a weakling of Earth, one fit to be only a woman's slave."

I looked at her, angrily.

"There are sleen in the House of Tima," she said. "Perhaps you desire to be fed to them."

"No," I said.

She looked at me.

"No, Mistress," I said. I put my head down, frightened. Well did I recall the fearsome, curved fangs, the long, sinuous bodies, the claws, the lithe muscularity, the incredible swiftness and agility, of the sleen in the House of Andronicus, leaping upward, ferocious, eyes blazing, mouths slavering, to tear me from the rope which suspended me over their heads.

"Look into my eyes, Jason," she commanded.

I lifted my head and met her eyes. She, and those who

were masters, held the power of life and death over me. They were all, and I was nothing. I was a slave.

"What are you, Jason?" she asked.

"A slave," I said.

"Do not forget it," she said.

"No, Mistress," I said.

"You may lower your eyes," she said.

"Yes, Mistress," I said. I put my head down.

"It is not necessary to hold him," she said to the two men who held me. They released me. I stood quietly on the platform. I had been well reminded that I must obey, and that I was a slave.

"Pretty Jason," said the Lady Tendite, stepping toward me. She touched the side of my face with the palm of her right hand.

I clenched my fists.

"Be warned, Jason," whispered the Lady Tima.

I opened my hands.

The Lady Tendite handed her whip to one of the attendants.

Gently, solicitously, the Lady Tendite, standing quite near to me, removed my necktie. "Is that not more comfortable, Jason?" she inquired. She then walked to the side of the platform and discarded the tie in the shallow bowl of burning wood. She then returned to me and, attentively, button by button, unbuttoned the shirt I wore, even the buttons on the sleeves. "Do not be upset, Jason," she said, sweetly. "Surely you remember me, Darlene, the little Earth-girl slave?"

"I trusted you," I said, bitterly.

"What a fool you were," she said.

"Yes," I said.

"I did not think I would be so successful in deceiving you," she said.

"Why?" I asked. "Did you fear the inadequacy of your English?"

"My English is excellent," she said.

"That is true," I said. Her English was indeed excellent. It was perhaps a bit formal and precise for a native speaker, a little too correct, perhaps, and it had been occasionally infected with certain oddities of expression and construction which had been surprising, but I had not weighed these factors heavily. I had discounted such matters in virtue of what I had conjectured were consequences of Gorean influence and a lack of practice, over years, in the language. "Why then," I asked, "did you fear you might not be able to deceive me?"

"Is it not obvious?" she asked.

"No," I said.

"Do you think that any real slave girl would even have dared to think of acting as I did?"

I said nothing.

"Do you know the penalties for such a thing?" she asked. "The little sluts know well the meaning of their collars."

"I understand," I said. I shuddered. From her few simple words I now understood more than I had before of the depth and significance of Gorean slavery.

She went behind me and removed my shirt, which she threw in the fire.

She then strode to the front of the platform. "We have a bid of a silver tarsk on this slave," she said. "Do I hear a higher bid?"

The crowd was silent.

"Come now, Ladies," said the Lady Tendite. "This is a superb silk slave. It is true he is somewhat untrained, but which of you is not capable of training a silk slave? He is from the planet Earth. He is fully tame."

But no bids were forthcoming from the crowd.

The Lady Tendite turned to me. "Remove your upper garment," she said, "that which conceals your chest."

I looked at her.

"Quickly," she snapped.

I pulled the garment, short-sleeved, of white cotton, a common T-shirt, over my head, and then held it. There is no specific Gorean word for this type of garment. The English expression for the garment was presumably unknown to the Lady Tendite.

Some of the women in the tiers had laughed, seeing my quickness in obeying the Lady Tendite.

Too, I was conscious of the women in the tiers regarding me with renewed interest, though caution. I stood very straight. I was not displeased to be regarded with interest. Too, I was not displeased to sense that certain of the women regarded me with considerable circumspection. I am large and strong. They were not certain, I conjecture, that I was fully tame. The feelings of a woman toward a man who may not be fully tame tend to be ambiguous. They are afraid of him, and yet they find him intriguing. They wonder what it would be to lie at his mercy, in his arms. What if, truly, he should not be tame? Then how would they be treated? What would be done to them? Would they not, in effect, be made his slaves, in the way of nature? But, too, I was apprehensive, for, in looking out on the tiers, I realized that one of these women could buy me, and that I would then have to obey her, and would be hers, fully, to do with as she pleased. I noted, too, that I was looked upon with a frankness, an openness of curiosity and sensual speculation, which I would not have expected from the women of Earth. I was being looked upon candidly as an erotic brute, a possible complement to their own urges and needs. Gorean women, not trained to be ashamed of their instincts, not tutored in the betrayal and suppression of their nature, tend to look upon males whom they find attractive with both honesty and pleasure. The concealment of feelings, particularly where male slaves are concerned, is a deceit not often practiced by Gorean women. Such a deceit tends not only to be rather beneath them, but, beyond this, would be almost meaningless to them. The male slave, you see, is an animal. Accordingly, he should be assessed as such.

The Lady Tendite approached me and held out her hand. I placed the T-shirt I had removed from my body in her hand and she went to the shallow bowl of burning cubes of wood and discarded it. I saw it burn.

She returned to me, speaking to the crowd. "Note," she said, "the breadth of the chest, the width of the shoulders, the narrowness of the waist, the flatness of the belly."

"One five!" called a woman. "I can use him in the stable bouts." I did not understand the reference to stable bouts. The bid, however, I gathered, was one silver tarsk, five copper tarsks.

"Stable bouts?" laughed the Lady Tendite. "Surely you jest?"

"Are you sure he is tame?" asked another woman.

"You saw with what alacrity he removed his garment at my command," said the Lady Tendite. "You see how he stands unheld on the sales platform."

"Lower your head," whispered the Lady Tima to me.

I did so.

"Regard him," said the Lady Tendite, "a fearful slave, awaiting your command."

"One six," called another woman.

The Lady Tendite turned angrily to me. "Take off your shoes and stockings," she said. "Leave them on the platform. Then kneel."

"Yes, Mistress," I said. I knelt down on one knee. I began to unlace my right shoe.

The Lady Tima, with her whip, stood near me.

"This is not a common work slave," said the Lady Tendite to the crowd, "a simple brute, an insensitive lout for your fields or stables. This is a valuable and highly intelligent silk slave. Furthermore, he is a male from Earth. From birth he has been taught to be deferential to the wishes of women, to adopt whatever values they have told him to adopt, and to believe whatever propositions they have told him to believe. Buy him. He has been trained since birth to be the slave of women. Have no fear. He will be sweet, tender, solicitous, understanding, sympathetic and obedient. You need not fear lust and power from him. You need not fear to be alone with him. He is a male of Earth. Bid for him. He will always be to you a lovely and complete slave."

I now knelt on my right knee and unlaced my left shoe.

"Tendite," said the Lady Tima to me, "is not skilled in conducting a sale. I am training her."

I did not respond.

"Is her skill in your language good?" she asked me.

"Yes, Mistress," I said.

The bids, slowly, without enthusiasm, increased to one eight.

"How is it," I asked, "that the Lady Tendite knows English?"

"She learned the language in connection with training Earth-girl slaves," she said, "in the House of Andronicus. At one time, two or three years ago, English was one of the Earth languages used in that occupation. Now, as you may know, Earth girls are trained substantially in, or entirely in, Gorean."

"Yes, Mistress," I said. I recalled that the Lady Gina had once told me something along these lines. The collared Earth girl would now learn her Gorean, or most of it, as a child learns it, or an animal, not through the medium of another language. According to the Lady Gina the method was efficient. I did not doubt it. Indeed, my own Gorean was largely a function of exactly this approach. The Lady Gina, who knew English, had, however, I must admit, given me occasional assistance. Although she had been strict with me, she had not, on the whole, treated me badly. I was sorry that I had disappointed her, in not becoming a man. But I was only a male of Earth, and a slave.

"Even after this change, of course," said the Lady Tima, "she continued in her employment in the House of Andronicus, continuing to be used particularly in her specialty, that of the training, though now generally brief, of naked, collared Earth sluts."

I swallowed, hard.

"The little Earth beauties learned to fear her whip well," said the Lady Tima.

I imagined it was true.

"I lured her to the House of Tima for higher wages," she said.

"But you are not satisfied with her performance?" I asked.

"Is she not beautiful?" asked the Lady Tima.

"Yes," I said.

"I will obtain the full value of my wages from her," said the Lady Tima, "even untrained as she is now. You will see. And, in time, she will conduct a sale as skillfully as any female slaver."

I now, sitting upon the platform, bent forward, removed my shoes and stockings. I then knelt.

"I will get at least four tarsks for you," said the Lady Tima. I assumed she meant four tarsks of silver. This was a high price. Lovely women often go for a silver tarsk or two. I did not think she would manage to get four silver tarsks for me. I was now being bid upon rather as might be a work slave, though there was some ambiguity in the bidding. The least valuable slaves are often female work slaves, purchased for the public kitchens or laundries. The next level of slaves, not generally thought to be of great value, tends to be male work slaves, usually used in cargo galleys, on the wharves, and in the fields or quarries. The next level of slaves, and the most common form of slave on Gor, is the female who can be used as a pleasure slave. It is my conjecture that some ninety percent of Gorean slaves are female, and that some eighty percent of these fit into the category of slaves who must figure into their duties the serving of the pleasure of men. Indeed, even the miserable females in the fields, or those in the kitchens and laundries, know that upon occasion they will be used, usually chained, to slake the lust of their

foremen or masters. The female slave on Gor, knowing herself owned, is usually in little doubt as to what can occur to
her in her slavery. The next level of slaves is that of male silk
slaves. These usually bring higher prices, on the whole, than
female pleasure slaves. This, it seems to me, is purely a matter of supply and demand. Female pleasure slaves, given
slave raids and the sackings of cities, are relatively plentiful
on Gor. Male silk slaves are not. The explanation for this, I
think, is reasonably clear. Gorean males seldom make good
silk slaves. The explanation for the much smaller number of
male as opposed to female slaves on Gor, speaking now generally of male work slaves, is also clear. First, the female
tends to be the desirated object of the slaver's seizure. She
brings higher prices than male work slaves. Secondly, in
battles, often male defenders have been slaughtered or driven
off. Their females thus remain as spoils for the chains of the
victors. Too, male captives are often killed. Female captives,
on the other hand, particularly if comely, are usually spared
for the collars of their conquerors. They learn to yield well to
their masters. The most valuable general category of slaves,
however, much to the chagrin of some male silk slaves, is
that of the particularly desirable female. These are usually
extraordinarily beautiful Gorean girls, once of high caste.
Sometimes they are dancers. Commonly they are highly
trained. Sometimes they are even passion slaves, girls literally
bred for the pleasure of men. The prizes purchased by Ubars
and rich men for their pleasure gardens usually belong to the
types of girls included in this general category. Girls of political interest, too, it might be mentioned, are usually included
in this category. For example, a captured, enslaved Ubara
would commonly bring a very handsome price. These general
remarks, of course, if they were to be made more accurate,
would require numerous qualifications. For example, the
prices of Earth girls have tended to improve in the past few
years on Gor. Gorean men tend to enjoy teaching them their
slavery. Too, once they have learned the meaning of their
collar, they are extraordinarily delicious slave girls. Some au-
thorities believe that Earth girls should be a special category
of slave. Others dispute this. I agree with those who dispute
it, regarding Earth girls as only being women like other
women. To be sure, there is a special spice and flavor in owning them. I have not mentioned exotics, incidentally, slaves
bred or trained for unusual purposes. I have not mentioned,

cithor, slaves with professional competences, such as medicine or law, or fighting slaves, in effect gladiators, men purchased for use as bodyguards or combatants in arranged games. The intricacy of the institution of slavery on Gor is prodigious. These general remarks, dealing only with major and obvious categories, should be understood as no more than a crude orientation to the subject matter as a whole. The utility of generality must not be permitted to blind us to the specificity of reality. There are always market variables, and buyer and slave variables. A girl who seems to most men only a low-grade kettle-and-mat girl may be to a given man very precious. She may be as valuable to him as a collared Ubara, one who must now, strictly, be taught her duties as a slave.

"I have now a bid of one sixteen," said the Lady Tendite. "Surely, noble buyers, you will bid more realistically for such a splendid property?"

"I will have at least four for you," said the Lady Tima to me.

"Why is the bidding not higher?" I asked.

"They are afraid of you," she said.

"I see," I said.

"But I will teach them they have nothing to fear," she said.

I looked at her, with apprehension.

"Bring on another slave!" called a woman.

"Bring on another slave!" called yet another.

The Lady Tendite, distraught, turned to the Lady Tima. "I shall close the bids," she said. She knew she had not done well. She was disappointed with her performance.

"May I continue?" asked the Lady Tima.

"Certainly," said the Lady Tendite, gratefully.

"Bring on a new slave!" called a woman.

The Lady Tima, suddenly, cracked her whip, the blades, loud, snapping in a staccato burst of leather, almost at my ear, the crowd instantly still, its attention arrested, stunned, alert.

"Stand!" ordered the Lady Tima. "Strip! Kneel! Knees wide!"

Startled, terrified, scarcely knowing what I was doing, I found myself kneeling before the buyers.

"Crawl to the Lady Tendite," ordered the Lady Tima. "Beg to be collared."

I found myself terrified, crawling to the Lady Tendite. The whip snapped again, behind me.

"Please collar me, Mistress," I begged.

"Louder!" said the Lady Tima.

"Please collar me, Mistress!" I begged the Lady Tendite.

"Stay on your hands and knees, head down!" ordered the Lady Tima.

A collar was brought, one which had been lying at hand, with other accouterments, at the rear of the platform. It was identical to that which I had worn in the room of preparation.

I felt it clasped about my neck and locked shut. I shuddered.

I saw the Lady Tima throw what garments I had just torn from my body into the shallow bowl of burning wood.

I was aware of applause, Gorean applause, from the tiers.

The Lady Tima, with her whip, indicated my shoes and stockings lying on the platform. "Take them, one by one, in your mouth," she said, "and discard them in the fire."

The whip cracked again.

I began to comply with her request, shattered, terrified, a slave.

I heard bids now from the crowd. "Two tarsks!" I heard. "Three tarsks!" I heard. "Three five!" I heard. "Three six!" "Three ten!" "Three twenty!"

The bidding was at four eighteen when I had jerked back my head from the flaming cubes, my right shoe thrown from my teeth into the fire. My knees hurt. I could feel the smooth wood of the platform beneath the palms of my hands. I was stark naked on Gor, save that I wore a steel collar. I saw the last of my clothing burst into flame. I saw fire licking about the shoes, which I had placed in the dish.

The whip snapped again. "Here, Jason!" ordered the Lady Tima, pointing with the whip to a place at her feet.

I crawled to her feet.

"Five tarsks!" I heard.

"Stand, Jason!" ordered the Lady Tima.

I stood.

"Here is the slave," said the Lady Tima. "You have seen him kneel naked to a woman and beg to be collared. Has not your lovely auctioneer, the Lady Tendite, well prepared him for his sale?"

"Six tarsks!" I heard.

There was applause for the Lady Tendite. I was bitter. I realized now only too well that the room of preparation had

been for me just that. It had been where the Lady Tendite
had prepared me for my sale, even to having me, unwittingly,
dress myself as a man of Earth. It was there that she had laid
the snares and set the traps, earning my trust, building up my
hopes, which had made me so additionally vulnerable to the
humiliations and miseries of my sale. She had done her work
well. What a fool she had made of me. What a splendid joke
for the Gorean women. I had thought to escape. I was now
naked, being sold.

"Seven tarsks!" I heard. "Seven five!" I heard.

What a fool I had been not to realize that she was not a
true slave girl. A true slave girl, I gathered, would not even
have dared to think of behaving as she had. They knew the
penalties. Besides the concern of a slave girl is not with male
slaves; their concern is with free men, their masters.

"Seven seven!" I heard. "Seven eight!"

"Show yourself to them as you were in the room of
preparation," said the Lady Tima to the Lady Tendite, "when
you pretended to be a miserable little Earth-girl slave."

"Lady Tima?" inquired the Lady Tendite.

"I know what I am doing," said the Lady Tima to her,
smiling.

"But I would be ashamed to be seen before free women so
clad," she said.

"There are only women here, and this slave, and our men,"
said the Lady Tima. "Do so."

The Lady Tendite looked at her, uncertainly.

"Do you wish to remain in my employ?" inquired the Lady
Tima.

The Lady Tendite smiled. She threw back the white gown
she wore, still fastened about her neck with its silver clasp. It
then hung back, over her shoulders, like a cape.

She stood there, then, in the Ta-Teera. She was exquisitely
beautiful.

The Gorean women in the tiers seemed for a moment
taken aback. Then, beginning one by one, they struck their
left shoulders.

"How beautiful she is," breathed more than one woman.

I saw many of the women looking upon the Lady Tendite
almost breathlessly, thrilled with her loveliness.

I then understood how brilliant indeed was the slaver who
was my mistress. The women in the tiers, almost overcome
with excitement, were identifying with the Lady Tendite.

Though it was she who stood there it was they who, in their imaginations, wore the shameful Ta-Teera and stood upon the wood of a slave platform. The Lady Tendite smiled, and lifted her hand to the crowd. Perhaps it was only then that she realized that her beauty had not been incidental to her hiring by the Lady Tima. I looked out on the women in the tiers.

"Remove the gown, and put on the collar," said the Lady Tima to the Lady Tendite.

"Yes, Lady Tima," she said. She unclasped the gown and dropped it to one side. From an attendant she retrieved the collar which she had earlier handed him. She stood before the crowd and, smiling, held the collar.

The crowd was intent and hushed.

The Lady Tendite, smiling at the crowd, closed the collar about her neck. The click was audible.

There was an intake of breath. There was a cry of pleasure. Then there was applause for the Lady Tendite.

She stood before them, as a collared slave girl.

There was much applause.

The women in the tiers, clearly, were identifying with the Lady Tendite, and her beauty, as a collared slave girl. The Lady Tima was appealing to, and exploiting, something deep in women which she, as a slaver, well understood, the deep, thrilling desire, profound in women, to be the owned slave of a strong man, to be mastered and to find themselves under the obligation of obedience. I do not know how many of the women clearly understood what was occurring on the platform. Perhaps many knew only that, for some reason that was not clear to them, they were excited and thrilled. And they could, of course, be innocent in feeling this thrill and excitement for, first, it was not truly they but the Lady Tendite who stood on the platform, and, too, she was not truly a slave, but only pretending to be one. How frightening, of course, it would have been had the collar been truly locked upon her!

"My congratulations to the superb actress, the Lady Tendite!" called the Lady Tima.

There was more applause.

I have little doubt, too, the fact that I stood in the near background to the Lady Tendite, a male large and strong, contributed to the scene intended by the Lady Tima. She was very small, compared to me.

"Caress the slave," said the Lady Tima to the Lady Tendite.

The Lady Tendite came near to me. She looked up into my eyes. She was exquisitely beautiful. Her breasts, swelling within the pathetic restraint of the Ta-Teera, made me want to cry out with pleasure.

"Please do not touch me," I begged.

She wore a steel collar.

"Please," I begged. I cried out with misery and shame.

"Ten tarsks!" I heard. "Ten five!" I heard.

"You may now remove the collar and take your whip from the attendant," said the Lady Tima. "Then, with the whip, display him as you will."

The Lady Tendite smiled, and went to the rear of the platform.

Bids continued. When the Lady Tendite returned, the collar removed, her whip in hand, they were at eleven six. I was then, guided by the voice of the Lady Tendite, and the deft touches of her whip, displayed to the crowd. There were tears in my eyes. Then I was made to kneel.

"Fourteen tarsks!" I heard.

"Jason," said the Lady Tima, "you did attempt to escape."

"Yes, Mistress," I said, shuddering.

"Speak up," she said.

"Yes, Mistress," I said.

"Too," she said, "you spoke at least once without permission this evening."

"Yes, Mistress," I said, loudly, knowing that I must speak so that I could be heard in the tiers.

"Do you beg to be whipped?" she asked.

"Yes, Mistress," I said. "Please have me whipped." I put my head down, miserable.

The Lady Tima gestured to one of the attendants who then stood behind me, and shook out the blades of a slave whip.

"Whip him," she said.

I shuddered as the lash fell upon me.

The bids continued, as I was beaten. I was sold for sixteen silver tarsks. I did not know who bought me. I was chained hand and foot. I remember realizing that I was no longer being beaten. I was dragged, bloody, from the sales platform. I remember hearing the sound of the gong once more. A new slave was being presented before the buyers.

# 13  THE LADY FLORENCE: I ENCOUNTER A SLAVE GIRL, WHOM I LEARN IS OWNED BY ONEANDER OF AR

"How pretty he is at your stirrup, Lady Florence," said the veiled woman, reclining in the palanquin, its draft slaves now halted.

"A lengthening of his hair, a white ribbon binding it back, a silken tunic make quite a difference, Lady Melpomene," responded the Lady Florence.

"I see you no longer have him chained there," said the Lady Melpomene.

"It was not necessary, as I soon discovered," said the Lady Florence. I kept my head down.

"I envy you such a sweet slave," said the Lady Melpomene.

"It is kind of you not to be bitter," said the Lady Florence, acidly. I held the reins of her tharlarion. It was not large. Its stirrup was at my right shoulder.

"Have you had him branded yet?" asked the Lady Melpomene.

"No," said the Lady Florence. "I keep my male slaves smooth-thighed."

"Interesting," said the Lady Melpomene.

The Lady Florence shrugged.

"Is he any good on the couch?" asked the Lady Melpomene.

"I use him when it pleases me," said the Lady Florence.

"Of course," said the Lady Melpomene.

"It is unfortunate that your resources, in the recent

markets, have become so limited, or you might have outbidden me," said the Lady Florence.

"My resources are quite ample," said the Lady Melpomene.

"Rumor has it," said the Lady Florence, "that your fortunes lie near ruin."

"Such rumors," snapped the Lady Melpomene, "are malicious and false."

"I thought so," said the Lady Florence, pleasantly. "It is unfortunate that they are so rampant."

"I was insufficiently interested in the slave to bid sixteen tarsks," said the Lady Melpomene.

"Of course," said the Lady Florence.

"Have you been long shopping in Ar?" asked the Lady Melpomene.

"Some four days," said the Lady Florence. "We left our house in Vonda a month ago, for my villa." The villa of the Lady Florence of Vonda lay some forty pasangs south and west of Vonda. Vonda was one of the four cities of the Salerian Confederation. The other cities of this confederation were Ti, Port Olni and Lara. All four of these cities lie on the Olni River, which is a tributary to the Vosk. Ti is farthest from the confluence of the Olni and Vosk; downriver from Ti is Port Olni; these were the first two cities to form a league, originally intended for the control of river pirates and the protection of inland shipping; later, downriver from Port Olni, Vonda, and Lara, lying at the junction of the Olni and Vosk, joined the league. The Olni, for practical purposes, has been freed of river pirates. The oaths of the league, and the primitive articles pertaining to its first governance, were sworn, and signed, in the meadow of Salerius, which lies on the northern bank of the Olni between Port Olni and Vonda. It is from that fact that the confederation is known as the Salerian Confederation. The principal city, because the largest and most populous, of the confederation is Ti. The governance of the confederation is centralized in Ti. The high administrator of the confederation is a man called Ebullius Gaius Cassius, of the Warriors. Ebullius Gaius Cassius was also, as might be expected, the administrator of the city, or state, of Ti itself. The Salerian Confederation, incidentally, is also sometimes known as the Four Cities of Saleria. The expression 'Saleria', doubtless owing its origin to the meadow of Salerius, is used broadly, incidentally, to refer to the fertile basin territories both north and south of the Olni, the lands over which the confederation professes to maintain a hegemony. The meadow of Salerius, thus, lies on the northern bank of the Olni, between Port Olni and Vonda; the area called Saleria, on the other hand, is, in effect, the lands controlled by the confederation. Ti, Port Olni and Vonda lie on the northern bank of the Olni; Lara lies between the Olni and the Vosk, at their confluence. It is regarded as being of great strategic importance. It could, if it wished, prevent Olni shipping from reaching the markets of the Vosk towns, and, similarly, if it wished, prevent shipping from these same towns from reaching the Olni markets. Overland shipping in this area, as is generally the case on Gor, is time consuming and costly; also, it is often dangerous. It is interesting to note that the control of piracy on the Olni was largely a function of the incorporation of Lara in the confederation. This made it difficult for the pirate fleets, following their raids, to descend the Olni and escape into the Vosk. It may also be of interest to note that what began as a defensive league instituted primarily to protect shipping on a river gradually, but expectedly, began to evolve into a considerable political force in eastern known Gor. Jealousies and strifes, rivalries, even armed conflicts, tend often to separate Gorean cities. Seldom do they band together. In this milieu, then, of suspicion, pride, autonomy and honor, the four cities of Saleria represented a startling and momentous anomaly in the politics of Gor. The league to protect shipping on the Olni, inadvertently but naturally founded in the common interest of four cities, had formed the basis for what later became the formidable Salerian Confederation. Many cities of Gor, it was rumored, looked now with uneasiness on the four giants of the Olni. The Salerian Confederation, it was rumored, had now come to the attention even of the city of Ar.

"We proceeded from my villa to my house in Venna," continued the Lady Florence, speaking lightly with the Lady Melpomene.

"I, too, have a house in Venna," she said.

"I did not know, with the state of your finances, that you had managed to retain it," said the Lady Florence. Venna is a small, exclusive resort city, some two hundred pasangs north of Ar. It is noted for its baths and its tharlarion races.

"Do you come often to shop in Ar?" asked the Lady Melpomene.

"Twice yearly," said the Lady Florence.

"I come four times yearly," said the Lady Melpomene.

"I see," said the Lady Florence, sweetly.

"I can afford to," said the Lady Melpomene.

"Do not permit me to detain you from your shopping," said the Lady Florence.

"I would not stay too long in Ar," said the Lady Melpomene.

"I do not think there will be trouble," said the Lady Florence.

"There was talk in the baths at Vonda," said the Lady Melpomene. "It is feared there will be an attack by Ar. Already troops have skirmished south of the Olni."

"Men are barbarians," said the Lady Florence. "They are always fighting."

"If hostilities should break out," said the Lady Melpomene, "it might not be well to be a woman of Vonda caught in this city."

"I do not think there will be trouble," said the Lady Florence.

"You may risk a steel collar if you wish," said the Lady Melpomene. "I am leaving Ar tonight."

"We are leaving in the morning," said the Lady Florence.

"Excellent," said the Lady Melpomene. "Perhaps I shall see you in Venna."

"Perhaps," said the Lady Florence.

"And perhaps you will let me enjoy your slave," said the Lady Melpomene.

"Perhaps—for a fee," said the Lady Florence, coldly.

"A fee?" asked the Lady Melpomene.

"Sixteen tarsks," said the Lady Florence. "The pitiful price which you could not afford to pay for him."

Sixteen tarsks was actually a high price to pay for a male silk slave. Most would go from four to six tarsks.

"I wish you well," said the Lady Melpomene.

"I wish you well," said the Lady Florence.

The Lady Melpomene then clapped her hands. "Proceed!" she called to the draft slaves, those bearing upon their shoulders the poles of her palanquin.

In a moment or two they had proceeded down the street.

"What a hateful woman," said the Lady Florence. "What a pretender she is! How I despise her! Her fortunes are ruined. She is almost penniless. If she does retain a house in Venna she is sure to lose it soon. How bold she is, even to dare to speak with me. She is probably in Ar trying to negotiate a loan, or sell the house in Venna, if indeed she still owns it. Even the palanquin and slaves are rented! She does not fool me! How I hate her! I hate her! Did you see how sweetly she spoke to me? But she hates me, too. Our families have been enemies for generations."

"Yes, Mistress," I said.

"She even bid against me for you," said the Lady Florence. "Would a friend have done that?"

"I do not know, Mistress," I said.

"No," said the Lady Florence.

"Yes, Mistress," I said.

"And she had the nerve to ask for your use," said the Lady Florence. "I will share you only with those women who please me."

"Yes, Mistress," I said. It is a common Gorean hospitality to offer the use of one's slaves to guests, if they should find them attractive. The Lady Florence of Vonda, she to whom I belonged, could give or assign me, as any slave she owned, to whomsoever she pleased. She had, however, at least thus far, kept me for herself. Sometimes when there were guests at her villa southwest of Vonda I was kept locked in my kennel.

"This way, Jason," she said. "I wish to purchase veil pins at the shop of Publius. Then I wish to proceed to the avenue of the Central Cylinder, to examine the silks in the shop of Philebus."

"Yes, Mistress," I said. I proceeded down the street in the direction indicated, leading the tharlarion by its reins. Small saddle tharlarion are generally managed by snout reins. The huge war tharlarion are commonly guided by voice signals and the blows of spears on the face and neck. Draft tharlarion are harnessed, and can be managed either by men, or usually boys, who walk beside them, or by reins and whips, controlled by drivers, men mounted in drawn wagons.

We passed a woman in the street, a woman of Ar, followed by a silk slave. He looked at me. I suppose he was wondering what I had cost.

A slave girl passed, a short-legged beauty, clad in a gray rag, chewing on a larma fruit. She spit against the wall as I passed.

"Do not mind her, Jason," said the Lady Florence.

"No, Mistress," I said. But I wished I could have gotten my hands on her.

"Such girls are unrefined," she said.

"Yes, Mistress," I said. But the girl had had good ankles.

"Stop here, Jason," she said.

"Yes, Mistress," I said.

"You will tether the tharlarion, Jason," said the Lady Florence.

"Yes, Mistress," I said.

"When you have finished with that," she said, "you will return here, and wait for me."

"Yes, Mistress," I said.

The sun was high now, and it was past noon. We were stopped now before the shop of Philebus, which specializes in Turian silk. This shop is located on the great avenue of the Central Cylinder, which is more than four hundred feet wide, an avenue used in triumphs, dominated by the Central Cylinder of Ar itself, which stood at one end of it. There are many trees planted at the sides of this avenue, and there are frequent fountains. It is a very beautiful, and impressive, avenue. I was pleased to look upon it. Shops on this avenue, of course, if only because of the rents, are extremely expensive.

She glanced to the looped chain at the side of her saddle.

"Does Mistress wish to chain Jason, her slave?" I asked. If she wished this I would fetch her the chain, when I had tethered the tharlarion. There were slave rings, a foot or so from the sidewalk, in the front wall of the shop of Philebus. Such rings are common in public places on Gor. A slave girl, sitting, her hands bound before her body with cord, by a shortened neck-leash, was chained at one of these rings. At another, also sitting, fastened there by a two-loop fitting, running to a collar ring, was a silk slave.

"No, Jason," she said. "You may drink from the spillings of the fountain while I am inside."

"Yes, Mistress," I said. "Thank you, Mistress."

The fountain had two levels, a great bowl and, lower, near the walk level, a shallow bowl. From this shallow bowl slaves might drink.

The Lady Florence looked up at me. I could not read her expression. "Perhaps you will like what I will buy," she said.

"I am certain that I will, Mistress," I said. I was not lying. She had, I had learned, exquisite taste.

She swiftly turned and went into the shadowed, cool recesses of the shop.

"She did not chain you," said the male silk slave to me.

"No," I said.

"What did you cost?" he asked.

"Sixteen tarsks," I said.

"That is not much," he said, puzzled.

"Of silver," I said.

"Liar," he said.

I shrugged.

I led the tharlarion into a small, sanded, sunny area near the shop of Philebus, looping its reins twice about a tharlarion ring there. As I tethered it, it could reach water, from a run from the nearby fountain. These tharlarion rings are quite similar to slave rings. Indeed, the only real difference between them is their function, the one being used to tether tharlarion and the other slaves. They have this in common, of course, that they are both animal rings.

I looked at the tharlarion.

It stood there, placidly. It slid a transparent membrane upward, covering its eye, as a broad-winged insect crawled on its lid. The insect fluttered away. The Lady Florence owned many tharlarion. Her stables were among the most extensive and finest of any owned by a citizen of Vonda.

I returned to the area before the shop of Philebus.

I glanced again at the male silk slave sitting on the walk, fastened at the ring.

"Liar," he said. I think he was angry that he, and not I, had been chained. I looked away from him. The broad avenue was beautiful, with its width, its paving and fountains, the buildings, the trees, the central cylinder in the distance. It was in that cylinder, as I understood it, that were housed many of the bureaus and agencies of Ar, many of the departments important to the functioning of the state; in it, too, met various councils; in it, too, were the private compartments of the Ubar of Ar, a man called Marlenus.

I leaned against the wall of the shop of Philebus. Most Gorean shops do not have windows. Many are open to the street, or have counters which are open to the street. These shops are usually shuttered or barred at night. Certain of the shops, usually those containing more precious goods, such as that of Philebus, are entered through a narrow door. Not unoften, inside, there is an open court, with awnings at the sides, under which goods are displayed. There was, in the shop of Philebus, such a court at the back, whence goods might be taken to be viewed in natural light, should the customer wish.

I looked, idly, at the people on the avenue. It was not excessively crowded on this day of the week, nor at this hour; yet there were ample numbers of shoppers and passers-by. Here and there there were borne palanquins, as richer individuals were carried about their business. Some light, two-wheeled carriages passed, drawn by tharlarion. I saw, too, more than one bosk wagon, drawn by gigantic, shaggy, wickedly horned bosk. Their hoofs were polished; their horns were hung with beads. One of these wagons had a cover of blue and yellow canvas, buckled shut with broad straps. From within I heard the laughter of slave girls. A man followed the wagon, walking behind it, with a whip. In such a wagon the girls are commonly chained by the ankles to a metal bar which runs down the center of the wagon bed. I saw a girl lifting up the canvas a bit, and peeping out. I wondered if she were pretty. She belonged to someone. Then the canvas was pulled down, quickly. All the girls might be whipped, I supposed, for such a transgression. They were slaves.

I glanced to the slave girl who was, by the shortened neck-leash, chained at one of the rings in front of the shop of Philebus. Her small wrists were secured before her body with cord, fastened with cunning knots. The cord, I supposed, had been woven about a core of wire. The knots were under the left wrist, to make it more difficult to reach them with the teeth.

She looked at me.

She wore a light, gray tunic, brief. I considered the lines of her thighs and calves.

"I am for free men," she said, angrily. "I am not for the likes of you, Slave."

"Do you yield well in their arms, Slave?" I asked her.

She looked away, biting her lip.

I examined her body. It was exciting and attractive. I would not have minded owning her.

"I expect you yield well indeed, Slave," I said to her.

She flushed crimson, from head to toe, at the ring. I saw that my speculation had been correct. I smiled to myself. Her shoulders shook with a sob.

I went to the fountain, which was only a few yards away, and, getting down on my hands and knees, putting my head down, from the lower bowl, from which slaves and animals might drink, satisfied my thirst.

I then returned to the shop of Philebus, to continue to wait for my mistress.

I looked up, hearing tarn drums in the sky. A squadron of Ar's tarn cavalry, the stroke of their wings synchronized with the beat of the drum, passed by, overhead. There must have been some forty birds and riders. The formation seemed large to be a patrol.

I watched the robes of free women, passing in the street, the wagons, the now increasing throngs, the palanquins of rich men, some with lovely, briefly tunicked slaves chained behind them, attached to the palanquins, an affectation of display.

My mistress was long in the shop. I assumed I would have many packages to bear.

I then saw a kaiila pass. It was lofty, stately, fanged and silken. I had heard of such beasts, but this was the first one I had seen. It was yellow, with flowing hair. Its rider was mounted in a high, purple saddle, with knives in saddle sheaths. He bore a long, willowy black lance. A net of linked chain, unhooked, dangled beside his helmet. His eyes bore the epicanthic fold. He was, I gathered, of one of the Wagon Peoples, most likely the Tuchuks. His face, colorfully scarred, was marked in the rude heraldry of those distant, savage riders.

"Slave," said a woman's voice.

Immediately I knelt, head down. I saw the sandals and robes of a free woman before me.

"Where is the shop of Tabron, who is the worker of silver?" she asked.

"I do not know, Mistress," I said. "I am not of this city. Forgive me, Mistress."

"Ignorant beast," she said.

"Yes, Mistress," I said. Then, with a turn of her robes, she had gone on.

I got again to my feet, and leaned against the wall of the shop of Philebus. I felt the collar at my throat, of sturdy steel. It was enameled white. In it, incised, in tiny, dark cursive letters, in a feminine-type script, was a message in Gorean. It read, I had been told, 'I am the property of the

Lady Florence of Vonda.' The lock on the back of the collar had a double bolt, the double bolt, however, responding to a single key. I was barefoot. The tunic my mistress had given me was of white silk.

I stood straighter then, by the wall, for I now heard the counting of a cadence. Passing now in the street before me, in ranks of four, was a column of men. The four files, as I counted that nearest to me, were fifty deep. The men wore scarlet tunics. Behind their left shoulders were round shields. On their heads were scarlet caps, with yellow tassels. Behind their left shoulder, over the shields, there hung steel helmets. Sheathed swords, short, were slung at their left shoulders. On their right shoulders they bore spears, with long, bronze, tapering blades. Their feet wore heavy, thick-soled sandals, which, almost like boots, with swirling leather, rose high about their calves. The sound of these bootlike sandals on the stones of the street was clear and regular. Behind the right shoulder, slung on the shaft of the spears, were light packs. I gathered the men were leaving the city. The Gorean infantryman usually marches light. Military supply posts, walled, occur at intervals on major roads. Indeed, one of the apparent anomalies of Gor is the quality and linearity of certain roads, which are carefully kept in repair, roads which often, seemingly paradoxically, pass through sparsely populated territories. The nature of these roads and their quality seems peculiar until one examines maps on which they occur. It then becomes clear that most of them lead toward borders and frontiers. They are then, in effect, military highways. This becomes clearer, too, when it is recognized that most of the supply posts occur at forty pasang intervals. Forty pasangs is an average day's march for a Gorean infantryman. I wondered why the troops were leaving the city. Too, such troops, as I understood it, usually departed from a city in the early morning, primarily, I supposed, that a normal day's march might be completed. I watched the troops disappearing down the street. They had been led by two officers, also afoot. The column had been flanked, too, by two other officers, presumably of lesser rank. The column's tread had been even. The unison had been unpretentious but, in its way, stirring and dramatic. One felt that what was passing was not at that moment simply a collection of men, an aggregate of diverse individuals, but a unit. This, I take it, was a tribute to the training of such men. At the head of the column, behind the officers, but a pace or two before the rightermost man in the first rank, there marched a fellow who bore a standard on which was mounted an image of a silver tarn. Many such standards are over a century old. The Gorean soldier is commonly a professional soldier, usually of the caste of Warriors. In a sense, given the cruel selections undergone by his forebears, he has been bred to his work. In his blood there is the spear and war.

The column had now disappeared. When departing from main roads such troops can be followed by bosk wagons or tharlarion wagons, bearing supplies. Too, by tarn, they can be supplied from the air. It should also be mentioned that it is not unusual nor impractical for such troops, which are usually in fairly small numbers, to live off the game-rich Gorean countryside. Levies, too, within certain territories, can be imposed on villages for their provisioning. Mobility and surprise are often features of Gorean warfare. Much of it is more akin to the raid than to the siege or the open conflict of large bodies of men over large areas. It would be extremely unusual, for example, for a Gorean city to have more than five thousand men in the field in a given time.

Uneasily I touched the collar on my neck. It read, I had been told, 'I am the property of the Lady Florence of Vonda.' I could not remove it, of course, for I was a slave and it had been locked on me. I looked down the avenue of the Central Cylinder, down which the troops had disappeared. I had heard, inadvertently from the Lady Melpomene, as I had stood at the stirrup of my mistress, that an uneasy situation existed currently between Ar and the Salerian Confederation. The Lady Melpomene had said she was leaving Ar that night. The Lady Florence, of course, if I were identified as her slave, would by my collar presumably be recognized as a citizeness of Vonda, one of the cities of the confederation. I did not think it would go easily with her if hostilities should break out openly and she be seized in Ar. Indeed, we might be sold from the same platform. I wondered what she might look like in a collar. I knew, of course, what she looked like naked, for I was her silk slave. Free women think as little of concealing their bodies before their silk slaves as the women of Earth would before their pet dogs. Too, of course, it would not be well to be a woman of Ar in Vonda, should hostilities break out. Immediate reduction to total slavery would surely be the least of what would

be inflicted on such a woman. I thought it would be desirable, from my mistress' point of view, to leave Ar in the near
future, and make her way to her house in the resort town of
Venna. I began to be uneasy. It seemed to me that the sooner
we departed from the walls of Ar the better it might be. My
alarm, of course, was not simply on behalf of my mistress,
but on my own behalf as well. Gorean men, I had learned,
are not patient with silk slaves. I did not wish to risk crawling
on my stomach, over stones, under whips, perhaps for
pasangs, to the nearest slave market.

Some fifty yards away, in the street, another palanquin
passed, borne by draft slaves, some lovely enslaved girls, in
brief tunics, chained by the neck to a bar at its back. Their
hands, too, were locked behind their backs in slave bracelets.
Perhaps the display was a bit ostentatious, but I did not object. The girls were slim-thighed and sweetly breasted.

I looked down to the girl who, wrists bound, on the shortened neck-leash, sat at the slave ring in front of the shop of
Philebus. It was later in the afternoon now, and it was hot. I
was surprised to see, though I gave no sign of this, that she
had been looking at me. She turned her head away. I continued to regard her. I think she was aware of this. She sat a bit
more straightly against the wall, putting her head back. I
thought again of the girls chained behind the palanquin I had
just seen, and the girl before me now, at the ring, fastened
there. How marvelous I thought to be on such a world, where
such women might be owned. I was not displeased then to be
on Gor. I regarded her ankles, her calves and thighs, the
sweetness of her belly and breasts, her throat, her face, her
hair.

"I am thirsty," she said.

"Kneel," I said.

"Never," she said.

I looked away.

"I am kneeling," she said.

I looked back at her. She was now kneeling.

"Slave!" said the male silk slave, fastened at the wall, at
the next ring.

Somehow I had known the girl would kneel to me. It is
difficult to say how I had known this. Indeed, perhaps I had
not known it. Perhaps I had only expected it.

She was kneeling. She had obeyed.

I recalled our earlier exchange, in which she had told me

that she was not for the likes of me, but for free men. "Do you yield well in their arms, Slave?" I had asked her. "I expect you yield well indeed, Slave," I had said to her. She had flushed crimson, and had sobbed. Our relationship was now quite different than it would have been, I sensed, had that exchange not taken place. In that exchange I had made it clear to her that she was a woman, and that, if she were to relate to me, she must do so as a woman. I would have it no other way. I had seen fit, by an act of my will, that of a male, to deny to her the convenient refuges of deceit, pretense and fraud. She now knelt at my feet. I had, by an imperious word, put her there.

She looked up at me. I saw that her eyes were angry. I saw, too, in her eyes that she knew she belonged at the feet of a man.

"I am very thirsty," she said.

"What of it?" I asked.

Her eyes flashed.

I looked away, out into the street.

"I am very thirsty," said the girl, after a time. "I am chained. Would you bring me water from the fountain, please?"

"You must pay me," I said.

The male silk slave at the next ring cried out with outrage.

"You must pay me," I said. "Do you understand?"

"Clearly," she said.

I went to the fountain and, from the lower bowl, scooped up a brimming, double handful of water which I carried, carefully, to the girl. I lifted it to her lips and she, kneeling, hands bound before her body, her neck on its chain leash fastened to the ring behind her, drank. My hands were in position, when she had drunk, to hold her head. She looked at me, frightened. "I know the feel of such hands," she said. "You are not a silk slave," she whispered.

"I," said the silk slave fastened at the next ring, "if I had been free, would have fetched you the water for nothing."

"I know your sort," said the girl. "You ask nothing, but you expect much." I thrust the girl back against the wall. I thrust my lips to her throat. "I prefer a man," gasped the girl, to the silk slave, "who takes command of a girl, and takes what he wants from her." Then she said to me, sucking in her breath, turning her head to the side, "And what do you want of me?" "Everything," I told her, "and more." "I feared so," she laughed. I thrust up her bound hands, to get them out of my way. I then understood why Goreans commonly bind the hands of women behind their back. Then her bound wrists, crossed, were behind the back of my neck, and her lips began to meet mine, eagerly. "Take me," she whispered, "—Master!"

"Stop!" cried the silk slave at the next ring. "Stop! I shall tell!"

"Take me, Master!" begged the girl. "Please take me!"

"Stop!" cried the silk slave. "Stop! I shall tell! I shall tell!"

I had been had numerous times on Gor by free women, usually chained or obedient to their commands, but I had not been permitted, myself, to take a woman, to hold her in my arms, owning her, and transform her into an obedient, squirming slave. Uncontrollable, wild, starved for the ownership of a woman, I thrust her back, brutally, against the wall. Then I dragged her, half lying, holding her helplessly, from the wall. Her head was up in the leash collar. "Oh," she cried, "oh!"

"Disgusting!" I heard from a free woman passing in the street.

"Animal!" I heard another woman say.

But these passers-by, and others, did not order us apart. We were slaves. Such scenes are not unknown on Gorean streets. They would attract little more attention than would the writhings of pet sleen. It is for such reasons that slave girls are sometimes sent from their houses locked in the iron belt. To be sure the slave girl is more likely to be attacked by young ruffians than male slaves, who are often closely supervised.

"Oh," moaned the girl in my arms. "Oh, Master."

"Please take me home, Publius, and touch me." I heard a woman, in robes of concealment, say to he who walked with her upon that street.

They hurried away.

I cried out with the glory of having her.

"Master!" she wept.

I withdrew from the girl, lifting her arms from about my neck, shuddering, gasping.

"You are ruthless, Master," she said. Then she reached out to me with her mouth, and kissed me, again and again, on the left forearm.

I stood up, and left her at my feet. I was breathing heavily.

"Wait until your Mistress comes," said the silk slave at the ring. "I shall tell her."

The girl, half sitting, half kneeling, her neck in the leash collar, her hands still bound before her, put her head against the wall. She was covered with sweat, and the smell of her pleasure. Her body was covered with deep crimson blotches. Demurely she smoothed down the hem of her tunic.

I turned about to look at the street. Some twenty yards away two palanquins, heading in opposite directions; were stopped. The men in them, facing one another, were talking, presumably greeting one another and passing the time of day with genial converse. The pace of life in a Gorean city, even a large city such as Ar, does not tend to be swift. Sometimes when there is an especially beautiful sky many people will close their shops and men will flock to the high bridges to watch.

"I shall tell," said the silk slave at the ring.

Behind the palanquins, as behind several of the others I had seen this day, were several chained girls, briefly tunicked and ribboned.

"Yes, I shall tell," said the silk slave.

One of the girls was looking at me. She was small, slender-legged and exquisite. She was collared. The short, loose silk she wore was hitched high, at her left hip. She was chained by the neck, in one of two eleven-girl coffles, between two other girls, each coffle chained separately to a bar at the back of the palanquin. Her hands, like those of the other girls, were fastened behind her back.

I shook with emotion. I had never realized she could be so beautiful.

She was looking at me.

Slowly, trembling, heart pounding, I moved toward her.

"Come back," called the silk slave. "Stay at the wall! I will tell! I will tell!"

I approached the girl. The masters did not notice, for they were in converse. Some servants, too, were speaking together, near the palanquins. Neither did they notice.

Then I stood before her. Her eyes were regarding me with horror. She stepped back, in the chain.

"I did not think I would ever see you again," I said.

She did not speak.

I looked at her fair, white throat; it was lovely and delicate; it wore, snugly, locked on it, the circlet of bondage.

"That girl," she said. "You raped her."

I stepped back from the girl, to look upon her. I could scarcely believe my eyes.

"Please," she said.

Objectively, I suppose, she was no more beautiful than thousands of other girls, but to me she was the most exciting woman I had ever seen.

"Please," she said.

I examined, with wonder and pleasure, the girl who stood before me, her small feet, bare, and trim ankles, her calves and thighs, the delicious curves of her body in the loose, scant silk, the loveliness of her slender throat, locked in its collar, the delicacy and beauty of her features, the loveliness of her eyes, sensitive and vulnerable, and the marvels of her dark hair, grown longer now, tied back with a silk ribbon.

"Please," she said, "do not look at me like that."

"Are you branded?" I asked.

She turned her left side from me. She pulled at the bracelets which fastened her hands behind her back.

"Oh, how beautiful it is," I said, having stepped to her left. There, her tunic had been hitched up to her hip, presumably the better to expose her beauty and the mark which identified it as merely that of an item of merchandise.

"You raped that girl," she said.

It was hard for me to take my eyes off the beauty. Her thigh, I had noted, bore the common Kajira mark of Gor. She, I understood, in spite of her beauty to me, was only a common Kajira.

"Are you not pleased to see me?" I asked. It seemed to me incredible that she should not be pleased to see me.

"You raped that girl," she said, angrily.

"Not really," I said. "She was paying for a drink of water which I had brought to her."

"Beast," she said.

I said nothing for a moment.

I looked at her. She was in the nearest coffle of eleven girls, one of two coffles fastened to the bar at the back of the palanquin. She was the tenth girl in her coffle. The coffle chain had its own collars, rounded and rather loose, which lay below the common collars of the girls; they could not, of course, be slipped. They were similar to what I have learned are called Turian collars.

"You are very beautiful," I said. I stood more closely to her.

She tossed her head. "Doubtless did you have me at a similar disadvantage," she said, "I would have been subjected to the same treatment."

I put my hands on her tunic. It had parted somewhat, apparently, in her walking, following the palanquin. Her hands fastened as they were, behind her, she could not draw the garment closed. Briefly I wanted to rip it down from her shoulders. She was woman enough to understand this. She shuddered. Then I drew it together more closely, that the loveliness of her small breasts might be the better concealed.

"You would strip and rape me on the street, if you could, wouldn't you?" she asked.

I wanted to take her in my arms. But I did not know, truly, she fastened as she was, how to do this. Secured as she was she could be taken in one's arms only as a captive or slave girl. That, of course, scarcely seemed proper in the context.

"Wouldn't you?" she asked.

"No," I said, "of course not."

"Oh," she said.

"You are not a Gorean girl," I said.

"That is true," she said.

I looked down at her. "You are looking quite well," I said. It was true. I had never seen her before looking so relaxed and beautiful. And yet she stood before me, helpless in chains. Slavery, of course, reduces tensions in a woman.

"You are looking well yourself," she said.

"I see that you are a display item," I said.

"Yes," she smiled.

"If I owned you, I would show you off, too," I said.

"Beast," she smiled.

"You are wearing a white ribbon," I said.

"So are you," she said.

"I am not white silk," I smiled.

"The ribbon is only to match my tunic," she said. "I am not truly white silk."

"Do you wish to speak in English?" I asked. "Would it be easier?"

She looked about, uneasily. The other girls were not paying us attention. "No," she said, continuing in Gorean. We had both spoken, naturally, in the language of our masters. Masters do not care to hear slaves speak in tongues they do not understand. The slave learns the language of the owner, and learns it well. Her Gorean was quite good. Mine, I thought, was better. Surprisingly, perhaps, we had spoken together in Gorean without really considering the matter. I do not think this was simply because we feared to irritate or offend passing Goreans, who tend to view languages other than their own as barbarous, or because slaves are expected to use a speech intelligible to their masters, but because, for most practical purposes, Gorean had become our language. I am sure, however, we could have conversed readily in English, had we so chosen. After a brief period of readjustment we would have become again at ease in it.

"I was white silk on Earth," she said.

"I did not know that," I said.

"It is scarcely the sort of thing a girl publicly discusses on Earth," she said.

"I suppose not," I said. Such information, of course, would be publicly brandished to buyers in a slave market. "Who first took you?" I asked.

"I do not know," she said. "I was hooded and thrown naked to keepers. I was raped and handed about, passed from brute to brute. They did with me what they pleased."

"I understand," I said. Her ravishing would have been thorough, accomplished by Gorean men. I looked at her. She was beautiful. I envied the brutes who had enjoyed her.

"I was then," she said, "though a girl of Earth, ready to be trained as a slave."

"Of course," I said. I did not press her on the nature of her training.

"I was trained in the House of Andronicus," she said, "and sold in Vonda."

"I, too, was in the House of Andronicus," I said. "I was later purchased by Tima, a slaver, mistress of the House of Tima. I was sold from the market of Tima. That is also in Vonda." I looked at her. "Were you naked, and auctioned?" I asked.

"Yes," she said. "And you?"

"I, too," I said.

She shrugged. "We are only slaves," she said. I looked at her. I realized she had been trained to give pleasure to men. She was beautiful. She would do it well. This pleased me. I envied the lazy brute in the palanquin who owned her. I wished that I owned her. But, of course, I reminded myself, she was not a Gorean girl. She was of Earth.

"You there!" I heard. "What are you doing there?"

I backed quickly away from the girl. I turned. I saw one of the servants, near the side of the palanquin, with a whip, gesture me angrily away. Then he turned again to talk with his fellows.

"Who is your master?" I called to the girl.

She looked at me, frightened, and now stood very straight, facing the back of the palanquin.

"Fearful slave," I said, angrily. She was afraid to speak.

"To whom do you belong?" asked a blond girl, she who was last in the coffle line.

"My Mistress is the Lady Florence of Vonda," I said.

"You belong to a woman?" she asked.

"Yes," I said.

"I do not believe it," she said.

"It is true," I said.

"You are a silk slave?" she asked.

"Yes," I said.

"I was once free," she said. She shrugged her shoulders, moving her wrists in the bracelets.

"Now you serve men well," I said.

"Of course," she said.

"Who owns you?" I asked.

"Beware," she said. "Strabar is coming!"

"Stand where you are!" I heard.

I turned about. The servant, with his whip, approached me. He stopped some dozen feet or so from me. "Do not move," he said.

I stood still.

He turned to the girls. "Which of you wenches dared to speak to this slave?" he asked.

The girls were silent.

"It was this one, wasn't it?" he grinned, touching the small, exquisite, dark-haired girl with whom I had been engaged in converse with his whip. She shuddered.

"It was she whom I accosted," I said. "If there is blame here, it is mine, not hers."

"Bold slave," he smiled.

"We are of the world called Earth," I said to him. "We knew one another there."

"It is not permitted for you to speak to her," he said.

"I did not know," I said, "I am sorry, Master."

He regarded me. Then he looked again at the girl. "She is a pretty one, isn't she?" he asked.

"Yes, Master," I said.

"Remain where you are," he said.

"Yes, Master," I said. I was puzzled that he had, originally, ordered me to stand, rather than kneel. The day was hot, of course. Perhaps he did not feel like beating me. Too, he did not seem too bad a fellow. I noted that I had now come to the attention of the two men in the palanquins. This made me somewhat uneasy. Then I saw the draft slaves turning about and both of the palanquins were borne near to me. Then, at a gesture from the masters, the palanquins were lowered to the ground. The draft slaves, who were not chained, then stood free. I found myself, thus, in the center of several individuals, the men in the palanquins, various servants, the slave girls, and the draft slaves. Too, some passers-by stopped to see what would occur.

"Who owns you?" asked one of the men in the palanquins, that behind which, with other girls, was chained the girl with whom I had been in converse.

I knelt. He was clearly a master. "The Lady Florence of Vonda is my mistress, Master," I said.

He gestured that I should rise. He took from a tiny box attached to the interior of the palanquin a circular glass mounted on a pearled wand. He then looked back at the girls chained behind his palanquin. He examined the girl with the glass, she to whom I had been talking. "Did you know that girl on your own world?" he asked.

"Yes, Master," I said.

"Was she free there?" he asked.

"Yes, Master," I said.

"Look upon her now," he said.

I did so.

"She is now a slave," he said.

"Yes, Master," I said.

The girl shrank back, suddenly, in her chains, and gasped. She looked at me in fear. I licked my lips. Then I shook my head, to clear it of the way in which I had suddenly, for an instant, seen her. I had seen her, in that instant, not in wonder and pleasure, as I had before, but from the point of view of uncompromising manhood, in triumph and pleasure, as the most suitable and fit object possible for the exercise of masculine power and desire, as what she now was, and only was, a beautiful female slave.

The masters, and the servants, laughed. Even some of the draft slaves laughed. The girl was sobbing. Again I shook my head, to clear away the violent and exciting memory, that recollection of the instant in which I had seen the girl as what she now was, and only was, a slave. It struck me with incredible force that not only could she be owned, but that she was owned, literally. When I had looked at the girl several of the other girls had quickly sucked in their breath. The breasts of some were rising and falling with excitement. The bodies of others, in their brief tunics, had blushed crimson. I saw more than one girl looking at me. Doubtless they, too, from time to time, here and there, had been looked upon honestly, as slave females.

"Did you see that?" asked one of the men in the palanquins, he whom I took to be the girl's owner, to his friend.

"Yes," said the other.

I blushed in shame, that I had, though only for an instant, looked upon the girl as a slave. How shamed, and offended, she must have been! But, of course, she now was a slave, only a slave.

"Granus, Turus," said the man in the palanquin, that to which the girl's coffle was chained.

I looked to the girl, but she would not meet my gaze. How sorry I was then that I had looked upon her as might have a Gorean male. She was not a Gorean girl. She was of Earth. Did I not know that? Yet she was surely beautiful, and a legally imbonded slave.

I heard a grunt near me. I spun about. A fist struck me in the side of the head. Then I was kicked, and punched in the side. I gasped, stumbling back. Two of the draft slaves were upon me, pounding and kicking. I rolled under one of them, and leaped to my feet, bloody.

"Granus struck him a goodly blow," said someone.

"I saw," said another.

"And he is again on his feet," observed another.

"Interesting," said someone.

"He is a strong fellow," said another.

I wiped blood from the side of my head. I stood, unsteadily.

The man in the palanquin gestured toward me with his glass, that on the pearled wand.

The first of the two draft slaves again approached me, his great fists balled into hammerlike weapons. "When I strike you again," he said, "do not get up. It will be enough for the masters."

I gasped for breath.

Then he lunged toward me. I tried to defend myself. His left fist struck into my stomach, doubling me over, and then his right fist struck me against the left side of the face. I sprawled sideways, losing my footing, slipping to the stones. I was half kneeling, half lying, on the stones.

The draft slave turned away from me.

"Look," called someone. "He is on his feet again!"

I stood, unsteadily.

The draft slave, he whom I took to be Granus, turned again, surprised, to face me. He and his fellow looked at one another.

"Run," said the servant, the fellow with the whip, who stood near to me. "Run."

I saw that none blocked my alley of retreat. "No," I said. "No."

"It is a fight!" called someone, excitedly.

Again the fellow in the palanquin indicated me, bemused, with the glass on the pearled wand.

Again the large draft slave lunged toward me. Twice more, brutally, he struck me, as I stumbled backward, and then I had seized him, holding him, trying to clear my head, trying not to let him gain again the leverage to strike such telling blows. I heard him grunt. My arms were tightening on him. I began to bend him backwards. There was blood on his body then, mine, and on my tunic. "No," he grunted. Suddenly I saw he was frightened. Further I pressed him backward. Then, suddenly, terrified, I realized what I might do to him.

"Stop!" called the man with the whip.

I let the draft slave fall. His back had not been broken. I knew nothing of fighting, but I had discovered, it frightening me, that there was in me, somehow, strength which I had not understood. I recalled lifting the bench in the cell in the House of Andronicus. The exercises and the physical trainings to which I had been subjected there I had, not really thinking about it, kept up.

"Are you a fighting slave?" asked someone.

"No," I said.

The man with the whip looked to the man in the palanquin. "Interesting," said the man in the palanquin.

"Is it enough?" asked the man with the whip.

"Yes," said the man in the palanquin. I suddenly realized that he did not wish to risk a slave.

The man in the palanquin lifted the glass on the pearled wand and, again, the draft slaves took their places. The man with the whip joined other servants beside the palanquin. In a moment the two palanquins, with their respective retinues, were taking their respective departures. I stood, bloody, unsteadily, in the street.

The crowd dissipated.

Suddenly, angrily, I ran after the departing palanquin, that behind which the exquisite, dark-haired girl, she to whom I had been earlier speaking, was one of the chained, displayed beauties. I slipped, unnoticed by the man in the palanquin and his servants, behind the blond-haired girl, she who had told me she had once been free, who was the last in the right-hand coffle, that lovely string of chained women.

My hand closed on the back of the blond girl's neck.

She gasped, startled.

"Who is your master?" I asked.

"We are not permitted to speak in coffle," she said. "Oh!" she said. My hand had tightened on her neck.

"Who is your master?" I asked, walking behind her.

"Oneander of Ar," she said, "of the merchants. He does business in Vonda."

I did not release her neck.

"You are not a silk slave," she said, in pain, held.

"Oneander of Ar?" I asked.

"Yes," she said.

"Yes, what?" I asked. My grip tightened.

"Yes—Master!" she said. I released her, and she stumbled ahead, following in her place. She looked back, frightened. Then she again set her eyes ahead. She was not an Earth girl, of course. She was only a Gorean girl, and a slave, a woman fit to be done with as men please.

I walked to the side of the street, looking after the palanquin, with its attached coffles.

I knew I should return to the shop of Philebus. If my mistress emerged from the shop and I was not there, she would not be pleased. But, on an impulse, I followed, for a time, behind it and on its left, the double coffle.

Doubtless I attracted some attention, for I was bleeding and, as I discovered, the silk tunic I wore had been soiled from the street and torn at the left sleeve; too, it was stained with my blood; but no one said anything to me. Perhaps they were wary of one who looked as though he might be distraught, or dangerous.

I followed the double coffle on its left, for it was on the left side of her body that the exquisite, dark-haired girl's short, loose silk had been hitched up, baring her branded thigh to the hip. I observed her in the coffle, neck-chained, her small wrists, above the rounded flesh of her palms and below the sweet, rounded flesh of her small forearms, locked in the steel of slave bracelets. She was surely the most exciting, and desirable and beautiful woman I had ever seen. Earlier I had been almost stunned with the sight of her beauty.

I smiled to myself.

I now knew who owned her, Oneander of Ar, a merchant who apparently did business in Vonda. It would have been in Vonda, I supposed, that he had purchased her. It seemed a shame that he apparently kept her primarily as a display item. Perhaps, upon occasion, he used her, and the other girls, or had them thrown to his men. I wondered if she would make a good love slave. I supposed not, for she was of Earth. It was difficult to imagine her kneeling before a man, helplessly aroused, weeping, begging to be raped.

I drifted about, to the right side of the coffle lines, and stopped, watching the lines, chained behind the palanquin, making their way down the street.

I saw the blond-haired girl, the last one in the right-hand coffle line, turn about, in her chain and collar. She was curious, apparently, to see if I still followed. She smiled. I grinned at her. I had made her use the word 'Master' to me. Then she looked ahead again. But her body moved, suddenly, as that of a slave girl. I smiled. She might once have been free but now, clearly, she was only a slave. She was aroused. When she returned to the house of her master I had little doubt but what she would kneel to the nearest keeper and beg to be used, perhaps to be given for an Ahn, hooded, to the male slave of his choice.

I stood on the stones of the avenue of the Central Cylinder. I looked after the palanquin, with its twin chains of enslaved beauties.

I considered, again, the small, exquisite, dark-haired girl. I had never expected to see her again. Then I had done so. What a transformation had been wrought in her. I had been almost overcome by her beauty. I could not drive it from my mind.

I reminded myself, interestingly, that Earth women were imported to Gor doubtless precisely to be love slaves. I wondered if Gorean men knew something interesting about the women of Earth that the men of Earth did not know.

The palanquin, with its chained girls, had now disappeared down the street.

The dark-haired girl on Earth, of course, had been extremely beautiful, but her beauty then, considerable though it might have been, could not even have begun to bear comparison with what it now was. I stood upon the street, recollecting her with astonishment. I would never have dreamed she could have become so delicately and incredibly beautiful. It seemed almost incomprehensible to me. It was the first time, of course, I had seen Beverly Henderson, of Earth, as a slave girl.

Then I turned about, to hurry back to the shop of Philebus.

"Jason! Jason!" cried the Lady Florence, angrily. "Where have you been?"

I quickly knelt before her, head down.

"Down the street, Mistress," I said.

"Look at yourself!" she cried. "You have been fighting!"

I glanced quickly at the silk slave fastened by the neck to the slave ring on the other side of the girl at the nearer ring. He grinned at me. I realized he must have told Lady Florence all that had occurred.

"I cannot leave you alone for a moment!" said the Lady Florence. "You have kept me waiting! I cannot turn my back for an instant but you are in trouble. Do you not know I have been finished shopping for a quarter of an Ahn!"

"No, Mistress," I said.

"He ran away," said the male silk slave.

"No," I said. "I was just down the street."

"Did you rape this poor slave?" demanded the Lady Florence, angrily gesturing to the leashed girl at the ring.

"Forgive us, Mistress," begged the girl, who was kneeling and trembling. She put her head down as far as she could, given the leash and collar.

"I took her," I admitted.

"Took her!" cried the Lady Florence.

"She was thirsty," I said. "She wanted water. I made her pay for it with her use."

"Beast!" said the Lady Florence.

"Yes, Mistress," I said.

"Your tunic is torn," she said. "You are bloody. Are you hurt?"

"No, Mistress," I said.

She spun to face the girl at the ring, who trembled. "You sold your use for a drink of water?" she asked.

"Yes, Mistress," said the girl.

"Slut!" cried the Lady Florence.

"Yes, Mistress," said the girl.

"Low, disgusting slaves!" said the Lady Florence. "How fit that you should be in collars!"

"He accosted a slave girl in a retinue, too," volunteered the silk slave at the ring on the other side of the girl. "It was there that he was fighting."

"I do not know what I am going to do with you, Jason," said the Lady Florence. "You did not wait for me here. You abused this poor girl. You accosted a strange slave. You have been fighting. Your tunic is soiled, and torn, and bloody. It is almost too much!"

"Yes, Mistress," I said.

"Do you think that you are a quarry slave, or a draft slave?" she asked.

"No, Mistress," I said.

"I am a lady," she said. "And you are a lady's silk slave!"

"Yes, Mistress," I said.

"Have no fear but what you will be well punished when we return to Venna," she said.

"Yes, Mistress," I said.

"It will be close chains for two days for you," she said.

I would not look forward to that. Usually, in close chains, the wrists and ankles are chained closely together. Over a period of time this builds up, understandably, a considerable amount of body pain. Usually after only five Ahn in close chains a girl is ready to serve delightfully and willingly.

"Do you understand, Jason?" she asked.

"Yes, Mistress," I said.

I glanced at the male silk slave, who was sitting on the

walk, coupled by his neck to the ring behind him, smiling. I
wanted to break in his face.

"Bring the tharlarion, Jason," said the Lady Florence.

"Yes, Mistress," I said.

In a few moments I had freed and fetched the tharlarion.

I felt a chain leash snapped about my throat. The Lady
Florence put it there. The other end was attached to her stirrup. "I am afraid this is necessary, Jason," she said.

"Yes, Mistress," I said.

"Help me into the saddle," she said. I lifted her sandaled
foot upward, and she took her place in the leather seat at the
side of the tharlarion's back. It has stirrups, into which I
helped her place her feet, but it is not exactly a saddle as
those of Earth would think of one, even of the sort usually
designated as a sidesaddle. It is somewhat more in the nature
of a stirruped seat. It is at the height of the beast's back,
cushioned, held there by straps. She hooked herself into the
seat, or, if one prefers, saddle. As I had lifted her into the
seat I had seen her ankle. It was a good one, as I knew. I had
never held her in my arms. When she used me, as she did
frequently, I was chained on her couch.

"Philebus!" she called.

A man, accompanied by a servant, appeared at the door of
the shop. He was balding, and benign. A servant, behind him,
carried several packages. I lifted the reins of the tharlarion to
the Lady Florence.

"Thank you, Jason," she said.

"Yes, Mistress," I said.

I looked at the eyes of Philebus. His eyes were troubled.
The servant came out on the walk and handed me several
packages. He looked at me, irritably. "Thank you, Master," I
said to him.

"Good, Jason," said the Lady Florence.

"Yes, Mistress," I said.

"I wish you well, Lady Florence," said the shopkeeper.

"I, too, wish you well, Philebus," she said. Philebus was actually of Turia. He managed his shop, however, in Ar. He
had lived in Ar for several years.

The Lady Florence guided her tharlarion out into the
street. I accompanied her, carrying the packages, chained by
the neck to that stirrup in which was placed her left foot. Her
body was turned somewhat in the saddle, so that she might
the more easily guide the beast she rode.

"You embarrassed me today, Jason," she said.

"Forgive me, Mistress," I said.

"Did you truly use the slave girl at the ring?" she asked.

"Yes, Mistress," I said.

"Disgusting," she said.

"Yes, Mistress," I said.

"Did you use her," she asked, "—as a slave girl?"

I thought about the matter. "Yes," I said.

"Ah," she said. She looked down at me. It was not easy to read her eyes.

Then she looked away, again guiding the tharlarion. "What of the little slut in the refinue?" she asked.

"Mistress?" I asked.

"Was she pretty?" she asked.

"Yes, Mistress," I said.

"Was she in coffle?" she asked.

"Yes, Mistress," I said.

"How is it then that you, a slave, dared to speak to a girl in coffle?" she asked.

"I did not know it might not be permitted," I said.

"It is fortunate that your tongue was not cut out," she said.

"Yes, Mistress," I said.

"Did you know her?" she asked.

"I had known her on Earth," I said. "We are now both slaves."

"Of course," she said.

"Yes, Mistress," I said.

"Jason," she said.

"Yes, Mistress," I said.

"We are leaving Ar tonight, not tomorrow, as I had planned."

"Why, Mistress?" I asked.

"I spoke to Philebus," she said. "He advises me to leave the city soon. I fear there may be trouble between Ar and the Salerian Confederation."

I nodded. I had gathered that there might be trouble brewing. I myself had seen the movement of troops.

"You would not like to see me in a collar, would you, Jason?" she asked, a smile in her voice.

I did not respond.

"Jason?" she asked.

"I think you would be very beautiful in a collar, Mistress," I said.

I saw her hand reach for a quirt at the side of the saddle, but then she did not grasp it. She put back her head, and laughed, merrily. "You are a beast," she said.

"Yes, Mistress," I said.

"We will leave the city within the Ahn," she said, "by the great gate."

"Yes, Mistress," I said.

# 14 A MISTRESS EXPRESSES CURIOSITY AS TO THE TOUCH OF MEN; A MISTRESS COMMANDS HER SILK SLAVE TO TAKE HER IN HIS ARMS

"Is that you, Jason?" she asked, not turning to look.

"Yes, Mistress," I said. She knew that it was I. She stood on the wide balcony, with its low balustrade, outside her chamber. I stood within the chamber. We were within her house in the resort city of Venna, noted for its baths and tharlarion races. It was early evening.

She turned, and entered the chamber. I knelt, in silk.

"Am I pretty?" she asked. She turned before me, the gown of sheer, scarlet silk, almost diaphanous, like slave silk, swirling about her.

"Yes, Mistress," I said. She was indeed pretty, even beautiful. She was some five feet five inches in height and sweetly figured. Her face was rounded, rather oval. Her eyes were blue; her hair, which was long, and now unbound, was auburn.

"You are even beautiful, Mistress," I said.

"How obsequious are silk slaves," she laughed, but was pleased.

"It is true, Mistress," I said. It was true.

"Do you like the gown?" she asked.

"Yes, Mistress," I said.

"I thought you might like it," she said. "I purchased it at the shop of Philebus, in Ar."

I thought that might be true. I had not seen it before.

"Do you think it is too much like—like slave silk?" she asked.

"I do not know, Mistress," I said.

She laughed.

We had been in Venna now for five days. Two of these days I had spent in close chains, being punished for my behavior in Ar. I was still somewhat sore. This was the first night, since our return to Venna, that she had commanded me to her chamber. My relationship with the mistress, interestingly, was now somewhat different than it had been before our trip to Ar. Though she had professed distress at my actions and had subjected me to appropriate discipline, I sensed that she was not entirely displeased with me. She was rather proud, I think, though she would not have admitted this, to be the mistress of a possibly unruly slave. That I had been a bit forward and rowdy, I think, had pleased her. She did not fear me, personally, of course, for I was her slave. Once, after our return to Venna, I had heard her discussing me with some of her women friends. "Are you not afraid to own such a slave?" asked one. She had laughed. "I keep him on his knees," she had said. Another time, in the halls, she had passed me while I was polishing a large, brass vase. Two slave girls, too, owned by my mistress, barefoot, in collars and tunics, had been in the vicinity, chatting, balancing wicker laundry baskets on their heads. "Better keep the slave girls away from this one," she had said to a nearby keeper, indicating me. They had laughed. It had been a joke, of course. To so much as touch one of the mistress' slave girls without her permission could be punishable by death. Yet I thought it of interest that the mistress had made the joke. She was not truly displeased, I think, that I had misbehaved in Ar. The girls had then, the baskets on their heads, laughing, fled away. Their bare feet had pattered on the tiles. The one on the right, Taphris, short-legged and luscious, was not without interest.

"Rise, Jason," said my mistress.

I rose to my feet. I reached to my tunic, to discard it. "Shall I take my place on your couch, Mistress?" I asked. I glanced at the broad, furred couch, and the cunning chains upon it, which had so often confined me for her pleasure.

"No," she said. I could not read her expression. Standing, of course, I towered over her. I dropped my hands, leaving the tunic alone.

"Jason," she said.

"Yes, Mistress," I said.

She turned away from me, and went out onto the balcony. The three moons were now high. We could hear insects in the hedged gardens beneath and beyond the balcony. We could see the lights of Venna, too. The baths were still open. The house of the Mistress was in the Telluria section, which is in the northwest part of the city, on a hill. It is the preferred residential section of Venna. The house, situated as it was, provided us with a lovely panorama of the small city.

"Jason," she said, not looking back, "come with me out upon the balcony."

I joined her on the balcony, near the balustrade.

"I am very rich, Jason," she said, "but, too, I am very lonely. Too, I am restless. I do not know why."

I did not speak. Mistresses, I knew, often spoke intimately to their silk slaves.

"I am certain that there are needs in me, longings," she said, "which are not satisfied."

"Yes, Mistress," I said.

"But I do not know, truly, what they are," she said.

"Yes, Mistress," I said.

"I know only that I am desperately unhappy," she said.

"I am sorry, Mistress," I said.

"I saw the coupling of sleen today," she said. "The female fought. Then the male seized her by the throat with his fangs. She became immediately docile. Soon she writhed in heat. I have seen the male urt drive his female into a corner, whence soon she squeals with pleasure. The female larl, her flanks bleeding, yields to the male, after which she bears his young and hunts for him. The verr and bosk select out the females that please them and herd them to the place of their choice." She looked out, bitterly, over the gardens. "In all these relationships," she said, "it is the male, always the male, who is master. And the females, disgustingly, do not seem discontent. What is the meaning of it?"

"I do not know, Mistress," I said.

"Today," she said, "I saw slave girls, meaningless sluts in collars, with scarcely a rag to cover their nakedness. They seemed joyful and happy! What is the meaning of it?"

"I do not know, Mistress," I said.

"Nor I," she said, bitterly. She looked out over the gardens. "They are slave, and are happy," she said. "I am free, and am unhappy. I do not understand it."

I said nothing.

"No one is concerned to make them happy," she said. "It is they who must make others happy. It is they who must yield, and obey, and serve, and love and be pleasing."

"Yes, Mistress," I said.

"So why, then," she asked, "should they be happy, and I not?"

"I do not know, Mistress," I said.

"I am advised, Jason," she said, "by certain of my friends to accept a companion."

"I did not know that," I said.

"Many men, young and rich, have desired to become my companion. Such matches, in many cases, would profitably increase our common holdings. Yet I have until now, at least, turned them all away. I have remained independent."

"Yes, Mistress," I said.

"I have seen many companionships," she said. "Yet more often than not I have seen the male companion keep sluts of slave girls on the side, and, I think, it is only those sluts he cares for." Her voice was bitter. "Why," she asked, "should a man forsake a noble companion, serene and beautiful, independent and regal, for a slut in a steel collar who will crawl to his feet and beg to lick them with her tongue?"

I did not speak.

"Beast!" she said.

"Yes, Mistress," I said.

"How I hate men!" she cried.

"Yes, Mistress," I said.

"Yet," she said, "they stir me. Oh, I do not mean you, Jason, a silk slave, but true men."

"Yes, Mistress," I said.

She continued to look out over the gardens. "They disturb me," she said. "They make me uneasy."

I said nothing.

"I am curious about them," she said. "I wonder, sometimes, what it would be like to be naked in their arms."

I did not speak.

"I have never been in the arms of a man, Jason," she said. This did not, truly, surprise me. She had used me many times, of course, but she had never permitted me to hold her in my arms. I had, of course, under her direction, kissed, licked and caressed her. I had given her much pleasure but she, a woman of lofty position, of high social station, rich and free, had never let me hold her. It had been one of the enraging frustrations of my slavery that I had never been permitted, truly, to hold a woman and subject her to my will. The only girl I had truly had on Gor was a slave who had been leashed to a ring outside the shop of Philebus in Ar. It had been a joy to have her. I did not even know her name, or master, nor had she known my name or the name of my Mistress. We had been only two slaves, one leashed and tied, coupling in the shadow of a slave ring on a hot day in Ar.

She turned about, suddenly, and faced me. "Take me in your arms, Jason," she said.

I took her, suddenly, in my arms, and began to press kisses about her throat. "No," she whispered. "Oh," she cried. The gown lay about her ankles. "Jason," she said. I lifted her, naked, from her feet and carried her toward the couch. Her weight was nothing for me. Her hands were behind my neck. She kissed me under the neck, then she turned her head away, horrified that she had put her lips to the body of a slave. I stopped before I reached the couch. She looked up at me. She kissed me on the chest. "No, no," she said, weeping. But I carried her then again toward the couch. "No," she said. I placed her on the couch. I sat beside her. I then pulled her by the arms into a sitting position, and held her. "No," she said. "No!" My arms tightened on her. She struggled, but could not begin to free herself. "Is this what it is to be in the arms of a man?" she asked, weeping. "This is only the beginning of what it is to be in the arms of a man," I told her. "You're holding me too tightly," she said. "You are hurting me!" "Oh!" she cried, as my grip tightened yet more upon her. I then pressed her to her back on the deep furs of the couch. She looked up at me, wildly. I lowered my head toward her small, fair mouth. "Stop, Slave!" she cried. "Stop!"

I released her, and stood up. She knelt on the couch, trembling wildly, crying. She pointed at me. "Get out!" she cried. "Get out!"

I left her chamber.

"I will have you beaten!" she cried after me. "I will have you beaten!"

# 15   I AM BEATEN;
## THE MISTRESS SPEAKS
## WITH ME

I stood below the whipping ring, my wrists crossed and tied over my head.

I jerked under the second blow of the snake. I did not cry out. Present were only two keepers, one of whom wielded the whip, and the Lady Florence.

I felt blood running down my back.

"Hold," said the Lady Florence. She came to stand quite near to me, near my left shoulder. We were on a colonnaded porch on the south side of her house.

"Do you understand why you are being whipped, Jason?" she asked.

"I displeased my Mistress," I said.

"You are not weeping under the lash," she said.

I shrugged. I was angry.

"I have thought much about what happened last night," she said. "It has been much on my mind."

I said nothing.

"I did not sleep well," she said.

"I am sorry, Mistress," I said. A tincture of bitterness, or irony, doubtless, infected my voice.

"Are you angry, Jason?" she asked.

I shrugged. My back hurt. I felt sick.

"I was not entirely displeased, as I now think about it," she said, "that you took me in your arms." She spoke softly. The others, standing back, could not hear.

"I thought Mistress commanded me to take her in my arms," I said. "It seems that I was mistaken."

"It is how you took me in your arms," she said.

"Oh?" I asked.

"I am a Lady," she said.

"Yes, Mistress," I said.

"You held me too tightly," she said.

"You would direct a man on how to take you?" I asked.

"Take me?" she said, angrily.

"Of course," I said.

"I am a free woman," she said.

"Yes, Mistress," I said.

"I could have you beaten to death," she said.

"Yes, Mistress," I said.

"Are you angry with me, Jason?" she asked.

"No, Mistress," I said.

"I am Mistress," she said.

"Of course, Mistress," I said. "I understand that well, Mistress."

"Yet your hands were not entirely displeasing on my body," she said.

"Mistress should be a slave girl," I said.

"Surely you understand that you are tied, and at my mercy," she said.

I moved my wrists in the leather bonds that held them. I had been tied, expertly, by a keeper. I was held fast.

"Yes, Mistress," I said.

"I could have you beaten to death, or tortured, and slain," she said.

"Yes, Mistress," I said.

"Yet you dare to speak to me so boldly?" she asked.

"Yes, Mistress," I said.

"Beat him," she said. She stepped away from me. Three more times the snake fell against my back.

"Hold," she said.

I was still on my feet. I struggled to remain so. I could scarcely see. "He is strong, Lady Florence," said the man who had struck the blows. He was a short, powerful man, Kenneth, a free man, a keeper and the first groom in her stables. I had not once lost my footing. I recalled that in the House of Andronicus I had once received five blows of the snake. After the second I had hung in the straps, helpless, weeping, crying out for mercy.

"Do you still think your Mistress should be a slave girl?" she asked.

"Yes, Mistress," I said.

"Beat him," she said. Five more times the snake fell upon my back. Then, again, she cried out, "Hold."

"Do you still think your Mistress should be a slave girl?" she asked.

"Yes, Mistress," I said, through gritted teeth.

"Why?" she demanded.

"Because you are exciting and beautiful," I said.

"Flattering slave!" she laughed.

I did not speak.

"But I am exciting and beautiful as a free woman," she said.

"It is true, Mistress," I said. "But the excitement and beauty of a free woman is as nothing compared to the excitement and beauty of a slave girl."

"Beast!" she laughed. But I think she knew that it was true.

"Is he to be beaten further?" asked Kenneth, the keeper and groom.

"Do you wish to be beaten further, Jason?" she asked.

"No, Mistress," I said.

"Beg my forgiveness for your insolence." she said.

"I beg forgiveness for my insolence," I said.

"Are you ready to obey me in all particulars and be fully pleasing?" she asked.

"Yes, Mistress," I said.

"Very well," she said. "I forgive you." Then she turned to the fellow with the whip, Kenneth. "Five more blows," she said.

I looked at her.

"I have forgiven you, Jason," she said. "But surely you must understand that punishment for your insolence must still be meted out to you."

"Yes, Mistress," I said.

Five more times the snake fell against my back.

"He is still on his feet," said one of the two men in the room, he who did not hold the whip.

"That he is," said he who wielded the whip, Kenneth, the groom.

"He is strong," said the Lady Florence, my mistress. There was a pride in her voice.

"Is he to be beaten further?" asked Kenneth.

"No," she said, "it is enough." She walked about to where

she could look at me. "Cut him down," she said. "Then with-draw. I will tell you when to fetch him to his kennel."

The strap which held my bound wrists was cut away from the ring to which it was tied.

I crouched down, under the ring. I did not collapse to the tiles. I was sick. I was aware of the blood on the tiles, beneath me and on my feet. I was aware of the sweat and blood on my body. My hands were still tied before my body. I was conscious of the collar of steel on my neck. I had received fifteen blows of the snake. I knew that twenty blows of that fearsome whip could kill some men.

I felt the small hand of my Mistress on my naked shoulder. "You are strong, Jason," she said, "very strong. That pleases me."

I did not speak.

"You must clearly understand, of course, that I am Mistress," she said. "Is that clearly understood?"

"Yes, Mistress," I said.

"I like you, Jason," she said. "You excite me," she whispered. Women think little of speaking intimately to their silk slaves, for such are only their animals.

I felt sweat under the tight leather bands confining my wrists. I breathed heavily.

"Are you angry with me, Jason?" she asked.

"No, Mistress," I said.

"Sometime," she said, "perhaps, if you are a very good boy, I may let you take me again in your arms."

The air was soft and gentle. I could smell flowers in the gardens.

"But you must not hold me too tightly," she said, "and you must do exactly as I tell you."

"Yes, Mistress," I said.

"Kenneth, Barus!" she called.

The two men returned to the area. They had been waiting inside the house, near the portico.

"Return him to his kennel," she said. "Put balm on his wounds. Feed him later. Let him rest. Tomorrow he will run certain errands for me. Tomorrow, in the evening, send him to my chambers."

"Yes, Lady Florence," said Kenneth, who stood first among the two men.

The Lady Florence, then, with a movement of her robes, departed from the porch.

"Have you ever fought?" asked Kenneth, lifting me up, his fellow assisting him.

"No," I said. "No."

"Do not throw up until you reach the kennel," he said.

"Yes, Master," I said.

# 16 THE PERFUME SHOP OF
## TURBUS VEMINIUS;
### I AM CAPTURED

I knelt in the cool recesses of the shop of Turbus Veminius, a perfumer in Venna. Venna has many small and fine shops, catering to the affluent trade of the well-to-do, who patronize the baths and public villas of the area. I, a slave, unaccompanied by a free person, would wait until free customers were waited upon and served. I could smell perfumes and their mixings in the long shop behind the counter. There, at various benches, attending to their work, measuring and stirring, were apprentice perfumers. Though one is commonly born into a caste one is often not permitted to practice the caste craft until a suitable apprenticeship has been served. This guarantees the quality of the caste product. It is possible, though it is seldom the case, that members of a caste are not permitted to practice specific caste skills, though they may be permitted to practice subsidiary skills. For example, one who is of the Metalworkers might not be permitted to work iron, but might be permitted to do such things as paint iron, and transport and market it. Caste rights, of course, such as the right to caste support in time of need and caste sanctuary, when in flight, which are theirs by birth, remain theirs. The women of a given caste, it should be noted, often do not engage in caste work. For example, a woman in the Metalworkers does not, commonly, work at the forge, nor is a woman of the Builders likely to be found supervising the construction of fortifications. Caste membership, for Goreans, is generally a simple matter of birth; it is not connected necessarily with the performance of certain skills, nor the attainment of a given level of proficiency in such skills. To be sure, certain skills tend to be associated traditionally with certain castes, a fact which is clearly indicated in caste titles, such as the Leatherworkers, the Metalworkers, the Singers, and the Peasants. A notable exception to the generalization that women of a given caste normally do not engage in caste work is the caste of Physicians, whose women are commonly trained, as are the boys, in the practice of medicine. Even the physicians, however, normally do not admit their women to full practice until they have borne two children. The purpose of this is to retain a high level of intelligence in the caste. Professional women, it is well understood, tend not to reproduce themselves, a situation which, over time, would be likely to produce a diminution in the quality of the caste. Concern for the future of the caste is thus evinced in this limitation by the physicians on the rights of their women to participate without delay in the caste craft. The welfare of the caste, typically, takes priority in the Gorean mind over the ambitions of specific individuals. The welfare of a larger number of individuals, as the Goreans reason, correctly or incorrectly, is more important than the welfare of a smaller number of individuals. I do not argue this. I only report it.

"My thanks, Lady Teela," said Turbus Veminius, proprietor of the shop, accepting coins and handing to a robed woman a tiny vial of perfume. She then left.

The woman of the Physicians, at the age of fifteen, in many cities, wears two bracelets on her left wrist. When she has one child one bracelet is removed; when she has a second child the second bracelet is removed. She may then, if she desires, enter into the full practice of her craft.

Turbus Veminius then turned his attention to another customer.

Caste is important to the Gorean in ways that are difficult to make clear to one whose social structures do not include the relationships of caste. In almost every city, for example, one knows that there will be caste brothers on whom one may depend. Charity, too, for example, is almost always associated with caste rights on Gor. One of the reasons there are so few outlaws on Gor is doubtless that the outlaw, in adopting his way of life, surrenders caste rights. The slave, too, of course, has no caste rights. He stands outside the structure of society. He is an animal. It is said on Gor that only slaves, outlaws and Priest-Kings, rumored to be the rulers of Gor, reputed to live in the remote Sardar Mountains, are without caste. This saying, however, it might be pointed out, as Goreans recognize, is not strictly true. For example, some individuals have lost caste, or been deprived of caste; some individuals have been born outside of caste; certain occupations are not traditionally associated with caste, such as gardening, domestic service and herding; and, indeed, there are entire cultures and peoples on Gor to whom caste is unknown. Similarly, caste lines tend sometimes to be vague, and the relation between castes and subcastes. Slavers, for example, sometimes think of themselves as being of the Merchants, and sometimes as being a separate caste. They do have their own colors, blue and yellow, those of the Merchants being white and gold. Too, are the bargemen of the Southern Cartius a caste or not? They think of themselves as such, but many do not see the matter in the same light. There are, on Gor, it might be mentioned, ways of raising and altering caste, but the Gorean seldom avails himself of these. To most Goreans it would be unthinkable to alter caste. He is generally too proud of his caste and it is too much a part of him for him to think in such terms. It is, too, recognized that all, or most, of the castes perform necessary, commendable or useful functions. The Leatherworker, accordingly, does not spend much time envying the Metalworker, or the Metalworker the Leatherworker, or either the Clothworker, and so on. All need sandals and wallets, and clothes, and metal tools. Each does, however, tend to think of his own caste as something special, and, somehow, I suspect, as being perhaps a little bit preferable to the others. Most Goreans are quite content with their castes; this is probably a function of caste pride. I have little doubt but what the caste structure contributes considerably to the stability of Gorean society. Among other things it reduces competitive chaos, social and economic, and prevents the draining of intelligence and ambition into a small number of envied, prestigious occupations. If one may judge by the outcome of Kaissa tournaments, amateur tournaments as opposed to those in which members of the caste of Players participate, there are brilliant men in most castes.

"Is the perfume of the Lady Kita of Bazi ready?" Turbus Veminius called to the back of the shop.

"No," a voice answered him.

"Do not hurry," called Turbus Veminius. "It must be perfect."

"Yes, Turbus," I heard.

Turbus Veminius then turned, sternly, toward the Lady Kita. She was a small, delicate, brown-skinned woman, with a light yellow veil, common in Bazi. She shrank back. "When was your perfume to be ready, Lady Kita?" he inquired. He did not seem deterred by the two large, smooth-skinned, brownish guards, arms folded, who stood behind her.

"At the fifteenth Ahn," she said, timidly.

"It is now the fourteenth Ahn," he said, casting a meaningful glance at the water clock on the counter to his right.

"I am early," she explained.

"Obviously," he said.

"Yes, Turbus," she said.

"Return at the fifteenth Ahn, and not before," he said.

"Yes, Turbus," she said.

The Lady Kita turned about and hurried, followed by her guards, from the shop.

Turbus Veminius looked after her. He, like many perfumers, and hairdressers and cosmeticians, treated his female clientele almost as though they were slave girls. Indeed, he was famous for once having said, "They are all slave girls." Yet, in spite of the gruff, authoritarian way in which they might be handled, and the rude, peremptory fashion in which they might be addressed, women, and high-caste women, for no reason that was clear to me, flocked to his shop. He was, of course, one of the foremost perfumers of Gor. His prices, it might be mentioned, were beyond the reach of all but the very wealthy. It might also be mentioned that he did not deal at all in slave perfumes.

"Will the perfume of the Lady Kita be ready at the fifteenth Ahn?" Turbus called back to someone in the shop.

"I do not know," said the voice.

"Do not hurry it," he said. "If it is not ready, I will order her to wait, or to return tomorrow. It must be perfect."

"Yes, Turbus," I heard.

I smiled at the thought of ordering a free woman to wait, or to come back tomorrow, and knowing that she would obey you. "They are all slave girls," Turbus Veminius was once reputed to have said.

He then turned his attention to a new customer. She hurried deferentially forward.

I knelt on the tiles. It was warm outside, but cool inside, in the shade. I smelled the perfumes of the shop, many of which were being blended by hand from signature recipes in the back of the shop. Signature recipes are unique, and secret. They are the result of a perfumer's consultations and experiments, the outcome of an effort to devise the perfect perfume for a given woman, though perhaps relativized to a time of day and mood. A wealthy woman may have as many as ten or fifteen signature recipes, each different. They are called signature recipes not only because they are individualized to a given woman but because the recipe bears the perfumer's signature, indicating that he accepts it as a perfume worthy of his house. These recipes, interestingly, are kept on file in the perfumer's strong boxes. The ingredients and processing remain the secrets of the perfumer. There are also, of course, perfumes associated with a given house, which may be purchased by more than one woman. These recipes are sometimes, by an extension of usage, also called signature recipes. They are, at any rate, supposedly unique to given houses. Also, of course, there are hundreds of more standard perfumes, the preparation of which is widely understood by the perfumers of many cities. Slave perfumes, of course, are an entirely different area. These are usually heavier scents, and more sensual, than those used by free women, scents more fitting to a woman who must obey, and perfectly. There are hundreds of slave perfumes, as there are hundreds of perfumes for free women. The perfumes of Gor, as those of Earth have not, have given special attention to the development of perfumes for slaves. There is thus, on Gor, a subtle and complex variety of slave perfumes available, exciting, provocative, sensuous and unmistakable. There are perfumes for the slave in any woman on Gor. Sometimes, though this is more expensive, a girl is brought in to the perfumers by her master for a consultation; the perfumer then questions the girl, orders her about, and may even caress her; then, in the light of her background and history, and intellectual and physiological nature, he recommends a perfume, or blend of perfumes, for her; this perfume, or blend of perfume, is thus, in its way, matched to her unique beauty and bondage. Most slave girls, however, feel that an individualized perfume is not necessary. Too, they often wish to use a variety of perfumes, depending on various factors, such as the time of day and their own moods, and those of the master. Too, many girls are stimulated by wearing a perfume that they know, like the collar and the brand, is common to many slaves. It can make them feel their bondage even more deeply and sensuously. Perhaps, as one slave girl once said, "What difference does it make what slave perfume we wear? They all excite us. They all teach us that we are slaves."

Turbus Veminius had now finished with the customer on whom he had been waiting.

He looked at me. I put my head down, before a free man. He did not summon me forward. I must still wait.

I heard a man outside in the street, selling bread.

I lifted my head. Turbus Veminius was no longer paying me any attention.

"Is the perfume of the Lady Kita of Bazi ready?" he called to the back of the shop. He cast a glance at the water clock.

"It is done," said a voice. "It requires now only your approval."

Turbus then left the counter, and went to the back of the shop.

It is not unusual, on Gor, incidentally, for the articles sold in a shop to be manufactured on or near the premises. This is often the case with craft products, such as glassware, metalware, particularly gold and silver work, rugs and mats, sandals and jewelry. The tradesman, thus, closely supervises the production, and controls the quality of the articles he markets. There are also, of course, many shops which specialize in the sale of, so to speak, foreign goods. A major difference between Gorean shopping and that on Earth is that on Gor there are few stores of a general nature, handling a large variety of goods. One tends, usually, to go from one shop to another, garnering what one needs from a place which specializes in that sort of product. This is inconvenient, perhaps, in some respects, but, at least, one knows that the shopkeeper one visits knows his goods and that the quality of his livelihood is intimately connected with the excellence of his merchandise. The place of general stores is taken largely by bazaars and markets where, quite close to one another, in various booths, sometimes of canvas, one may find a large variety of goods. There are, of course, shopping districts in all Gorean cities, where one may find clusters of shops, often specializing in different items. Sometimes, of course, certain areas specialize in, or are known for, given types of services or products. Each city usually has, for example, its "Street of Coins." On such a street, or in such an area, its banking will largely be done. Similarly most cities will have their "Street

of Brands," on which street, or in which area, one would expect to find the houses of its slavers. It is to one of these
houses, or one of the markets in the area, that one would go
if one wished to buy a woman. As I have mentioned, most
Gorean slaves are female.

Turbus Veminius was still at the back of the shop.

I, glancing to the side, saw two men, large, in brown
tunics, in the doorway of the shop. They seemed an unlikely
pair of fellows to be patrons of the shop of Veminius. They
glanced at me, and then to the back of the shop. They looked
at one another. Then they looked at me again. Then they
turned about and left the shop. I did not know what their
business was. I had seen them twice earlier, this morning,
when I had been on another errand for my Mistress. Once I
had thought they might be following me, men put upon my
trail by my mistress to spy upon me, to see if I were discharging her errands perfectly, or if my eyes might stray to the
ankles of slave girls, but then, as they had turned aside, it
had seemed to me that I must be mistaken. Too, I reminded
myself, to my chagrin, it was unlikely that my mistress would
send men to spy upon me. She was too confident in her control over me, and doubtless rightly so, to feel that there
would be any point in such an action. My Mistress now took
me for granted. No longer did she even give any thought to
any possible recalcitrance on my part. I was now only a
docile, obedient slave. I had been beaten with the snake. The
two men, I surmised, might be ruffians hired to hunt down a
strayed or tardy silk slave. I did not fear them, however, for,
as far as I knew, my collar was in order. It read, I had been
told, 'I am the property of the Lady Florence of Vonda.'
They needed only check my collar to see that I could not be
he whom they might be seeking.

Turbus Veminius had now returned to the counter. He had
with him a small vial of perfume which he had obtained in
the back of the shop. He placed it in a cabinet to one side. It
was doubtless that which had been prepared for the small,
brown-skinned woman, the Lady Kita of Bazi. He glanced at
the water clock. It was five Ehn to the fifteen Ahn. The
Gorean noon is the tenth Ahn. The shadows were now long
outside, on this warm, summer afternoon.

I moved so that I might look a bit out the door. I saw no
sign of the two men in brown. Something about them had
made me apprehensive. I did see two slave girls hurrying

past. It was a bit late now, and they were hurrying home.
When their master arrived home they would be expected to
greet him, kneeling, his meal prepared.

Turbus Veminius looked at me. Again I put my head
down. If he wished me to come forward, he would summon
me.

My hands were bound behind my back, with Gorean binding fiber. Slaves are sometimes sent on errands, thus secured.
About my neck, on a leather string, was tied a small sack. It
contained a note, and coins. I could not read the note, of
course, for I was illiterate in Gorean. I had run my errands
this morning, too, similarly bound and accoutered. I looked
up. The attention of Turbus Veminius was now again elsewhere. He was straightening vials in one of the cabinets on
the side. I moved my hands in the bonds. I shifted my position a little, kneeling now again in the background, aside
from the door. Twice earlier, too, I had been the only one in
the shop but, still, I had not been waited on. Turbus Veminius and one of his fellows had merely spent those times engaged in conversation, pertaining to the tharlarion races. I
had not objected, nor did I object now, of course. I did not
wish to be kicked or beaten, or have a tag wired to my collar,
which would be seen by my Mistress, saying perhaps 'This
slave was impudent. I recommend twenty lashes.'

I thought again of the two slave girls who had been hurrying past, doubtless to arrive home in time to prepare their
masters' meals and then to be ready, bathed, perfumed and in
a bit of silk, kneeling, to greet him. I began to get a bit
uneasy then on my own account. This night, I knew, I was to
be ordered to the chamber of my Mistress. I did not think
she would be pleased if I were late in returning to the house.
I would not relish being whipped again, though presumably it
would not be with the snake, nor being perhaps confined for
another day in close chains.

"May I speak, Master?" I asked.

"No," he said.

"Yes, Master," I said. I glanced at the water clock. It was
now shortly after the fifteenth Ahn.

"Ah," said Turbus Veminius, as the Lady Kita, with her
two guards, entered the shop.

"Is the perfume ready?" she asked.

Turbus Veminius handed her the vial. She removed the
tiny cap and lifted it to her face, which was veiled. She in-

haled delicately through her nose. I saw the veil draw inward.

"What is the meaning of this?" she asked, horrified. "Surely this is slave perfume!"

"No," said Turbus Veminius, "but it, by design, resembles it."

"Surely you do not expect me to pay for this?" she asked.

"Only if you wish to, Lady Kita," he said.

Her eyes, over her veil, were angry.

"You wished a perfume, did you not," asked Turbus Veminius, "to distract your companion from his slave sluts, did you not?"

"Yes," she said.

"This perfume," said Turbus Veminius, "will remind him of what he has forgotten, that you are a woman."

She looked at him, her body rigid with rage.

"But it, in itself," he said, "will do little to improve your situation."

"I do not understand," she said.

"You are, I suspect," said Turbus Veminius, "a pretty little thing. If your companion bought you, naked and collared, in a market, he would doubtless prize you highly."

"Turbus!" she cried, angrily.

"But as his companion you are too much taken for granted," he said.

"It is true," she suddenly sobbed.

"If you would improve your situation somewhat," he said, "I recommend that you learn the arts of the slave girl, and practice them with diligence."

"That would only improve my situation somewhat?" she asked, puzzled.

"Yes," he said, "for you would still be free, and no free woman, because she is free, can truly compete for the attention and affection of a man as can a slave girl."

"Why?" she asked.

"I do not know," said Turbus Veminius. "Perhaps it is simply because the slave girl is a slave girl, truly, and is owned."

"What then am I to do?" she asked.

"You could risk slavery," he said, "expose yourself to possible capture, walk the high bridges at lonely Ahn, picnic in the country, go to paga taverns alone, take dangerous sea voyages."

"But what if I were caught, and enslaved?" she asked.

"You would then be a true slave girl," he said, "and would

doubtless be taught, thoroughly, and more deeply and sensuously than you could ever hope to learn them as a free
woman, for you would then be a slave, the arts of the female
slave."

"But I might never again come into the possession of my
former companion," she said.

"Presumably you would not," he said. "But presumably
you would come into the possession of some man who truly
wanted you, and who was willing to pay good money for
you."

"I brought a large companion price to my companion," she
said. "Perhaps he wanted that more than me."

"I do not know," said Turbus, shrugging.

"He did," she said, bitterly. "He did."

"Perhaps it would be just as well, then," said Turbus, sym-
pathetically, "if you did not come again into his possession."

She put her head down.

"The girl who is bought off the—block," said Turbus,
"knows that it is she herself, and only herself, who is desired.
Nothing else, you understand, is being sold, only the girl."

"Yes, Turbus," she said. "I understand."

"I will take back this perfume," he said. "Obviously you
will not want it."

"No," she said, quickly, lifting her head. "I will take it."

"The price is high," he said, "a golden tarn disk."

"I will pay it," she said, giving him the coin from a small,
beaded purse she held in her hand.

She turned to leave, but then, again, turned to face him.

"Yes?" he asked.

"Do you sell slave perfume, true slave perfume?" she
asked.

"We do not sell perfume for slave sluts in the shop of Veminius," he said, sternly.

"Forgive me, Turbus," she said.

"Try the shop of the Steel Bracelets," he smiled. "It is near
the house of Hassan, on the Street of Brands."

"Thank you, Turbus," she said. She turned again, to leave.

"And do not let them overcharge you," he called after her.
"Five two-hort vials should cost you no more than a copper
tarsk!"

"Yes, Turbus," she said. "Thank you, Turbus." She stopped
in the doorway, but did not turn to face him. "I wish you
well, Turbus," she said.

"I, too, wish you well, Lady Kita," he said.

She looked up at one of the two large guards who stood beside her. Then she lowered her head. He was looking at her, with a curiosity and interest that must have been unsettling for her. She hurried then from the shop, followed by the guards.

Turbus Veminius looked at me.

"Approach, Slave," he snapped, "and lower your head."

I hurried to him, and put my head down. He took the loop of leather, with its tiny sack, from my head.

"You are Jason," he asked, "the slave of the Lady Florence of Vonda?" He was looking at the note, extracted from the sack.

"Yes, Master," I said.

"Her perfume was ready yesterday," he said. He went to one of the cabinets. From the sack he took the coins. They were five silver tarsks. He put them in a drawer. He wrote something on the note, and then he put the note and the vial of perfume in the sack. I again put down my head and he put the sack, on its leather string, about my neck.

"Be careful with that perfume," he said. "It is expensive. It is a signature perfume."

"Yes, Master," I said.

"Is your Mistress beautiful?" he asked.

"Yes, Master," I said.

"Would she look well in a collar?" he asked.

"I am only a poor slave," I said. "How could I form an opinion on that?"

He looked at me, sternly.

"Yes, Master," I said. "She would look well in a collar."

"You are a big fellow," said he. "Have you ever been entered in the stable bouts?"

"No, Master," I said.

"It is growing late," he said. "Perhaps you should hurry home. Your Mistress, hot in her robes, will be wondering where you are."

I said nothing.

"Must I beat you from the shop with a whip?" he asked.

"No, Master," I said. I turned about.

"It seems a shame for a beautiful woman to waste her time with a silk slave," he said. "She should be crawling, collared, to the feet of a true man."

I said nothing.

"Run!" he said, suddenly. "Run, Slave!"

I ran from the shop.

Outside, almost immediately, I struck against two men. "Forgive me, Masters," I said. But my arms were then held, each arm by one of the men. "I did not mean to strike against you," I said. I was being pulled then along the street. The shadows were long. It was warm, and late in the afternoon. There were only a few people on the street. I saw that the two men who held me were the fellows in the brown tunics whom I had seen earlier. "I am sorry, Masters," I said. "Beat me, and let me go, please." I realized then they were pulling me toward an alley. My feet, bare, scraped on the flat stones of the street. My hands, tied behind me, as they had been while I had run the errands of this morning and the errand of this afternoon, fought the binding fiber. A passing Baker glanced at us. "What do you want of me?" I asked. I was dragged into the alley. "I am Jason, slave to the Lady Florence of Vonda," I said. "I cannot be he whom you seek. Look at my collar. Call a guardsman!" I was thrust along the alley. About fifty yards down the alley was a high-sided tharlarion wagon. It had a canvas cover. I was thrown brutally, back first, against a building near the wagon. My feet were half kicked out from under me. My own weight then half pinned me in place. I saw that these men were accustomed to handling slaves. "Who are you?" I asked. One of the men, from his tunic, drew forth a slave hood. "Who are you? What do you want?" I cried. Then the wadding connected with the hood was thrust into my mouth; in a moment, by buckled straps, fastened behind my neck, it was secured in place. One of the men then threw aside the cover on the wagon. Inside I saw a slave sack and, formed of wood, a small, stout, cord-bound, thick-barred slave cage. Such cages are quite adequate for bound slaves. The hood was then drawn over my head and, by straps, buckled shut under my chin. My feet were kicked then fully from under me. In a moment I felt myself being thrust, doubled up, in a heavy leather sack. My head was then thrust down. The sack was tied shut over my head. The two men then lifted me, helpless in the sack, and placed me in the slave cage. I heard its wooden gate slide down into place. The gate then would have been tied shut.

"Throw down and buckle the cover," I heard.

The canvas on the wagon, then, would have been shut and secured.

In a few moments I could feel the movement of the iron-rimmed, wooden wheels of the wagon over the stones of the alley.

I struggled for a time, but, in the sack, could obtain no leverage. At times I felt my body, captive in the sack, press futilely against the thick, stout bars of the slave cage. I tried to free my wrists but could not begin to do so. They were held perfectly, and would continue to be held perfectly, each a prisoner to the other, until masters might free me. Slave knots had been used, and Gorean binding fiber, designed for the perfect control of slaves and prisoners.

Again I struggled, futilely, irrationally. Then I ceased struggling.

Resistance was useless.

# 17 THE LADY MELPOMENE; THE VENGEANCE OF THE LADY MELPOMENE

"Ah, Jason," said the woman. "You are awake."

I struggled to move, but could not well do so. When the tharlarion wagon had arrived at a house in Venna, I had been removed from the slave cage and slave sack. When the hood, with its gag, had been removed from me, I had been forced, sitting in the courtyard, my head back and nose held, to swallow a draft of water, into which a reddish powder had been mixed. I had shortly thereafter lost consciousness.

I closed my eyes. The image of the woman had been blurred.

"I know you are awake," she said.

I opened my eyes. I moved my arms and legs a little, but they were, on the whole, effectively restrained. I lay on my back on a large, round couch, on deep furs. I was chained, hand and foot.

"Do you know me?" she asked.

I now recognized her, but I thought it wiser on my part to deny this. Though she had been veiled when I had seen her on the streets of Ar, in her palanquin, it was not difficult to recall the eyes, the character of the cheekbones, the voice.

"No, Mistress," I said.

"I am the Lady Melpomene of Vonda," she said.

"Yes, Mistress," I said.

She stood near the couch, looking at me. "Your Mistress," she said, acidly, "insinuated in Ar that I could not have bid sixteen tarsks for you. That is false. It was rather that I did not think you were worth sixteen tarsks."

"Yes, Mistress," I said.

"You are her preferred silk slave, are you not?" she asked.

"I think so, Mistress," I said.

"Is she fond of you?" she asked.

"She finds me in some respects not unacceptable," I said.

"You are now chained on my couch," she said.

"Yes, Mistress," I said.

"You are a pretty male," she said, "sleek and strong."

I said nothing.

"I have complimented you," she said.

"Thank you, Mistress," I said.

"You have recovered more quickly than I had anticipated from the Tassa powder," she said. "But it does not matter. You may watch me while I prepare myself." She went to a vanity and knelt there, and, looking in the mirror, began to comb her hair. It was long and dark.

I looked about the room. It was large, but shabby. The hangings were old. There were cracks in certain of the walls. It was not kept up.

The Lady Melpomene slowly, luxuriantly, delighting in its beauty, and well displaying it for me, combed her hair. She used a comb of kailiauk horn. She wore a yellow gown, long and almost transparent. Her feet were bare.

"Lady Melpomene has beautiful hair," I said.

"Silk slaves are such flatterers," she said. But I could see she was pleased. It was true, of course, that she had beautiful hair.

There was dust on her bare feet, and on the floor of the room. I had heard that she had had to sell her slaves, or most of them. My Mistress spoke occasionally about her. She hated her. The two families, of which these two young women were scions, were ancient rivals in Vonda. The investments of the family of my Mistress, however, had prospered, while those of the family of the Lady Melpomene had languished. Indeed, most of the members of the family of Lady Melpomene had left Vonda over the years. She, of that family, had remained in Vonda, reigning over the shreds of what had once been a considerable number of assets.

"In the courtyard below," I said, "I was drugged."

"It was done by Tassa powder," she said.

"It was tasteless, and effective," I said.

"Slavers sometimes use it," she said. "It is well for a girl not to drink with a strange man," she laughed.

"It shows up, of course," I said, "in water."

"It is meant to be mixed with red wine," she said.

"Of course," I said.

I wondered how many girls, accepting the apparent generosity of a stranger, had found themselves suddenly, inexplicably, swooning, only to awaken later in some unknown place, naked and in the chains of a slave.

The Lady Melpomene then laid aside her comb. She then touched perfume to her body.

"I did not enjoy my conversation with your Mistress in Ar," she said.

Deftly she touched the perfume to her body.

"She insinuated that my fortunes were in sorry order," she said, "indeed, that I was almost destitute."

"Perhaps she meant no harm," I said.

"I am not a fool," she snapped. Then she rose to her feet and turned to face me. Like many Gorean women, she did not use cosmetics. Free women in Ar commonly use cosmetics, but, outside of Ar, usually it is only the bolder women who resort to them. My Mistress, for example, did not use cosmetics either. Many free women regard cosmetics as only for-slave girls. Slave girls, of course, use them often. The Lady Melpomene regarded me. Then she slipped the yellow gown from her body. She was extremely lovely, though, I think, not so lovely as my Mistress. My eyes, inadvertently, wandered to her throat. It would have looked well in a collar. The collar, like a brand, enhances the beauty of a woman, particularly when she is naked. It, of obdurate, locked, circular steel, indicative of harsh, uncompromising bondage, contrasts well with the delicious, feminine softness which it encircles and confines. "But now," she said, "Jason, her precious silk slave, lies chained upon my couch."

I did not speak.

She came to the couch and sat near me. "You are a pretty slave," she said.

I did not speak.

She looked at me, sternly.

"Thank you, Mistress," I said.

She touched me. "I see that you find me attractive," she said.

"Yes, Mistress," I said.

She lowered her head, letting her hair fall about my face. "Do you smell the perfume?" she asked.

"Yes, Mistress," I said.

"It is that of your Mistress," she said. "What did it cost?"

"Five silver tarsks," I said. "It was purchased, as you perhaps know, at the shop of Veminius."

"Once," she said, "I could afford five tarsks for perfume. Once I, too, could shop at the shop of Veminius."

I looked about the room, lofty, but disreputable, covered with dust. She, of course, a free woman, and one once of means, would not concern herself with such work as dusting and cleaning. It was beneath her. She had had, apparently, to sell all, or most, of her slaves. I had not even been washed and combed, apparently, before being placed on her couch. The men who had captured me had doubtless, for their small fee, brought me to the room and had then left, after which she had, while I lay unconscious, locked her chains on me.

"It is true, then," I asked, "that Mistress has had misfortunes in her financial affairs?"

"I have had difficulties, Jason," she said. "It is common knowledge."

I did not speak.

"I was in Ar negotiating the sale of this house," she said. "The very palanquin in which you first saw me, that in which I rode in Ar, was rented."

"My Mistress," I said, "had suggested to me that it might be."

"But now you lie chained at my mercy," she said.

"Yes, Mistress," I said.

"I was successful in selling the house," she said. "I am leaving it tomorrow."

"Mistress has now recouped her fortunes?" I asked.

"Only a small portion of them," she smiled. "I remain still much in debt."

"Mistress has," I said, "a house in Vonda. Perhaps she might sell that. too."

"I could sell ten houses," she smiled. "and not recoup my fortunes. I owe the merchants of a dozen cities."

"What will you do?" I asked.

"Tomorrow." she said. "with the moneys I will have from the sale of this house I will recoup all, in a single afternoon. I will become again one of the richest women in Vonda."

"In what way can Mistress possibly accomplish this?" I asked.

"I am assured of certain winners in the tharlarion races," she said.

"You have information?" I asked.

"Yes," she said.

"Is it wise to venture your capital in such a way?" I asked.

"I shall do with it as I please," she said.

"Yes, Mistress," I said.

"There are many notes against me," she said. "I must do something."

"Yes, Mistress," I said.

"But have no fear, pretty slave," she said. "Lady Melpomene of Vonda will win, and then will be again one of the richest women in Vonda. Perhaps, even, in time, she may ruin your Mistress, and force your sale." She smiled at me, and idly fingered my arm. "She might then, if she wished," she said, "buy you for her very own." She then, idly, touched my belly. "Would you like that, Jason?" she asked.

"No, Mistress," I said.

"Why?" she asked. "Am I not beautiful?"

"You are beautiful, Mistress," I said.

"Then, why not?" she asked.

"I am a man," I said.

"No," she said, "you are only a silk slave." She looked down at me. "Indeed," she said, "you are a male of the world called Earth. You are fit, thus, only to be a woman's property."

I did not speak. I was bitter. I knew that many of the men of Earth were, in effect, the property of their women. It was not particularly their fault. They had been raised to be such. Rhetoric, conditioning and social controls kept them in their place. Only occasionally did they dream of the subverted biological hegemonies which were theirs by nature. One must own, in effect, or be owned. The women of Earth, in effect, owned their men. But the women of Earth were unhappy. Perhaps they wished, in some deep part of themselves, that it was they who were owned by the men.

"Is it your intention to return me to my Mistress?" I asked.

"Perhaps," she said.

I suddenly reared up, struggling, my shoulders some two or three inches above the surface of the couch.

"Do not be afraid, Jason," she said. "I am only caressing you."

I struggled, futilely.

"You are helpless, Jason," she told me. "The room may be

in disrepair, but I assure you that the chains are new, and adequate. I have checked them."

I cried out with rage.

Again, I struggled, but was held helplessly and perfectly in the sturdy steel.

"What a chained larl you are!" she laughed. "How fortunate for me that your hands are not free. If they were free, I, though a free woman, could scarcely dare conjecture my fate!"

Again I struggled, and was again held helplessly and perfectly in the steel.

"Cease your struggles," she said, suddenly, angrily. "Or I will geld you."

I ceased my struggles.

"That is better," she said.

"What are you going to do with me?" I asked.

"Are you not slave enough to know?" she asked.

I looked at her, in fury.

"Do you think you can resist me?" she asked.

"No," I said. "I do not." No man, chained as I was, could resist any woman. And she was exciting, and beautiful.

She mounted me.

"Unchain me," I said. "Let me take you in my arms."

"I am not a fool," she said. "I will not be made a slave by any man."

"Aiii!" I cried.

"Thus," she laughed. "I, the Lady Melpomene of Vonda, take the silk slave of my enemy, the despicable Lady Florence of Vonda!"

I looked up at her, shuddering.

"It is only the beginning," she said to me.

She used me several times that night. It was only later that I realized that she, in spite of the fullness of her use of me, had never once kissed me. She did not wish to soil her lips by touching them to my body, that of a slave.

# 18 THE INSPECTION OF THE STABLE SLAVES

"The stable slaves are ready for inspection, Lady Florence," said Kenneth, head keeper of the Mistress' slaves. Barus, who assisted him, stood near him.

We knelt in the sunlit, central stable yard of the Mistress' stables, which were extensive. There were barns about, and equipment and feed sheds. These structures were generally painted yellow and trimmed with shades of blue. These colors tend to be cultural for Goreans with respect to housings for domestic animals. Blue and yellow, too, of course, are the colors of the slavers. There may be a connection here, for the slave is, of course, regarded as a domestic animal. To be sure, in barns and such the color yellow usually predominates, whereas in the colors of slavers, exhibited in such places as in the blue and yellow of the canvas covering slave wagons or in the blue and yellow of the tenting of slave pavilions, the blue and yellow is, or tends to be, more equally distributed, almost invariably occurring in stripes.

I knelt near the end of the line. The Mistress, with a long, tharlarion quirt, had begun her inspection.

When the Lady Melpomene had finished with me, after that long night of her use of me, she had held for me another draft of water, discolored by the reddish Tassa powder. I had not wished to drink this. Then she had held her dagger to my body. I drank. Soon I was unconscious.

"Kneel more straightly, Slave," said the Lady Florence to another stable slave, down the line from me.

Apparently the two men in the hire of the Lady Melpomene, those two who had originally captured me, and carried me to her house in Venna, returned for me. I did not regain consciousness until, painfully, I was aware of being thrown upon a hard surface. I heard two men hurrying away. I was,

knees drawn up, and head down, fastened in a slave sack.
Within the sack itself my ankles were crossed and tied, and
my hands, too, were similarly fastened, behind my back.
"What is going on here?" I heard cry. "Stop!" It had been the
voice of Kenneth, the head keeper of my Mistress' slaves, the
Lady Florence of Vonda. I had heard a wagon rattling away,
swiftly. "What is going on?" I had heard, a woman's voice,
that of my Mistress. Over my head I had felt the sack being
untied. "It is Jason," had said Kenneth. He had drawn me
from the sack by a bound arm. I felt my head slapped to the
side. "You are in the presence of the Mistress," had said
Kenneth. I had then knelt before her. I was on the porch of
her house in Venna. I was naked. "There is a note tied to his
collar," said Kenneth. Men and women of the household, including male and female slaves, domestic slaves, house slaves,
such as short-legged, luscious Taphris, had gathered about.
The note on my collar was taken and handed to the Mistress.
She read the note in fury, and then crumpled it, and cast it to
the side. She looked down at me, in fury. "Send him to the
stables," she said.

"Yes, Lady Florence," had said Kenneth.

"Have the rest of you nothing better to do than gawk at a
stable slave?" she snapped.

Quickly the small crowd dissipated, the free persons turning aside to their duties and the slaves, barefoot, including
Taphris, scurrying quickly to their tasks. Lady Florence, Kenneth and myself were alone left on the porch.

Kenneth unbound my ankles and threw aside the binding
fiber which had restrained them.

I kept my head down.

Kenneth stood up. "Lady Florence," he asked.

"Yes?" she said.

"When we return to your villa near Vonda," he asked, "is
the slave to be returned to the house or is it your intention
that he serve there, as well as here, in the stables, not your
private stables but the great stables?" The Lady Florence
owned more than a thousand tharlarion. She bred and raised
tharlarion, and her stables were among the finest in the vicinity of Vonda.

"He is a stable slave," she said, angrily. "Use him as such."

"In the great stables?" he asked.

"Yes," she said.

"As a full stable slave," he asked, "subject to all the conditions and strictures of such?"

"Yes," she said.

"Excellent," he said.

Then, in fury, she had spun about and left, robes swirling.

I lifted my head. Kenneth was chuckling. For some reason he seemed pleased.

"Master," I said.

"Yes?" he said.

"May I know what was in the note which was affixed to my collar?"

"I, too, am curious," he grinned. He picked up the note. " 'My sweet friend and compatriot, Lady Florence of Vonda,' " read Kenneth, " 'Thank you very much for the use of your lovely silk slave, Jason. I enjoyed him very much. It is easy to see why you are so fond of him. Incidentally, thank you, too, for the lovely gift of perfume. I wore it while using him for my pleasure. Thank you again, my sweet and understanding friend, and generous friend, for your kindness in these matters. I wish you well. Melpomene, Lady of Vonda.' "

Kenneth then dropped the note, muchly where he had found it.

He pulled me to my feet and thrust me, stumbling, to my right, down the steps and toward the wagon way leading about the house, toward the stables.

At the corner of the house we stopped.

"Look," he said.

I looked back. The Lady Florence had come out again on the porch. She looked about, but did not see us, as we were some distance away, at the corner of the house, and shielded by trees. She bent down, furtively, and snatched up the note which had been attached to my collar. Then she hurried again into the house.

"She is a woman," said Kenneth.

"Yes, Master," I said.

"She cannot bear that it might be found," laughed Kenneth. "Too, perhaps she wants it, that she may, regarding it, hate the Lady Melpomene even more than she has in the past, if that is possible."

"Yes, Master," I said.

"Did you see how furtive she was," he asked, "so fearful of discovery?"

"Yes, Master," I said.

"She is, for all her wealth and freedom," he said, "only a woman."

"Yes, Master," I said.

"Is she pleasant in the furs?" he asked.

"It was I, a silk slave," I said, smiling, "not she, who must needs be pleasant in the furs."

"Of course," he said. Then he said, "Would she look well in a collar? Would she look well naked, upon a slave block?"

I was startled. "May I respond to such questions?" I asked.

"Yes," he said.

"Yes," I said, "she would look well in a collar, and would look well naked, upon a slave block."

"I had guessed as much," he grinned.

"If I may speak, Master," I said, "you seem pleased to learn that I have been consigned to the stables."

"I am," said he. "I expect that you will make coins for Barus and myself."

"Master?" I asked.

"Can you fight?" he asked.

"No," I said.

He laughed. "You are a big fellow," he said, "and strong. Too, you seem fast. Too, you are clearly intelligent. That is important, more important than many fools understand."

"I do not know how to fight," I said. I was very conscious of the binding fiber confining my wrists behind my back.

"Tighten your belly," he said.

I did so. He then, as I anticipated, struck me, heavily, in the gut. I was, of course, in good condition, and set for the blow.

"Good," said Kenneth.

"I do not know how to fight," I told him.

"In the stables," said Kenneth, "authority is mine. You will, for all practical purposes, belong to me. Is that understood?"

"Yes, Master," I said.

"Do you wish to live?" he asked.

"Yes, Master," I said.

"You will then do as you're told," he said.

"Yes, Master," I said.

"In the stables," he said, "we have, too, besides the male slaves, some Kajirae, stable sluts, as we call them. I can assign these as I please."

I looked at him. I thought of Gorean Kajirae. I inadvertently licked my lips.

He laughed, and turned about, leading the way about the corner of the house, treading upon the wagon way.

"Come along, Stable Slave," he said.

"Yes, Master," I said, following him.

The line of kneeling, male stable slaves was straight. I knelt near the end of that line. The Mistress, not hurrying, continued her inspection. Kenneth and Barus followed her. Occasionally she stopped to speak to a slave, sometimes to put him under questions, pertaining to his duties and his discharging of them. She could be quite thorough, my mistress, the lofty Lady Florence of Vonda. Many of the slaves feared her, her demands and her quirt. She held over them, of course, the power of life and death. She was only a few slaves from me now. It had rained the night before, and the ground was soft. She wore a full, beige skirt, the hem of which fell to within some six inches of the ground, and slim, high, black-leather boots; a beige blouse, and a beige jacket, belted, which fell to her thighs; too, she wore a loose hood, attached to the jacket by hooks, of matching beige material, and an opaque veil, also of beige material. Such garments, far less formal than the common attire of the Gorean free woman, are sometimes worn by rich women in the supervision and inspection of certain sorts of holdings, such as orchards, fields, ranches and vineyards. They constitute, for such women, so to speak, a habit for work.

The mistress was now but five slaves from me.

The skirt's hem, some six inches from the ground, protects the skirt from being soiled by water or mud. Doubtless that is the principal reason for its height. Also, however, interestingly, it functions as a slave control device. The sight of the Mistress' ankle, of course, even booted, is tantalizing; it is exciting and provocative. The male slave, thus, if he is vital, finds himself powerfully drawn to look upon it. On the other hand he knows that such an act can be punished by death. Thus, when he is in the presence of his Mistress, she in such a habit, he becomes fearful and ill at ease. She, in effect, flaunts herself in front of him, acting however as though no such thing is going on. She knows that he is in misery. She exploits this in her control of him.

The Mistress was now some four slaves from me. I was the

thirty-fifth in a long line of male slaves, some forty-two in length. We knelt, in brief brown tunics, in the soft earth. The sunlight was bright; the air was Gorean in its exuberance and freshness. The homely smells of the stable yard and the barns, with their straw-filled stalls, are not really objectionable, when one grows used to them. The odors are distinctive but, when one grows accustomed to them, familiar and not really unpleasant. I rather liked the odors of the stables and barns, such complex mixed odors, ranging from straw, and hay and leather, to the organic wastes of our huge charges, some four species of draft tharlarion. We did not, in the great stables, raise saddle tharlarion, though in the house stables, here in the Mistress' villa, some forty pasangs south and west of Vonda, there were several saddle tharlarion. The Mistress did not breed and raise racing tharlarion, incidentally. These are usually larger and more agile beasts than common saddle tharlarion and are smaller, of course, than either draft tharlarion or war tharlarion, the latter used almost exclusively in the tharlarion cavalries of Gor, huge, upright beasts, several tons in weight, guided by voice commands and the blows of spears. The Lady Mélpomene of Vonda, incidentally, I had heard, for such stories reach even the stables, had fared badly in the tharlarion races in Venna. I recalled that she had hoped to recoup her lost fortunes in such races. Apparently she had failed to do so. As the story went, and my own knowledge, as far as it went, corroborated the story, she had wagered what were, in effect, her last serious financial resources, the proceeds garnered from the sale of her house in Venna, on the outcomes of certain tharlarion races. She had thought herself, in virtue of the possession of significant and secret information, assured of certain winners in these races. Unfortunately for her this information, as I suspect is often the case in such matters, proved unreliable. Her wagers had, at any rate, proved uniformly disastrous. She had become a ruined woman. She had had to flee from Venna under the cover of darkness, that she not be delivered to the mercies of her creditors. Such creditors often come for a woman with a collar and chain. She resided now in Vonda, in a tiny, dingy holding, where she, as a citizeness of that city, would have, at least against foreign creditors, the protection of its Home Stone. The Lady Melpomene of Vonda, impoverished, ruined, had little now to pride herself on save the name of her family and the splendor of her lineage. The Lady Florence, though she must have been aware of these things, never, it was said, at home or abroad, mentioned the name of the Lady Melpomene. She had, perhaps, forgotten about her.

The Mistress was still some four slaves from me. She was sharply questioning one of my fellow slaves. Stammering and cringing, he was trying to satisfy her. I observed the Mistress' ankles, which, below the swirling hem of the beige skirt, were well turned in the high, slim boots. A slaver, of course, would remove such boots before shackling her. I saw Kenneth, behind her, grinning at me. I decided I had best look away from the Mistress.

We had worked hard, the last two days, preparing the stables and the animals for the inspection of the Mistress. I did not know if she would find fault or not, but, to me, objectively, it seemed the holding was in splendid condition. Kenneth, who had held an earlier inspection, had been satisfied, and he was, I suspected, harder to please than would be the Mistress. Indeed, it was a bit unusual that the Mistress conducted her own inspections. Too, it seems she was spending longer with the slaves than one would normally expect. This sudden, exacting concern with the details of the operation of the great stables was unusual for her. She was Mistress, of course, and might do as she wished.

"Do you wish to be whipped, with the snake?" she asked a fellow down the line from me.

"No, Mistress," he said, swiftly.

"Then do your work well, Slave," she said.

"Yes, Mistress," he stammered.

I considered again the polished, black leather of her trim, high boots. A free woman, of course, if she owns slaves, does not polish her own boots. That would be done by one of the house slaves. I suspected that it was Taphris, short-legged and luscious, who polished her boots.

I saw a frown on the face of Kenneth. I then looked away from the Mistress.

I smiled to myself. Kenneth did not wish me to be torn to pieces between tharlarion, driven in opposite directions.

I no longer wore the collar of the silk slave. I now wore, like other stable slaves, a common work collar, of black iron, with an attached ring. On it was the legend 'I belong to the Lady Florence of Vonda.' I, like other stable slaves, was chained at night.

The Lady Florence was now two slaves from me.

Besides the line of forty-two male stable slaves, with which my Mistress was now concerning herself, there knelt to one side, backs straight and heads up, a line of five Kajirae, who were stable sluts. These were barefoot and bare-armed, and wore brown tunics which, as they now had them belted, with binding fiber, would have failed to their knees, rather demurely for slave girls, had they stood up. There were two blonds and three brunets. All were Gorean wenches. On the throat of each, though much more slender and graceful than those of the males, was a collar, too, a work collar, of black iron, with an attached ring. I relished the sight of them.

"Slave!" snapped Kenneth.

"Yes, Master," I said, quickly, startled.

The Mistress, her eyes angry, stood before me. She slapped the quirt in the palm of her left hand. She was not pleased that I had not noticed when she had moved before me.

I knelt very straight. I stared ahead, inspected. I could see the hint of her sweet thighs beneath the beige skirt. Lifting my eyes I recalled the latitudes of her white belly, now concealed beneath her skirt, and blouse and jacket; I saw the loveliness of her breasts swelling within the blouse and jacket. I remembered the slender softness of her body and shoulders, the beauty of her throat, and face and hair, now muchly concealed by the jacket, and hood and veil. I inspected her. Her lineaments, for I had once been her silk slave, were not unfamiliar to me.

Above the veil, briefly, I saw her eyes flash in anger. But then she controlled herself. She would say nothing. How could she, in such a situation, call attention to the fact that she had been inspected, and as a woman, by one who was a mere slave.

"Is this not a new slave in the stables?" she asked Kenneth.

"Yes, Lady Florence," said Kenneth, "but, still, he has been with us now for some five weeks."

"What is his name?" she asked.

"Jason," said Kenneth.

"He seems familiar," she said, lightly.

"Perhaps you remember him, Lady Florence," said Kenneth. "He was once your silk slave."

"Ah!" she said, as though suddenly recollecting the matter. "Is it truly you, Jason?" she asked.

"Yes, Mistress," I said.

She stepped back two or three feet, and looked upon me. "What a sturdy brute you have become," she said.

I said nothing.

"Your face and features," she said, "seem to have coarsened. And there is a scar on your lower left cheek."

I said nothing. I had had the scar from a cut received some four weeks ago. I had been careless.

"I have, inadvertently, from time to time, overheard the speakings of slaves," she said. "Is it true that you are the champion in the stables?"

I smiled to myself. Her informant in such matters was Taphris. Kenneth had told me this.

"Is it true?" she asked.

I considered the line of men. "Yes, Mistress," I said.

"He is splendid, Lady Florence," said Kenneth, warmly. "He is a true champion. He has beaten already the champions of five stables, those of Kliomenes, Policrates, Gordon, Dorto and Miles."

"I abhor violence," she said, shuddering, the quirt in her hand.

"Of course, Lady Florence," said Kenneth. "Forgive me. They are, of course, only slaves who are set at one another."

"That is true," she said. "It is not as though they were people. They are only animals."

It was true. Slaves, both male and female, are animals. Anything may be done with them.

"When he does well, or is successful," she asked, as though merely curious, "is he rewarded?"

"Yes," said Kenneth, "it is useful in the training."

"And how is he rewarded?" she asked.

"An extra round of rations," said Kenneth, expansively, "some pastry upon occasion, sometimes with even a bowl of cheap wine."

"I see," she said.

I looked over at the line of stable sluts, kneeling in the soft earth, in their brown tunics. I had had all of them, and more than once. Kenneth had been generous. Not unoften he would bring one of them to my stall at night, where I was chained, and chain her by the neck, beside me in the straw. My favorite was the blond, Telitsia.

"And is he, upon occasion," asked the Lady Florence, "rewarded with things of another sort?"

"Of course, Lady Florence," said Kenneth.

"With what?" she asked.

"With meaningless little things, trivialities, baubles, things of no account or worth," said Kenneth.

The Lady Florence looked over to the line of kneeling Kajirae. "To be sure," she said, acidly.

"If Lady Florence disapproves," said Kenneth, "we shall, of course, discontinue the practice."

"Why should I disapprove?" she asked, angrily.

"I do not know, Lady Florence," said Kenneth. "I only thought—"

"The sluts are on their slave wine, are they not?" she asked.

"Of course," said Kenneth.

"In what else could I possibly have been interested?" she asked.

"I do not know," he said.

"If there is to be breeding done upon them, I will, of course, supervise it," she said.

"Of course, Lady Florence," said Kenneth.

Slaves are domestic stock. They are bred if and when, and as, the masters please.

"How strong your arms seem to have become," mused the Lady Florence, looking down upon me. Like the other slave tunics, mine was sleeveless.

I said nothing.

"It is nothing whatsoever to me," said the Lady Florence to Kenneth, "whether this slave, a mere slave, is or is not used in the stable bouts. See, however, that he performs his full share of labors."

"Of course, Lady Florence," said Kenneth.

The Mistress then turned from me, and surveyed the next slave in line. She stayed before him, however, only a moment. And, indeed, she was soon finished with our line of slaves. She turned about.

"Does the Lady Florence wish to inspect her Kajirae?" inquired Kenneth.

The body of the Mistress suddenly stiffened. "Yes," she said.

Then, in a moment, in her swirling skirt, and hood and veil, and boots, quirt in hand, she stood before the five Kajirae, members of her own sex, briefly tunicked, wearing feminine work collars, with rings, who knelt before her.

"Which of these," she asked, "is the favorite of the fighting slave, he named Jason?"

"Telitsia, this one," said Kenneth, puzzled.

Blond Telitsia looked up at her Mistress, frightened.

"Sell her," said the Lady Florence, and turned away.

The training beam, about a foot Gorean square, sunk a yard deep in its wood-lined well, braced, too, within the wooden-floored, high-roofed barn, shook with the blows struck against it. On my hands I wore the gunni, training devices, curved weights of lead, several pounds heavy, with handles, cushioned with cloth. The value of these devices is twofold. First, they strengthen the muscles of the shoulders, back and arms, building up incredible strength; second, when they are removed, it seems as though the hands, relieved of such weights, can fly like hornets. I stayed close to the beam. The fist moves most swiftly and has the greatest power within the first six inches of its motion, with the back and arm behind it. Too, it is similar to the loosened arrow, which has its greatest swiftness, and maximum striking power, immediately after being sprung from the string, immediately after leaving the bow. The concave surfaces of the gunni face the user of the devices, and the handles are recessed within these surfaces. The outer surfaces, or striking surfaces of the gunni are usually shallowly rounded, being slightly convex. This tends to prevent excessive splintering of the beam. The blows thus, in a sense, compress and pack the beam, causing it to last longer, until it finally, after a few finishing blows, shatters. These beams are frequently replaced. It may seem surprising but a strong man, determined, and working against time, can break through a training beam in a matter of only a few Ehn. The gunni, in weight, are similar to the heads of sledge hammers. One may, of course, break through walls with such devices or bend iron.

I struck at the beam, denting it, causing it to shudder in its well and braces.

It had been yesterday that we had been inspected by the Mistress. After she had inspected me, it had seemed to me that she had brought her inspection to a rather swift termination. She had been cursory with the rest of the slaves in my line and she had barely glanced at the Kajirae.

I struck again and again at the beam. It is important to maintain one's balance. This permits maneuverability and reduces the opponent's opportunities to take advantage of a misstep or a momentary clumsiness in the distribution of one's weight; too, it provides greater impact for the blows which one strikes. My feet seldom moved more than some twenty inches apart; earlier in my training my ankles had been shackled; now, kinesthetically, habitually, without thinking, I tended almost invariably to maintain a sensible measure between my feet; I stayed, too, generally on my toes; this reduces friction and enables quickness of movement; too, in the fighting pit, the toe, gouging into the sand, the body moving forward, increases leverage. Many slave fights are little more than bloody brawls, which free persons are pleased to witness. Kenneth and Barus, on the other hand, who bet on such matters, took these fights seriously. They had, over the years, devoted time and intelligence to the training and development of fighting slaves. The stables of the Lady Florence of Vonda had been, as a result of this, particularly in the last four or five years, unusually successful in the stable bouts. Indeed, Kenneth and Barus had accumulated small fortunes as a result of their efforts in this area. Gorean free persons of high caste, of course, tended to take little note of these matters.

I struck again and again at the beam, pummeling it. It groaned. I heard it crack. Again and again, over and over, I struck at it. The ceiling of the high-roofed barn and its walls rang with the sound of the blows on the weakening wood. I sensed that it would soon give way. I increased the number and speed of my blows.

Sometimes as often as every fourth or fifth day I was hooded and chained, and placed in a wagon, usually with some fellow slaves, fighters, too. I would then be unchained and unhooded, in my turn, in a shallow pit, about which free persons, almost always of low caste, would be gathered. In the pit, too, would be another slave. Our hands would be wrapped in leather that they might not be easily broken. One might kick but holds to the death were not permitted. One fought, with occasional rest periods, for this makes the fight last longer, the fighters being briefly refreshed, until one man or the other could no longer fight. There would be much shouting and betting. I had lost my first matches in our own stables but, in time, with training and advice, and pit experience, I had begun to do well. I had won my last seventeen bouts, five of which had been outside our own stables. I was usually one of a team of five fighters, divided by weight. I was in the heaviest weight class. Some small men, as is well known, are extremely fine fighters, though, of course, they do not have the size and weight to consistently best larger men, assuming that the distribution of skills is similar.

The beam splintered suddenly away, shattering back from the weights on my hands.

I threw back my head, sucking in air.

I sensed her suddenly beside me, the small, blond female, collared, in the brown rag.

"Telitsia," I said.

She removed one of the gunni, that which clothed my left fist. It was heavy for her. She carried it, with two hands, and placed it on the shelf to one side.

"Does Kenneth know you are here?" I asked.

She returned to my side and, from my right fist, removed gently the heavy, curved weight with which it was clad.

"Does Kenneth know you are here?" I asked.

She placed the second weight beside the first on the shelf. She turned and looked at me. I looked at her. She trembled. She put down her head, and went to a water-filled wooden bucket in the corner of the barn. There was a gourd dipper near the bucket. She lowered the gourd dipper into the water and then, the dipper brimming, returned to my side. I took the dipper and drank. I handed the dipper back to her and she returned it to its place. Her small, bare feet dislodged sawdust on the floor of the barn. She returned to my side with a large, coarse towel, and began, gently, to towel my body. I was soaked with sweat. We were alone in the barn. There were several stalls in the barn. These were empty, but filled with clean straw. She continued to towel my body.

I thrust back the hair from my eyes.

She was now on her knees beside me, head down, trembling, toweling my legs.

"Does Kenneth know you are here?" I asked.

She continued, head down, to towel my legs.

"Speak, female," I told her.

"No," she whispered.

She looked up at me, suddenly. "The wagon is to come for

me this afternoon," she said. "I am to be taken to the market.
I am to be sold."

"I know," I said.

"I do not want to be sold," she wept.

"You are a slave," I told her. "Your wishes are unimportant."

"I know," she whispered.

She continued to towel my body. "The wagon will be here
soon," she said.

I nodded. She would then be hooded and bound, and
placed in the wagon for transport to the market.

Suddenly she flung away the towel and, sobbing, looked up
at me, tears in her eyes. She was quite beautiful, kneeling
barefoot before me, clad only in the brief, sleeveless brown
rag of a slave, her blond hair about her shoulders, her blue
eyes moist, her throat graced by the narrow collar of dark
iron, slave iron. "Telitsia is at your feet," she whispered, piteously, "—Master."

I lifted her into my arms and carried her to one of the
stalls, where I placed her gently on the straw.


"Telitsia! Telitsia!" we heard. It was the voice of Kenneth,
master keeper of the slaves of the Lady Florence.

The bar for the tenth Ahn, the Gorean noon, had already
been struck.

"I must escape," wept Telitsia. I touched her brand, I fingered her collar, as she lay naked in the straw, looking up at
me.

I shook my head. "No, Telitsia," I said. "There is no escape for such as you, a Gorean slave girl."

She turned her head to the side. "I know," she said.

"Telitsia!" said Kenneth, standing before the stall. We
drew quickly, guiltily, apart. We both, immediately, knelt,
heads down, before a free person.

"Where have you been?" said Kenneth.

"Here, Master," she whimpered.

"Get your rag on," said Kenneth. "The wagon is ready."

"Yes, Master," she said, hurrying to pull her tiny, pathetic
garment over her head.

"You, Jason," said Kenneth, sternly. "Were you given permission by some free person to engage in slut sport with this
bond girl?"

"No, Master," I said, head down.

"You understand that you could be slain for this?" he inquired.

"Yes, Master," I admitted.

"How was she?" he asked.

"Lovely, and slave hot," I said.

The girl blushed, all the exposed parts of her body turning red, even her legs.

I smiled. I did not think Kenneth truly objected to my rutting with the lovely, neck-ringed stable slut. Indeed, he had not kept her chained by the neck to her ring in the kennels for stable sluts this morning, a precaution which is not uncommon for a girl who is to be soon sold. Rather he had let her wander free. I think that he was not, in his way, unkind. He had doubtless suspected that she would seek me out, or another male slave of her choice. There had been no great search for her. Kenneth, it seemed, had come almost directly to the barn where I was training.

Kenneth threw me some binding fiber and a leash. "Tie and leash her, and bring her to the wagon," he said.

"Yes. Master," I said. I went to Telitsia and bound her wrists behind her back with the binding fiber, and snapped the leash on her collar ring.

Too, however, it should be noted that Kenneth, permitting the bedding of the lovely slave girl at this time, had assured himself that she would be warmed for her sale. His motivations, thus, were doubtless not entirely altruistic. A vital, passionate woman, of course, displays herself very differently on the block than one who is inert, cold or frigid. There are degrees in these things, of course. For example, a truly frigid girl is almost certain to be a first-sale girl. Frigidity is a neurotic luxury which Goreans do not see fit to indulge in female slaves. It is permitted only to free women. The same girl who in her first sale was frigid is likely to be, by the time of her second sale, even should it be within the year, a wonder of lascivious appetition, needful of love and the touch of an uncompromising owner.

"Come along," said Kenneth.

I followed him, leading Telitsia on her leash.

"Greetings, Kenneth," said Borto, the driver of the low-bedded tharlarion wagon. "I see you have the slave."

"Greetings, Borto," said Kenneth. "Yes, and I think she is now well ready for her sale."

Borto laughed.

"I bring you another, a replacement," he said, indicating a prone figure, in a slave sack.

"Good," said Kenneth. "We are short on stable sluts. They are useful in keeping the male slaves content, and may well be applied to lighter labors, on which a man's strength would be wasted."

Borto smiled, and handed Kenneth a note, from inside his tunic.

Kenneth took the note and read it, frowning. "I see," he said.

"Put her in the wagon," said Kenneth, "kneeling position, leashed-legs tie."

"Yes, Master," I said.

Telitsia looked up at me. Her hands were bound behind her back. There were tears in her eyes. She lifted her lips to mine. I kissed her. I then lifted her into the wagon, kneeling her on the boards. Her breasts were loose and sweet within her small garment. It was high on her thighs. I then, using the leash, passing it before her body and between her legs, crossed and bound her ankles, thus fastening her in that same kneeling position in which I had originally placed her. She could not rise and the fastening on her collar kept her head down. It is a standard submission tie on Gor for a female slave.

The girl in the slave sack squirmed angrily, irritably.

Kenneth looked at the sack move, responding to the luscious girl curves within it.

"Does she not know she is not to squirm?" asked Kenneth.

Borto laughed. "Apparently not," he said.

"There is nothing in the note," said Kenneth, "to indicate that she is not to be a stable slut."

"Doubtless she will have to be taught a few things," said Borto.

"Barus!" called Kenneth.

"Yes," answered Barus, who was nearby, tallying feed sacks.

"Bring a stable collar," said Kenneth.

Barus put aside his tallying board and marking stick, and went into a nearby, small building, an equipment shed.

"Hood her," said Kenneth to me.

Telitsia sobbed. I took the slave hood from the wagon bed and drew it over her head, adjusting the straps and buckling them under her chin. I then descended from the bed.

Kenneth threw the key to Telitsia's collar to Borto, who caught it and placed it in his pouch. Her collar would be removed only when a new one was ready to replace it, probably the house collar of some slaver's emporium.

"Remove her from the sack," said Kenneth. "We will have a look at her."

Borto untied the ropes at the foot of the sack.

Barus came to the wagon, handing Kenneth a stable collar, a light, hinged circle of iron, with an attached ring, that of the sort which is often used to loop the throats of stable sluts.

Borto lifted the sack somewhat, shaking and sliding the girl somewhat from it. Then she was on her knees, with the sack still covering the upper part of her body. I saw she had good legs. She also wore, I saw, a brown tunic, similar to those which are worn by stable sluts. It was, however, a little long.

Borto then drew away the sack.

"Ah!" said Kenneth.

I, too, was surprised. Kneeling before us, on the wagon bed, her hands braceleted behind her back, two small keys dangling from her enameled collar was Taphris, who was one of the personal serving slaves of the Lady Florence.

"It seems you have fallen from the Mistress' favor, Taphris," said Kenneth.

"Perhaps," she said.

He looked at her.

"Perhaps, Master," she said.

"On your belly," he said, "head over the end of the wagon."

Angrily Taphris lowered herself to her shoulder, and then to her belly, and put her head over the end of the wagon.

Kenneth, removing one of the keys from the enameled collar she wore, removed it from her, putting it, and its key, back in the wagon, to one side. He then, she briefly shuddering, locked the stable collar on her throat.

He let her lie there for a moment. Then he said, "Descend from the wagon bed, and stand here, before me."

She struggled up and then, carefully, that her tunic not be drawn upward, put her legs over the edge of the wagon bed and lowered herself to the ground.

Kenneth regarded her. Taphris was a luscious wench. "You

are no longer a house slave," he said. "There are strong men in the stables. Stand straight, and beautifully."

"Master has, I trust," she said, acidly, "read the note which has accompanied me."

Kenneth removed the note from his tunic, where he had placed it, and read it again, to himself, with apparent care.

She tossed her head.

"I see nothing in here to the effect that you are not a stable slut," he said.

"Master!" she protested.

"Are you not now a mere stable slut?" he asked.

Taphris quickly looked at me. "Yes, Master," she said. "I have fallen from the favor of the Mistress. I am now only a mere stable slut."

"It is true," said Kenneth, grimly. He put the note again in his tunic.

"Master?" she asked.

"Bring heavy shears," said Kenneth to Barus.

"Master?" asked Taphris.

Barus returned in a moment with a heavy pair of large-handled iron shears, procured from the nearby equipment shed. They were of the sort which could be used for shearing the wool of the bounding hurt. The Lady Florence did not raise hurt, though some were raised on nearby ranches. Miles of Vonda, for example, raised hurt as well as tharlarion. They were used in the stables for a variety of cutting tasks, ranging from opening feed sacks to shearing the hair of Kajirae, which is unexcelled for the braiding of catapult ropes. Slaves, incidentally, were not allowed in the equipment shed. A careful accounting is kept in the stables of bladed equipment.

Kenneth, shears in hand, stepped back and regarded Taphris. "Your tunic has sleeves," he said. "Let us bare your arms, that you may work more efficiently."

"Work?" she said.

Kenneth, with the shears, cut away the sleeves of her tunic, so that her arms were bared.

Her hands tensed in the slave bracelets, confining them behind her back.

"Let us free, too, your legs," he said, musingly.

He then, with the shears, considerably heightened the hemline on the skirt of her tunic. This did not displease me. He handed the shears to Barus.

"Wait until the Mistress hears of this!" she cried.

"And this," said Kenneth, angrily, "I do for the pleasure of my men."

She shrank back. Angrily he tore away two additional horts from the tunic's freshly sheared hem. She cried out with misery, so exposed. "And this, too!" he said angrily. "Please, no, Master!" she wept. But his hands then tore open the tunic, that the beauty of her breasts be but ill concealed. Lastly he tore open, to the hip, on the left side, the now ragged, scandalously brief skirt of her tunic. I saw that she wore the common Kajira mark of Gor. It is that mark, lovely, small, a Kef in cursive script, the first letter of 'Kajira', which is worn by most Gorean slave girls.

He then kicked her legs out from under her, and she knelt sobbing in the dirt at his feet.

"Give me the shears," he said to Barus.

"The note, the note, Master," said the girl, looking upward, pathetically.

"Is it not time," Kenneth asked Barus, "that the hair of this Kajira was harvested?"

"I think so," said Barus.

Taphris had long, dark hair.

"The note, the note, Master," begged the girl.

"Have no fear, Slave," said Kenneth. "You will be treated in accordance with the exact letter of the note. But beyond that you are only and fully a stable slut."

He then, holding her hair, sheared it away at the base of her neck.

"Put a string on this and put it in the sack," he said to Barus.

The girl was sobbing.

Kenneth normally did not shear the hair of his stable sluts, even in the fall. He did occasionally use shearing, however, as a disciplinary device. Goreans tend, culturally, to be fond of long hair on a woman. The shorn girl, thus, in her collar, tends to be an object of scorn and ridicule. Girls will go to great lengths to please a man, that they not be shorn. The girls who are regularly shorn are usually slaves who work on the great farms or on the large, commercial hurt ranches, or low girls who are used in large numbers in such places as the mills, or the public laundries and kitchens. Any girl, of course, may be shorn, even a high pleasure slave, if she displeases the master. The girls know that there is always a market for their hair.

I watched Barus going toward the equipment shed. He carried the shorn hair and the shears. The sack in which the shorn hair of Kajirae was kept until it was marketed was in the equipment shed, where the shears were kept.

"Stand, shorn slave," said Kenneth to the girl.

She quickly stood.

"Remember," said he, "you are now no longer a lady's house slave. You are now a stable slut."

She then, fearfully, stood straight and beautifully. To see her in the brief rag of a stable slut, she standing so beautifully, the narrow collar on her throat, was to desire to rape her.

"Not bad," commented Kenneth.

The girl trembled. Her small hands were still locked behind her back, in slave bracelets.

"Not bad at all," said Kenneth.

Barus was now returning to the vicinity, having bound and discarded the hair in the hair sack. Too, he had replaced the shears in the shed.

"Ah," said Barus. "She is not unattractive for a shorn slave."

"Yes," said Kenneth.

"She will be a pleasant addition to the Kajirae in the stables," said Barus.

"I think so," said Kenneth.

"I must be on my way soon," said Borto, who was the driver of the tharlarion wagon.

Barus went to the discarded, enameled collar, now open, which lay in the wagon bed. He removed the second key from it, that which opened the slave's bracelets. He went behind the girl and freed her hands. He threw the opened bracelets, leaving the key in one of the bracelet locks, to the wagon bed. Borto lifted up the rear gate of the wagon and, with two hooks, fastened it in place.

"I wish you well," said Borto to the two free men.

"I wish you well," said Kenneth to him.

"I wish you well," said Barus to him.

In a few moments Borto had climbed to the wagon box and, with a crack of his whip, had urged the two tharlarion whose reins he controlled into motion.

Borto began to sing.

I watched the wagon departing, its wheels leaving tracks in the soft dust of the stable yard. In the wagon, hooded, head down, tied on her knees, bound hand and foot, her shoulders shaking, was Telitsia, an animal bound for the market.

I turned again to regard Taphris.

"Turn your hip out," said Kenneth. "Place your feet like that," he said, kicking her right foot. "Suck in your gut. Put your palms on your thighs. Lift your head."

Taphris was learning quickly that she was no longer in the house, but in the stables, a province in which she was a woman and in which men were supreme.

"Bend over at the waist," said Kenneth. "More!"

Her knees were flexed. Her head was then at his hip.

Kenneth stepped back from her. I could see that he was not displeased to have the lovely Tahpris at his mercy.

She did not dare raise her head.

"Barus," said Kenneth, "will show you your kennel, and your duties."

"Yes, Master," she said.

Barus placed his hand in her hair, grasping it firmly. She winced.

She had not moved her head, of course, for she knew she had been placed in a common leading position for slave girls.

She tried to look up at Kenneth, but the hand of Barus did not permit it. She must look to the dirt at her feet.

Barus turned away from us, leading her.

"Barus," said Kenneth.

"Yes," said Barus, stopping, and looking back.

"See that the new girl is worked well," said Kenneth.

"The south stables should be cleaned," said Barus.

"Shoveled and scrubbed," said Kenneth.

Barus grinned.

"And then water must be drawn and carried to fill the tanks in stables six through ten."

"Yes," said Barus. He turned then and strode away, pulling the half-running Taphris beside him.

Water is drawn from wells. It is then carried, in yoked buckets, to great wooden tubs in certain of the stables.

I did not envy the beautiful Taphris.

Kenneth turned to me. "You cannot read," he said.

"No, Master," I said, "not Gorean." Slaves are commonly kept illiterate. It makes them more helpless. It gives the masters more control over them. Besides, it is said, why should a slave know how to read?

"I do not think out little friend, Taphris," said Kenneth, "has fallen in the favor of the Mistress."

"Oh, Master?"

"No," he said.

"But she has been sent to the stables," I said.

"And she will learn what it is to be a stable slut," said Kenneth, grimly.

I smiled. I had little doubt but what Kenneth said was true.

"May I inquire as to the contents of the note, that which accompanied her?" I asked. I gathered that Kenneth would have been willing to let me read it, had I been able to do so.

"It specifies that she is to be exempt from assignment to male stable slaves, that she is not to be given to them for wench sport."

"That is interesting," I said.

"And, further, it specifies that under certain conditions she is to be granted certain freedoms of observation and movement. Too, once, weekly, she is to be sent to the house on some errand or other."

"What are these conditions under which she is to be granted movement and freedom of observation?" I inquired.

"Conditions deemed pertinent to the cognizance of a certain male slave's whereabouts and activities," he said.

"Mine?" I asked.

"Yes," said Kenneth, grinning.

I said nothing.

"Our lovely Taphris, it seems," said Kenneth, "has business in the stables."

I said nothing.

"It seems the Mistress has not forgotten her former silk slave."

I did not speak.

"Taphris is a spy," said Kenneth. "She has been sent to the stables by the Mistress to spy on you."

"I see," I said.

"Beware of her," he said.

"I will," I said.

# 20 I LEARN THAT THE MISTRESS WILL HAVE HOUSE GUESTS

I reeled back, sprawling in the sand. I could feel blood about my mouth.

I grunted, kicked. He threw himself at me, fists striking.

I heard the screams of the crowd, in the tiers. I rolled to one side, eluding the attacker.

I staggered up. He, too, then, was on his feet. I tried, gasping, to thrust him away. He struck me in the gut with his head, driving me half to the wall. He again lowered his head. I clasped my hands, and flung them upward, catching him under the chin and he staggered backward. I spit blood into the sand. He again rushed at me, seizing me, and flung me against the low palings. "Fight! Fight!" I heard. "Jason!" I heard. "Kaibar!" I heard. "Now you have him!" I heard. "Get away from the wall!" Kenneth was screaming. The slave, Kaibar, then, of the stables of Shandu, holding his hands together, slashing sideways, struck me with his left elbow, and then his right. "Get away from the wall!" I heard. I grunted, taking a blow in the gut and then another, the fists now, like battering rams. "Get away from the wall!" screamed Kenneth. But it was not he, the bastard, who was pinned against it. I clenched Kaibar, holding to him, gasping. He tried to shake me from him. "Do not delay the fight!" warned the referee, moving about us. I felt his whip lash at me. Then he was between us, forcing us apart. But I was now in the center of the pit. Kaibar and I faced one another. We were both bloody, and exhausted. He struck at me with his balled fist. I blocked the blow. He was strong. My arms ached. Even to parry the blows of a strong man takes its toll.

251

My shoulders and arms ached. I could scarcely lift them. Kaibar staggered toward me again. Again I seized him, holding to him.

We heard then the bar being struck.

"Here!" called Kenneth. I, turning about, followed the sound of his voice and in a moment he had seized me and pulled me down on the box. Barus, with a sponge, dipped in a bucket, squeezed water over my head.

"You are doing splendidly," Kenneth assured me.

I could not even answer him.

Barus sponged sand and blood from my body.

"Drink," said Kenneth to Taphris, who knelt at our side.

She thrust the bottle filled with water, thick with sugar, to Kenneth who, holding it for me, poured some of it down my throat. I spit the rest of it away into the sand. Kenneth pushed the bottle back to Taphris.

Barus now toweled my body. Weakly I pushed him away. The sweat and water on my body, I hoped, would tend to slide blows away, were they struck at oblique angles.

He then dried the leather on my fists, that it would grip when it struck flesh.

The bar was again struck, a sharp, ringing note.

"You have him now," said Kenneth. "Finish him quickly."

I was half thrust to my feet and staggered toward the center of the pit. Kenneth, I decided, was insane. Yet he had seen hundreds of such bouts.

I took the first blow, staggering to the side. I straightened and, stumbling, smashed my fist into the gut of Kaibar. He reached for me, and I struck aside his hands, and struck him on the left side of the face. We stood in the sand, unsteadily.

"Fight!" cried the referee. "Fight!" cried the crowd. The crowd, mostly, was an excited and motely assortment of low-caste males, but, here and there, there were veiled women amongst them, generally these, too, of low caste. There were, in favored seats, some upper-caste Goreans, recognizable by the colors and qualities of their robes, and among these, here and there, heavily veiled, erect and lovely, some upper-caste women. At one end of the enclosure, where it was entered, there was a barred gate. Behind this, pressed against it, watching, excited, holding to the bars, were collared, half-naked slave girls, stable sluts, crying out for the champions of their various stables.

"Fight!" cried the referee. His lash fell on Kaibar.

I suddenly felt chilled. I realized then I should have permitted Barus to towel my body, drying it. I feared I might be seized with muscle cramps. The sweat and water, too, now that I had paused, sticky on my hot body, formed an adhesive surface which I feared might hold the leather of Kaibar.

"Fight!" cried the referee. His lash stung my back. The referee's lash again then fell on Kaibar, and again on me.

Kaibar and I again staggered toward one another. I had survived the eighteenth fighting period.

Then suddenly it seemed that the gunni were again on my hands and that I stood in the training barn before the great post. I could hear, but only as in the distance, the crying of the crowd, the screaming of the women, slave and free. I must work against time. Did not Kenneth hold the vial of sand? Blows it seemed I rained with an avalanche of lead on the reeling post shuddering in its braces. I must beat the sand. I could, and would. I lunged against the post, inches from it, blow after blow. Then spitting blood from my mouth, my legs covered to the knees with sweat and sand, pounding, laughing, exultant, terrible, I saw the post shatter away, falling from me.

"Stop! Stop!" was crying Kenneth. He ran to me, holding me. I stood bloody in the sand. At my feet, bloody, covered with sand, unconscious, lay Kaibar.

"Is he dead?" someone was crying.

"No," called the referee.

I was dragged to the center of the sand and my hands, one by the referee, the other by Kenneth, the trainer, were lifted in victory.

I threw back my head, sucking in air. My hands were swollen. The bloodied leather was cut from my hands.

"I shall have a champion who can beat your Jason!" cried Miles of Vonda, from the side of the wall.

"Bring him then forth!" cried Kenneth. "The stables of the Lady Florence of Vonda will await him!"

I had beaten the champion of the stables of Miles of Vonda two weeks ago. It had been that match which had established my precedence among the fighting slaves of the stables in the vicinity of Vonda. It had been that match which had resulted in my being named the local champion. This victory had not set well with Miles of Vonda. It was not merely that his own champion had been defeated and that he had lost a goodly bit of coin on the wagering involved, but

that he had been, in the past, like several other young swains
in the vicinity, an unsuccessful suitor, in the matter of the
companionship, for the hand of the Lady Florence of Vonda.

I was half dragged, half pushed, by a crowd, Kenneth and
Barus close to me, Taphris behind, through the barred gate
leading to the sand pit. Another match, to hold the interest of
the crowd, would soon be beginning. I pressed through people,
slave and free, who pressed about me, congratulating me,
many trying to touch me, even free persons. Slave girls, their
eyes bright, their breath hot, tried to press themselves piteously against me. Some fell to their knees as I passed, trying
to seize my legs, and kiss at my thighs and ankles as I passed.
Women know that they are the natural spoils of conquering
males. I saw even the eyes of free women bright and wild over
their veils.

"Well done, Jason," said Kenneth. "Well done."

We heard the striking of the long bar from near the pit.
Another match was beginning.

We walked around, behind the tiers, still pressing through
an admiring throng. Slave girls pattered behind, hoping for
another look, but fearful now, away from the gate, of jostling
free persons.

"Back," begged Kenneth, "back! Return to the tiers!"

We were now near the corridor gate leading from the
small arena, to the stables where we were prepared for
combat.

"The Mistress!" said Kenneth.

I looked up. Before us, standing, near the corridor gate,
were two free women, veiled, in flowing, lovely robes.

Swiftly I knelt. I was owned by one of these women.

"Congratulations, Jason," said the Lady Florence of
Vonda. "You did well."

"Thank you, Mistress," I said. I looked up at her. My
throat was locked in her collar. I was still breathing heavily.

Though she was robed and veiled I would have recognized
her, of course, from her eyes, her attitude, the lineaments of
her body. Silk slaves recognize the bodies of their mistresses,
even when they are robed and veiled, with much the same
ease with which a master recognizes the bodies of his slaves.
Too, I had, as I had learned on Gor, a good eye for woman
flesh. Too, to my amazement, I recognized the woman who
stood beside her.

"May I present, Kenneth," said the Lady Floronoo of
Vonda, "my dear friend, the Lady Melpomene of Vonda."

"I am charmed, Lady Melpomene," said Kenneth, bowing.

"Jason," said the Lady Florence, "perhaps you remember
my good friend, the Lady Melpomene of Vonda, my city."

"Yes, Mistress," I said, putting my head down.

"We have patched up our differences, Jason," said the
Lady Florence, "and we are now the best, and fastest, of
friends."

"I am pleased to hear that, Mistress," I said.

"Lady Melpomene will be staying with us for two or three
days," said the Lady Florence. "And, soon, we shall have
some house guests."

"Yes, Mistress," I said.

"You will see that the grounds, and the stables, are tidy,
won't you, Kenneth?" asked the Lady Florence.

"Surely, Lady Florence," said Kenneth.

"And you will keep the stable sluts on their chains, won't
you?" she asked.

"As Lady Florence wishes," said Kenneth.

"We would not wish the sight of them to embarrass or offend our guests."

"No, Lady Florence," said Kenneth.

"Oh, Kenneth," asked the Lady Florence, "is the new girl
working out?"

"Yes, Lady Florence," he said.

"What is her name?" she asked, absently.

"Taphris," said Kenneth.

"Oh, yes!" she said. "Is she doing well?"

"Yes," said Kenneth, "she has the makings of a superb
stable slut."

"Oh," said the Mistress.

Taphris, in her stable collar, reddening, gasping, shrank
back.

"It seems her tunic has been torn," said the Lady Florence,
"and, too, it seems her hair has been cut."

Taphris, with two hands, tried to pull together the sides of
her tunic, but it did her little good. She was now as exposed
as any stable slut. Kenneth had seen to that. The Mistress'
spy was now only a dream of pleasure to any man who might
lay eyes upon her.

"Surely Mistress recognizes that her tunic is now more fit

for the arduous and crude labors of the stable slut than before."

"Of course," said Lady Florence.

"And her hair had value," said Kenneth, "so, as she is merely a stable slut, I saw fit to shear it."

"Of course," said the Lady Florence. She would not interfere, of course, with Kenneth's management of the slaves.

Kenneth smiled.

"Again, Jason," said the Lady Florence, turning away from Kenneth, "permit me to congratulate you on your victory."

"Thank you, Mistress," I said.

"I did not know, Lady Florence," said Kenneth, "that you were a partisan of the bouts."

"I am not," she said. "It is only that the Lady Melpomene and I thought it might be amusing, for the afternoon, to see how some of those of the lower castes see fit to spend their time."

"I see," said Kenneth. "Did Lady Florence enjoy the bouts?" he asked.

"As a woman of taste, and one of refined sensibility," she said, "I could not enjoy them."

"I see," said Kenneth.

"They are far too brutal," she said. She turned to the Lady Melpomene. "How did you find them, my dear?" she inquired.

"Disgusting, simply disgusting," said the Lady Melpomene, quickly.

"Most disgusting of all, perhaps," said the Lady Florence, "was the disgraceful sight of those half-naked slave girls pawing after the fighters."

"Yes," said the Lady Melpomene.

"They are only slaves," pointed out Kenneth.

"This is true," admitted the Lady Florence.

"Yes," said the Lady Melpomene. "What can one expect of collared sluts?"

"I wonder, though, what it would be like to feel such emotion," mused the Lady Florence.

"They wear only a rag and a collar," said the Lady Melpomene. "They are owned. They must serve. They are not permitted pride. Under such circumstances it is doubtless easy to feel emotion."

"Perhaps," shuddered the Lady Florence.

"With your permission, Lady Florence," said Kenneth, "I

would like to get Jason to the stall, that we may dry and warm him. He is hot and sweaty. I do not wish him to take a chill."

"I trust you take as good care of my tharlarion as you do of your fighters," said the Lady Florence.

"Of course," grinned Kenneth.

"You may kiss my feet, Jason," said the Lady Florence. I bent, putting my lips to her slippers, kissing them. "Now those of the Lady Melpomene," she said. Again I bent, this time pressing my lips to the slippers of the Lady Melpomene, too, kissing them.

"He has become a sturdy brute, hasn't he?" asked the Lady Florence.

I lifted my head.

"And a handsome brute, too," she said.

"Come, Jason," said Kenneth, drawing me to my feet. He half pushed me down the corridor.

"Kenneth!" called the Lady Florence.

Kenneth stopped and turned.

"Is he to be rewarded?" she asked.

"Surely," said Kenneth. "Was it not a splendid performance? Did he not do excellently?"

"Double rations, and wine," she said.

"Of course," said Kenneth.

I was angry.

"And no slut!" she said, clearly.

"He is a male slave, a fighter," protested Kenneth. "He needs a collared slut squirming in his arms. He has earned her."

"No slut," she said.

"Let me at least chain Taphris at his side," said Kenneth. "She is the least of the sluts, and has been shorn."

Taphris shrank back.

"No, Kenneth," said the Lady Florence. "Do not give him a woman."

"He is a man," said Kenneth. "He needs meat and a slave girl."

"He is not to be given a woman," she said. "Is that clearly understood, Kenneth?"

"Yes, Lady Florence," he said, angrily.

"Kenneth," she said.

"Yes, Lady Florence," he said.

"I will later find a slut for him," she said. "I have a slut in mind."

Kenneth looked at her, puzzled. "Very well, Lady Florence," he said. Then he turned about, to thrust me ahead of him down the corridor, I looked back, seeing again, at the gate, the Lady Florence and, beside her, the Lady Melpomene. Then I yielded to the pressure of Kenneth's arm and was guided down the corridor, toward the stall set aside for our fighters. Barus was close behind us, and then Taphris. Back, behind the gate, from the tiers, I could hear shouting. Another match was in progress.

# 21 THE INCUBATION SHED

I was naked and sweating profusely. It is hot in the incubation shed.

"The Mistress seems in a good mood," I said.

"Shhh," Barus, who was stripped to the waist, cautioned me. "Listen." He put his ear down to the warm sand.

I joined him, listening. Beneath the warm sand, say a foot below the surface, we heard a tiny noise, a scratching.

"It will be coming out soon," said Barus, grinning, straightening up.

"Yes, Master," I said.

"Taphris," said Barus, "put more sticks in the flame ditch."

She looked at us. She was naked. Barus had made her remove her clothes in the incubation shed. She was covered with sweat. Her flesh, in the light from the flame ditch, it almost encircling the buried clutch before us, glowed reddishly. Girths cloths lay at hand. These, sewn from feed sacks, are used to dry and wrap the hatchlings. Snout straps, too, coiled, used to secure their jaws, also lay nearby.

"I should not have to do this work," said Taphris.

"Get on your hands and knees," said Barus. "Carry the sticks, one by one, in your mouth."

"Yes, Master," she said, angrily. I smiled to myself to see the Mistress' spy, commanded by a free man, obeying.

"It is too bad she is not to be used," said Barus. "She needs raping."

I shrugged. What Barus said was doubtless true.

"Kenneth, too, is displeased with her," said Barus to me. "One can scarcely make a move in the stables without knowing that the little she-sleen is going to report it to the Mistress."

I nodded.

We watched Taphris, on her hands and knees, carry a stick

to the edge of the flame ditch and, shutting her eyes, drop it in, then quickly drawing back. She then looked at us.

"Continue, Slave," said Barus.

"Yes, Master," she said, returning on her hands and knees to the box for another stick.

"It is irritating, having such a spy about," said Barus. "Too, she thinks she is important. She thinks she is still a house girl, and not a stable slut. Her presence in the stables is not good for the discipline of the other girls."

That was true. If she were not to be whipped and chained, and disrobed and raped, as might be the others, and for no obvious reason, such as being the favorite of one of the keepers, a reason a slave girl can understand, then puzzlement, and perhaps even consternation and dissension, might soon manifest itself in the kennels. The other girls might then soon want the same privileges. And if such matters were allowed to proceed unchecked soon half-naked slave girls might aspire to the pretensions of free women, desiring to be the mistresses of their own clothing and bodies. But matters, of course, would never be permitted to reach that point. Long before that point was reached the leather would have been removed from its nail in the whipping shed.

"We must do something about Taphris," said Barus.

I shrugged. It seemed to me now, objectively, that Taphris was under sufficient discipline. She was crawling about, naked, on her hands and knees, carrying sticks in her mouth, feeding the slow fires in the flame ditch. To be sure, it had for a moment this afternoon seemed otherwise.

"Taphris," said Barus, sharply.

"Yes, Master!" she said, startled.

"Bring water," he said.

"Yes, Master," she said. She got to her feet and went to the side of the shed, where the water bucket was placed, to get the yellow, half-gourd dipper.

We watched her.

"She is pretty," said Barus.

"Yes," I said.

"It is a pity she is not to be raped," he said.

"Yes, Master," I said.

She filled the half-gourd dipper.

"It will not be difficult to get rid of her when we wish," said Barus. "Kenneth has already intimated to the Mistress that she has the makings of an excellent stable slut."

"I see," I smiled.

"Soon the Mistress will fear to trust her in the stables, where you are," he said.

"I see," I said.

"Two of the sluts in the kennels have been whining for you," said Barus.

"Might I inquire which ones?" I asked.

"Tuka and Claudia," he said. "And I do not think Peliope or Leah would much mind having your hands on them either."

I shrugged.

"They sweat in their chains," he said.

"I wish I could have them," I said.

"It is not the wish of the Mistress," he said.

"Your drink, Master," said Taphris.

He looked at her and, suddenly, frightened, she fell to her knees. She put her head down. She pressed the yellow, rough-skinned half-gourd, brimming with water, deep into her belly. Then she lifted the yellow side of the gourd to her lips and, lingeringly, turning her head, kissed it; then she lifted it to him with both hands, her head down between her extended arms.

Barus took the gourd and drank. He had seen that the Mistress' spy had served him well.

He held the cup. "Are you under perfect discipline, Taphris?" he asked.

"Yes, Master," she said, trembling.

"It did not seem so this afternoon," he said.

"Forgive me, Master," she said, trembling. "Please do not have me slain." Taphris, a Gorean slave girl, knew that she was at the complete mercy of free persons. Barus, as one of the Mistress' slave keepers, could kill her, or have her killed, at a whim. The Mistress, she knew, could always send another spy to the stables, perhaps Pamela or Bonnie, other house slaves. Neither Pamela nor Bonnie, incidentally, were Earth girls, though they wore Earth-girl names. Such names, as I have mentioned, are often used as slave names on Gor.

Taphris kept her head down.

"Do not kneel me with those sluts!" she had cried out, angrily.

The other girls, kneeling in a circle, referred to as sluts by one who was herself obviously only a stable slut, even to the rag and collar, cried out in protest, in outrage.

"Kneel," had said Barus.

"Yes, Master," had said Taphris, and she had knelt, taking her place in the circle.

She had not been pleased, but she had obeyed.

The other girls, I had seen, had glanced at one another. The outburst of Taphris had not been punished. She had not been slapped until she cried out for mercy, or kicked, or disrobed or beaten. Obviously, in some way, she was special. Barus, I had seen, had been angry.

"Sew," he had said, irritably.

He threw the girls feed sacks. To Tuka he gave a pair of scissors. To all of them he gave a needle and thread. The sacks were to be used to make girth cloths for the expected hatchlings.

The incident had occurred in the sewing shed, which has a large window. The stitching on the sacks is opened, and then the sacks are cut into appropriately sized strips, which are then joined and hemmed. Commonly this is a pleasant time for the girls, kneeling on cloths on the wooden floor, sewing and chatting, but today they were quiet and, heads down, worked and did not speak. The finished girth cloth is about ten feet in length and a yard in width. Taphris, too, sewed. She had a slight smile about her lips. The cloth of feed sacks, incidentally, though it is a coarse cloth, is seldom used for slave garments. The wool of the hurt is usually used for male slave garments; it absorbs perspiration well; and rep-cloth is commonly used for female slave garments; it is quite thin and clings well to the curves of the female body.

"We are going to chain them, with the exception of Taphris, by the fifteenth Ahn today," Barus had told me.

"The guests of the Mistress," I had said, "I have been told, would not begin to arrive until after dark."

"We think not," said Barus. "But some might arrive early. Some of these guests, at least, are apparently of refined sensibility. The Mistress does not wish to embarrass or offend them by the sight of stable sluts on the premises."

"If the guests are male I do not think they would be embarrassed or offended," I said.

"Perhaps not," smiled Barus.

"Why are the guests of the Mistress arriving after dark?" I asked. "It is unusual, is it not, to travel on Gorean roads at night?"

"Yes, it is unusual," said Barus, "particularly in times like these, what with the tense political situation existing between Ar and the Salerian Confederation. That is a situation in which many spears may mix the brew." It was a Gorean saying. The political situation was indeed complex, and might, by various parties, allies and enemies, and others, and even bystanders, be diversely influenced or exploited.

"I trust the guests will arrive safely," I said.

"I think they will," said Barus. "They are doubtless well fixed and can afford armed escorts."

"But why, in any case, should they choose to arrive after dark?" I asked.

"I do not know," had said Barus.

I had, in the afternoon, not speaking, watched the girls sew. They were lovely.

Barus, after the ringing of the bar for the fourteenth Ahn, had looked occasionally out the window, judging the position of the sun.

Early in the morning we had been in the southeast meadow, Barus, and I, and others in a work crew of male slaves. Taphris, too, had been with us, ostensibly to carry water. We had been placing sharpened posts, leaning inward, braced with abutments, at the edge of the meadow. These serve to keep the ponderous tharlarion which graze in the meadow confined.

"Look!" had called Barus, pointing upward.

Overheard we had seen some one hundred and twenty-five tarnsmen. They were moving generally southward. We could see their spears, mounted at the right stirrup, like needles, at the distance, and the shields, seeming small and round. The pennon of the standard bearer, long and narrow, fluttering back some twenty feet from his spear, was that of Vonda. Yet Vonda, herself, I knew, did not have tarnsmen. The men were mercenaries.

"It is a patrol," said the man next to me.

"It is large for a patrol," I said.

"I have been working on the fencing for the last four days," said the man. "I have seen them four times before. They return usually before dark."

"Doubtless Ar, too, has mounted such patrols," said another man.

"Yesterday," said yet another, "I saw a single tarnsman, flying northeast. He might have been a scout of Ar."

"Do you think there will be trouble?" asked a man of Barus.

"There has already been trouble," said Barus, "skirmishes in border areas, in disputed territories."

"But such things have occurred before, have they not?" asked a man.

"Yes," said Barus.

"And nothing ever came of it," said a man.

"No," said Barus.

"You do not think there will be serious trouble, do you?" pressed one of the men.

"No," said Barus, "I do not think so." He looked after the disappearing tarnsmen. "There is a party in Vonda which wishes war," said Barus, "but, as I understand it, there is little sympathy elsewhere in the confederation for conflict with Ar."

"But what of Marlenus of Ar, her Ubar?" asked one of the men.

"He does not need trouble with the confederation," said Barus. "He has his hands full these days with Cos and his troubles in the valley of the Vosk." There was a reference to the rivalry of Ar and Cos for the markets and resources of the broad regions drained by the Vosk. Both states desired to extend their hegemony into these areas. Small cities and towns, usually ruggedly independent, even belligerently so, along the river, such as Ven and Turmus, found themselves, to their discomfort, half coerced by armed might, half enticed with alliances and treaties, embroiled in the struggles of major powers.

"Hah!" laughed Barus. "How clever you scoundrels are! You engage me in conversation, and then, you shirkers, you dally in the performance of your fitting and lowly labors! Do you think you are free persons who may stop to pass the time of day? No, you are collared brutes! Now work, you neck-ringed sleen, if you would live to see the sunset, work! Work!"

Laughing, with a will, we turned again to our labors.

"Away!" cried Barus, waving his cloak at a tharlarion, browsing near the posts. It blinked, and turned away, its huge tail twitching.

Later in the morning, on the dusty road outside the posts, a two-wheeled cart passed, drawn by a small tharlarion, driven by a single driver. Behind it, her neck tied by a rope to the back of it, in a brief slave tunic, her hands braceleted behind her back, walked a slave girl. She turned, as she walked, to regard me. Our eyes met. She smiled, shyly. I grinned. She was a slave. Suddenly she hurried two or three steps forward and then, with the slack in her rope which she had gained, she turned suddenly to face me. She strained at the bracelets, twisting her body. Then, suddenly, flexing her legs, she thrust her lower abdomen toward me and kissed at me with her lips. I grinned. She quickly turned then and hurried that she might not be pulled from her feet by the rope. It had been a slave girl's gesture. I tossed a kiss after her. Too, she did not wish to alert her master to her action. He, however, stopped the tharlarion wagon and looked around. But he saw her only docilely behind his wagon, his rope on her neck, her wrists fastened behind her back in his bracelets, her head down. He looked at me, and I bent to my work. In a moment the wagon was moving forward again. I lifted my head. I saw the girl looking back. She pursed her lips and kissed to me. I brushed her a kiss in the Gorean fashion. She then turned about and followed her master's wagon.

"She wanted to be had by you," said Barus.

I said nothing.

"She presented her body to you as though to that of a rape master," he said. "Interesting," he said, "for you are only a collared slave."

I said nothing, but bent to my work. I did consider, however, the power which a free man might have over a slave girl.

I saw Taphris glaring at me. She was angry. I did not doubt but what the Mistress would hear of my interlude with the passing slave.

Barus was relieved at the edge of the southeast meadow at noon, and he, wanting help later in the incubation shed, returning to the stables, took me with him. Taphris, leaving the waterskin with the work crew, followed us.

"Who is the captain of the mercenaries who fly for Vonda?" I asked. "Is it such men as Terence of Treve or Ha-Keel, once of Ar?" These were two well-known mercenary captains. Others were Oleg of Skjern, Leander of Farnacium and William of Thentis.

"Vonda does not pay so high," he had smiled. "It is one called Artemidorus."

"Artemidorus of Cos?" I asked.

"Yes," had said Barus.

"Vonda plays with fire," I remarked.

"Perhaps," said Barus. Though such a captain as Artemidorus was a free captain, certainly the sympathies of Cos would ride with him. Too, if there were trouble it would not go unnoticed by those of Ar that they were dealing with Cosians.

"It seems a potentially dangerous choice," I said.

"Even if Vonda were willing to afford such men as Terence or Ha-Keel," said Barus, "it is unlikely they would be willing to take saddle in her behalf. Terence, being of Treve, would not be eager to ride against Ar. Such an action could precipitate a new expedition into the Voltai by the tarnsmen of Ar." Several years ago I knew there had been war between Ar and Treve. The tarnsmen of Treve, over the snow-capped crags of the scarlet Voltai range, had turned back the squadrons of Ar. It had been one of the fiercest, bloodiest tarn battles ever fought in the history of the planet. Ar had never forgotten that she had been checked in the Voltai, nor had Treve forgotten the cost of having done so. Terence, I conjectured, would not be willing to ride against Ar unless he had removed the insignia from his helmet and shield. It did not seem likely he would do so. Men of Treve commonly disdain to conceal their identity. "And Ha-Keel," said Barus, "though he was banished from Ar, would not, I think, care to ride against her."

Ha-Keel had been banished from Ar. It had been a matter of murder. A woman had been involved. He had captured, raped and enslaved her, then selling her. "Be sold as the slave you are," he had said to her. It was said, however, in the long years since his banishment, that Ha-Keel had never forgotten Ar, or the woman. He had never found her again, of course. It is difficult to trace a female slave. They often change names and masters.

"I understand," I said.

"What I fear," said Barus, "is that it is no accident that Artemidorus was given fee in this matter."

"You see in that a desire on the part of those in Vonda who favor war with Ar an artifice to provoke a full-scale conflict between Cos and Ar, a conflict in which Cos and the Salerian Confederation would then find themselves natural allies?"

Barus looked at me, soberly. "Of course," he said. "Yet I

think neither Cos nor Ar, nor the confederation, truly desires a full-scale war."

"They could be maneuvered into it, perhaps," I said, "by those who do."

"It is possible," said Barus. "Matters are delicate." He looked south. "Kaissa," he mused, "is sometimes played for high stakes." Kaissa is an intricate board game popular on Gor.

Barus then regarded Taphris. "The pretty spy accompanies us," he said.

"Yes, Master," I said.

Taphris looked down, reddening.

"After you and Jason have been swilled and watered," he said, "we are going to the sewing shed."

"Yes, Master," she said.

"Can you sew, Taphris?" he asked.

"Yes, Master," she said.

"I am glad there is something you can do," he said, "which is appropriate for a female slave."

"Yes, Master," she said, angrily.


"Chain them," said Barus.

"Yes, Master," I said.

I had, in the afternoon, not speaking, watched the girls, including Taphris, sew. They were lovely.

Barus, after the ringing of the bar for the fourteenth Ahn, had looked occasionally out the window, judging the position of the sun.

How skilled, too, were the girls, even though they had worked only on common girth cloths. How swift and nimble were their fingers, how fine and exact their work. How rude and clumsy would have been the large hands of a man for such work, and how delicate and perfect for it were the small, lovely hands of females.

I had seen Barus again look through the window. It had then been shortly before the fifteenth Ahn.

I had looked again at the girls, their scanty garments and collars, with the dependent chain loops.

How marvelous it is to be on a world where such lovely, delicious creatures may be owned.

"Chain them," had said Barus.

"Yes, Master," I had said.

The girls looked up at me, Tuka, Claudia, Peliope, Leah and Taphris.

"Tuka," I said, "open the sewing cabinet and replace the scissors on their peg; Claudia, replace the needles in the pin cushion in the cabinet; Peliope, replace the thread spools on the spool spindles in the cabinet; Leah, fold the girth cloths; Taphris, place the girth cloths on the table near the window. When you have finished your tasks, kneel by the door, in the order of descending height."

"Yes, Master," they said, for I, even though only a slave, had been placed in authority over them.

In a few moments I went to the sewing cabinet. The scissors were on their peg. I counted the needles. Five had been returned to the pin cushion. And the five spools of thread, I counted them, were residing on their spool spindles. I shut the sewing cabinet. Barus locked it. He picked up the folded girth cloths from the table near the window. "I shall meet you in the incubation shed," he said.

"Yes, Master," I said.

"On your feet," I said to the girls.

Taphris looked over her shoulder to Barus. "Surely," she said, "I am not to be chained."

He thought for a moment. He shrugged. He nodded at me. "Do not chain her," he said, "at least for the time." If she were chained, held by her collar in the kennel, confined by a linkage of steel, how could she keep her eye on me?

She tossed her head. "I am an exception," she said.

"Perhaps," I said.

"The rest of you," I said, "to your kennels, hurry!" I clapped my hands.

"Yes, Master," said the girls, with the exception of Taphris, scurrying from the sewing shed.

I glanced at the sun. They would be in the kennels well before the fifteenth Ahn.

I snapped the heavy lock, on its chain, on the collar loop of Tuka.

The girls had hurried to their kennels before me. When I arrived there I found them waiting, kneeling on the boards of their kennels, before their chain rings, in the position of pleasure slaves, back on heels, heads up, hands on thighs, backs straight, knees wide.

"Take your hands off her," said Taphris. My left hand had strayed to her right thigh, and my right hand to her left hip. It is hard to keep one's hands off a female slave. They have been made to be handled, and mastered.

"That slave," snapped Taphris to Tuka, referring to me, "is not to be pleasured. It is the will of the Mistress."

"But what of my pleasure, my needs?" asked Tuka.

"Be silent, slave," snapped Taphris.

"Yes, Mistress," said Tuka, for she sensed that Taphris had power with the Mistress. Taphris was not even being chained.

"Scream, squirm, sob, bite at your chain, tear with your fingernails at the floor of your kennel, if you wish," advised Taphris, smiling. "I am sure the Mistress will not object to that."

"Yes, Mistress," moaned Tuka.

Angry, I went then to Claudia and locked her chain on her collar.

"You have chained me," she whispered.

I grinned at her. "Yes," I said. Her breasts heaved. On Gor it is generally understood that a man who chains a woman has full rights over her.

"Master," she whispered to me.

"Slave," I said to her.

"Yes, Master," she whispered.

"Do not fraternize with the sluts," ordered Taphris.

I then, in turn, secured Peliope and Leah in their kennels. Both drew in their breath briefly, briefly, too, closing their eyes, when the heavy lock was closed about their collar loops. They then looked at me, the weight of the chain dragging down their collars. I saw that either, at a snap of my fingers, would have thrown themselves on their backs on the boards before me.

"Do not dally," said Taphris, "or I shall make a report of it to the Mistress."

I rose to my feet.

"Surely you have tasks to perform," she said.

"I must go to the incubation shed," I said. "I think it will be quite warm there, perhaps even uncomfortable. You need not accompany me there."

"I will come with you," she said.

I looked at her. "Very well," I said. "Doubtless something can be found for you to do there."

"I am not to be used for the pleasure of men," she said.

I turned about and left the kennel shed. I heard the bare feet of Taphris pattering after me. I heard, too, Tuka cry out with misery, jerking at her chain. I heard the other girls, too, moan. Then I had left the shed, Taphris with me. I paused only long enough to bar the door, from the outside.

On the way to the incubation shed, I heard the ringing of the bar which signified the arrival of the fifteenth Ahn. The stable sluts, with the exception of Taphris, were now shut away from the sight of the Mistress' guests, should they arrive early. They would not now be seen during the visit of the guests unless the guests should request to look upon them.

In the incubation shed, Barus, looking down at Taphris, held the half-gourd cup. "Are you under perfect discipline, Taphris?" he had asked.

"Yes, Master," she had said, trembling.

"It did not seem so this afternoon," he had said.

"Forgive me, Master," she had said, trembling. "Please do not have me slain." Taphris, a Gorean slave girl, knew that she was at the complete mercy of free persons. Barus, as one of the Mistress' slave keepers, could kill her, or have her killed, at a whim. The Mistress, she knew, could always send another spy to the tables, perhaps Pamela or Bonnie, other house slaves. Neither Pamela nor Bonnie, as I have mentioned, were Earth girls, though they both wore Earth-girl names. Such names, as I have mentioned, are often used as slave names on Gor.

Taphris kept her head down.

"We know you are the Mistress' spy," said Barus.

"Yes, Master," she said.

"Serve Jason water," he cried.

"Jason!" she cried.

He handed her the cup formed from the yellow half-gourd. She looked down at it, clutched in her hands. "Do you wish me to repeat a command?" he asked.

"No, Master!" she cried and leaped to her feet, hurrying to the water, in its wooden bucket, at the side of the shed. Quickly she returned with the half-gourd brimming full. She looked at Barus, and then she knelt before me, and pressed the half-gourd into her naked belly, head down, then lifted it to her lips, and lingeringly kissed it, then proffered it to me, kneeling, arms extended, trembling, head down between her arms.

"Speak," I told her.

"I bring you drink, Master," she said.

I took the cup and drank, looking upon her. How fit she seemed, in her place in the order of nature, naked, kneeling before a man. At this point it is common to rape the female.

"Let me throw her to her back in the sand," I begged Barus.

She shrank back, regarding Barus. At his least word or gesture, the smallest token of his permission, she knew she would be raped.

She trembled.

"No," said Barus, at last, regarding her, "she is not to be used for the pleasure of men, and the Mistress has given strict orders that you, unless receiving her explicit permission, are to be denied the pleasures of slut sport."

I turned away and, furious, helpless, an aroused, collared slave, struck with the side of my fist at the wall of the incubation shed.

"Return the dipper to the bucket, Taphris," I heard. I had, in fury, cast the dipper down to the sand. Barus had not reprimanded me.

"Yes, Master," I heard.

I sobbed in anger at the wall.

When I turned about Taphris, again, had been set about her homely duties, naked, on her hands and knees, carrying the sticks in her mouth, of feeding the fires in the flame ditch. I glared at her. How right she seemed for seizing and raping. She did not dare to meet my eyes.

"Here, Jason," said Barus. "Come here! Listen!"

I went to where he now knelt in the sand. The sand there began to sink down slightly. I saw it stir. Then, suddenly, the horny snout of a tharlarion thrust up from the hot sand. Its eyes blinked. Its tongue darted in and out of its mouth, licking sand from about its jaws. Its head was some eight inches in width.

"Snout strap," said Barus.

I picked up one of the long, leather, coiled snout straps lying at hand.

The head of the tiny hatchling, some eight inches wide, some foot or so in length, was now fully emerged from the sand. I saw one clublike foot, clawed, strike up out of the sand. It hissed.

I looped the snout strap about its jaws and tied them shut. It squirmed and half pulled itself from the leathery casing which had contained it, drawing it up, half out of the sand.

"Girth cloth, Taphris!" called Barus.

Together Barus and I drew the hatchling out of the sand. With my foot I thrust back the clinging shell.

"Watch out for the tail!" said Barus to Taphris. She stepped back.

Barus and I threw the hatchling on its back and, rolling it, then, wrapped its torso in the folds of the girth cloth. This tends to protect it against the tunnel air when it is carried to the nursery. I bent down and, with the help of Barus, got the hatchling to my shoulders. The head, with its strapped-shut jaws, rotated on the neck, some two feet in length. It struck against my thigh. The young beast weighed, I conjecture, some one hundred and forty to one hundred and fifty pounds. Barus slid back the bolt and lifted up the large trap door at one side of the shed and I, carefully, in the light of the fires of the incubation shed, descended the dirt ramp. At the bottom the tunnel, in its center, is floored by a set of single boards, laid end to end. This permits it to be traversed in the darkness. One need only keep one or both feet on the board. With the help of the boards, and a bit of practice, usually following a torch the first time, it is not difficult to find one's way about the tunnels in the darkness. Strings, depending from the ceiling, through which one brushes, indicate side tunnels. Inclines indicate exits. The strings contain knots on the side on which the side tunnel occurs. If one encounters, as in side tunnels, approaching the main tunnel, a fully knotted, dependent wall of strings, then one knows that a left-and-right branching is imminent. This occured in the tunneling under the domain of the Lady Florence only where the main tunnel was approached.

"Jason," called Kenneth, from the shed above me.

"Yes, Master," I said, turning, on the ramp, the hatchling quiet, puzzled, on my shoulders.

"When you have delivered the hatchling to the nursery, return to the incubation shed. Doubtless other eggs will hatch this night."

"Yes, Master," I said.

"Tomorrow you may rest," he said.

I was puzzled. "Yes, Master," I said.

"Jason," said he.

"Yes, Master," I said.

"Tomorrow night you are to report to the house."

I did not understand this.

"You were right earlier," he said, "when you suggested that the Mistress seemed in a good mood. She is."

"Yes, Master," I said.

"Her guests are arriving this evening, most, it seems, under the cover of darkness," he said.

"Yes, Master," I said.

"She is looking forward to tomorrow evening," he said. "She has planned, it is rumored, an exotic entertainment for them."

"I am to report to the house tomorrow evening?" I asked.

"Yes," he said.

"Am I to be implicated in this entertainment?" I asked.

"It is not impossible," he said.

"Do you know its nature?" I asked.

"No," he said, "but I can well conjecture what it may be."

I stood in the tunnel, puzzled.

"The hatchling must not chill," he said. "Get it to the nursery."

"Yes, Master," I said, and turned away.

"Wait, Master!" I heard Taphris cry.

I turned about, again, and saw her, drawing her tiny slave rag over her head, carefully descending the ramp, her small feet leaving prints in the incline's dust.

I turned away again and strode down the tunnel.

I heard the trap door close above and behind us. The tunnel was immediately plunged into total darkness.

I began to traverse the tunnel, toward the nursery, keeping my right foot on the center board.

"Wait, Slave!" she cried, peremptorily.

But I did not wait. I knew the tunnel well.

"Wait, Slave! Wait, Slave!" she cried angrily. Then I heard her stumbling in the darkness, half running to follow me.

"I am furious that Barus made me kneel to you!" she cried. "I am in the Mistress' favor! I am in the Mistress' favor! I am a house slave, a house slave! I am not a stable slut! I am a house slave!"

I continued down the tunnel.

"I am a house slave!" she cried.

Taphris was a bother, a nuisance. I was tired of being followed about by her. Kenneth and Barus, too, were weary of her constant spyings and reportings to the Mistress. They would not have been displeased to rid the stables of her.

"Wait, Slave!" she cried.

I considered putting the hatchling down and turning on Taphris, raping her in the darkness of the tunnel to within an inch of her life. But I did not do so. It was not that I feared the Mistress. It was rather that I did not want the hatchling to become chilled. I had stood the vigil of its hatching. I felt responsibility for it. Too, I respected it. It was a free animal. It was not a slave.

# 22 THE HOUSE GUESTS OF THE LADY FLORENCE; THE VENGEANCE OF THE LADY FLORENCE; I AM GIVEN A SLAVE TO SPORT WITH

"I do not know how I can ever thank you, Lady Florence," breathed the Lady Melpomene.

"It is nothing," said the Lady Florence, "for we are sharers of a Home Stone and are, too, fast friends."

"How I regret our former differences," said the Lady Melpomene, clasping in her two hands those of the Lady Florence.

The Lady Florence nodded, her features visible behind the light house veil, suitable for an informal dinner with friends. The Lady Melpomene, too, wore such a veil. Both were richly robed.

I stood with Kenneth behind a curtain. Through the curtain we could hear and see what took place within the lofty hall in the house of the Lady Florence, she of Vonda. The hall was lovely, too, as well as lofty, with its mosaics and tiles, its hangings and slim pillars. In the hall was an open circle of small tables, at which a handful of guests, on cushions and mats, reclined. There were four men and two women at these tables, other than the Lady Florence, the hostess, and her guest of the past several days, the Lady Melpomene. The tables were covered with cloths of glistening white and a service of gold. Before each guests there were tiny slices of tospit and larma, small pastries, and, in a tiny golden cup, with a small golden spoon, the clustered, black, tiny eggs of the white grunt. The first wine, a light white wine, was being deferentially served by Pamela and Bonnie. Both girls were beautiful, in flowing, classic white. Their arms, of course, were bare, as is common with slave girls. On the throat of each was a lustrously polished silver collar, and on the left wrist of each, locked, with a chain loop, should one desire to secure them, a matching bracelet. Both girls, of course, were barefoot.

"When these papers are signed," said the Lady Melpomene, happily, lifting some papers from the table in front of her, "I shall be free of my debts."

There was polite applause, the striking of the left shoulder, from those at the tables, including the Lady Florence.

"And all this I owe to my dear friend," said the Lady Melpomene, "the Lady Florence!"

There was again light applause, but this time, the Lady Florence, being the object of the commendation, merely bowed her head graciously.

"I lift my wine to the Lady Florence of Vonda!" said the Lady Melpomene.

"We lift our wine to the Lady Florence of Vonda," said the guests.

All then drank, save the Lady Florence, who, smiling, did not lift her cup. Free women, drinking, commonly lift their veil, or veils, with the left hand. Low-caste free women, if veiled, usually do the same. Sometimes, however, particularly if in public, they will drink through their veil, or veils. Sometimes, of course, free women will drink unveiled, even with guests. Much depends on how well the individuals are known, and who is present. In their homes, of course, with only members of their families present, or servants and slaves, most free women do not veil themselves, even those of high caste.

"I thank you, citizens of Vonda and others, friends, all," said the Lady Florence. "And now I, in turn, lift my cup."

All lifted their cups, save the Lady Melpomene.

"I lift my cup," said the Lady Florence, "to the beautiful Lady Melpomene of Vonda, who is beautiful enough even to wear the collar of a slave!"

There was laughter at this bold toast, and the Lady Melpomene, reddening, smiling, put down her head. "Please, Lady Florence," she chided. "There are those here who are not of

Vonda." She looked across the tables, across the space between them, to where three men sat, one of Venna, and two of Ar. "What will your guests think?" she asked.

"Fear not, Lady Melpomene," said one of the men, one of Ar, who raised his cup. "I am sure that the toast of the Lady Florence is true in all particulars."

There was again laughter, and all drank, save the Lady Melpomene, who, embarrassed, smiling, was the object of the toast.

Pamela and Bonnie, heads down, silent effacing themselves, as is proper with slaves, again filled the small golden cups. It was again a serving of the first wine. In a Gorean supper in a house of wealth, in the course of the supper, with varied courses, eight to ten wines might be served, each suitably and congruously matched with respect to texture and bouquet not only to one another but to the accompanying portions of food.

I looked about, through the curtain, at the guests of the Lady Florence, other than the Lady Melpomene. The fellow from Venna, clad in white and gold, was Philebus, a bounty creditor. He was known to the merchants of several cities. Such men buy bills at discount and then set themselves to collect, as they can, their face value. They are tenacious in their trade. I did not know the business of the two men from Ar. They were Tenalion, and his man, Ronald. The fourth man was Brandon. He was from Vonda. He was a prefect in that city. His certifications on certain documents would be important. The two ladies, both of Vonda, were Leta and Perimene, both friends of the Ladies Florence and Melpomene. As free citizens of Vonda they could witness legal transactions.

"The Lady Melpomene is richly garbed," I noted to Kenneth, who stood beside me.

"The garments are those of the Lady Florence," he said.

"I see," I said.

"Even the perfume she wears is that of the Lady Florence," said Kenneth.

"I see," I said.

As we spoke some five musicians entered the room and took their places to one side. There was a czehar player, two flutists, a kalika player, and a player on the kaska, a small hand drum.

Between the tables there was a large, tiled scarlet circle,

some twelve feet in width, with an iron ring at its center.

"What is the entertainment you have planned for us, Lady Florence?" inquired the Lady Melpomene.

"It is to be a surprise," said the Lady Florence.

"I can hardly wait," said the Lady Melpomene.

"You are so secretive, Florence," laughed the Lady Leta, as though chiding the Lady Florence. Yet from her laugh I through it not unlikely that she knew well what was in store.

Philebus, across the tiled circle, cleared his throat. "Let us conduct our business," he said. "We may then proceed to the amusements of the evening."

"A splendid idea!" said the Lady Florence.

"A splendid idea!" said the Lady Melpomene.

"Before you Lady Melpomene of Vonda," said Philebus, "lie several papers, detailing the consolidation of your debts. These papers are certified by the bank of Bemus in Venna, and are witnessed by the signatures of two citizens of that city. Do you acknowledge that the tallies are correct and that the debts are yours?"

"I do," said the Lady Melpomene.

"I now," said he, "by my purchased rights, charge you with these debts and demand payment."

"And, thanks to my friend, the Lady Florence, she of Vonda," said the Lady Melpomene, "you shall have your payments, and now. The Lady Florence has graciously agreed to lend me the full amount of the due notes and at no interest."

This seemed to me incredibly generous of the Lady Florence. Kenneth, near me, behind the curtain, was smiling.

"I herewith publicly sign," said the Lady Melpomene, "this loan note, made out to the Lady Florence of Vonda, for the full sum of one thousand, four hundred and twenty tarns of gold."

"And I," said the Lady Florence, "herewith publicly sign this draft, marked in the same amount, drawn on the bank of Reginald in Vonda, and properly certified, made out to Philebus of Venna."

She handed the draft to the Lady Melpomene. The Lady Melpomene handed her back the loan note. Philebus of Venna went to the table of the Lady Melpomene and took the draft. He looked at it, and was satisfied, and placed it in his pouch. The loan note was carried by the Lady Florence herself to the prefect and to the Lady Leta and the Lady

Perimene. These, with their signatures, and the prefect with a stamp also, certified and witnessed the loan note. Pamela and Bonnie, incidentally, the two enslaved Gorean beauties in attendance on the tables, did not fetch or carry the documents about. This had been done by Philebus of Venna and the Lady Florence. Slaves, generally, are not permitted to touch legal documents. They are slaves.

"You are now my full and only creditor, Lady Florence," said the Lady Melpomene. "I trust that you will be merciful, and kind, to me."

"You will be treated precisely as you deserve," the Lady Florence assured her.

"Let us all, together rejoicing," called out the Lady Melpomene, "prepare to lift our cups to our lovely and generous hostess, she with whom I share a Home Stone, my dearest friend, the Lady Florence of Vonda!" The Lady Melpomene reached for her cup.

"Do not touch that cup, Slut," said the Lady Florence.

"Florence!" cried the Lady Melpomene.

"Have you paid for the wine?" asked the Lady Florence. "Can you pay for it?"

"I do not understand," stammered the Lady Melpomene.

The Lady Florence reached to the tiny cup of wine, and seized it up, and hurled its contents against the Lady Melpomene. It struck against her veil and the upper portions of her garments.

"What are you doing?" demanded the Lady Melpomene angrily.

"What perfume are you wearing?" demanded the Lady Florence.

"Yours, as you know!" said the Lady Melpomene, coldly. "That from the shop of Turbus Veminius in Venna." I recalled the perfume which I had fetched for the Mistress, when I had been waylaid by the henchmen of the Lady Melpomene. I supposed it was the same perfume, replaced.

"Not mine," said the Lady Florence. "I use it only as a slave perfume. I use it to souse my stable sluts before I throw them chained to the men." That was not true. The Lady Florence did not permit her stable sluts perfume, even slave perfume. On the other hand the smell of their sweat and fear, and the precipitated odors of their hot love oils, indicative of their helpless arousal, were more than sufficient to excite the brutes who took them in their arms.

"Whose garments do you wear?" asked the Lady Florence.

The Lady Melpomene sprang to her feet. "I will not remain here to be insulted," she said, furiously. She drew up her robes, to her ankles, and in fury, with a sob, fled toward the door. But there she was met by two large fellows, who barred her way. "Durbar! Hesius!" she said. "Take me home." I recognized the pair. They were the fellows who had, long ago, captured me in an alley in Venna and carried me, bound in a slave sack, to the house of the Lady Melpomene, where she had used me for her pleasure. I had been returned similarly helpless to my Mistress, with a note. After that my Mistress had sent me to the stables.

The two men now each held an arm of the Lady Melpomene. "Take me home!" she cried.

"We are now in the fee of the Lady Florence," said one of the men, he whom I took it was named Durbar.

They then turned the Lady Melpomene about and, she stumbling, they forced her back to a place between the tables. The three of them then stood on the red tiles. The two men, each one holding an arm, held the Lady Melpomene so that she must face the Lady Florence.

"What is the meaning of this?" cried the Lady Melpomene.

"Whose garments do you wear?" demanded the Lady Florence.

The Lady Melpomene struggled, but helplessly. "Yours! Yours!" she then cried, held.

"Remove them," said the Lady Florence, coldly. The two men released the arms of the Lady Melpomene and stood back some feet and to the side.

"Never," said the Lady Melpomene.

"The slippers first," said the Lady Florence.

The Lady Melpomene stepped from the slippers. "She bares her feet before free persons," said the Lady Florence. The Lady Leta and the Lady Perimene laughed.

"Now throw back the hood and remove your veil," said the Lady Florence, harshly.

"Never!" cried the Lady Melpomene. The veil bore the stain from the wine which had been thrown upon it.

"You will do these things or they will be done for you," said the Lady Florence, indicating Durbar and Hesius.

The Lady Melpomene, angrily, threw back her hood, and then, pin by pin, lowered her veil. Her hair, as I recalled, was long and dark. Her cheekbones were high, her eyes dark. She was a very lovely woman.

"She face strips herself before free persons," said the Lady Florence.

"Why are you doing this to me?" cried out the Lady Melpomene. There was again laughter from the Lady Leta and the Lady Perimene.

"Remove your clothing now, all of it," said the Lady Florence, coldly.

With a sob the Lady Melpomene suddenly fled from the hall, to the anteroom beyond it. The Lady Florence indicated to Durbar and Hesius that they were not to pursue her. We heard the Lady Melpomene in the outer room, pounding on a door. It was apparently barred from the other side and whoever guarded it, probably Borto, one of the men of the Lady Florence, had been instructed not to open it in answer to her entreaties.

"Let me out! Let me out!" cried the Lady Melpomene.

"Come back, Lady Melpomene," called the Lady Florence, "and hurry, lest we become displeased."

The Lady Melpomene hurried back to the tables, sobbing, and fell on her knees at the low table of the Lady Florence. She extended her hands to the Lady Florence. She tried to touch the Lady Florence but the Lady Florence drew back. "What are you doing to me?" begged the Lady Melpomene.

"Go, stand there on the tiles, where you were before," said the Lady Florence, pointing.

With a sob the Lady Melpomene rose to her feet and went to stand where she had stood before.

"Now remove your clothing, all of it," said the Lady Florence, "or it will be done for you."

Trembling, garment by garment, the Lady Melpomene removed her clothing. Then she stood on the scarlet tiles, naked, near the iron ring.

"That is the sum of your resources," said the Lady Florence. "That is what you have, nothing."

"Please, Florence," moaned the Lady Melpomene.

"Am I not your single and full creditor?" asked the Lady Florence.

"Yes," whispered the Lady Melpomene.

Then, grandly, loftily, the Lady Florence lifted up the loan note from the table before her.

"I demand payment," said the Lady Florence. "I demand

that you now pay me the sum of one thousand, four hundred and twenty tarns of gold."

"I cannot pay you now," said the Lady Melpomene. "You know that."

The Lady Florence turned to look upon Brandon, who was a prefect in Vonda. He jotted down something on a paper before him.

"You cannot do this!" cried out the Lady Melpomene.

"Such notes as that I hold," said the Lady Florence, "are due, as you must know, upon the demand of the creditor."

"Yes, yes!" cried the Lady Melpomene, clenching her small fists. "But I did not dream you would desire to achieve so hasty a closure on your note."

"Such is my prerogative," said the Lady Florence, imperiously.

"You must give me time to recoup my fortunes!" cried the Lady Melpomene.

"I do not choose to do so," said the Lady Florence.

"Is it your intention to bring about my total ruin?" asked the Lady Melpomene.

"My intentions go far beyond your ruin," said the Lady Florence.

"I do not understand," said the Lady Melpomene.

"A demand for payment has been made, Lady Melpomene," said Brandon, a prefect of Vonda. "Can you pay?"

"You have lured me here," cried out the Lady Melpomene to the Lady Florence, "away from Vonda, beyond the shelter of her walls!"

"The walls of Vonda," said the prefect sternly, "would no longer afford you protection, for your debt, in its plenitude, is now owed to one who is a  itizen of Vonda."

The Lady Melpomene shuddered. "I have been tricked," she said.

"Can you pay?" pressed the prefect.

"No," she cried in misery, "no!"

"Kneel, Lady Melpomene, free woman of Vonda," said the prefect.

"Please, no!" she wept.

"Would you rather this be done on the platform of public shame in the great square of Vonda, where you might bring shame upon the Home Stone?" inquired the prefect.

"No, no," sobbed the Lady Melpomene.

"Kneel," said the prefect.

"What is to be my sentence?" she cried.

"Kneel," said he.

She knelt, trembling, fearfully, before him.

"I pronounce you Slave," he said.

"No," she cried, "no!" But it had been done.

"Let her be collared," he said.

The girl put her head down, sobbing.

The Lady Florence cried out with pleasure and clapped her hands together in triumph. The Lady Leta and the Lady Perimene, too clapped their hands and laughed with pleasure. Then, for a moment they struck their left shoulders in Gorean applause, congratulating the Lady Florence on her triumph over her long-term enemy.

"On your hands and knees, Slave Girl," said Tenalion of Ar, who had risen to his feet. From the box beside him he had taken a collar, with a chain loop, and a length of chain.

"May I present our friend Tenalion in a new light to you?" inquired the Lady Florence of the naked, shuddering slave near the ring. "I was somewhat obscure, as seemed fitting, concerning his business to you. He is, of course, a slaver, as is his man, Ronald."

There was a decisive click as Tenalion locked the collar on the slender, lovely throat of the new slave. It fitted, snugly. Slavers can tell a woman's collar size at a glance. She sobbed, head down, on her hands and knees, at the ring. She was now collared. Tenalion crouched beside her. It interested me that Tenalion, a slaver of Ar, was in the vicinity of Vonda. I was curious as to what the reason for that might be. It was doubtless only a coincidence, I assumed. The chain loop depended from the girl's collar. Her breasts, now those of a slave, given her posture, depended beautifully from her body. Tenalion snapped the lock at the end of the length of chain he carried about the chain loop on the girl's collar. Such women, thriftless, then indigent, on my old world, Earth, I supposed, might be supported indefinitely at public expense. Tenalion then snapped the lock-loop at the other end of the length of chain about the iron ring in the tiles. The former Lady Melpomene of Vonda, now a nameless slave, collapsed to her belly, sobbing, on the scarlet tiles, chained by the neck to a slave ring. Goreans do not see fit to reward improvidence.

"Bring a slave whip!" cried the Lady Florence, leaping to her feet.

Pamela hurried from the room.

Brandon, though a prefect in Vonda, rose to his feet and carried papers to the Lady Leta and the Lady Perimene. They were, after all, free women. They affixed the seal of their witnessing signatures to the documents. He then returned to his place and himself signed the papers.

Pamela hurried back, pressing into the hands of the Lady Florence a long-handled, five-bladed Gorean slave whip.

She seized the whip with two hands and turned to look at Brandon.

I heard the stamp of Brandon strike on the papers before him. He looked up at the Lady Florence, and smiled. "The papers are in perfect order," he said.

"I have waited long for this moment!" cried the Lady Florence. "We have been rivals, and enemies, for years!" she said to the prone slave. "How I have despised you in your pride and pretensions, how I hated you, how I held you in contempt! And now you are fully mine, helpless and at my mercy!"

The girl sobbed.

"I name you Melpomene!" cried the Lady Florence.

The girl shook with uncontrollable sobs.

"Kneel to the whip, Melpomene!" she ordered her.

Melpomene then, sobbing, knelt, her legs close together, her wrists held crossed under her, as though bound, her head down, touching the floor, the bow of her back exposed, a slave girl awaiting punishment.

"Triumph! Joy!" cried the Lady Florence. Then, holding the whip with two hands, she lashed savagely down at the slave. She struck her again and again, as though in maddened fury. The struck girl, crying out with misery could not hold the position.

"Do you dare to obstruct a blow of the whip!" cried the Lady Florence to the girl who lay now terrified and supine, in pain, wild, her hands trying to fend the leather away, at her feet.

"No, no!" cried the girl.

"No, what!" cried the Lady Florence.

"No, Mistress!" cried the girl.

"On your belly," said Tenalion to the slave. "Hold to the slave ring with both hands."

The girl obeyed. The Lady Florence then again, wildly, angrily, laid the leather to the lovely back of her former rival. I smiled to myself. Tenalion, though doubtless a strict master, was merciful. He was helping the girl to endure her first beating. Usually, of course, a girl is tied or chained for her beatings. Sometimes, however, she is not secured but merely ordered to hold the ring. After the first two or three strokes it is sometimes difficult to pry her fingers from the iron. The most merciful thing, is my opinion, however, is always to tie or chain the girl. The beating can then be straightforward and efficient. The Lady Florence was now gasping. Holding the whip clenched in her hands, standing over the slave, gasping for breath, she stopped.

"Do you beg to be whipped?" she asked.

"No, Mistress!" wept the girl on her belly at the ring.

"Beg!" cried the Lady Florence.

"I beg to be whipped, Mistress," she wept.

"Very well," cried the Lady Florence, and then, again, she struck at the girl. Then, after a few blows, five blows, she stepped back, and threw aside the whip. The girl lay at her feet, sobbing, shuddering, her hands white on the ring, her back richly striped with the blows of the whip. The Mistress returned to her place, exhausted. The Lady Florence was not strong. She had only a woman's strength. I observed the back of the girl. It was red, and covered with an intricate pattern of deeper reds, as stripes, but it was not bleeding, nor was it cut. The Gorean slave whip is made to punish a girl, and terribly, but it is not made to permanently mark or scar her. A girl with a scarred back brings a lower price in the markets. Melpomene sobbed in pain and disbelief at the ring. She had not known what it could be to be beaten. I had no doubt she would now be docile, helpless and obedient, a true slave girl. Yet I could not help smiling to myself. I wondered what would have been her reaction had she been beaten not by a mere woman, but by a man, with a man's strength.

"On your knees, Melpomene," snapped the Lady Florence.

"Yes, Mistress," wept the girl.

"Feed and water the slave," said the Lady Florence to Bonnie.

"Yes, Mistress," said Bonnie. She brought forth a pan of crusts and one of water, which she placed before Melpomene, on the floor.

"You see what an indulgent Mistress I am, Melpomene," said the Lady Florence. "I permit a slave to eat before our supper is finished."

"Yes, Mistress," whispered Melpomene.

"From whom do you receive your food and water?" inquired the Lady Florence.

"From you, Mistress," said Melpomene. The chain dangled from her collar, down, between her thighs, to the ring.

"Eat," said the Lady Florence.

"Yes, Mistress," said Melpomene. She reached for one of the crusts.

"Melpomene!" said the Lady Florence.

"Mistress?" asked the girl, frightened.

"Do not use your hands," she said.

"Yes, Mistress," said the girl. She then bent forward and, the palms of her hands on the tiles, began to eat from the pan. Too, as she ate, she lapped at the water.

"Pamela, Bonnie," called the Lady Florence, "we are now ready for the second course of our supper."

"Yes, Mistress," they said, and hurried to fetch the second course.

"It is a small dish," said the Lady Florence, "the white meat of roast vulos, prepared in a sauce of spiced Sa-Tarna and Ta wine."

The guests expressed a murmur of pleasure and anticipation. "It will be wonderful," said the Lady Leta.

The Lady Florence turned to the musicians, who were sitting to one side. "You may play," she said.

"Yes, Lady Florence," said the czehar player, their leader.

I looked at the girl at the ring, head down, feeding as a she-sleen.

"Why have I been brought here?" I asked Kenneth.

"Be patient," said Kenneth.

"Yes, Master," I said.

The dinner proceeded in a leisurely fashion through seven of its courses. There was light banter and charming conversation. The playing of the musicians was pleasant, and unobtrusive.

When the tiny plates and cups of the seventh course had been cleared away the Lady Florence looked over to the chained slave, kneeling at her ring. She had finished her own meager provender even to, at the Mistress' command, licking the pans. They had then been taken away by Bonnie.

"It is time for you to entertain us, my dear," said the Lady Florence to the slave.

The girl looked at her, frightened.

"Surely you do not think slaves are kept about only to be pampered and fed?" she inquired.

"No, Mistress," said the girl.

"I had intended to rent a dancing slave in Vonda," said the Lady Florence to her guests, "a decorous girl in blue silk and a golden collar, who might by the loveliness and grace of her movements please us, but it slipped my mind. I am so forgetful! I am afraid we must make do with poor Melpomene."

The Lady Leta laughed.

"Pamela," said the Lady Florence, "bring dancing silks for our slave."

"Oh, Mistress," said Pamela, smiling, "this is a house of refinement. We do not have such scandalous garments here."

"Ah, poor Melpomene," said the Mistress. Then she snapped to Melpomene, "On your feet, Slave!"

Swiftly Melpomene leaped to her feet, tears in her eyes. The chain fell to the ring from the chain loop on her collar.

"Tenalion, my dear," said the Lady Florence, "would you please relieve our lovely Melpomene of the impediment of her chain?"

"Certainly, Lady Florence," said Tenalion. He had been considering Lady Florence, doubtless surmising the configuration of her body beneath the ornate robes.

In a moment Tenalion had taken the chain from Melpomene, unlocking it first from the iron ring in the floor and, secondly, from her collar loop. The order of these events was not arbitrary. It was the opposite, too, of course, of the order in which she had been originally secured, where the chain had been first placed on her collar loop and only then locked about the ring in the floor. Commonly, in a Gorean tethering or chaining situation, of this sort, where neither fastening has as yet been effected, that bond which is on, or near, a woman's body is the first to be placed; similarly, of course, it is the last to be removed. In many situations, of course, there is only one fastening to be effected, that on the woman. It is not unusual for a master, for example, to keep a chain attached to the slave ring at the foot of his couch. It only needs, thus, when he wishes, to be put on the woman. Tenalion coiled the chain, and returned to his place. He put the chain in the box, which reposed near him. Melpomene then, now unchained, but naked, and wearing her collar, stood on the red tiles near the slave ring.

The Lady Florence looked to the leader of the musicians.

"Surely you are not going to dance a naked slave in mixed company?" laughed the Lady Leta.

"Is this a rude house?" laughed the Lady Perimene.

"Scandalous!" laughed the Lady Leta.

"Oh," cried the Lady Florence, in mock dismay, "I wished to obtain a dancing slave from Vonda, but it slipped my mind, so silly am I, and we have now on hand only poor Melpomene."

"She will have to do," said the Lady Leta.

"She seems a poor slave," said the Lady Perimene.

"Many slaves are like that at first," said Tenalion, soberly, "but with diet and exercise, and training, and discipline, they become wonders."

"I see," shuddered the Lady Perimene.

"To be sure," said the Lady Florence, "to dance a naked slave in mixed company seems scarcely to comport with the dignity of a refined house, but remember, too, I am a hostess, and we have men present, and we all know what beasts they are." The women laughed. "Yes," said the Lady Leta. "And so," said the Lady Florence, smiling, "as a good hostess I am under the obligation, surely, of providing a little something for the men."

"Of course!" agreed the Lady Leta.

"The beasts!" laughed the Lady Perimene.

The men laughed, and Melpomene reddened, totally.

The Lady Florence again turned to the musicians.

"Mistress," cried Melpomene, suddenly, in misery, "I do not know how to dance!"

"What!" cried the Lady Florence, as though in astonishment.

"I was a free woman," wept Melpomene. "I have been locked in a collar but this night. I know nothing of the lovely and sensuous dances of the female slave."

"Bring a slave whip," said the Lady Florence to Pamela, who swiftly brought it to her, from where she had earlier cast it aside.

I saw Tenalion smile. To be sure, many of the dances of female slaves are lovely and sensuous; others, of course, are piteous and orgasmic. In all fairness, though, one must note that there is a large variety of slave dances on Gor, and that there is some variation from city to city. The institution of female slavery on Gor is doubtless thousands of years old; accordingly it is natural that there should be great complexity and refinement in such a delicious art form as slave dance. There are even, it might be mentioned, hate dances and rebellion dances, but most dances, as might be expected, are display dances, or need dances, or love and submission dances; even the hate and rebellion dances, of course, conclude, inevitably, with the ultimate surrender of the girl to her master as a love slave.

"I do not know how to dance, Mistress," whimpered Melpomene. "Please do not whip me."

The Lady Florence stood up.

"I will dance! I will dance!" cried the girl.

The Lady Florence sat down, smiling. "And as you dance, Melpomene," she said, "do not neglect to dance your beauty to the men, and dance it as the slut and slave you are."

"Yes, Mistress!" she wept.

The Lady Florence then signaled to the musicians. There was a swirl of music and a beating on the drum, and then a pause, and then began, with the czehar prominent, the strains of a slow Gorean melody. And Melpomene, the collared slave, danced, entertaining the guests of her Mistress, the Lady Florence of Vonda.

"It is natural in a woman," said Kenneth.

"I think so," I said.

Though doubtless Melpomene was untrained and lacked the thousand precisions and controls, the brilliancies and techniques, of the trained dancer, she was not unattractive on the tiles. She strove to please and dance well. I have little doubt but what the disposition to, and the fundamentals of, slave dance are instinctual in a woman. No other explanation seems compatible with the readiness with which they can acquire such dance. Many of the expressions, the gestures and movements of the body, of course, are clearly reminiscent of those of need and desire, of love and submission. I have little doubt but what these dispositions and talents have been naturally and sexually selected for in the course of evolution, such women being more often spared and sought.

The musicians now played more swiftly.

"Earlier, I suspect," said Kenneth, "she has danced so only in the privacy of her chambers, naked, before her mirror."

"Perhaps," I said.

"What a slave she is!" called the Lady Leta.

"It is for the men," laughed the Lady Florence.

"Surely I must avert my eyes!" laughed the Lady Leta.

"I, too!" laughed the Lady Perimene.

"Dance, you slut, dance!" cried the Lady Florence.

"Yes, Mistress!" wept Melpomene. "Yes, Mistress!"

Neither of the other two women, I noted, had averted their eyes.

"To the men!" ordered the Lady Florence. "To the men!"

Sobbing, the slave then danced her beauty to Brandon, a prefect of Vonda. He threw back his head, laughing at the humiliation wrought upon her, once a proud free woman. She spun from him and, crying, danced before Philebus, bounty creditor of Venna. He grinned and lifted before her eyes the bank draft, drawn on the bank of Reginald in Vonda, certified, and signed by the Lady Florence, for one thousand, four hundred and twenty tarns of gold. His trip had been quite successful, and he had now, too, the pleasure of seeing she who had been the elusive debtor now dancing as a naked slave before him. She then spun about and danced before Tenalion and Ronald, his man. She, a slave, I noted, danced most helplessly and lasciviously before them. They were strong men, and slavers. Too, Tenalion had put the collar on her.

"Continue to dance here," said Tenalion, indicating a place before his small table.

"Yes, Master," she said, commanded.

Then, as she danced before him, he took forth a small pad and, with a marking stick, jotted notes upon it. He was doubtless appraising her, and considering how she might be improved.

After a time, he said, "You may now dance elsewhere."

"Yes, Master," she said.

But a moment after this the Lady Florence stood up and signaled to the musicians to discontinue, for the time, the music.

Melpomene then, of course, knelt, head down, facing her Mistress.

"How do you like my little dancer?" she asked.

"Excellent, for a raw slave," said Tenalion. "Obviously she has slave fire in her belly."

"Do you hear that, Girl," said the Lady Florence to Melpomene, "you have slave fire in your belly."

"Yes, Mistress," said Melpomene, head down, shamed.

"I knew it!" said the Lady Florence.

"Yes, Mistress," said Melpomene, sobbing.

"How right that you wear a collar, Slave Girl," sneered the Lady Florence.

"Yes, Mistress," sobbed Melpomene.

The Lady Florence regarded her new female slave. "Have you been shamed sufficiently, Melpomene?" she asked.

"Yes, Mistress," said Melpomene.

"No, you have not been," said the Lady Florence. "It is no dishonor for you, a slave, to dance before free persons. Rather have I accorded you a privilege in permitting you to do so."

"Yes, Mistress," said Melpomene.

"Now I think that I shall truly shame you," she said.

"Mistress?" asked Melpomene.

"Now you shall dance," she said, "before a male slave!"

"Oh, no, Mistress," begged Melpomene, "please, please do not so shame me!"

The two women, the Lady Leta and the Lady Perimene, clapped their hands with pleasure. Brandon and Philebus laughed. Tenalion and Ronald, his man, smiled.

"Please, no, Mistress," begged Melpomene, extending her hands to her Mistress. She could not believe what was being done to her. There can be no greater degradation for a slave girl than to be made to serve a slave.

"Be silent, Girl," snapped the Lady Florence.

"Yes, Mistress," wept Melpomene.

"Kenneth!" called the Mistress. "Jason!"

"Precede me," said Kenneth, holding back the curtain.

"Yes, Master," I said.

I strode into the room. I was stripped to the waist. I wore the half tunic of a stable slave.

I heard the women, the Lady Leta and the Lady Perimene, draw in their breath.

"You!" breathed Melpomene, putting her hand before her mouth.

I stood a few feet from her, my arms folded. I looked down upon her. She seemed very small and vulnerable, so white, so soft, in a steel collar, kneeling on the tiles.

I looked to the men. We measured one another, as men do. I did not flinch before their gaze, though I was slave and they were free. I had stood against men such as Gort, of the stables of Miles, and Kaibar, of the stables of Shandu, in the pit of leather and blood. Brandon, a prefect of Vonda, and

Philebus, the bounty creditor of Venna, seemed troubled. Inwardly I smiled. I could tear either of them to pieces, should it please me. I did not think Brandon would care to speak to me, unless he had guardsmen at his back. I did not think Philebus would care to pursue me for my debts. More respect I entertained for Tenalion and his cohort, he called Ronald. They were slavers. They would know the martial arts. They would be, secretly, armed. It was possible they could slay me before I could get my hands on them. Such men, though mostly they deal with collared wenches, must know the handling of the larger and more dangerous animals, the Kajiri. I saw that they did not fear me. They saw, too, however, that I did not fear them.

"Look at his body," breathed the Lady Leta.

"Where have you been keeping him, my dear?" inquired the Lady Perimene.

"He is a fighting slave, is he not?" inquired Brandon.

"I understand," said the Lady Florence, "that he has been upon occasion used in the stable bouts." Indeed, I was champion of the local stables, those within a perimeter of some fifty pasangs. Even Gort, of the stables of Miles, and Kaibar, of the stables of Shandu, had been unable to best me.

"This is Jason," said the Lady Florence, introducing me to her guests. "He is one of my less important stable slaves. He is, however, apparently not totally unattractive to certain sorts of low women."

The Lady Leta and the Lady Perimene laughed.

"According to my reports," continued the Lady Florence, "some of my stable sluts are half mad with passion for him."

"Imagine what it would be," said Tenalion, "if he were free, and they were his."

"I do not think I would mind being a slut in your stables, my dear Florence," said the Lady Perimene, "if I were to find myself at the mercy of such beasts."

"I deny him women, of course," she laughed.

"That could be dangerous, Lady Florence," said Tenalion, "unless he is kept closely chained."

"Except occasionally, of course," she laughed. She looked at Melpomene who, kneeling, in her collar, shuddered.

"Why do you limit his rations of love flesh?" asked Tenalion.

"It is my will," said the Lady Florence angrily, defensively.

"I see," said Tenalion. He smiled. He looked at the Lady Florence as though he had stripped her.

"Oh, I let him have a snack of love flesh upon occasion," she said, "if it suits my whim." My face was expressionless. I had not had a woman since I had had Telitsia in the training barn, the morning before she had been sold. "Indeed," laughed the Lady Florence, "I might let him have one tonight."

There was laughter.

"Jason," said the Lady Florence, "may I introduce one of my slaves to you, a new one. I call her Melpomene."

"Yes, Mistress," I said. I regarded Melpomene. She was visibly trembling.

"Do you remember Jason, Melpomene?" asked the Lady Florence, sweetly.

"Yes, Mistress," whispered Melpomene.

"Do you think she would make a suitable snack of love flesh for a fighting slave, Jason?" asked the Lady Florence.

"Yes, Mistress," I said.

"To his feet, Girl," snapped the Lady Florence. "Lick and kiss them!"

Melpomene fled to me. I felt her lips on my feet, and her small tongue.

There was laughter from the Lady Leta and the Lady Perimene.

"Now beg to dance for him," said the Lady Florence.

Melpomene lifted her head. There were tears in her eyes. I saw the collar on her throat, with its chain loop. "I beg to dance for you, Master," she said.

I glanced to the Lady Florence. Then I said, "You may do so."

Melpomene rose to her feet and backed away a few feet from me, and lifted her hands over her head, the wrists back to back. Her knees were flexed.

The Lady Florence regarded the slave, who, not moving, and afraid to meet her eyes, now held, trembling, one of the lovely attitudes of a dancing slave. Then, slowly, not hurrying, the Lady Florence returned to her place, behind the small table. She knelt there, making herself comfortable, and adjusting her robes.

There was silence in the room.

The Lady Florence then signaled to the musicians, and they began to play.

And Melpomene danced before me.

"If you are not pleased with her, Jason," said the Lady Florence, "let me know, and I will have her slain before morning."

Melpomene turned white, for her very life had then been placed in my hands.

"Yes, Mistress," I said.

"Please find me pleasing," begged Melpomene. "Please, Master!"

My face was expressionless. I stood regarding her, arms folded. I looked at her. I remembered her well from that night in Venna, in her house, when I had lain chained at her mercy, subject to her pleasure and abuse.

"Please find me pleasing, Master," she begged, dancing naked before me.

"I will not find you pleasing unless you are pleasing," I told her. It was true.

She moaned. The music began to swirl and flame. Piteously, and more piteously, she danced her beauty before me.

"Do you find her of interest, Jason?" asked the Lady Florence.

"The slave is not without interest," I said.

Suddenly a look of joy came into the eyes of Melpomene, as she sensed that she might be spared, and then, as suddenly, a look of astonishment, as though she could not understand what was occurring within her, and then, suddenly, a look of heat and passion.

"See the flanks move," said Tenalion to Ronald.

"Note the belly," said Ronald.

"Excellent," said Tenalion.

"Slut! Slut!" cried the Lady Florence.

The music became ever more wild and primitive.

"Slave!" cried the Lady Leta.

"Slave!" cried the Lady Perimene.

I smiled. There danced now before me an aroused slave girl, eager to please her Master.

The music suddenly stopped and Melpomene fell to her knees, putting her head to my feet.

"Has her dance pleased you, Jason?" asked the Lady Florence.

"Yes, Mistress," I said.

"Beast," she said.

"Yes, Mistress," I said.

"Pamela," cried the Lady Florence, "bring love furs!"

"Yes, Mistress," she said.

"Tenalion," said the Lady Florence. "May I trouble you to shackle my little Melpomene by the ring?"

"Of course, Lady Florence," said Tenalion. He smiled. The Lady Florence and Melpomene were of quite similar height and weight. The Lady Florence might have been an eighth of a hort taller.

Melpomene rose to her feet and stood by the ring, head down, while Pamela spread the love furs on the tiles between the tables. While she stood there Tenalion snapped an ankle ring on her left ankle. It had a chain loop. He then took the length of chain he had used before and snapped one end of it about the chain loop on her ankle ring. The other end of it he snapped about the slave ring set in the tiles. The lovely slave then stood there, shackled in place.

"You remember, Jason," said the Lady Florence, "when after your victory over Kaibar, of the stables of Shandu, I ordered that you not be given a woman."

"Yes, Mistress," I said.

"But I told Kenneth," she said, "that I would later find a slut for you, and that I had a slut in mind."

"I remember, Mistress," I said.

"This is the slut," said the Lady Florence, indicating Melpomene.

"Yes, Mistress," I said.

Melpomene stood at the edge of the love furs. She looked down at them.

"To the furs, Slave," I told her.

Melpomene looked up at me, frightened.

With the back of my hand I struck her to the furs.

She looked up at me from the furs where she half lay, half knelt. There was blood at her mouth.

"When you are ordered to the furs, move swiftly," I said.

"Yes, Master," she said.

The two women, the Lady Leta and the Lady Perimene, gasped with pleasure. I sensed that they wished that it had been they, and not Melpomene, who had been struck to the furs for their raping.

"I see that you well know how to handle a slave girl, Jason," she said.

I shrugged. I looked at the Mistress. I thought that she herself might make some man an excellent slave.

"Melpomene," said the Lady Florence to her new slave, who was now kneeling on the love furs, "when you were a free woman and dared to steal my silk slave for your pleasure, did you kiss him?"

"Of course not, Mistress," she said. "I was a free woman. I would not put my lips to the body of a slave."

"Recline on the love furs, Jason," said the Lady Florence. I did so, dropping aside the half tunic I wore. The Lady Leta and the Lady Perimene drew in their breath with pleasure.

"Melpomene," said the Lady Florence, "you understand that you are now no longer a free woman but only a slut of a slave."

"Yes, Mistress," said Melpomene, quickly.

"Furthermore, you understand that Jason is no longer a silk slave, but only a stable slave, a lowly stable slave."

"Yes, Mistress," said Melpomene.

"Kiss his body," said the Lady Florence, "every inch of it."

"Yes, Mistress," sobbed Melpomene.

"Begin at the extremities," said the Lady Florence.

"Yes, Mistress," said Melpomene.

The Mistress then clapped her hands. "Pamela, Bonnie," she said, "begin now to serve the eighth course of our supper."

"Yes, Mistress," they said.

In time my body had been covered with the kisses and tears of the new slave.

It was then that the Mistress, pausing in her meal, looked at me and said, "Congratulations on your victory over Kaibar, of the stables of Shandu."

"Thank you, Mistress," I said.

"You have had various other victories, too, I gather," she said.

"Yes, Mistress," I said.

"I have heard that, some two weeks ago, you became the local champion."

"Yes, Mistress," I said.

"That was by defeating Gort, of the stables of Miles, was it not?" she asked.

"Yes, Mistress," I said.

"I heard of that," she said. "Miles is one of my rejected suitors," she said. "Your victory over his champion gave me great pleasure."

"Thank you, Mistress," I said.

"Enjoy her," said the Mistress, indicating Melpomene, the shackled slut at my side.

"Thank you, Mistress," I said. I took Melpomene and threw her to her back beneath me, on the furs. The Lady Leta and the Lady Perimene cried out with pleasure.

I looked down into the eyes of Melpomene. She looked up at me, and then she lifted her lips softly, delicately, to mine. "Enjoy me, Master," she whispered.

"The collar is becoming on you, Melpomene," I said to her.

"Thank you, Master," she whispered.

Many times, while the guests had supped and conversed, I had forced Melpomene to yield to me, and as a slave. Often, as I caressed the helpless, squirming slut, the guests paid us little attention. They continued to enjoy their supper, served by Pamela and Bonnie, and engaged one another in conversation. Often they discussed politics. The carryings on of slaves were of little interest to them. But sometimes the Lady Leta or the Lady Perimene would pause to observe the helpless passion of the slave girl and laugh at her, or insult her for her weakness. But she only kissed and clutched at me all the more. "Slave!" once chided the Mistress. "Yes, Slave, Mistress!" cried Melpomene, joyfully. "Slave!" "Scandalous!" once said the Lady Leta. "She has no choice," said the Lady Perimene. "She must obey, and yield like that. She is a slave girl." "Look at her," said the Lady Leta. "Do you think she wants a choice?" "No," said the Lady Perimene, "she does not want a choice. Choiceless, she wishes to yield fully and totally." "That would be her choice," said the Lady Leta, "to have no choice." "Would it not, too, be your choice?" asked the Lady Perimene. The Lady Leta was silent. "How else could one yield totally to a male?" asked the Lady Perimene. Later in the evening, however, the moans and cries of the helpless slave must have become somewhat obtrusive. "Must we gag the little slut to keep her quiet?" demanded the Lady Florence, angrily. I then, from time to time, placed my hand over the mouth of the slave, that her whimperings, her moans and cries not disturb the free persons. The last time, however, I let her scream the submission of her slavery to me. "I am your slave, Master," she screamed. "I am your slave, Master!"

The guests then rose to their feet. I crouched beside Melpomene. She lay on her back, on the love furs. She was panting; her nipples were delicately rigid; her skin, from the dilation of capillaries, was a patchwork of red and white. The collar was obdurate on her throat. She reached to touch my hand. I permitted it, though she was a slave.

The Lady Florence came about the small tables to stand near the love furs, over her new slave girl.

"You are a slave, Melpomene," she said.

"I am not discontent, Mistress," said Melpomene.

The Mistress suddenly, viciously, with her small, slippered foot, kicked the supine girl. Melpomene cried out with pain.

"Kneel," I told Melpomene.

Swiftly then she knelt before the Mistress, head down. I saw then that the Mistress was mollified. I did not think then she would order Melpomene slain within the Ehn.

"Your vengeance on the slut was exquisite," said the Lady Leta.

"It was perfect," said the Lady Perimene.

"Thank you," said the Lady Florence, regarding her former enemy, now her naked slave, at her feet.

"Will you keep her as a personal serving slave?" asked the Lady Leta. "That might be amusing."

"She is too sexual to be a serving slave," said the Lady Florence.

Melpomene, head down, smiled.

"Will you keep her as one of your collared stable sluts?" asked the Lady Perimene.

The Lady Florence glanced at me. I had donned again my half tunic.

"No," she said. "I will not send her to the stables." I found that disappointing. Melpomene, I thought, would make a superb stable slut. Just the sight of her about the stables would drive the male slaves wild with desire, let alone the occasional opportunity to get their hands on her.

"No," said the Lady Florence. "I will have her sold in Ar. That is why I have invited Tenalion to my house this evening. He has a cage for her waiting in his wagon." She looked to Tenalion. "You may take her, Tenalion," she said.

Tanalion rose to his feet and went to the girl. "On your hands and knees, head down, Slave," he said.

Immediately the girl assumed this posture.

He removed his chain from the slave ring and also from the chain loop on her ankle ring. He then attached that end of the chain which had been attached to the chain loop on the ankle ring to the chain loop on her collar, that it might serve, if he wished, as a leash for her. He then threw the chain back between her legs. He then removed the ankle ring from her and threw it to Ronald, his man, who placed it in the box which resided near what had been Tenalion's place, behind his small table.

"Do you think she is good slave meat?" asked the Lady Florence.

"She is raw, and untrained, and needs diet and exercise, and discipline," he said, "but I think that, in time, she will prove superb slave meat." He then looked evenly at the Lady Florence. I conjectured that Tenalion thought it likely that the Lady Florence, too, under similar circumstances and conditions, might prove superb slave meat. I supposed that the cage on his wagon was large enough for two.

"I thank you for your supper and for the evening," said Brandon, a prefect of Vonda. "I must now rejoin my men and return to the city." "I, too, extend my thanks to you for our business, and for the supper and evening," said Philebus, bounty creditor of Venna. He looked down at the naked slave, on her hands and knees, the chain depending from her collar, trailing back between her legs. "I had not thought to collect so readily or in so full an amount my bills."

The two men, then, with felicitations and pleasantries exchanged with the Mistress, withdrew from the room. The door to the anteroom, I noted, was no longer barred. No longer was there a need that it be shut.

The Lady Florence looked down at the stripped, humbled Melpomene. "Get this slut from my sight," she said. "Put her in a cage. Take her to Ar. Sell her. Auction her naked from a block."

Tenalion smiled. "She is a piece of property," he said, "an item of merchandise. I am not a raiding slaver. I am a business slaver. I cannot simply remove her from your premises."

"She is worthless," said the Lady Florence. "I give her to you."

"She is not worthless," said Tenalion, appraising the lines of the slave.

"Give me then," said she, "a tarsk bit, the tenth of a copper tarsk. It is more than she is worth."

"I am an honest man," said Tenalion. "Permit me to give you a competitive price for her, compatible with the month's markets."

"What is she worth?" asked the Lady Florence, curious.

Tenalion placed in her hand a silver tarsk.

"So much?" asked the Lady Florence.

"Yes," said Tenalion. "She is beautiful, and in her belly is slave fire. Men will pay high for such a slut."

The hand of the Lady Florence closed on the silver tarsk. Melpomene now belonged to Tenalion of Ar.

"I have sold you, Melpomene," said the Lady Florence to the girl. "You are a sold slave!"

"Yes, Mistress," said Melpomene. "Master," she said.

"Yes," said Tenalion.

"May I speak?" she asked.

"Yes," said Tenalion.

"For what was I sold?" she asked, head down.

"A silver tarsk," said Tenalion.

"Ah," breathed Melpomene.

"See that you prove worthy of having been sold for a silver tarsk," said Tenalion.

"Yes, Master," said Melpomene.

"Doubtless, Tenalion," said the Lady Florence, "you will soon have her branded." She spoke lightly, but I could see that she was interested in the question.

The eyes of the Lady Leta and of the Lady Perimene shone above their veils.

"I will have her branded in my camp before sundown of the day after tomorrow," said Tenalion.

"I see," said the Lady Florence.

"Have no fear, Lady Florence," he said, "her thigh will soon know, and well and deeply, the kiss of the burning iron. Soon she will be a properly and fully marked slave."

"Good," said the Lady Florence. Then she added, "Do not permit her to escape."

"Slaves do not escape from Tenalion of Ar," he said. He looked at her evenly.

She shuddered. "I see," she said.

I smiled to myself. Even if the security of Tenalion were not perfect, as is that of most slavers, making escape impossible, where would a naked woman in a collar go. If she should escape one master, surely she would soon fall to another. They have been made slaves, and they will remain slaves.

"Your vengeance on your enemy, Lady Florence," said the Lady Leta, looking down at Melpomene, "is surely now complete and perfect."

"Yes," said the Lady Perimene, regarding the collared slave, "you have reduced her to slavery, you have shamed and humiliated her, you have made her entertain your guests, you have made her dance for a stable slave, and then lie for him, and have now sold her."

"Yes," said the Lady Florence, "surely now my vengeance is complete and perfect, but if this is so, then why do I feel somehow dissatisfied?"

"I can explain that to you, Lady Florence," said Tenalion, "if you wish to listen."

She regarded him, puzzled.

"Girl," he said to the slave.

"Yes, Master," she said, quickly, frightened that she had been abruptly spoken to. Had she not been fully pleasing?

"Are you pleased that you are a slave?" he asked her.

There was a silence. Then the girl whispered, "Yes, Master, I am pleased that I am a slave."

The women, the Lady Leta, the Lady Perimene, the Lady Florence, gasped in astonishment.

"That is why you are dissatisfied, my dear Lady Florence," said Tenalion.

"I do not understand," said the Lady Florence.

"You have liberated the slave in her," said Tenalion. "She is now free to be the slave that she is, fully."

"I do not understand," said the Lady Florence.

"She will come to know emotions, and degradations and joys of which you, a free woman, cannot even dream. You have returned her birthright to her."

"Her birthright?" asked the Lady Florence.

"Woman is born to the collar, and love," said Tenalion. "You have put her in a collar. And she must now, helplessly, seek the other."

"Good night, Tenalion," she said, angrily. "I wish you well."

"And good night, too, to you, Lady Florence," he said. "And I, too, wish you well."

Then he spoke to the slave. His voice was quite different when he spoke to the slave from what it had been when he had spoken to the free woman. After all, he was then addressing himself to one who was only a bond girl. "Go to the back entrance, Melpomene," he said. "My wagon is there. Beg the driver to lock you in the slave cage."

"Yes, Master," she said. Suddenly she put her lips, and then the side of her head to the side of my knee. I felt her kiss, and then her tears.

"Slave!" cried the Lady Florence.

"Yes, Slave, Mistress," said Melpomene. Then, head down, she crawled from the hall on her hands and knees. She had not been given permission to rise. The chain, fastened to her collar, dragged behind her.

"I wish to thank you for a lovely evening," said the Lady Leta.

"It was marvelous, simply exquisite," said the Lady Perimene.

Tenalion and Ronald, his man, took their leave. Ronald, in one hand, carried the slaver's case, with its chains, and rings, and bracelets and collars, with him.

The two women, the Lady Leta and the Lady Perimene, too, took their leave.

As they left, I heard the Lady Perimene say to the Lady Leta, "But who would not be a slave in the arms of such a brute?"

The Lady Florence signaled that the musicians might leave. Pamela and Bonnie knelt at one side of the room, waiting for permission to clear.

"I should get the slave back to the stables," said Kenneth. "It is late."

"Of course," said the Lady Florence.

I turned away.

"Oh, Jason," she said.

I turned about.

"You did well tonight," she said. "I am very pleased."

"Thank you, Mistress," I said. Again I turned away.

"Oh, Jason," she said.

"Yes, Mistress," I said, turning again to face her.

"It is nothing," she said. "Nothing." She looked at me. She seemed angry. "Go," she said. "Get out!"

"Yes, Mistress," I said.

"You may clear," I heard her tell Pamela and Bonnie.

I glanced about once before leaving the room. I saw Pamela and Bonnie attending to the tables. The Mistress stood alone in the room. Suddenly, angrily, she picked up a plate and flung it across the room. Pamela and Bonnie kept their heads down, pretending not to notice. Angrily the Mistress left the room.

"Come along, Jason," said Kenneth.

"Yes, Master," I said.

# 23  A GIRL IN THE TUNNEL

I stood in the absolute darkness of the tunnel. It was the central tunnel of that network of tunnels under the lands of the Mistress, by means of which various buildings, such as storage sheds, the incubation shed, certain of the stables, and the nursery, are connected.

My back was sore. Twice this week had I been beaten, and well.

Last night, while chained by the neck in my stall, I had received two visits, one from Taphris and one from Kenneth.

"Do you see now the power I have over you?" had asked Taphris.

"Yes," I had said, miserable in the straw, lying on my stomach, sick.

"I have the favor of the Mistress," said Taphris. "I can have you beaten when and as I wish."

"It is true," I admitted.

"Will you meet me now in the tunnel?" she had asked.

"No," I told her.

She stood at the open end of the stall, beyond my reach. She was angry. "I see that tomorrow," she said, "you will seize Claudia in your arms, crush her to you and rape her lips with the kiss of the Master."

I looked at her.

"It will be only my inadvertent discovery of your indiscretion," she said, "and my crying out that forced the separation of you guilty, discovered slaves."

"And I will be beaten again," I said.

"Of course," she said.

"I see," I said.

"Will you meet me now in the tunnel?" she asked.

"No," I said.

"Very well," she said.

I was silent.

"Are you not curious as to my designs on you?" she asked.

"What are they?" I asked.

"I wear a collar," she said. "I am a slave. I must obey. But I would be Mistress!"

"Mistress?" I asked.

"I will have you, when I wish, in the secrecy of the tunnels as my own silk slave," she said. "There you will obey me, and do as I command."

I was silent.

"I find your body not disagreeable, Jason," she said.

"I see," I said.

"Too, you are a strong, powerful man. I hate such men. You are the sort of man in whose arms a woman could weep herself slave. I hate such men! It will be especially delicious to break and humble you."

"I see," I said.

"Meet me in the tunnel," she said.

"No," I said.

"Very well," she said, and turned about and left.

———————◆———————

I stood in the absolute darkness of the tunnel, waiting.

I heard nothing.

"I saw Taphris sneak from the barn," had said Kenneth, when he had come to see me in my stall yesterday evening.

"Yes, Master," I had said, struggling to my knees, the chain on my neck. I did not wish to be slain for disrespect.

"Do not bother to kneel," said Kenneth, crouching at the end of the stall.

I had then sat in the stall, in the straw.

"How is your back?" asked Kenneth.

"Sore," said I, grinning. "Barus belabored it well."

"We had no choice," said Kenneth. "Taphris was watching." Kenneth looked at me. "Taphris was here," he said. "What did she want?"

"Nothing," I said.

"Speak," he said.

"She wants me to meet her in the tunnel," I said. "She wishes to force me to be her silk slave."

"The she-sleen," laughed Kenneth. "What did you say?"

"I refused," I said.

"Doubtless she will then have you beaten again," he said.

I shrugged. "Doubtless," I said.

"This sort of thing could spoil you for the bouts," he said. "Too, more grievously, it is needless and irrational. It interfers with proper discipline." Kenneth took from his belt a flask, which he handed me. "It is wine," he said.

"Thank you, Master," I said, and drank some swallows of the beverage. It was a Ta wine, from the Ta grapes of the terraces of Cos. Such a small thing, in its way, bespoke the intimacy of the trade relations between Vonda and Cos. In the last year heavy import duties had been levied by the high council of Vonda against the wines of certain other cities, in particular against the Ka-la-nas of Ar.

I handed back the flask to Kenneth.

"I am scarcely master any longer in the stables," grumbled Kenneth. "It is not just you. Taphris interferes in many ways. The men may not train as long or well for the bouts now. The stable sluts live in terror of her, fearing that because of her false reports they might lose their ears or feet. Even Barus and myself must watch our step." Kenneth threw back his head and finished the wine. He then hung the flask again at his belt. He then stood up. "Every day she grows prouder, and bolder and more insolent," he said.

"She is determined to have her way," I said.

"But she is a collared slave," he said.

I shrugged.

"I think we must find a way to remind our little Taphris of what she is," he said.

I looked up at him.

"Tomorrow," said he, "meet her in the tunnel, near the junction between the central tunnel and the side tunnel to Storage Shed Four, at the fifteenth Ahn."

"Master?" I asked.

"I have a plan," he said.

"Yes, Master," I said.

***

I stood in the absolute darkness of the tunnel, waiting. I heard nothing. It was near the fifteenth Ahn. The junction to the side tunnel, also in pitch blackness, to Storage Shed Four was to my right.

Then, from several yards away, I heard, soft and light, the movement of bare feet on the central board, that guide board set in the floor of the tunnel.

"Jason?" I heard. It was the voice of Taphris.

"Mistress?" I asked.

"Ah, you call me 'Mistress,'" she said, "excellent!"

She approached me carefully, in the absolute darkness. I felt her small hand touch my chest. "You are standing," she said. "Kneel, Slave!"

"Forgive me, Mistress," I said. I knelt before her. I heard her draw her slave tunic over her head and drop it to one side. As the tunic had passed over her head I had heard the chain loop on her collar, with a small sound, lift and then fall back into place.

"I belong to the Lady Florence of Vonda, of course," I said to her.

"Here in the tunnels," she said, "you belong to me."

"I do not think the Lady Florence of Vonda would be pleased to hear that," I said.

"Who cares for what she thinks!" laughed Taphris. "I hate her! She is a cold, arrogant woman. It is she who should be the slave, not I! Indeed, one of the pleasures of having you as my silk slave will be that you were once her own silk slave. I a mere slave, use her former silk slave as my own silk slave! Thus do I demean her!"

"I did not earlier this week," I said, "steal a kiss from Tuka nor did I, two days later, with two hands, intimately caress the leg of Peliope near the first feed shed."

She laughed. "Yet," she said, "you were beaten for both offenses."

"Why did you lie?" I asked.

"It pleased me," she said. "And did it not bring you before me, on your knees, in the tunnel, a cringing silk slave?"

"It seems to have done so," I said. "Have you lied often to the Mistress?"

"I have lied to her a hundred times," said Taphris. "The silly, pretty fool believes me. In time, though I wear a collar, I shall be, for all practical purposes, Mistress in the stables!"

"I see," I said.

"Now, Slave," she said, imperiously, "serve my pleasure!"

I reached with my right hand across to her right ankle, and with my left hand across to her left ankle.

"What are you doing!" she cried. My hands were tight on her ankles.

"Oh!" she cried. I pulled her from her feet and turned her, so that she fell away from me, heavily, on her belly and hands. Then I knelt across her body and, with the tharlarion snout strap I had had coiled to one side, knotted her hands behind her back. I then threw her roughly on her back under me.

"What are you doing, you beast!" she cried.

"I am going to use you for my pleasure, pretty Taphris," I told her.

"I will tell the Mistress!" she cried. "Oh, no! No! Please! No! Oh, oh!"

<hr />

Taphris lay weeping in my arms, trying to kiss me in the darkness.

"Are you now Mistress?" I asked.

"I did not know such feelings could exist," she said.

"Are you now Mistress?" I asked.

"No," she said, "no. I am only a slave! I was a slave before, but did not know it. You are the first to have taught me, truly, that I am a slave."

"Do you think you will forget it?" I asked.

"No," she said, "I will never forget it. I will remember it, lovingly, always."

I began to kiss her about the shoulders and throat.

"I am a slave!" she cried, happily. "I am your slave, Master!"

"Enough!" cried the Mistress. "Light! Light!"

I heard a fire maker strike in the darkness. There was a shower of sparks and then a tiny flame.

Taphris squealed in terror, squirming helplessly under me.

Then Kenneth had lit the torch and held it. Taphris, on her back in the dirt, naked, blinking against the light, her hands bound behind her, looked up in terror at the stern figure of her Mistress.

"Discovered slaves!" cried the Mistress.

"Forgive me, Mistress!" cried Taphris.

"The tunnel is often used as a trysting place for slaves," said Kenneth.

"Disgusting!" cried the Mistress.

"Forgive me, Mistress," begged Taphris. "Forgive me, Mistress!" She struggled to her knees in the dirt and put her head down to her Mistress' feet.

"I should put a pin through your ankles, Taphris," cried the Mistress, "and hang you up by the heels from a Tur tree, smeared with your own blood, for the jards!"

"Did you hear all, Mistress?" begged Taphris.

"All!" said the Mistress, savagely.

Taphris, with a moan, threw herself to her belly in the dirt before her mistress. "Mercy," she begged, "mercy, please."

"Sell her!" screamed the Mistress. "Sell her!"

"On your feet, Taphris," said Kenneth, "head down, in leading position." He bent down to retrieve her slave rag. I drew on my tunic.

Taphris stood, bent over, her knees bent, too, her head at the hip of Kenneth.

"I am your slave, Master," she whispered to me, tears in her eyes.

"You will be the slave of any man who makes himself your full master," I said.

"Yes, Master," she said.

"Sell her as a pot girl," said the Mistress.

"But she is now an ignited slave," said Kenneth, smiling.

"Are you an ignited slave?" asked the Mistress.

"Yes, Mistress," sobbed Taphris.

"Very well," said the Mistress, "when she is placed naked on a block and sold to the highest bidder let it be in a market which sells pleasure slaves."

"Yes, Lady Florence," said Kenneth.

"Thank you, Mistress," said Taphris.

The Mistress turned away from her, angrily. "Slut!" she said.

"Yes, Mistress," said Taphris.

Kenneth then thrust Taphris' slave rag in her mouth. She was to hold it there. She was not to speak, of course, until it was removed.

"Take her away," said the Lady Florence.

Kenneth then led Taphris down the tunnel, his left hand fixed in her hair, his right hand holding aloft the torch.

The Lady Florence looked about the tunnel, and at the retreating figure of Kenneth. She then looked at me. I stood there, regarding her, my arms folded. She then turned about and hurried after Kenneth, and the light of the torch.

# 24 ANOTHER GIRL IN THE TUNNEL

I stood again in the absolute darkness of the tunnel, the central tunnel of that network of tunnels under the lands of the Mistress, by means of which various buildings, such as storage sheds, the incubation shed, certain of the stables, and the nursery, are connected.

"Go to the tunnel at the fifteenth Ahn," had said Kenneth. "Wait in the central tunnel, near its juncture with the side tunnel leading to Storage Shed Four."

"Yes, Master," I had said, puzzled. It was there, yesterday, at that very spot, that Taphris had ordered me to meet her in clandestine rendezvous. It was there that we had been discovered slaves, caught by the Mistress. "The tunnel is often used as a trysting place for slaves," had said Kenneth. "Disgusting!" had cried the Mistress. Taphris, naked, and chained in a slave sack, was now on her way to a market in Vonda.

"May I ask, Master," I inquired, "as to why I am to go to the tunnel at the fifteenth Ahn?"

"Because you are told to do so," he said.

"Yes, Master," I said.

He smiled. "There is a 'new slave,'" he said. "She is to be sent to you in the tunnel."

"But would the Mistress approve?" I asked.

"She has ordered it," he said.

"That is interesting," I said. "Generally the Mistress has ordered women kept from me."

"She now sends you one," said Kenneth.

"Yes, Master," I had said.

I now stood quietly in the tunnel, waiting. I thought it must now be the fifteenth Ahn.

I then heard the footsteps approaching me. They were light, quick footsteps, feminine, not the stride of a man. Interestingly from the sound of the footsteps on the central board, as they touched it, I detected that she was wearing slippers.

"I am here," I said, in the darkness.

"Oh!" she said, and stopped, not more than a yard or two from me.

I let her stand there for a moment. She said nothing.

"Are you naked?" I asked.

"I wear a light slave gown," she said.

"Remove it," I said. I heard light silk dropped to the dirt.

"Are you now naked?" I asked.

"Yes," she said.

"No, you are not," I said. "You are wearing slippers."

"Yes," she said.

"Remove them," I said. I heard the two slippers kicked softly to the side.

"Are you now absolutely naked?" I asked.

"Yes," she said.

"Kneel," I said.

"Kneel?" she asked.

"Must a command be repeated?" I asked.

"No," she said. I heard her kneel.

"Are you now kneeling?" I asked.

"Yes," she said. "I am now kneeling." I had wished to hear from her own lips this confession that she had now adopted this posture of submission before me.

"Crawl to me on your knees," I said.

She hesitated. But then she did so.

"Kiss my feet," I said. She gasped, but then, putting forth her hands, finding me, did so.

"Straighten up," I told her. She did so.

I put forth my hands and felt her head, and her shoulders. Briefly I put my two hands in her hair, that she might know I could control her by means of it, should I choose to do so. Then I stepped back a foot or so from her.

"Lie down, on your back," I told her. I threw my tunic to the side.

"Are you now lying down?" I asked.

"Yes," she said.

I slipped down beside her, quickly, with my hands, checking that she had assumed the position to which I had ordered her.

As my hands touched her, she gasped with pleasure. She

lifted her hands to put them about my neck but I pressed them away. Then she lay quietly beside me, her arms at her sides. Her breathing was deep.

"You are a new slave?" I asked.

"Yes," she said.

I felt her throat.

"You wear no collar," I said.

"Kenneth has not yet put me in a collar," she said.

I felt her left thigh. Most girls are branded on the left thigh. Perhaps this is because most masters are right-handed. The brand, then, as one controls the slave, may be easily caressed. But her left thigh wore no brand. Her right thigh, too, as I soon noted, did not wear the slave mark, nor did her lower left abdomen. These are the three standard marking places, following the recommendations of Merchant Law, for the marking of Kajirae, with the left thigh being, in practice, the overwhelmingly favored brand site.

"You are not branded, are you?" I asked.

"Your hands," she said, "they are so possessive!"

"No," I said, "you are apparently not branded."

"No," she gasped, "I am not branded!"

I had examined her body, fully, for slave marks.

"As you now doubtless know," she said.

"Why not?" I asked.

"The Mistress has not yet seen fit to brand me," she said.

"Why not?" I asked.

"I do not know," she said. "Do you think me privy to the secrets of the Mistress? She does with me what she pleases."

"You are only an ignorant and lowly slave?" I asked.

"Yes," she said, "I am only an ignorant and lowly slave."

"Why do you think you were sent to the tunnel?" I asked.

"I do not know," she said.

"It seems then," I said, "that you are not only an ignorant and lowly slave, but one who is stupid and foolish as well."

"I am not stupid and foolish!" she exclaimed, angrily.

"Kiss me," I ordered her.

I felt her lips, warm and soft, sweet, wet, on mine. "I see that you well know why you were sent to the tunnel," I said.

"Yes," she said, "I well know why I was sent to the tunnel."

"Your use is mine," I said.

"My 'use'!" she exclaimed.

"Of course," I said.

"Yes," she then said, half purring with delight, "my 'uoo' has been given to you by the Mistress."

"You are then mine, for an Ahn or two," I said.

"Yes," she said.

"I am then, for an Ahn or two, your Master," I said.

"Yes," she said.

"And you should address me as such," I said.

"Yes," she whispered, softly, "—Master."

She tried then to kiss me, but I held her from me.

"Has the Mistress owned you long?" I asked.

"No, Master," she said. "I am a new slave."

"Where were you purchased?" I asked.

"In Vonda," she said.

"Why has the Mistress sent you to me?" I asked.

"I do not know, Master," she said.

"What is your name?" I asked.

"The Mistress has not yet given me a name," she said. "If you wish, you may give me a name, for your use of me."

"I shall not bother," I said. "It is sufficient for me that I simply hold you in my arms as a nameless slut."

Her body became suddenly rigid, but then she relaxed. "Yes, Master," she said.

"Doubtless your Mistress will soon give you a name," I said.

"Yes, Master," she said.

"It is convenient for a slave to have a name," I said.

"Yes, Master," she said.

"It is then easier to order her about, to serve and fetch," I said.

"Yes, Master," she said.

"It is interesting to me that you are not collared and branded," I said.

"Yes, Master," she said.

"Do you expect to be soon collared and branded?" I asked. I smiled to myself.

"Probably," she said, sadly.

"You sound sad," I said.

"Should I not be?" she asked.

"No," I said. "The collar and brand are splendid on a woman. They make her a hundred times, a thousand times, more beautiful."

"Oh," she said.

"Kiss me, nameless slut," I said.

"Yes, Master," she said. Then she lay back. I felt her finger at my shoulder.

"Do you think that I am more beautiful than the Mistress?" she asked.

"Probably," I said. "It is difficult for a free woman to even begin to compete with a slave in beauty."

"Is the Mistress attractive?" she asked.

"She is a quite beautiful woman," I said. "If she were made a slave, she would probably become dazzlingly and desirably beautiful."

"If the Mistress and I were both slaves," she said, "who do you think would be the most beautiful?"

"I do not know," I said. "I would have to stand you both naked in your collars before me, side by side, and see."

"That would be difficult to do," she laughed.

"Why?" I asked.

"Nothing," she said.

"Why?" I asked.

"Oh," she said, quickly, lightly, but frightened, "because Mistress is a wonderful free woman, and I am only a lowly slave."

"I see," I smiled.

"What are you going to do with me now?" she asked.

"Why use you for my pleasure, and as a slave," I said.

"Yes, Master," she breathed.

"But first I shall see if you are hot," I said.

"Master?" she asked. "Oh!" she cried.

"I see that you are hot," I said.

"Yes, Master," she said.

I held her.

"Your arms are strong," she said.

I did not move. I felt her beauty squirm against my chest and thighs. "Master, Master," she whispered. "Please, Master!"

"What do you want me to do?" I asked.

"Have your hot slave," she begged.

"Very well," I said.

I made her scream and sob muchly in the darkness of the tunnel. She seemed piteous in my arms. "I did not know it could be like this," she whispered, hoarsely.

"Be silent, slave," I told her.

"Yes, Master," she whispered, kissing and moaning.

"Do it to me again, Master," she begged. "Please, Master!"

"It is growing late," I said.

"Please, Master," she said.

"It is time to send you back to your Mistress," I said. "She will surely be wondering where you are."

"Please, Master," she begged.

"Surely you do not wish to spend time at the whipping ring," I said.

"The Mistress will not whip me," she said.

"How do you know?" I asked.

"I am sure of it," she said. "Please, please, Master!"

"It is late," I said.

"But one more time, I beg of you," she said. "But one more time, I beg of you, my Master," she said.

"Very well," I said.

She lay on her back in the dirt, beside me. She was very quiet.

I rose to my feet, found my tunic, and drew it on.

"Get on your knees," I told her.

She did so.

I reached to her hair and, holding her head with one hand, with the other jerked a few hairs from her head.

"Oh!" she cried. "Why did you do that?"

"It pleased me," I said.

"You hurt me," she said.

"Be silent," I said.

"Yes, Master," she said.

I put the bit of hair to one side, where I might retrieve it later.

"Find your things," I said, "and hold them in your hands."

She felt about in the darkness. "I have them," she said.

"Are you now again kneeling before me?" I asked.

"Yes, Master," she said.

"Kiss my feet," I said.

I felt her lips kissing at my feet in the darkness.

"Straighten up," I said.

"Yes, Master," she said.

"I now dismiss you," I said.

"You dismiss me!" she cried.

"Should I not now return you to your Mistress?" I asked, smiling.

"Yes, Master," she said, angrily.

I heard her move to get up.

"Wait!" I said.

"Master?" she asked, acidly.

I crouched beside her. I took the two slippers and the light gown from her hands. "Open your mouth," I told her. I put a bit of the silk across her lower teeth, and then thrust the open heels of the slippers into her mouth. "Close your mouth," I told her. She did so, with a sound of anger. I then, by the arms, jerked her to her feet, and turned her about.

"Return to your Mistress," I told her.

She made an angry noise.

"Run!" I told her. I gave her a swift and stinging slap below the small of the back.

She then ran down the tunnel, sobbing, away from me.

I retrieved the bit of hair which I had put on the floor of the tunnel, and placed it in my tunic.

I heard her running down the tunnel, sobbing, away from me.

I smiled in the darkness.

# 25   I FIGHT KRONDAR, SLAVE OF MILES OF VONDA; TARNSMEN

The leather slave hood was pulled from my head. I heard the cry of the crowd. Barus rubbed my back. Kenneth was wrapping the long strips of leather about my hands. I saw slave girls, in their brief rags and collars, at the gate, some standing on the bars of the gate. "Jason! Jason!" some of them called. "Krondar!" cried several of the free persons in the crowd. "Jason!" cried others.

There was a new cry from the crowd as a burly, short, thick-bodied man was led into the sand-floored, circular pit. He pulled against the manacles which confined his hands behind his back. "He is eager," I thought.

"Krondar! Krondar!" cried men in the crowd.

"I have not heard of this slave," I said to Kenneth. "Is Gort not the champion of the stables of Miles of Vonda?"

"Here," cried one of the referee's men, pointing to me, "is Jason, champion of the stables of the Lady Florence of Vonda!" There was a cheer at this. "Jason! Jason!" cried several of the slave girls. The women present at the pit of sand, whether at the gate leading into it, or in the tiers looking down upon it, were excited. Women grow excited when men are to do battle. This is because they know that they are the natural spoils of the wars of men. This is obvious in any woman, whether slave or free, but it is particularly and almost pathetically obvious among female slaves, who already know themselves explicitly and legally as properties and spoils. Too, their half-naked bodies, collared and branded, make it difficult for them to conceal their excitement, or other emotions and feelings.

"He seems strong," I said to Kenneth.

"Yes," said Kenneth, not looking back, but continuing to wrap the leather about my hands.

"His body," said I, "is muchly scarred."

"It should be," said Kenneth. I did not understand his remark.

"Krondar!" cried free persons in the tiers.

"Jason!" cried others.

I looked to the tiers and there saw the proud and regal figure of Miles of Vonda. He was smiling. I recalled that he had once been one of the rejected suitors of the Lady Florence of Vonda. He was one of the main tharlarion ranchers in the area. I did not think so proud a man would have taken his rejection cooly. The Lady Florence was not this day present at the bouts. For no reason that was generally clear to her employees and slaves she had claimed to be currently indisposed, and had chosen to remain in seclusion in her house. When I had asked Kenneth about this, he had merely grinned, and asked, "Do you not know?" "Perhaps," I had smiled.

Miles of Vonda gestured to one of the referee's men, and he removed the slave hood from the head of the burly man opposite me, across the sand.

"Aiii," I whispered.

There was a gasp of horror from the crowd.

"This," called another of the referee's men, pointing to the burly fellow, whose seconds were now removing the manacles from his wrists, freeing his hands from behind his back, "is Krondar, newly purchased slave to Miles of Vonda, and new champion of his stables!"

Krondar struggled, but was held by his seconds. One of the referee's men whipped forth steel, a Gorean blade, short and wicked, and, leveling it, thrust it a quarter of an inch into the burly man's gut. Krondar ceased struggling. He well knew the meaning of Gorean steel. Such a blade, with little effort, can disappear into a body and divide flesh.

But Krondar's eyes sought mine. They were small, under hanging brows. His face was a mass of scar tissue.

"That is no ordinary fighting slave," I told Kenneth.

"No," said Kenneth, not looking back. "That is Krondar. He is a famous fighting slave of Ar."

"His face," I said, half in awe.

"In the pits of Ar," he said, "he has fought with the spiked leather, and with the knife gauntlets."

"Doubtless he has cost Miles of Vonda much," said Barus, rubbing my back.

"Why should Miles of Vonda have purchased such a slave?" I asked. "Can the championship of the local stables mean so much to him?"

"More is at stake here," said Barus, "than a local championship. Miles is not pleased at having had you best Gort, his former champion. He is not pleased, so to speak, to have had his stables lose to those of the Lady Florence, whom he once courted in vain. Too, it is well known you were once a silk slave to Lady Florence. Thus I think he would not be entirely displeased were you to be humiliated and crushingly defeated in the pit, perhaps even broken, disfigured and maimed."

"Surely he could not be jealous of me," I said. "He is a free person, and I am only a collared slave."

Kenneth laughed.

Across the pit, Krondar's seconds were wrapping leather about his hands.

"Do not delude yourself," said Kenneth, "he will rejoice in each blow that is struck upon your body. When you fall broken and bloody at the feet of Krondar, unable to move and at his mercy, will that not be a sweet vengeance for him, against you, and, in its way, against the Lady Florence?"

"Doubtless," I said.

"Beat and mark his face well, Krondar!" called Miles of Vonda to his slave.

"Yes, Master," growled the slave.

"When Krondar is through with him," laughed a man in the tiers, "a she-tharlarion would not have him for a silk slave!" There was laughter at this.

"Krondar seems a formidable antagonist," I said.

Barus laughed.

"He is one of the finest fighting slaves of Ar," said Kenneth.

"It seems he could tear me to pieces," I smiled.

"I do not think it is impossible," said Kenneth, finishing with the leather on my hands.

I began to feel sick. "Do you think I can win?" I asked.

"Of course not," said Kenneth.

"Why then am I fighting?" I asked.

"You are champion," said Kenneth. "You must fight."

"Have you bet upon me?" I asked.

"No," said Kenneth.

"Have you bet on Krondar?" I asked.

"No," said Kenneth.

"Why not?" I asked.

"Such a bet would cast suspicion on the honesty of the bouts," said Kenneth.

"Such a bet could be placed secretly, through agents," I said.

"Doubtless," said Kenneth.

"But you have not done so?" I asked.

"No," he said.

"Why not?" I asked.

"I will not bet against my own men," said Kenneth.

"Does Master speak the truth?" I asked.

"A bold question," he smiled.

"Its answer?" I asked.

"Yes," smiled Kenneth, striking me on the shoulder. "I speak the truth!"

"Bet," I told him.

"Bet?" he asked.

"Yes," I said, grinning. "I am going to win."

"You are mad," said Barus.

"After the first few blows," said Kenneth, "feign disorientation, then when another is struck, fall to the sand."

"And then?" I asked.

"Why pretend unconsciousness," said Kenneth, "or inability to rise."

I regarded him.

"Krondar will probably kick you a few times, that your ribs may be broken, or pull you by the hair to your knees, that he may break loose your teeth or shatter your jaw, but you will live."

"As an overwhelmingly humiliated and defeated slave," I said.

"Of course," said Kenneth.

"Does Master command me," I asked, "as the collared slave I am?"

"I advise you," said Kenneth, "to adopt that course of action which is in your own best interest."

"Does Master command me," I asked, "as the collared slave I am?"

"I have watched you, Jason," said Kenneth. "The collar

does not belong on your throat. You are not a woman, born to lie-licking and loving at a man's feet. In you there is the stuff of masters."

"I am not then commanded," I said.

"No," said Kenneth. "I do not command you."

"Thank you, Master," I said. I measured Krondar across the sand.

"The bar will soon be struck," said Barus.

Krondar was eager. I was pleased at this. I decided that I would make short work of him.

"I have done all that I can do," said Kenneth.

"Not all," I said.

"What else can I do?" asked he.

"Why bet," said I.

"You are indeed mad," said Kenneth.

The bar then suddenly sounded and I leaped to my feet and moved quickly onto the sand.

I was not before him, however, when Krondar, raging, hurled himself toward me. He reeled, struck in the side of the head, against the wooden palings at the side of the pit of sand.

The crowd seemed stunned.

I did not pursue my advantage. "There are fighters other than in Ar," I told Krondar. "I hope that you understand this clearly."

He glared at me.

"A golden tarn disk on Jason!" I heard Barus cry.

"Taken!" called a man in the tiers.

"But ten to one!" called Barus.

"Granted!" called the man. "Let me bet, too," cried another.

Furious Krondar head down lunged at me. He was thus not in a position to protect against the upward stroke with which I caught him. Fortunately we did not engage with knife gauntlets or his head might have been torn from him. Even the cruel cestae of the low pits might have cut away his lower jaw. I still felt the shock in my right arm and shoulder. He staggered backward and to one side. I did not, again, pursue my advantage. "I tell you," I said, "that there are fighters, too, in what you might consider the wilderness or the outlands." He was breathing heavily. "Even in the stables of Vonda," I said, "there are champions." There was a cheer at this from many in the tiers. Even the slave girls, in their rags and collars, cried out with pleasure.

"A golden tarn disk on Jason!" cried Barus. "At ten to one!" There was silence. "Eight to one!" cried Barus. "Five to one!"

"Taken," said a man, uncertainly.

Again, maddened, Krondar, again head down, hurled himself toward me. This time I did not strike him, but let him, sand kicking behind him, plunge past me. He turned quickly, startled, at the palings. He knew that I had not struck him.

"Let us take one another seriously," I said.

"A golden tarn disk on Jason!" called Barus. "Five to one! Five to one? Three to one? Two to one? Even odds! Even odds!"

"Taken!" said a man. "Taken!" said another.

In that squarish, hideously scarred countenance of Krondar there was, for a moment, a sudden understanding that though he were now in the vicinity of Vonda he with whom he shared that shallow pit of sand, collared and slave, too, might be one perhaps not unworthy to be called a fighter.

"A golden tarn disk on Jason!" cried Barus. "Even odds! Even odds!"

There were no answers from the crowd.

Again Krondar charged, as though maddened, but I had earlier seen his understanding that I might be dangerous. This time I stood to the right and, as he thrust forth his hands to seize me, I struck upward with my left fist. I then struck him crosswise with my right fist, and then similarly again with my left fist, this time to the gut. This brought his head into position for the upward stroke of my right first again. The combination was swift and delivered at close range. The crowd was screaming. I could conceive of the post in the training barn shattering. Krondar shook his head, backing away. I followed him, warily. Swiftly, with his right foot he dug into the sand to hurl its granular shower at me, but I was too quickly upon him. Such an action puts a man off balance. I struck him four times before he struck against the palings and twisted away.

"You would not try that trick, surely, in the pits of Ar," I chided him. "Do you think you can dare to put yourself so off balance with me? Do you think to shame me? Next time I will press my advantage with severity."

Krondar grinned, and wiped blood from his face. He shrugged. "You are fast," he said.

"There are champions in Vonda!" cried a man in the tiers. "Yes!" cried others.

"A silver tarsk on Jason!" called Barus. "Even odds! Even odds!"

But no one responded to his proposal.

Krondar came carefully toward the center of the sand. He beckoned to me, "Come here," he said. "Let us become better acquainted."

"Do you think I fear to close with you?" I asked.

He suddenly lunged toward me and we, our hands even bound in leather, grappled. He grunted savagely trying to hurl me off balance into the palings. We stood locked together, swaying, breathing heavily, on the sand.

The slave girls screamed.

Krondar struck brutally against the palings. They shook. There was blood on them.

There was screaming and cries from the crowd. Krondar shook his head. He was still conscious.

"A silver tarsk on Jason!" cried Barus. "Odds of two to one in favor of Jason! Four to one? Ten to one in favor of Jason!"

The bar then rang and the first fighting period was terminated.

The crowd was screaming.

I stood unsteadily in the center of the sand. It was in the fourth fighting period. Kenneth and Barus ran to me. I felt my bloody, leather-bound fists raised in victory. Gold showered into the pit. Half-naked slave girls knelt at my feet, weeping, pressing their lips to my feet and body. I saw free women in the tiers, their eyes wild, half glazed, over their veils. Men were cheering. Many were pounding their left shoulders in Gorean applause. I saw that Miles of Vonda had left. I broke loose from the crowd and lifted Krondar, bloody, to his feet. We embraced. "You could fight in Ar," he said. Then he was pulled from me, and hooded and shackled. Kenneth and Barus drew me from the fighting area. We forced our way through the crowd. Slave girls clung about me. Even free women reached out to touch me, my body covered with sweat and sand.

Soon, at the gate leading to the stalls used as dressing rooms, the men of the bouts interposed themselves between us and the crowd. "Back! Back!" they cried. "Back, you collared she-sleen!" they cried to the slave girls, drawing their whips. And the leather of their whips, to cries of dismay and pain, fell liberally on the half-stripped bodies of the imbonded beauties. Even free women among them cried out in misery, struck. Then the women, bond and free, fell back, crying and frightened, for all women, whether slave or free, understand the whip. The gate closed behind us. Barus threw a towel about my shoulders and began to dry me. Kenneth thrust me happily down the corridor and into the straw-filled stall. "Well done, Jason!" he exclaimed. Barus reached to a peg in the stall to get my slave hood and shackles. "I want a woman," I gasped. I felt my hands pulled behind me. "I want a woman," I said. I felt the manacles, heavy and obdurate, snapped shut on my wrists. "I want a woman," I said. "Would that I could throw you a wench," said Kenneth. "You have well earned her."

"But the Mistress would not approve?" I asked.

"I do not think so," said Kenneth.

"What of the 'new slave,'" I smiled, "she who was sent to me in the tunnel?"

Kenneth grinned. "I do not think the Mistress would approve," he said.

"I want a woman," I said.

"I am sorry," he said. Then the slave hood was drawn over my head and its strap looped twice about my throat and then buckled shut under my chin.

I was not then to speak. I was a slave.

Barus continued then to towel and dry my body. I heard cries from the area of the bouts, but they were not the usual cries, those of excitement or exultation which often accompany the bouts.

"What is going on?" called Kenneth.

"Men of Cos, tarnsmen, have struck at the suburbs of Ar!" cried a man.

"It will mean war!" cried another man.

"Infantrymen from Vonda and Ar have engaged north of Venna!" called another man.

"It will be war," said Barus.

"By what right have the men of Vonda intruded so far to the south?" asked a man.

"It is done," said another.

"The entire Salerian Confederation may become involved," said Kenneth.

"Tyros, too," said another man.

"It is a grim Kaissa that is being played," said a man.

"Are the reports accurate?" asked Kenneth.

"There seems little doubt about them," said a man.

"The first steel has been bloodied," said Kenneth, grimly. "It has come at last. It is war."

"Ar and Venna are faraway," said a man.

"That is fortunate for us," said another.

Barus continued to dry and towel my body. In a few minutes I heard again the usual cries coming from the area of the bouts.

"Our men are finished," said Kenneth. "Let us get them in the wagon."

"I will first collect our bets," said Barus.

"Join us at the wagon," said Kenneth.

"I will do so," said Barus.

I felt Kenneth's hand on my arm and I felt myself being guided from the stall toward the slave wagon in which I and my fellows, other fighting slaves, were brought to the bouts.

"The fighting is faraway," I heard a man say. "We have nothing to fear."

We had been some two Ahn upon the road, returning to the lands of the Lady Florence of Vonda.

I do not know the identity of the fellow who hailed us. He may have been a peasant or a tharlarion rancher, or perhaps even a patrolling guardsman. "Beware of brigands!" he cried. "They are in the vicinity. They have already struck at the holdings of Gordon and Dorto!"

"Our thanks, Friend," called Kenneth to him. To Barus he said, "Keep watch. Have the keys ready."

"I will do so," said Barus.

I stirred uneasily in the chains.

There are varieties of slave wagons on Gor. A common type, used to transport female slaves, is covered with blue and yellow canvas. A central metal bar, hinged at one end, near the wagon box, and locked at the other, near the wagon bed's gate, usually occurs in such wagons. The girls' ankles are then chained about this bar. When the bar is freed and lifted they may then, still in their shackles, be removed through the rear of the wagon, the wagon gate being lowered. Another common type of wagon used generally in the transportation of women is the flat-bedded display wagon, with its mounted iron framework. The girls chained and manacled in various positions within and to this framework, sometimes compellingly attractive positions, are then visible. Sometimes buyers follow such wagons to the markets toward which they are bound. Sometimes, however, the girls are sold directly from such wagons, the wagons being in effect themselves traveling markets. In such cases usually one side of the flat wagon bed is used as an auction platform, a small but suitable scaffolding on which may be well displayed the lineaments of the girl's beauty, and on which may be exacted from her the provocative performances demanded by cruel and merciless vendors of their beautiful, degraded merchandise. Another common type of slave wagon on Gor is the cage wagon which, depending on the stoutness of its bars and security, may be used for either men or women. The particular slave wagon in which I was fastened combined the features of the cage wagon and common slave wagon. It was a converted tharlarion wagon and, with bars and extra planking, was unusually stout, probably because its purpose was to transport fighting slaves. It was a heavy wagon, with high sides and covered with a brown canvas. About the whole a cage had been built, with heavy bars, which opened by means of a small door in the back. Within the wagon, in low-sided, heavy stalls, by means of rings at the front and back of the stall, and on the side of the stall near our necks, we were chained by the ankles, wrists and neck. We had, thus, far less freedom of movement than is commonly accorded to females. On the other hand this additional security was only to be expected. We were male slaves, and fighting slaves. I pulled against the chains. They held me well. Gorean masters, for most practical purposes, simply do not lose slaves.

"Do you think there is danger?" asked Barus of Kenneth.

"I do not know," said Kenneth.

The wagon then began to move again. I heard chains near me move. One of my fellows struggled angrily. He, too, of course, was absolutely helpless. We were both only Gorean slaves, efficiently chained by masters.

"Look to the right," said Barus, after a time.

"I see it," said Kenneth.

"And to the right of there," said Barus.

"Yes," said Kenneth.

I did not understand this conversation, and, I suppose, neither did my fellows.

"Look there," suddenly said Barus. "In the sky!"

"I see!" said Kenneth. The wagon stopped.

I heard someone descend from the wagon box. In moments I heard the lock rattling at the rear of the wagon. I then heard keys, swiftly, being inserted into locks. "Get out of the wagon," I heard Barus ordering someone down the line from me. In moments I felt a key being thrust into the locks on my ankle shackles, and then, an instant later, I felt my manacles, fastening my hands behind my back, freed of the ring to which they were attached. My neck chain, a moment later, was pulled loose of my collar ring and fell against the side of the wagon, behind me. "Out of the wagon!" ordered Barus.

"Hurry!" called Kenneth. "He will return with others in moments!"

Barus half pulled me from the stall and pushed me toward the end of the wagon. I was still hooded. Still were my wrists confined behind my back.

"Our of the wagon!" I heard Barus order another man.

I struck against the bars at the end of the wagon. I then lowered myself to the floor and, feet first, slipped through the small, barred gate. It is made so as to admit the entrance or exit of only one man at a time. I then stood barefoot in the dust of the road.

To my amazement I felt Kenneth thrusting a key into the locks on my manacles.

"He is coming now, with others!" said Kenneth.

"Out of the wagon!" Barus ordered another man.

The manacles were pulled away from my wrists and cast through the bars into the wagon.

"Unhood yourself!" said Kenneth. He was then opening the manacles of another man. I fumbled with the buckles and then drew the hood away. The fresh air felt cold and wonderful. "Unhood yourself!" said Kenneth to another man.

"They will be here in an Ehn or less," cried Kenneth.

"Out of the wagon!" ordered Barus, addressing himself to the last man.

I looked back and to the right. There were two columns of smoke in that direction, far off. I also saw what I took, at first glance, to be a flock of birds in the sky, back and to the right.

"They are coming quickly!" said Kenneth.

I then realized that what I saw in the sky, in the distance, were birds, indeed, but tarns, and that doubtless mounted upon them, armed and purposeful, were men.

"What is going on?" cried one of the slaves.

Kenneth pointed to the sky. "Tarnsmen!" he said.

"Men or Ar?" asked a slave.

"That, or worse," said Kenneth. He then freed the last man. "Unhood yourself," he ordered him. The man, blinking, did so.

I watched the approaching riders, some pasang or so distant, some four or five hundred feet in the air.

"What do you think they will do with you?" asked Kenneth.

We stood there, uncertain, confused.

"Do you think you are lovely women, naked and alluring, whom they will simply chain up and take back to their camp, to be fitted with slave collars?"

We looked at him.

"Run!" said Kenneth. "Scatter!"

Confused, startled, we fled, scattering in various directions. I looked back once and saw Kenneth and Barus, too, hurrying from the vicinity of the wagon. I did not look back again until I had attained the refuge of an extended, linear terrain of trees and brush bordering a small stream. I saw the wagon burning. The tarnsmen then, in a moment or two, again took flight. They did not pursue us. They returned toward the twin columns of smoke in the distance. I saw the tharlarion which had drawn the wagon, cut loose and stampeded, lumbering away. I was breathing heavily. My heart was pounding wildly. I felt with my fingers the heavy collar of iron, with its ring, fastened on my neck.

# 26    I MAKE THE LADY FLORENCE MY PRISONER; WE FLEE THROUGH THE TUNNELS

There was a tearing of cloth. "No!" she cried, twisting away from him, terrified, running to the wall.

He beckoned to her with his left hand. His right hand held a sword. "Come here, my beauty," he coaxed her.

"No, please!" she cried. She was breathing heavily. She was terrified. Her right hand held her robes about her left shoulder, from which they had been torn.

The rough fellow, bearded, grinning, sheathed his sword.

"Show me mercy!" she begged.

"I will show you the mercy which a master shows his slave," he laughed.

He approached her and, as she wept, he tore down her robes to the waist.

I heard a girl screaming in the outer hall. It was probably Bonnie.

The rough fellow then, laughing, snapped slave bracelets on the wrists of the Lady Florence.

She cried out with fear as I seized the fellow by the back of the neck, thrusting my hand up under the helmet, and hurled him head-first into a wall. Stunned he turned about. I was on him in an instant. He could not free his sword or dagger. I thrust his helmeted face back again, the side of it, forcibly, against the wall. I then jerked loose the helmet strap and, by the crest, tore away the helmet, backward, almost breaking the fellow's neck. I then turned him about, measuring him. He could not defend himself. He must wait for my

329

blow. I struck him on the left side of the jaw. His head snapped to the side and he sank, senseless, to the floor. I then stepped back. He was senseless at my feet.

"Jason!" cried the Lady Florence.

I looked at her.

She reddened, blushing from the waist up. "I am braceleted!" she said, lifting her small, encircled wrists.

"You look well in slave bracelets," I told her.

She blushed, even more darkly.

"Free me," she said.

I regarded her.

"Free me!" she begged.

I went to the pouch of the fallen man and found there the key to the slave bracelets. I took them from her wrists. She rubbed her wrists, for the man had braceleted her tightly. "How horrifying is the feel of slave steel on a woman's body," she said.

"It is not horrifying," I said. "It is joyful and delicious."

"Surely I am the judge of that," she said.

"If it was horrifying," I said, "you would not now be sexually excited and filled with desire."

"I am not!" she said.

"Do you think such things cannot be told from your breathing, the mottling of your skin, the condition of your nipples, the timbre of your voice?"

"No," she said, "no!" Quickly she pulled up the robes about her body, holding them at her throat. I could still see her shoulders.

I shrugged.

"There are others about," she said, frightened. "More brigands."

"I am well aware of that," I said. "And these, or others like them, have struck at the holdings, too, of Dorto and Gordon."

"Where are the guardsmen of Vonda?" she asked.

"If any have escaped in the direction of Vonda," I said, "perhaps they may be here tomorrow, by nightfall."

"Tomorrow, by nightfall?" she said, in dismay.

"Perhaps," I said.

Then we were suddenly quiet, for we heard men in the hall outside. We heard, too, the crying of a girl. We stood, not moving. Through a crack in the door we saw two men pass.

One of the men was dragging a girl, nude, at his side, she bent over, his hand in her hair. It was Bonnie.

"Save me from these men," moaned the Lady Florence.

"Why?" I asked.

"Why they will make me a slave," she said.

"You would make a lovely slave," I told her.

"Please, Jason," she said, intensely, looking up at me. "Please, Jason!" How small and weak then seemed the Mistress, how pathetic and needful, and how far removed from the proud and imperious woman who had once, so casually and insolently, commanded me. "Please, Jason!" she said.

I looked down at her, not speaking.

"I will free you," she said suddenly, intensely.

I did not speak.

"You are free," she said. "You are free."

She fled from me to a small vanity by the wall, near her bed. She seized out a key from a drawer and fled again to me, holding her robes about her with her left hand.

"Remove the collar," I told her.

"Please, Jason," she said.

"Remove it," I said.

Blushing she allowed her robes to fall about her hips and, with two hands, holding the collar with her left and inserting the key with her right, she removed it from my throat. She bent down and placed the collar and key on the floor. She hesitated, for the briefest instant, realizing that she had bent her body before me, and then, quickly, she straightened up. I still held the slave bracelets I had removed from her in my right hand. The key I had placed in a fold-in the cloth belt of my half tunic.

She smiled. "You are now a free man, Jason," she whispered.

"Today, earlier," I said, "I defeated Krondar, a fighting slave of Ar, purchased by Miles of Vonda."

"My congratulations on your victory," she said.

"I want a woman," I said. "Do not touch your robes." Her hands hesitated, but did not touch her robes. Her body was small and soft, and beautifully rounded, before me. How incredibly beautiful women are!

"Of course," she said, nervously. "That is understandable. You may have your pick."

I threw the slave bracelets to the bed. They landed on the

wide bed, striking into the soft covers. She looked at them, nervously.

"Jason?" she asked.

I looked at her.

"You may have your pick!" she said.

"I know," I said.

She looked up at me, trembling.

"Take your clothes off, completely," I told her. "Get in bed."

"No," she whispered. "No!"

"Lie on the bed, on your stomach," I told her.

"No!" she said.

"Must you be beaten?" I asked.

"No," she said, frightened. "No." She stepped from her robes and slippers and went to the bed. She lay down upon it, on her stomach. I sat down beside her on the bed. "You may have your pick," she moaned. I pulled her wrists behind her. "The brigands are about," she wept. I snapped her wrists in the slave bracelets. "Oh," she said, for they were tight. I held her by the arms, from the back. "But you may have your pick!" she wept. "I know," I told her. I then flung her on her back, on the broad bed. She looked up at me, frightened. "I pick you," I told her.

She who had been my Mistress gasped in my arms, and then she, her head back, breathed deeply. Her small wrists pulled futilely at the slave bracelets and then her struggles subsided.

"Do you know what you have done?" she asked.

"Yes," I told her. "Shhh!" I said to her, suddenly, for I heard men speaking, out-of-doors, near the window. Her body tensed in my arms, frightened.

"Have you caught the stable sluts?" a man was asking.

"One is still at large," he was answered.

"What of the house slaves?" asked the first voice.

"They wear our chains," he was answered.

"Tie them to the saddle rings," said the first voice. "We must soon take flight."

"Where is Orgus?" asked a man.

"He went after the Mistress of the house," said another voice.

"Where is he?" asked the first voice.

"Doubtless he is richly enjoying her," said a voice. I smiled. There was laughter.

"Are you the sort of woman who can be richly enjoyed?" I asked the helpless, braceleted wench in my arms.

"I am not the sort of woman who can be enjoyed," she hissed. "I am a free woman! I am the Lady Florence of Vonda! Oh! Oh!"

I laughed softly to myself. How little she understood the potentialities of her beauty.

"Oh, oh," she moaned.

"You have underestimated yourself, lovely Lady," I assured her.

She glared up at me.

"To be sure," I said, "you are a far cry from a slave."

"Sleen," she said, but then closed her eyes and yielded to the pleasures which I saw fit, she at my mercy, to inflict upon her. "Oh," she wept. "Oh."

"But not too far a cry," I added.

She did not even respond to me, but only cried out softly, moaning. The fullness of a woman's orgasms, of course, in the totality of their physiological and psychological dimensions can be attained only by the female slave, the woman who is fully owned and finds herself at the complete mercy of a dominating and powerful master. Nonetheless I found the responsiveness of the Lady Florence, even though it was still well within the ranges attainable by the free woman, to be quite impressive. I was proud of my former Mistress. I had little doubt but that if she were made a slave she could learn well the arts of pleasing a master.

"By the way," I asked, "where is that 'new slave' whom you sent to please me in the tunnel?"

She looked up at me, frightened. "I sold her!" she said, quickly.

"She was a tasty little pudding," I said.

"A tasty little pudding!" cried the Lady Florence, angrily.

"Yes, rather like yourself," I said.

She looked at me in fury.

"Relax," I said. "For the time be content to be a tasty little pudding."

"Oh!" she said, closing her eyes. "Ah," she said. "Ah!"

"That is it," I said.

"You beast," she said, softly.

I kissed her.

"You shame me in my own bed," she whispered. "Oh, no!" she said. "Do not make me yield again!"

"Orgus! Orgus!" we heard cry.

"Do not make me yield again!" she begged.

"Yield!" I said.

She cried out, yielding, helpless.

"Hear her scream," laughed a man outside.

"Orgus is still busy with her," laughed another man.

"You bold sleen," wept the girl. "Surely we shall both be discovered!"

"Did you catch the other stable slut?" asked one of the men outside.

"Yes," said a voice. "She says her name is 'Tuka'. She is a hot one. I beat her well for being troublesome. She is now well chained at my stirrup."

"Good," said the first voice.

"Her name is now whatever we please to call her," said another man.

"Of course," said another.

"Fetch Orgus," said the first voice. "We wish to take flight."

I smiled. The girl looked at me, frightened. Then she gritted her teeth, gasping. We half reared from the surface of the bed. Then we were still. She was sobbing. Then I thrust her back to the covers. The marks of my hands on her arms were deep. I then left the bed. I went to the side of the room and picked up a bench.

The girl had then struggled to her knees on the bed. Her hair was about her face and body. Her body was covered with sweat. Her hands were braceleted behind the small of her back. "What you did to me!" she cried.

"Would you rather have spent the time wandering about the garden?" I asked.

She looked at me with anger.

"Kneel down beside the bed," I said, "facing it, your head down."

"I am a free woman!" she screamed. "You do not command me!"

"Do you want your neck broken?" I asked.

Swiftly she knelt beside the bed, facing it, head down.

"Ah," said the fellow, coming through the door, "there she is, stripped and braceleted." He looked about. "Orgus!" he cried. "What has happened?"

"Greetings," I said.

He spun about. His sword was but half from its sheath when the bench piled into his gut. Then I lifted the bench and broke it across his back.

"May I move, Jason?" asked the girl, not looking about.

"Yes," I said.

She leaped to her feet and turned about.

I was kneeling near Orgus. I tore away his weapons and accouterments. I slipped his tunic from his body and drew it on. I also put on his sandals.

"You are strong, Jason," said the Lady Florence, looking at the broken bench, "very strong."

"When these fellows revive," I said, "I do not think it would be wise for us to be in their vicinity." I drew on the weapons and accouterments of Orgus. I did this primarily that they might contribute to my makeshift disguise. I did not know the uses of Gorean steel. I had little doubt but what one who was the master of such skills could make short work of me.

"When Orgus and Andar return," said a voice outside, "burn the house."

"Have you emptied it of all valuables and slaves?" asked a voice.

"Of all but the Mistress," said another voice, "she whom Orgus has apparently been introducing to her new duties and condition."

There was laughter.

The girl looked at me, frightened.

I drew on the helmet of Orgus.

"What are we to do?" begged the girl.

"Run to me, and turn your back," I said.

"How fierce you look, in the helmet," she said, shrinking back.

"Must I repeat a command?" I asked.

She ran to me, and turned her back. "No Jason," she said.

I freed her of the bracelets and threw the key and bracelets to the tiles.

"Head in leading position," I said.

"I am the Lady Florence!" she said.

I took her head by the hair and held it at my hip. "Oh," she sobbed. It was thus that I had seen one of the brigands leading Bonnie into her new slavery, one in which she would serve not a woman, but men.

"Oh," said the girl, in pain. "Please, you're hurting me. What are you going to do?"

"Be silent," I said. "I have a plan."

"Oh," sobbed the girl, running beside me, bent over. Though she were the Lady Florence, a free woman of Vonda, I conducted her beside me as though she might have been a slave girl.

I strode rapidly through the halls of her house. Furniture had been cut open and thrown about. Hangings had been torn down. Chests had been broken open. I exited through the main entrance of the house and made my way rapidly about the house, taking the path leading to the stable area.

"Ho, Orgus!" cried a voice from the garden. "Ho, Orgus!"

"We are here!" called another voice.

I continued purposefully toward the stables.

"Have you not enjoyed her enough yet?" called a voice. "Bring her along! Chain her with the others! You can enjoy her at your leisure in the camp. Orgus!"

I continued to walk rapidly toward the stables.

"Orgus!" I heard. "Orgus!"

I did not break my stride.

"We are ready to depart!" called a voice. "Orgus!"

"Is that you, Orgus?" cried a voice.

At this point I released the girl's hair and seized her right hand with my left hand, and broke into a run for the stables. I had no doubt but what, in an instant, there would be swift pursuit of me and my fair prisoner.

"After them!" I heard.

I half dragged the girl behind me. I held her right hand, of course, for she was right-handed, and with my left, for I, too, was right-handed. Her most efficient and skilled hand was thus the prisoner of my grip, making her more mine, whereas, of course, my own most efficient, skilled hand, also the right, was freed for use. This same principle is generally used, it might be mentioned, for single-wrist leashes.

I looked back. Four men were now running towards us. "Hurry!" I cried to the girl.

We fled before our pursuers, she stumbling and gasping.

I reached the door of the nursery and kicked it open, thrusting her in front of me through the door. I joined her within and flung shut the door and threw down the bar, barring it.

A moment later. I heard the hilts of short swords pounding on the door.

"We are caught!" she wept.

"You are caught, not I," I told her. I looked about. I took two snout straps, those of the sort used to secure the jaws of newly hatched tharlarion. She looked at me. One of the snout straps I thrust, coiled, behind my belt. With the other I tied her wrists together before her body, leaving enough strap to lead her by, as a wrist leash. "By me," I told her. She gasped. There was pounding on the door.

I hurried to the trap door in the floor, that through which newly-hatched tharlarion, through the shelter of the tunnels, are brought from the incubation shed to the nursery.

Window glass shattered inward, to the side. "Stop!" we heard.

I, dragging the Lady Florence by the wrist leash, hurried down the smoothly sloping dirt ramp leading to the tunnel.

Behind us we heard men forcing open the door. We heard another breaking through the glass and wood at the window.

"Hurry, Prisoner!" I cried.

"Prisoner!" she cried.

But some fifty yards into the darkness of the tunnel I halted. As I had expected the men did not follow us blindly into the darkness. We might be presumed to know the tunnels. They would not. And I was armed, for now the steel of Orgus, the brigand, hung at my left shoulder.

"Bring torches!" I heard someone cry.

Chuckling I dragged the Lady Florence by her wrist leash through the darkness.

"I am not your prisoner!" she said.

I turned about. "Oh," she said, stumbling into me. in the darkness. I lifted her from her feet and sat her against one side of the tunnel. I crossed her ankles. "What are you doing?" she whispered. "I am going to tie your ankles," I told her. "I shall use the free end of the leash strap. I shall take the strap up then to your wrists, so that the knot will be where you can reach it neither with your fingers or teeth."

"No, no!" she said.

"Why not?" I asked.

"They will capture me," she said.

"Yes," I said.

"Do not leave me here," she said.

"Who wants a woman who is too stupid to know that she is a prisoner," I said.

"Do not leave me here," she begged.

"You will be left here as a trussed, female fool," I said, "to be a prisoner for others, others who presumably will be less particular about the intelligence of their captives."

"I am not stupid," she said, struggling futilely. "I am not a fool. I am not unintelligent!"

I stood up.

"Do not leave me here," she begged.

I turned away.

"I know that I am your prisoner," she wept.

I hesitated.

"Captor!" she cried.

"Yes," I said.

"Please do not leave me here," she begged. "Take your prisoner with you."

"Are you a prisoner?" I asked.

"Yes," she said.

"Whose?" I asked.

"Yours, yours!" she said.

"Is it true?" I asked.

"Yes," she said. "You know it is true, you beast," she said.

"And you knew it before, as well, did you not?" I asked.

"Yes," she said, angrily, "I knew it before."

"But only now have you admitted it," I said.

"Yes," she said, angrily, "only now have I admitted it."

I laughed.

"Do you laugh at your prisoner?" she asked.

"Yes," I said.

She cried out in rage.

I turned away again.

"Please do not leave me here," she begged. "Take your prisoner with you."

I turned, again, to face her. I heard her squirm, piteously, in the darkness.

"Do you beg it?" I asked.

"Yes, my captor," she said.

"Very well," I said. I whipped loose the strap from her ankles. I jerked her gasping to her feet and pulled her behind me. She ran behind me, gasping, uneasily, her wrists in my tether, her bare feet soft in the loose dirt of the tunnel.

We ran for something like a minute, and then we stopped.

"Why have we stopped?" she asked.

"Do you remember this place?" I asked.

"It is dark," she said.

"It is where you once caught two slaves rutting in the darkness," I said, "and where you once, kindly, sent me a "new slave" to content my needs."

"Let us hurry on," she said. My hands were on her arms. Then, suddenly, I thrust her arms up, and back, so that her bound wrists were now over her head. "No," she said, "you beast!"

"Are you not my prisoner?" I asked.

"Yes," she said.

"I think that I shall amuse myself with my prisoner," I said.

"No," she said.

"I shall assert the rights of the Gorean captor over his beautiful female prisoner," I said.

"Beast, beast!" she said. I forced her down. Then she was on her back in the dirt. She squirmed. "You are mad," she said. "They are in the tunnel now. Their torches are coming! Oh! Oh!" She lowered her arms, with their bound wrists, putting them about my neck. She kissed at me, helplessly. I pulled her to her feet. I dragged her beside me in the darkness. "I hear them ahead!" shouted a voice. I heard the clank of weapons. We sped on, the girl, naked, my former mistress, running and stumbling beside me. No longer did I conduct her by the wrist leash. It trailed behind her. I had felt how her body had clasped me in the darkness. I now held her by the hair. I now ran her beside me, bent over, her head at my hip.

# 27 I SEE TO IT THAT
# THE LADY FLORENCE
# PERFORMS FOR ME

"Clean it," I told her.

"I am doing so," she said, angrily. She was facing away from me, on her knees, a large brush grasped in her two hands, a bucket of water at her side.

"Do you think they have gone?" she asked.

"Yes," I said. "We waited sufficiently. Such men, too, must make their escape. They must not linger too long in the vicinity of their brigandage."

"Then we are alone, absolutely alone," she said, "on my estates."

"On the remains of your estates," I said: "The house, and many of the buildings, were burned."

She sobbed.

"Continue your work," I told her.

"Yes, Jason," she said.

I watched her.

"You are a clever man, Jason," she said. "I had thought we would have been captured. Yet you saved us."

"No," she had cried, "it is madness. No!" But I had thrown her to her side on the sand of the incubation shed and freed her wrists from before her body. I had then turned her to her belly and rebound her wrists behind her back and, pulling up her ankles and crossing them, lashed them to her wrists. I had then taken her by the arms and thrown her, in a kneeling position, onto the blackened sticks and gray ashes of the flame ditch. I had then kicked sand from the sides of the ditch about her. I jerked her head back as she cried out in misery. I kicked and scooped sand about her until only her eyes, and her nose and mouth, were exposed. I had then heard men pounding at the trap door leading into the incubation shed. I had flung shut its bolt. "Open this door!" I heard. I hurried across the shed and kicked open the outer door to the shed. I scuffed away my tracks back to the flame ditch. I heard pounding at the trap door, men straining beneath it. I looked down at the Lady Florence and saw her terrified eyes. Then I hurled a tharlarion blanket over her. Then I kicked and dug into the sand near her and, as the trap door splintered up, drew the tharlarion blanket over my head. My left hand clutched her hair, tightly. If she moved so much as a muscle I would know it, and she, too, would know that I would know it. The short sword was grasped in my right hand. The point of it, ever so slightly, was entered into her back. We heard several men come up the ramp through the trap door. We heard them talking, casting about. "This way," had said one of them, and they had exited through the outer door. We had remained hidden in the sand for several Ahn, and probably long after the brigands had departed. About the seventeenth Ahn I had eased myself from the sand and reconnoitered. The brigands, indeed, had taken their departure, bringing their tarns to flight, their loot sacks bulging and, tied helplessly at their saddle rings, lovely, naked slaves. I had drawn the Lady Florence from the sand. "Release me," she had demanded but then had gasped, lying on her back, the point of my sword thrust into her belly. "Forgive me, Jason," she begged. "Be silent now," I said, "or I will fill your mouth with sand." "Yes, Jason," she had whispered. I had then left her on her back, her knees drawn up, tied, in the incubation shed, while I had investigated certain buildings and sheds, gathering such supplies as I thought I might wish.

"Does it amuse you, Jason," she asked, "that I am cleaning your stall?"

"Are you finished?" I asked.

"Yes," she said. She was beautiful, on her knees, in the light of the small lantern, it hanging from an outjutting perpendicular fastened to one of the stall posts.

"Empty the water," I said. "Rinse and dry the bucket. Rinse the brush. Then put these articles back where you found them."

I watched her as she did these things. In a few moments she stood again before me. "I have done as you ordered," she said.

"Put now fresh, clean straw in the stall," I said.

I watched her.

Then she was standing in the stall, the clean, fresh straw to her knees.

"I have done as you have ordered," she said. "What do you want of me now?"

"I was successful many times in the bouts," I said.

"That is known to me, Jason," she said.

"Put it on," I told her, throw the rag against her flesh. She caught it, against her body, and took it in her hands, looking at it in disbelief. I had brought it from one of the supply sheds.

"Never!" she whispered intensely. "I am a free woman!"

I shook out the coils of the slave whip.

"No!" she said. Then, swiftly, she drew over her head and body the brief Ta-Teera. She backed away from me, toward the back of the stall. She tried to pull down the hem of the garment, frightened. It was cut at the sides. Then, frightened, she stood facing me, her back about a foot from the back of the stall.

"Why have you done this to me?" she asked.

The Lady Florence, my former mistress, wore now the rag of a stable slut.

"How do you like the garment?" I asked.

"Please give me something to wear," she begged.

"You have something to wear," I pointed out.

She moaned.

"How does the garment make you feel?" I asked.

"Please, Jason," she begged.

"Feel it on your body," I told her, "its texture, its meaning, how it touches you."

"Jason," she protested.

"Close your eyes," I told her. "Pay close attention to your sensations, to the fabric, its brevity, its snugness, to the feel of it on your body, to the feel, too, of where it is not on your body, to what, too, it proclaims about the woman who wears it."

She shuddered, her eyes closed. "Would you have whipped me?" she asked.

"Yes," I said.

She shuddered, and opened her eyes.

"How does such a garment make you feel?" I asked.

"It is the first time I have ever worn such a garment," she whispered.

"How does it make you feel?" I asked.

"Vulnerable!" she said. "Helpless!"

"And?" I asked.

"Do not make me speak," she begged.

"Speak," I said.

Her voice became a whisper. "And warm, and receptive," she said.

I smiled. That is a common feature of many female slave garments, most of which are brief and open at the bottom. It has been discovered that a woman who has been placed in such a garment can usually be brought to a succession of orgasms much more quickly than one who has been more traditionally clothed. Perhaps that is why masters often put their slave girls in such garments. Two other features of such garments, of course, are that they teach the woman who wears them that she is a slave and that they expose her beauty brazenly and deliciously to the vision of masters.

"What are you doing to do with me, Jason?" she asked. "No!" she wept. "Not that! Please, no!"

"I won many bouts for which I was not adequately rewarded," I said.

"Do not put the collar on me," she begged. "Please, no!"

She was backed against the rear of the stall. I stood quite close to her. I encircled her neck with the collar, but I did not yet close it.

"I am sorry!" she wept. "Please, Jason, do not close the collar!"

"Do you remember Telitsia?" I asked.

"Do not close the collar," she begged.

"Do you remember Telitsia?" I asked.

"Yes, Jason," she said.

"She pleased me," I said. "You sold her."

"No!" she wept, as the collar snapped shut about her throat. Then I threw her to my feet. Instantly I crouched beside her and, with the chain and ring in the stall, snapping the chain lock about the ring on her collar, fastened her in place. I then stood up. She, on her knees, tears in her eyes, trembling, her small hands on the chain depending now from her collar, looked up at me. "I am the Lady Florence," she said, disbelievingly. "You have chained me at your feet as a stable slut."

"I won many bouts for which I was not adequately rewarded," I said. "Too, I was fond of Telitsia, whom you sold."

"What are you going to do with me?" she asked.

"I am going to see that you yourself serve me well the pleasures which you denied me from others."

"You are going to make me stand proxy for the services of Telitsia and others?" she asked.

"Precisely," I told her.

"I cannot do that," she said. "I am free."

I crouched then beside her and thrust her back in the straw. I thrust the scrap of a slave rag she wore up over her hips. "I would have to serve you as a slave," she said, horrified.

"You will," I told her, "and many times."

She lay in my arms.

"You have treated me these many times as a slave," she chided.

"Yes," I said.

"Touch me again," she begged.

"As a free woman?" I asked.

"No," she said, with her left hand moving the chain on her collar, which lay partly across her body, to her left, "as a slave."

"Do you beg it?" I asked.

"Yes," she said.

"Yes, what?" I asked.

"Yes—Master," she said.

"Master," she whispered.

"Yes," I said.

"What time do you think it is?" she asked.

"I think it must be about the second Ahn," I said. The lantern had burned out. We were in the darkness.

"Let your girl please you again," she begged. "Oh!" she cried, delighted.

"Very well," I said. Then suddenly I seized her.

"Aiii!" she suddenly cried.

"So soon?" I marveled. She shuddered in my arms. Then I realized she had been lying heated at my side, awaiting my least touch.

"Ho, there!" I heard. "Do not move!"

We sprang apart.

"Do not move!" said the voice. A lantern, unshuttered, was lifted. We were in the pool of its light, lying in the straw. The girl gasped, and drew her legs up, tightly, under her. "A pretty one," said a voice. I tensed. "Do not move," warned another voice. I could see, dimly, that there were some five men a few feet from us. Three held drawn crossbows. The quarrels were trained on me.

"Are you a brigand?" asked a voice.

"No," I said. "You then, too," I asked, "are not brigands?"

"Call Miles," said a voice. One of the men left the barn. When he left, through the large door, I could see that it was still dark out. I saw the light of the Gorean moons on the earth outside. The stars were still bright in the sky.

"You, then, are not brigands?" I asked.

"No," said the man.

"Are you guardsmen then?" I asked. I did not think they were guardsmen. Too, I did not think guardsmen would be likely to arrive before morning. Too, many estates in the area may have been struck by the brigands.

"No," said the man.

A tall figure then entered the barn. With him there were some five men, two with lanterns. One of the men was he who had gone to fetch another man, he called Miles. This Miles, I assumed, was the tall man. He was, too, I assumed, their leader.

"These are the only two upon the estate," said one of the men. "Even the tharlarion were turned loose and scattered."

"The brigands were cruel, and thorough," said another.

Two more lanterns were lifted, and unshuttered, well exposing the girl and me in the straw. I blinked against the light. I could not well see the features of the tall man. He carried a drawn sword in one hand, and, in the other, his left, a dangling set of light slave chains, suitable for a female.

"Who are you?" asked the man.

"I am Jason," I said.

"The fighting slave?" he asked.

"I was freed," I said.

The tall man's gaze wandered to the girl beside me, the chain depending from her collar. His gaze lingered upon her, examining her beauty casually. She shrank back. "Does she not know she is in the presence of free men?" he asked.

"Position, Slut!" I snapped to the girl.

Swiftly the Lady Florence, frightened, knelt in the straw. She knelt back on her heels, her back straight, her head up, her hands on her thighs. She knelt in the position of the house slave. I looked at her sternly. Swiftly she spread her knees. She knelt now in the position of the pleasure slave, the slave of interest to men.

"Lift your chin, Jason," said the man. "Bring a lantern closer," he said to one of his fellows.

I did as he commanded.

"Indeed," said the man. "Your throat no longer wears a collar."

"The Mistress freed me," I said, "even before the brigands departed from the estates."

"I wonder if that is true," said the man.

"It is," I said. "Had I been a slave, interested in flight, surely I would not have dallied upon the estates."

"It is true," said one of the men. "He is known here, and in this area."

"You fought well today, Jason," said the man. "You cost me many tarn disks."

"You are Miles of Vonda, are you not?" I asked.

"Yes," said the man.

"He cost me twenty copper tarsks," said another man.

"And me fifteen," said another.

"It was a splendid fight," said another man, admiringly.

"Yes," agreed another.

"Thank you," I said. I now felt somewhat relieved. I did not feel these men were motivated by any particularly hostile intent. If I watched my step, I did not think I truly had anything to fear from them.

"Why are you here?" asked the girl.

"Your slave needs discipline," said Miles of Vonda.

I turned about and took the startled girl by the chain at her collar. Swiftly I lashed her face, back and forth, striking her twice, first with the palm of my hand, and then with the back of it. Then I threw her to her side in the straw. She looked up at me in disbelief, horrified. There was blood at her mouth. I do not think she had ever been struck by a man before. Indeed, as a Gorean free woman, it is possible that she had never been struck, truly and seriously, by anyone before.

"Position," I told her.

Then she struggled to her knees and knelt again in the position of the pleasure slave, that of a woman who is of interest to men.

"Why are you here?" I asked Miles of Vonda.

He smiled. "It is of no concern of yours," he said. "Where is she who was your Mistress?"

"I do not know," I said. The girl trembled. Miles of Vonda, of course, would not be likely to recognize her, for, hitherto, he would have seen her only in the robes of a free woman and heavily and modestly veiled. I did not think him likely to identify the lofty Lady Florence, a rich, high-born woman of Vonda, with the scantily-clad, exciting, punished girl who knelt chained as a slut beside me.

"Did she escape?" he asked.

"I think she escaped the brigands," I said.

"Where is she now?" he asked.

"Perhaps safe in Vonda, or in its vicinity," I said. "Why do you seek her?"

"These are hard times," said Miles of Vonda. "There is a breakdown of law and order."

"I see," I said. "But why, in such times, would you be searching for she who was once my Mistress?"

"Who knows what could happen to a woman in such times?" he asked. He lifted the light slave chains before me. They rustled in the palm of his hand.

"I see," I said.

"She is not here," said Miles of Vonda to his men. "We shall search elsewhere, in the vicinity, in the brush near the roads leading to Vonda." He turned again to face me. "Enjoy your slut, Jason," said he. He smiled. "You have well earned her."

"Thank you," said I, "Miles of Vonda."

The men then departed from the barn. I took the back of the girl's neck, over the collar, in one hand, and held my other hand over her mouth, that she might not speak until I was sure the men had gone. Finally, after several Ehn, I removed my hands from the back of her neck and mouth.

"Did you see that?" she whispered. "He was looking for me, and he was carrying slave chains."

"Yes," I said. I smiled. Miles of Vonda had been one of several unsuccessful suitors for the hand of the proud Lady

Florence of Vonda. He had not been successful in winning her to be his in Free Companionship, nor had his many competitors. The Lady Florence had held herself to be too good for men. Now, perhaps he reasoned, if she could not be enticed to kneel across from him at his table in the honorable resplendent robes of free companionship she might at least, perhaps, more appropriately, crawl to him naked, on her belly, under the whip, across the tiles of his slave quarters.

She looked at me, frightened.

"On your back, slut," I told her.

She lay back in the straw, the chain on her throat. She brushed it to one side with her hand.

"You struck me," she said.

"Yes," I said.

"I was never struck before," she said. "It is a strange feeling, to have been struck by a man."

I looked down at her.

"I must obey you, mustn't I?" she asked.

"Yes," I said.

"Are you going to strike me again?" she asked.

"If it pleases me," I said.

"Do not strike me again," she said. "Kiss and caress me instead."

"I will do either, or both, as it might please me," I said.

"Then I am, in your arms, no better than a slave," she said.

"Yes," I said.

She sat up, angrily, pulling at the collar that encircled her throat. It remained well fastened on her.

"Do you really think to remove it?" I asked her.

"No," she said, angrily. She sat forward, holding her knees. "What a fool Miles of Vonda is," she said. "He looked upon me and could not even tell the difference between the Lady Florence of Vonda and a mere slave girl."

"The light was poor," I said. "He did not examine your thigh for a brand."

"But he looked at me!" she said.

"That is true," I admitted, smiling. I well remembered the casual care with which the chained beauty at my side had been examined.

"How could he not have recognized me as a free woman?" she asked.

"He did not examine your thigh," I said.

"Light the lantern, Jason," she said, "please."

I found the lantern on its outjutting perpendicular and, in a few Ehn, adding some oil, turning up the wick and striking some pyrites together, relit it. I rehung the lantern on the perpendicular.

"Look at me, Jason," she said. "Do you think that I am a slave?"

"I know that you are a free woman," I said. Then I snapped, "Position!"

Angrily she assumed the position of the house slave. I continued to look at her. Angrily she spread her knees.

"It is difficult to talk to a man as a free woman in this position," she said.

"Doubtless that is true," I said.

"May I assume another position?" she asked.

"No," I said.

"Look at me, Jason," she said. "Can you not see that I am a free woman?"

"I know that you are a free woman," I said.

She tossed her head, irritably. There was a sound of metal, that of the collar with its ring, and of the chain, with its lock, depending from the ring. "Suppose you did not know," she said. "Then what would you think?"

I smiled.

"No!" she said. "No!"

"I could, of course, examine your thighs, your lower left abdomen, your body generally," I said. The thighs and the lower left abdomen are the brand sites recommended by Merchant Law. Masters, of course, may brand a girl wherever they please. She is theirs. Sometimes brands are placed on the left side of the neck, on the left calf, the interior of the left heel, and on the inside of the left forearm. The customary brand site, incidentally, is high on the left thigh. That is the site almost invariably utilized in marking Gorean kajirae.

"No," she said. "No!" She regarded me, in fury. "Can you not simply look upon me and see that I am free?"

"Perhaps if I saw you in the robes of concealment, and veiled, being carried in a palanquin through the streets of Vonda by slaves," I said, "I would think you free."

"It has nothing to do with such things!" she said. "Free women are different from slave girls. They are simply different! Free woman are noble and fine! Slave girls are only meaningless, lascivious, sensuous, little sluts!"

"Many slave girls are as large, or larger than you, Lady Florence," I said. "Too, where do you think slave girls come from? Very few are bred slaves."

"Did you see how Miles of Vonda looked at me?" she asked.

"Yes," I said.

"As though I might have been a slave girl!" she said.

"Yes," I said. I smiled to myself. It had indeed been a frank, bemused scrutiny to which Miles of Vonda had subjected the lofty Lady Florence, the sort of scrutiny commonly reserved for, and accorded to, slaves. Such a scrutiny, of course, would be inappropriate, even scandalous, if applied to free women. On the other hand, it did not seem out of place to me if applied to property girls. Indeed, in their case, it is fully rational and appropriate, for such girls are only slaves, lovely items of purchasable livestock.

"But I am not a slave girl!" she said.

"Not legally," I said.

"How could a mere legal convention make me a slave," she asked. "It is meaningless."

"Tell that to girls who wear collars, and find themselves at the total mercy of masters," I said.

"Miles of Vonda is a fool!" she snapped.

"Do not break position," I warned her.

She looked up at me. "Look at me, Jason," she said.

I did. It was a pleasure.

"Do you think a woman such as I could ever be a slave?" she asked.

"Yes," I said.

"Do I look like a slave?" she asked, angrily.

"Yes," I told her.

She cried out in anger.

"Do not break position, Lady Florence," I warned her.

"Very well, Jason," she said, icily.

"You seem cold," I said. "Perhaps I can warm you."

"Do not dare to touch me!" she cried.

"Perhaps you have forgotten that you are a prisoner," I said.

She looked up at me, frightened. "No," she said. "I have not forgotten."

"On your back, Slut," I said.

She obeyed. She threw the chain from her body to one side. "Please do not speak to me in that way," she said. "Please do not call me a slut," she said.

"You forget that I have held you in my arms," I said.

"I am the Lady Florence," she said.

"The Lady Florence," I said, "is a lovely slut."

"No!" she said.

"Do not forget that I have held you in my arms," I said.

"I am the Lady Florence," she said. "I am not a slut!"

"You wear the Ta-Teera of a stable slut," I pointed out.

"It is meaningless!" she said.

"Then remove it," I said. I tore it from her body. "Yes," I said, "the Lady Florence is indeed a lovely slut."

"Beast," she said. "What are you going to do with me?"

"I have fought well," I said. "I have won many bouts."

"Beast!" she said.

"I think you are suitable," I said.

"Suitable?" she asked.

"I have fought well," I said. "I have won many bouts."

"Yes," she said.

"It is customary to reward a successful pugilist," I said.

"I denied you such rewards," she said.

"Yes," I said.

"But now you have decided that I myself, formerly your Mistress, am yet again to be your reward."

"Yes," I said.

"I am not a man's reward," she said.

"How is it then," I asked, "that you lie chained in my stall?"

"I am not accustomed to thinking of myself as a man's reward," she said.

"Grow accustomed to it," I told her.

"Very well," she said, angrily, "I am a man's reward! You have decided it!"

"Yes," I said.

"Do you really think I am pretty enough to be a man's reward?" she asked.

"I think so," I said. "I see that that thought pleases you."

"No," she said. "No!"

I looked upon her sternly.

"Yes," she said, "that thought pleases me. Please do not strike me."

I smiled.

"It is only," she whispered, "that I am not accustomed, not accustomed, truly, to thinking of myself as a man's reward."

"Yet," I said.

"Yet," she whispered.

"It is one of the many things that a woman such as you is good for," I told her.

"I see," she said.

"Smile," I told her.

"Smile!" she cried.

"And lift your arms to me," I told her.

She tried to smile. She lifted her arms to me.

"Say, 'You fought well. You won many bouts,'" I said.

"You fought well. You won many bouts," she said.

"Say now, 'Your girl hopes to please you,'" I said.

"Your girl hopes to please you," she said.

I then crouched beside her, and took her in my arms. She gasped.

"Why are you doing this to me?" she asked.

"I have well earned you," I told her.

"Collect your earnings, yet again," she begged me.

"I shall," I told her.

"Kiss and squirm well, Slut," I said.

"Yes, I am a slut," she wept. "I am a slut!"

"Kiss and squirm," I said.

"Yes," she wept. "Yes, yes!"

"In your arms, you have taught me that I, the Lady Florence, am a slut," she whispered, bending over me. We were in the darkness. The lantern had again burned out. I felt her hair on my chest, the chain, too, depending from her looped, iron collar.

"I did not know that I was a slut," she said.

"Your excitement, your responses, have proved it," I said.

"I did not know I could have such feelings, or behave in such ways," she said.

I took her in my arms and threw her again beneath me.

"You must never let anyone know that I am a slut," she said. "You are the only man in the whole world who knows that."

"For the moment," I told her.

She stiffened in my arms, frightened. "Let it be our secret," she begged "Tell no one!"

"Why not?" I asked.

"No one must know that I am sexually responsive," she said.

"Why not?" I asked.

"It would be the ruin of my reputation," she said.

"Surely men have a right to know," I said.

"No," she said. "No!"

I laughed.

"Do not make my sexual responsiveness public," she said, "I beg of you!"

"Why not?" I asked.

"I am a free woman," she said.

"But one that is a luscious slut," I pointed out.

"Respect me!" she begged.

"You will not be respected," I told her. "You will be wanted."

"How much we women are at the mercy of you brutes," she said.

"You do not even know what it is to be at the mercy of a man," I said.

"Oh?" she asked.

"Yes," I said, "you are a mere prisoner."

"And not a slave," she said.

"Yes," I said.

"That shred of pride, at least, I have," she said.

I smiled to myself. As responsive as she was as a free woman, it was hard to even conjecture what her responses would be if she were made a female slave.

"A slut," she said, "is at least higher than a slave."

"Yes," I said, "a slut, if free, is at least a thousand times higher than a slave."

"Yes," she said, and kissed me.

"Are you ready to perform again, Lady Florence?" I asked her, courteously.

"As the slut you have proven me to be?" she asked.

"Of course," I said.

"Yes, Jason," she said.

"Do so, Lady Florence," I said, courteously.

"And if I do not?" she asked.

"You will then be whipped," I said.

"Could you do that?" she asked.

"Yes, and mercilessly," I said.

"I will perform," she said.

"And well, and as the slut you are," I said.

"Yes, Jason," she said, "I will perform, and well, and as the slut I am."

"Perform, Lady Florence," I said.

"Yes, Jason," she said.

# 28 THE ANKLES OF THE LADY FLORENCE ARE NOT BOUND

She lay on her stomach. "Why are you tying my hands behind my back?" she asked.

It was shortly before dawn. With the key I unlocked the collar from her throat. I threw it and the chain to one side.

"It is morning," she said, her head to the side. "Guardsmen will doubtless soon be here."

"I doubt that," I said. "Many estates must have been struck and plundered. Yet, doubtless, guardsmen, sooner or later, will arrive here."

"I am prepared to deal with you, Jason," she said. "Jason," she said, "why are you tying a strap on my throat?" I knotted the strap under her chin. I took the strap, then, and wrapped it several times about her throat, and then tucked in the loose end. It might thus, if unwrapped, if I chose, serve as a leash.

"I do not understand," I said.

She struggled to a sitting position, her hands bound behind her, the dark strap wrapped several times about her throat.

"You have much abused me," she said. "But I am tolerant. I can forgive much."

"Lady Florence is generous," I said.

"Free me," she said. "Untie me. Remove this horrid strap from my throat. It is too much like the leash of a slave."

"It is much like the leash of a slave," I admitted.

"Please, Jason," she said.

"Position!" I snapped.

Swiftly, as she could, she assumed the position of a slave and, this time, automatically, as she could, the position of a pleasure slave.

"You were going to deal with me," I said.

"Please, let me assume another posture," she said.

"No," I said.

"It is difficult to speak with you as I wish," she said, "while I am bound, while I wear leather on my throat, while I am kneeling before you, and in the posture of a slave."

"Speak," I told her.

"I am prepared to be lenient with you," she said. "I am prepared, even, to overlook to some extent your indiscretions of yesterday and last night."

"You are indeed generous, Lady Florence," I said. I smiled to myself. It amused me to hear the rapine to which I had subjected her, and the paces through which I had put her, suitable almost for a slave, referred to as indiscretions.

"I am prepared, even," she said, "to consider permitting you to remain on my estates."

"Why should you do that?" I asked.

"You saved me from brigands," she said, "and from the unspeakable fate of slavery." She smiled. "Were it not for you, Jason," she said, "I might even now have felt beneath my feet the sawdust of a slave block and have been auctioned to the highest bidder."

"Perhaps," I said. Actually I doubted that things would have happened that fast. Most girls are not sold for a few days after their capture, and some girls, if subjected to professional slave training, in a slaver's pens, not for weeks or months. Trained girls, of course, other things being equal, bring higher prices.

"And as a reward for this great service which you have rendered me," she said, "I am prepared not only to overlook your occasional and somewhat casual disregard for my dignity but to offer you a handsome employment upon my estates."

"Such generosity is almost overwhelming," I said. "Your conditions?"

"They are two," she said.

"And what is your first condition?" I asked.

"That you must never speak of my weakness, my sexual responsiveness to anyone," she said.

"But that is preposterous," I said. "You are helplessly and deliciously responsive. That is an important fact about you. Man have a right to know it. They have a right to know the delicious pleasures which may be derived from you."

"No!" she said.

"Ah, but yes, my dear Lady Florence," I averred.

"Do not tell my secret," she said.

"Under the touch of a strong man," I said, "your own body will tell it."

She shuddered.

"Such facts," I said, "about women such as yourself, like their height and weight, and the coloring of their hair, are usually made public."

"Public?" she asked. "About women such as myself? I do not understand."

"What is your second condition?" I asked.

"That you, in my hire," she said, "will obey me in all things, that you will do whatever I wish."

"That I would be, in effect, your hired slave?" I asked.

She tossed her head. "Yes," she said.

"I reject your offer," I told her.

"No, Jason," she said. "Please."

I went to the door of the barn and opened it. It was now light, shortly after dawn. I must be swiftly upon my way. I did not wish to dally. Though I did not think the guardsmen would arrive for several Ahn, even if they arrived today, I did not wish to risk encountering them.

I looked back at the girl.

"I will pay you much," she said.

"No," I said. Actually I did not think, any longer, though I was not interested in her offer, that the Lady Florence was truly in a position to extend a handsome employment. Her house, and several of her buildings, had been burned. The tharlarion had been released. Though doubtless she retained assets the Lady Florence, I suspected, stood upon the brink of being a ruined woman.

"Do you intend to flee the guardsmen?" she asked.

"Certainly," I said.

"Do not do so," she said. "I will intercede with the guardsmen. I will not permit them to hurt you. Remain with me on the estates."

"As your hired slave?" I asked.

"Yes," she said.

"No," I said.

"You have nowhere to go," she said. "You have no money!"

I looked at her. She shrank back.

"Do not break position," I said.

She held position, kneeling back on her heels, her knees wide, her back straight, her head high, her small wrists tied behind her back, the dark leather strap coiled about her throat.

"Do not look at me like that," she said. "I am not a slave!"

I smiled.

"I am not a slave!" she said.

"I must go," I told her. I gathered some supplies, which I had, yesterday evening, brought to the barn. Among them was food and water, and the blade I had taken from the brigand, Orgus.

"Are you determined in this matter?" she asked, bitterly.

"Yes," I said.

She pulled at her bonds. "Surely you will not leave me behind like this, to be found by guardsmen, as a naked, tied slut."

"No," I said.

"Bring me clothing," she said.

"No," I said.

"I can find my own clothing," she said. "I know you wish to move swiftly. Simply unbind me."

"No," I said.

"I do not understand," she said.

"Surely you have noted that your ankles are not bound," I said.

She looked at me.

"On your feet, Lady Florence," I said.

"No!" she cried.

I glanced to the slave whip.

Swiftly she rose to her feet.

I thought she would make a lovely traveling companion, for a portion of my journey.

# 29 WE MOVE SOUTH; THE TALE TOLD BY A STRAND OF HAIR; I DECIDE TO PREPARE THE LADY FLORENCE FOR SLAVERY

"It is madness!" she said. "You cannot seriously intend to take me with you!"

I looked at her. She trembled.

"It would be a difficult and delicate matter to hold me for ransom," she said.

"That is doubtless true," I admitted.

"Abandon, then, the idea," she said.

"I have never held it," I said.

"I do not understand then," she said.

"I seek an Earth girl," I said, "one called Beverly Henderson, who was brought with me, as a slave, to this world. She is owned, I believe, by Oneander of Ar."

"She may have had many owners by now," said the Lady Florence.

This was true. Slave girls often change hands.

"I must seek her out," I said.

"To put her at your feet?" asked the Lady Florence.

"Of course not," I said. "It is my intention to free her from the collar of bondage."

"But she is an Earth girl," said the Lady Florence. "Earth girls are natural slaves. They belong in the collar."

"No," I said. "No!"

"It is common knowledge," she said.

"Do you wish to be whipped?" I asked.

"No, Jason," she said.

I thrust her toward the door of the barn, and, in moments, we were crossing the meadows, beyond the ruins of several buildings, the sun on our left.

"You are not going toward Vonda," she said. "You are going south."

"I know," I said. I scanned the skies. I pushed her again ahead of me.

"These are times of war," she said. "You may be moving toward the camps of Ar."

"That is possible," I said.

"But I am of Vonda," she said.

"Yes," I said.

"Surel you know what fate could befall me if I fell into the hand of soldiers of Ar," she said.

"Yes," I said.

Suddenly she stopped, and wheeled to face me. She pulled at her bound wrists. "Why are you taking me from my estates, Jason?" she asked. "How do I figure in your plans?"

"Have you not guessed?" I asked.

"Why are we going south?" she asked. "What are you seeking?"

"Do you remember she who was once the Lady Melpomene?" I asked.

"Of curse," she said, "the shameless slut!"

"I did not think her more or less responsive than you," I said.

The Lady Florence reddened. "I sold her as a slave," she said.

"To whom?" I asked.

"Tenalion of Ar," she said.

"His camp," I said, "given the times which were required to reach your house, and return to the camp, is not more than two days trek from here."

She looked at me, aghast. "Do not joke, please, Jason," she said.

"Slavers," I said, "follow the paths, and projected paths, of armies. Given the times I do not think it a coincidence that Tenalion of Ar was recently in the vicinity of Vonda. Too, being a slaver, I think it not unlikely that he may have dealings with various parties. To his camp, I suspect, come not only the captures of brigands, and the stripped females from the outskirts of the Salerian cities, taken by the raiding parties of Ar, but, too, even women taken by the warriors of Cos and of the cities of Saleria. Such a camp, in effect, is a truce ground, where men of various allegiances may in safety bring what prizes may have fallen to their ropes and chains."

"Tenalion knows me," she said. "Doubtless he would swiftly free me."

"He has doubtless, already in his mind," I said, "speculated on your slave potential."

"He knows me," she said.

"Do you think that will make a difference to him," I asked, "when, with the dispassionate objectivity of the slaver, he stands you upon his assessment platform and assesses your quality as slave meat?"

"Do not take me to Tenalion," she said. "I fear him."

"As well you might, female of Vonda," I said.

"It is all a joke you are playing on me," she laughed, suddenly.

"Yet you are bound, and have a strap on your throat," I said.

"You are keeping me for a time, as a hostage," she said, "that is all!"

"And then what?" I asked.

"And then you will release me," she said. "That is it." She laughed.

I turned her about and thrust her again before me, southward.

"Where are we going?" she asked.

"To the camp of Tenalion," I said.

"But for what reason, Jason," she begged, "for what possible reason?"

"He knows you," I said, "and he is familiar with various matters known in Vonda and within her vicinity. He will know, for example, that you have been much sought as a Free Companion by rich young swains of Vonda, but that you have held yourself too good for them, and have refused them all."

"Oh, Jason!" she cried.

I thrust her forward again. Now she was sobbing. "Hurry your pace," I told her.

She stumbled. I scanned the skies.

"Doubtless such young men," I said, "invited to a private

sale, one suitably secret, will bid high against one another to have you. Tenalion will doubtless receive a fine price for you, even though you are untrained, and he, knowing this, will doubtless make me an excellent offer for you."

"You cannot sell me!" she wept. "I am not a slave!"

"Times are grim, Lady Florence," I told her. "Keep moving."

"I am not a slave," she said. "You are mad to think you can sell me!"

"We shall see," I said. "Keep moving."

Suddenly she turned and knelt, sobbing, in the grass before me. "I know you can sell me," she wept. "But do not, please!"

"Why not?" I asked.

"I am not a slave!" she sobbed.

"Goreans think that in every woman there is a slave," I said.

"Return me to Vonda," she said. "I will get you another woman, a true slave, whom you can sell. Let me go! Sell some other woman, one who is a true slave."

"Do you think you could find me another," I asked, "one to take your place?"

"Yes," she said. "Yes!"

"There was a girl of interest to me," I said, "apparently one of your own girls."

"Yes?" she said, eagerly.

"One whom you very kindly sent to content me in the darkness of the tunnels beneath your lands."

She turned white.

"She did not even have a name, as yet, as I recall," I said. "She was referred to, if I recall correctly, merely as the 'new slave.' "

The girl trembled, and could not meet my eyes.

"She must have been a new slave, indeed," I said. "As I recall she had not yet even been branded or collared."

"Yes, Jason," whispered the girl.

"She was pleasant in my arms, in a servile, sluttish way," I said.

The Lady Florence looked up at me, angrily.

"She was a true slave, wouldn't you say?" I asked the girl.

"Yes," she said, angrily, "she was a true slave."

"Do you think you could get her for me?" I asked.

"No," she said, "no."

"Why not?" I asked.

"I told you," she said, "I told you in my room, before, I sold her! I sold her!"

"But you did not tell the truth," I said.

She looked at me, warily. "How could you know that?" she asked.

"Such news travels swiftly in the stables," I said. "If you had sold a slave, I would have heard of it."

"I see," she said.

"Why did you lie?" I asked.

"I—I was jealous of her," she said. "I wanted you to think she was no longer on the estates."

"But she was still upon the estates, wasn't she?" I asked.

"Yes," she said.

"What became of her?" I asked.

"Doubtless she was captured by the brigands, when they raided my estates," she said.

"I do not think so," I said. "I saw various slaves, indeed, house slaves and stable sluts, fastened at the saddle rings of the brigands, but I knew them all. No girl there was unknown to me. Thus none of them could have been the new slave."

"I do not know what became of her," said the Lady Florence, looking away, trembling.

"But you are certain, are you not," I asked, "that she was a true slave?"

"Oh, yes," said the Lady Florence. "That slut was a true slave."

"She belonged in the collar, wouldn't you say?" I asked.

"Yes, Jason," said the Lady Florence.

"I wonder if I shall ever see her again," I mused.

"You would not know it, if you did, would you," asked the Lady Florence, "since, by my will, she served you only in the total darkness."

"I might know," I told her.

"Oh?" she said, warily.

"Her height and weight, and the feel of her body," I said, "were not unlike yours."

She shrugged, angrily.

"Her thigh, too," I said, "was as smooth as yours, and her throat, like yours, was innocent of the obdurate circlet of bondage. Surely such omissions are unusual in the case of female slaves."

"I simply had not yet had her collared and branded," she said. "She was, after all, a new slave."

"But are not such things among the first things which are done to a female slave?" I asked.

"Sometimes," shrugged Lady Florence.

"Her voice, too, was not unlike yours," I said.

"What are you suggesting!" demanded the Lady Florence, angrily.

"Her hair, however," I said, "was it the same as yours?"

"No," she said, "no! Her hair was blond, quite blond." The Lady Florence straightened up then, and smiled.

"Your hair, then," I said, "is quite different."

"Yes," she said.

I walked slowly behind the Lady Florence. She knelt straight. "Your own hair," I said, "is a rich auburn."

"Yes," she said.

"Such hair," I said, "is very unusual."

"I am fond of my hair," she said.

"You might well be," I said. "Such hair would be the envy of many slave girls."

"You need not speak of it that way," she said.

"Did you know that auburn hair is highly prized in the slave markets?" I asked.

"I have heard that," she said. "Oh!" she said. I had jerked a strand of hair from her head.

I walked about, before her, and held before her a strand of hair. "Why did you do that?" she asked.

"Is this your hair?" I asked.

"Of course," she said. "Why did you take it from me?" she asked.

"To identify you by it later," I said.

"I do not understand," she said.

"Why did you lie to me?" I asked.

"About what?" she asked.

"About the hair color of the new slave," I said.

"I did not lie," she said.

"Does this appear blond to you?" I asked. I showed her the strand of auburn hair, which she had just identified as her own.

"No," she said, "of course not."

"This is yours, is it not?" I asked.

"Of course," she said.

"Interesting," I said.

"Why?" she asked.

"This hair, which you have identified as your own," I said, "I took a few days ago, in the darkness, from the head of the 'new slave.' "

"No," she said, "you just took it from me, now!"

"No," I said, opening my left hand, "this is the strand of hair which I just took from you. The other I have carried for some days, concealed in my tunic. I removed it from my tunic when I was behind you." I held both strands in my right hand, before her. "Note," I said, "how both strands are identical."

She looked sick.

"Greetings, New Slave," I said.

"Greetings," she said, looking at me, frightened.

"Greetings, what?" I asked.

"Greetings—Master," she said.

I thrust her back to the grass. It was high about us.

"What are you going to do with me?" she asked.

"You lied to me," I said.

"What are you going to do with me?" she begged.

"Rape you as a slave," I said.

"I only pretended to be a slave," she wept.

"That pretense will be abruptly terminated in the camp of Tenalion," I said, "when the iron is pressed into your thigh, when the collar is closed about your throat."

"Oh!" she said. "What are you doing, your hands!"

"I am preparing you for slavery," I said.

"Free me," she begged.

I placed my mouth over hers. I felt her lips, full and liquid and wet, beneath mine. "No," I told her.

# 30 WE RESUME OUR JOURNEY

In a few moments she knelt before me, in the grass, shuddering, her head to my feet.

"You treated me as a slave, truly," she said.

"You are a slave," I told her, "except for certain legalities, which will soon be satisfied."

"No," she wept, "no!"

"Between now and our arrival at the camp of Tenalion," I said, "you will be and act in all respects as though you might be a full and legal slave. This will help you to accomodate yourself to your future condition. Indeed, it may save your life."

"Take pity on me, Jason," she said, head down.

I pulled up her head by the hair and crouched beside her. "Oh!" she said. I slapped her twice.

"Does a slave dare to address her master by his name?"

"No!" she said, tears in her eyes.

"No, what?" I asked.

"No, Master!" she said. I released her hair. I stood up.

"I fear," she said, "that I will never be able to make the transition between a free woman and a slave."

I laughed at her, and she looked up, angrily.

"There is in actuality no transition for you to make," I told her.

"Why?" she asked.

"Because you are a woman," I told her. "On your feet, female."

She stood up, enraged, her hands bound behind her. "Turn about," I told her.

She did so.

"Do you not feel the leash will be necessary?" she asked. "Am I not to be led to the market on a strap, like a tethered she-tarsk?"

"I shall use the leash after dark," I told her. The use of

366

leashes differs among masters. Some masters use leashes for little more than tethering a girl. Others, of course, use them liberally as leading devices. They are often used with a proud, rebellious or recalcitrant girl, sometimes to publicly humiliate her. After being led on a leash it is not unusual for a girl to beg her master to be permitted to heel him, following him deferentially in her proper place. Leashes are generally used in cities, or in crowds. A loose slave can be a nuisance. They may be useful, too, of course, in broken or wooded areas, where a fleeing girl might attempt to find cover, or in dangerous places, where she might be stolen. A leash, it might be mentioned, aside from its convenience in controlling a slave, particularly the choke leash, is an extremely useful training device. Many trainers, the leash loop about their left wrist, hold the leash in their left hand and their training whip in their right. Girls, too, can be taught to use the leash to enhance their seductiveness, appearing to draw away, then approaching, using it about their body, kissing it, taking it in their mouth, fingering it, and so on. A test for slave potential used by some slavers is to leash a new girl and see if she, in her apparent rebellion and defiance, actually, subtly, perhaps in the beginning unconsciously, uses the leash to enhance her desirability and beauty. This indicates that she, in her heart, is not displeased to wear the leash of the master. Indeed, the leash, not uncommonly, can cause a woman to sexually blossom. This is presumably a function of such things as its actual restraint, which is quite real; its message to her that she is an animal, a slave; and its making clear to her, by a device, such as a bracelet, a brand or collar, what is the order of nature, who it is who controls her and who it is whom she must obey, who is the slave and who the master. A leash, even apart from questions of training, of course, can have a powerful emotional impact on a girl. It is a very useful way of convincing a girl that she is a slave; similarly it can always serve as an effective reminder. Some girls do not seem to believe they are slaves until they have been leashed. But after that, and after having been put through "leash paces," there is seldom any doubt in their mind. Some girls beg to be leashed, sometimes crawling to their masters, their leash held between their small, fine teeth. Most masters use the leash at one time or another. A Gorean saying has it that a lashed slave is a hot slave.

"So you will use the leash after dark," she said.

"Yes," I said.

"Apparently you have no intention of permitting me to escape from you," she said.

"No," I said.

"Let me negotiate for my freedom," she said.

"Begin moving," I said.

"Yes, Master," she said.

# 31 WE CONTINUE OUR WAY SOUTHWARD

It was the heat of the afternoon. The sun was high. "On your back," I told her. She lay down, and I took her. Then I put her on her stomach, and untied her hands from behind her back. Then I put her on her back and retied her hands, wrists crossed, before her body, holding them in place, at her belly, with a loop of strap. "On your feet," I told her, "and face again southwards."

"Why have you tied my hands in this fashion?" she asked, her back to me.

"Because you are beautiful," I said.

"I see," she said.

"Begin moving," I told her.

"Yes, Master," she said.

24

# 32 I DO NOT LISTEN TO THE
# ENTREATIES
# OF THE LADY FLORENCE

"I did not think you would have the nerve to leash me," she said.

We lay together on the soft dirt and leaves, in a small clump of trees in a meadow. I was on my back, looking up at the moons through the branches of the trees. The stars were fine and beautiful, bright in the black sky. She pressed herself against me. I had again tied her hands behind her back. She was tethered by the neck beside me, by the strap which had earlier served as her leash. The tether was fastened to a tree which I could reach out and touch. The knot was under her chin.

"How is it that you have dared to put me on a leash?" she asked.

"I do not understand," I said.

"I am still free, truly, you know," she said.

"Yes," I said, "legally."

"I am furious," she said, "that you have leashed me." She kissed me.

"Why?" I asked.

"I am free," she said, "and it is so degrading. It is like I am a slave girl."

"I see," I said.

"I suppose it was necessary to leash me," she said, "as a matter of prisoner security."

"I do not think it was necessary," I said, "but it was convenient."

"Convenient!" she cried. "You leashed me because it was convenient!" She struggled up to one elbow beside me, the tether on her throat.

370

"Yes," I said, "but, too, there was another reason."

"What was that?" she asked.

"Because you are pretty in a leash, Lady Florence," I said.

She looked at me, not speaking.

Shortly after dark, while we were still trekking, I had put her to her back, untied her hands, then put her on her stomach, tying her hands again behind her back. I had then put her on her back again and unwrapped the long strap from her throat. I had then, holding the coiled strap about two feet from her throat, jerked it twice, that she could feel the pull against the back of her neck. She had looked up at me. "Not bad," I said. She had gasped. Then, loosening the coils, giving her some slack, I had pulled her to her feet. She had looked at me, her eyes wide. "I am leashed," she had whispered, disbelievingly. Then I had turned about and pulled her after me. In a moment she was hurrying behind me, hands bound, on the leash. Twice, that she might rest, we had stopped. Each time she had knelt quite close to me. The second time she had looked up at me, piteously, the tether on her throat, and kissed me on the thigh. It is interesting, the effect that a device such as a leash can have on a woman. The common Gorean leash, incidentally, unlike the simple strap I was using, has a lock snap and closes either about a collar or a collar ring. It might be mentioned that there are also such devices as wrist leashes and ankle leashes.

"What are you thinking?" I asked her.

"I was thinking," she said, "that you were once my silk slave."

I did not speak.

"If you were a gentleman," she said, "and I more fully free, I might beg to attempt to earn my freedom, by the performance of intimate services for you."

"Any such services which you might perform," I said, "are already mine to command."

"That is true," she said.

"I command them," I said.

"That I might earn my freedom?" she asked.

"No," I said, "that you might, through practice, improve your skills as a slave."

"I am not a slave," she said.

"You will behave as one," I said.

She looked at me, angrily.

"Come here," I said. I held the leash.

"You hold my leash. I obey," she said.

When she was but inches from me, I pulled her by the leash even more closely to me. Her lips were then but the breadth of fingers from mine.

"Are you taking me tomorrow to the camp of Tenalion?" she asked.

"Yes," I said.

"Do not lead me in on a leash," she said.

"It is common to take a girl to and from a market on a leash," I said.

"But Tenalion has known me as a free woman," she said.

"You will soon be known to him only as a lovely slave," I said.

"Not on the leash, please," she wept.

"On the leash," I told her.

"My will means nothing?" she asked.

"Nothing," I told her.

She sobbed then, and I threw her beneath me.

"Do not sell me!" she begged.

"Be silent, lovely slave," I said.

"Yes, Master," she said.

"Tomorrow," she whispered to me, confidently, "you will return with me to my estates and free me."

"No," I told her.

"You cannot be serious about selling me," she said. "It is madness!"

"No madness is involved," I said. "You will be an object in a simple business transaction."

"You cannot sell me, after all I have done for you this night!" she wept. "I have behaved as a full slave to you!"

I pulled her again to me, by the leash. She moaned. Then I turned her to her back, and put my hand under her chin, forcing her head back. "As a full slave," she said.

I kissed her, on the lips. Then I lifted my head. "And you will do so again," I whispered.

"I must," she said. "You hold my leash."

She writhed in my arms, squirming and moaning. Then I held my left hand behind the small of her back and touched her well and fully with my right hand. The tether was on her throat. Her hands were bound behind her back. She lifted her body to me piteously.

"You will make some master a hot slave," I said.

"I am leashed," she said. "I must obey!"

"Your condition is that of a slave," I said. "It is a thing far beyond leashes and collars."

"Do not stop touching me!" she begged. She thrust herself, rearing, up against me.

"You are superb, Lady Florence," I said.

"I want—I want—" she whispered, terrified.

"Yes?" I said.

"I want to scream myself a submitted slave!" she wept.

"Do so," I told her.

"I am a slave!" she sobbed. "I admit it!" she sobbed. "I am a slave!" she cried out. "I am a slave!" Then she shuddered and shook in my arms, and I could scarcely hold her, and then she was crying, and sobbing joyfully. I continued to hold her, and kiss her, and then, as she was so beautiful, I entered her and, in fierce silence, exulted within her. "Thank you, Master," she whispered, and I then continued to hold her. "I am a slave, aren't I?" she asked. "Yes," I said. "I have always feared so," she said. "In itself it is nothing to fear," I said. "Fear rather the actual state of bondage, and those who will be your masters."

"I do fear it, and them," she said. "But should not a true slave, like myself, be placed in actual bondage, and have a master? Otherwise she could not be truly fufilled."

"On the world which I once knew, one called Earth," I said, "it is common to deny the fulfillment of slaves. Laws, even, are sometimes opposed to their fulfillment."

"Cruel laws," she said.

"The Gorean world, in many ways, is cruel," I said, "but its cruelties are unhypocritical and open. They are honest and comprehensible. They are not pernicious and insidious. It would not occur to a Gorean to deny a slave her collar. She would not be forced to thwart and frustrate her deepest biological dispositions and sentiments, her desire to be, fully, a male's female."

"I am a slave," she said.

"Yes," I said.

"I want to be a slave," she said, "but I am terrified to be a slave."

"As well you might be," I said.

"What can a master do to me?" she asked.

"Anything," I said.

"I am afraid," she whispered.

"As well you might be," I said.

Suddenly she scrambled from my side, miserably, scattering leaves and dirt about. She backed away, frightened, to the end of her tether. She struggled against it, her head down. She struggled to free her wrists, futilely. She was very beautiful as she tried to free herself. She could not do so.

"I do not want to be a slave!" she cried.

"By tonight," I told her, "you will have felt the iron and will wear the collar."

"I do not want to be a slave!" she cried.

"The decision is not yours," I said.

"I do not want to be a slave," she wept. She fell on her knees at my side. "Free me," she begged. "Free me!"

"Try to be pleasing to your masters," I said. "Perhaps then you will be permitted to live."

She looked at me, aghast.

"Now lick and kiss me," I told her. "It is dawn, and we must soon be on our way."

"Yes, Master," she said.

# 33 WE WILL ENTER THE CAMP OF TENALION; THE LEASH

"There!" I said. "That is it!" I indicated to her, in the shallow valley between the two sloping hills, some half pasang from the southern road, the blue and yellow canvas of the distant tents. Too, we could see cages, and palisaded pens, and slave wagons. In the late morning we had asked directions from a surly, armed fellow herding two trussed women, a stick bound behind the back of their necks. We had seen a tarnsman, too, flying in this direction, four girls tied at his saddle rings. We stood at the top of the hill, in the grass, in the shade of some Ka-la-na trees, the yellow wine trees of Gor. "It is the camp of Tenalion," I said.

"Yes, Master," she said.

I took the leash and wrapped it about her throat, tucking it in.

"Will you not take me into the camp immediately?" she asked.

"Are you so eager to be branded?" I asked.

"They will brand me, won't they," she said, "as though I might be any girl."

"You are any girl," I told her.

"Yes, Master," she said.

"We will rest here for a time," I said. "There are grapes here. Feed me."

I lay down on one elbow and watched her picking the grapes with her teeth. Then she came and knelt humbly beside me and, one by one, from her mouth, as I fed, placed the grapes in my mouth.

"Bring me water," I told her.

She went to a nearby stream and, lying beside it on her belly, in the gravel, took water in her mouth. She then returned to me and, as she knelt above me, I took the water from her mouth.

She straightened up, kneeling. "Were you not afraid I would try to escape?" she asked.

"No," I said.

She looked down at me. "There is no escape for me," she said.

I then took her and flung her, twisting her, on her back in the grass beneath me. "It is true," I told her. "There is no escape for you."

"Yes, Master," she said.

"I watched you bring me food and drink," I said. "You did well. I think you are learning swiftly."

"You have taught me much," she said.

"We are near the camp of Tenalion," I said. "Do you not now wish, again, to beg me piteously for your freedom?"

"No, Master," she said. "I now beg piteously only to be permitted to please you."

I later lifted my lips and hands from her body.

"Am I pleasing?" she asked.

"Yes," I said.

I then stood, unsteadily for a moment. I picked up the steel of Orgus, in its sheath, and looped it over my shoulder. She knelt in the grass, in the position of the pleasure slave, as she could, her hands bound behind her.

"Do you think I will make a good slave, Master?" she asked.

"Yes," I said. "I think you will make a superb slave, Lady Florence."

"Do you think I will bring a good price?" she asked.

"You are raw, and untrained," I said.

"Do you think I will bring a good price?" she asked.

"You are a free woman," I said. "You are quite beautiful. Too, your hair is auburn."

"Do you think I will bring a good price?" she asked.

"That is a slave's question," I said.

She tossed her head, irritably.

"Yes." I said, "I think you will bring a fine price."

"Yes," she said, bitterly, "because men of Vonda, spurned suitors, will pay high for me."

I laughed at her.

"Master?" she asked.

"Look at yourself," I said. "Do you truly think only a spurned suitor could find you of interest?"

"I do not know," she stammered.

"You are superb slave meat, Lady Florence," I said.

"Slave meat!" she said.

"Men seeing you will want you in their collar," I said. "They will pay high to take you from the block. As a free woman you are extremely beautiful. As a slave you will be a thousand times more beautiful."

"I will try to please my masters," she whispered.

"On your feet, Lady Florence," I said. "It is time to go to the camp of Tenalion."

I went to the crest of the hill and stood among the trees. I could see the camp in the distance, with the blue and yellow canvas, the cages, pens and wagons. I could see a warrior, with a spear, leading a woman in. Her robes of concealment had been torn away to her waist. Her hands were bound behind her. A leash was on her throat. The girl was now standing beside me. "Follow me," I said, starting down the slope.

"Master!" she called.

"Yes," I said, turning about, to look upon her.

"Have you not forgotten something?" she asked.

"What?" I asked.

"My leash," she said.

"Come here," I said. She stepped down the slope carefully, to stand before me.

"Do you wish to be led in on a leash?" I asked.

"Am I not to be a slave girl?" she asked.

I smiled, and unwrapped the leash from her throat. "Yes," I said. I then conducted her down the slope, leading the captive beauty, the Lady Florence, on her leash, towards the camp.

## 34 WE ENTER THE CAMP OF TENALION;
## I SELL THE LADY FLORENCE;
## I MUST NOW SEARCH FOR
## THE SLAVE,
## BEVERLY HENDERSON

We entered the camp of Tenalion.

There were some slave girls, in brief tunics, and collars, loose in the camp, performing various duties. They looked at the Lady Florence as I brought her in. They assessed her candidly, as a new girl. We passed between guards. I saw their admiring glance. This heartened me. They were slavers' men. They would have their pick of most of the girls in the camp, except for virgins. "This way," I told the Lady Florence, heading toward the center of the camp, where the assessment platform would be. "Yes, Master," she said. I heard the ringing of a metal worker's hammer on metal, where simple straps of iron were being curved about the necks of beauties, their heads and hair over the anvil, these serving as temporary collars. I smelled branding fires. I heard the sound of a girl being lashed. I saw girls in cages and, in places, I saw them, stripped, and crowded together, through the interstices of palings. "Which way is the assessment platform?" I asked a man. "That way," he said. I heard the scream of a girl some yards to my left, who was being branded. "I'm frightened," said the Lady Florence. I took up some of the slack in the leash, until I dragged her about a yard behind

378

me. I saw two warriors, one of Ar and one of Cos, enemy cities. They were talking about something or other. The camp of Tenalion was truce ground. At the feet of each, their heads down, stripped save for bonds of black leather, there knelt a girl. "Into the slave wagon," said a man, herding a set of girls in throat coffle. In another place I saw another slave wagon, the girls sitting in it facing one another. About their ankles were close-fitting ankle rings, joined by a short length of chain. The chains had been slipped beneath a long metal bar, set parallel to the wagon bed. A slaver's man then lifted the bar some two inches and dropped it in place, locking it in its socket. Another man was pulling down the canvas over the square frame mounted over the wagon. It would be buckled in place. This protects the merchandise from the sun and weather. Another slave wagon, empty, its canvas high on its frame, was entering the camp. "Take her to the whipping post," said a man to another slaver's man, who was holding a girl by the arm, her wrists tethered before her body. "I did not mean to be displeasing!" she wept. I saw little evidence of actual training going on in the camp. I did, however, see, through the flaps of a tent, a girl on her back on the ornate rug being taught to move. She was being guided by a pointed stick.

"Take your place in line," said a slaver's man, at the assessment platform.

I took my place in line, holding the Lady Florence close to me by her leash.

We heard the scream of another girl being branded. "A good catch," said the man in front of me, nodding at the Lady Florence.

"She is not without interest," I said. I then regarded the short, luscious, dark-haired beauty kneeling beside him, on a short leash. "She is superb," I said, indicating his own catch.

"She is not without interest," he shrugged. The girl looked up at me, as a slave.

The Lady Florence gasped. "May I kneel, Master?" she asked.

"Of course," I said.

Swiftly she knelt between me and the dark-haired girl.

"Your master is handsome," said the dark-haired girl to her.

"Your master, too, is handsome," said the Lady Florence to her.

"I am to be sold," said the dark-haired girl.

"I, too, am to be sold," said the Lady Florence.

I saw a blond girl, shackled and sobbing, being led past on a chain leash.

"I can give a man much pleasure," said the dark-haired girl.

"I, too, can give a man much pleasure," said the Lady Florence.

"I do not doubt it," said the dark-haired girl. "You are very beautiful."

"You, too, are very beautiful," said the Lady Florence.

"You, there!" said a voice, that of a slaver's man, approaching me. Behind him I saw Tenalion, stripped to the waist, on the assessment platform, paused in his labors, looking at me.

"You are Jason, the fighting slave, are you not?" asked the man who had approached me. He, too, like Tenalion, was stripped to the waist. He wore a blue-and-yellow wristlet. He carried a whip, coiled, in his right hand. I recognized him. He was Ronald. He had been with Tenalion in the house of the Lady Florence, his man.

"I am Jason," I said, "the free man."

"Jason," called Tenalion, from the platform, "bring your capture forward."

I moved forward, drawing the Lady Florence to her feet behind me. Then, in a moment, trembling, she had stepped upon the assessment platform.

"You are free now, Jason?" asked Tenalion.

"Yes," I said, standing below the platform.

Tenalion then turned to a bound, dark-haired woman who had been standing on the platform, her head down, her hair over her eyes. He thrust her from the platform. "Ten copper tarsks," he said to a scribe at a small table nearby, with papers and a box of coins. The scribe counted out ten copper tarsks to a fellow at the table. "Brand her, common Kajira mark, strap-collar her and put her in Pen Six," said Tenalion to one of his men. "Yes, Tenalion," said he, and took the woman by the hair and, bending her over, led her away.

Tenalion then turned to the other woman on the platform, the auburn-haired beauty who was trembling.

"What have we here?" he asked me.

"A female, for your consideration," I said.

"I would think so," said Tenalion.

"Where is Beverly Henderson?" I asked them.

"We do not know of her," said one of the girls, frightened.

"The woman Beverly!" I said.

"We know no woman, Beverly," said one.

"The slave girl, Beverly!" I said, angrily.

"We know no slave, Beverly," said one of them.

"She is small, and dark-haired, and exquisitely beautiful," I said.

"Veminia?" asked one of them, to another.

"She is from Earth," I said.

"Veminia!" said one.

"The barbarian!" said another.

"Yes," I said.

"She who came in chains from some market in Vonda?" asked another.

"That would doubtless be she," I said. "Where is she?"

"We do not know," said one.

I cried out in anger, and Tenalion lifted his whip.

"We do not know!" cried the first girl, shrinking back.

"Was she sold with you?" I asked.

"No, Master!" cried the first girl.

"Where is Oneander?" I demanded.

"We do not know!" wept the first girl. "Please do not whip us, our Masters!"

"Where do you think he is?" I asked.

"He was returning to Ar," said the first girl. "He is perhaps there."

I looked to Tenalion. "I would suppose he would be in Ar," said Tenalion, "but I would not know."

"I do not think I need to question these slaves further," I said.

Tenalion nodded, and he turned and went to the gate of the pen. When the door was opened he turned about and looked at the three girls kneeling by the palings. "You may break position," he told them.

"Thank you, Master," they said, lowering their arms, frightened.

"I must venture to Ar," I said to Tenalion, once outside the pen. "I think it likely that she whom I seek is in that city."

"Perhaps," said Tenalion.

I nodded. Miss Henderson was a slave. She could have

been put on the block and sold, like any other girl, like the girls inside the pen. She might be anywhere.

"We will be returning to Ar in a month or two," said Tenalion.

"I do not understand," I said.

"Leave the slave for the time in whatever collar she wears," said Tenalion. He smiled. "She will doubtless, on one chain or another, be kept quite safe."

"I do not understand," I said.

"You are a strong fellow, Jason," said Tenalion. "I have heard of you. You once defeated the fighting slave, Krondar. I could use a man like you in my service. Remain with me in the camp. I pay well, and the use of most of these women would be yours for the asking."

"Tenalion is generous," I said. "I am truly grateful. But I wish to depart as soon as possible for the city of Ar."

"Are you truly so anxious to have this woman naked and chained at the foot of your couch?" asked Tenalion.

I smiled. It seemed to me absurd to think of Miss Henderson in such terms. Yet she was attractive. I did not think she would look bad chained at the foot of a man's couch.

"I must be on my way," I said.

"There is a tarnsman in camp, Andar," he said, "who is leaving for Ar shortly. He is a greedy fellow. Doubtless he could be convinced, for a silver tarsk, to grant you passage."

"My thanks, Tenalion," I said.

"In three days," he said, "you will be in Ar."

"I am grateful," I said.

We heard then the scream of a woman being branded.

"Is it the Lady Florence?" I asked.

"Not yet," said he. "There are several before her. Here she must wait her turn. Here she is only another girl." He looked at me. "Do you wish to wait," he asked, "to see her branded and collared?"

"No," I said, "she is only another girl."